Greig Beck grew up across the rc  Sydney, Australia. His early days w ing, and reading science fiction on to study computer science, immer software industry, and later receiv spends his days writing, but still finds time to surf at his beloved Bondi Beach. He lives in Sydney, with his wife, son, and an enormous German shepherd.

If you would like to contact Greig, his email address is greig@greigbeck.com and you can find him on the web at www.greigbeck.com.

Also by Greig Beck

The Alex Hunter series
Arcadian Genesis
Beneath the Dark Ice
Dark Rising
This Green Hell
Black Mountain
Gorgon
Hammer of God
Kraken Rising
The Void
From Hell
The Well of Hell

The Matt Kearns series
The First Bird
Book of the Dead
The Immortality Curse
Extinction Plague

The Fathomless series
Fathomless
Abyss – Fathomless II

The Valkeryn Chronicles
Return of the Ancients
The Dark Lands

THE DARK SIDE

GREIG BECK

Pan Macmillan acknowledges the Traditional Custodians of country throughout Australia and their connections to lands, waters and communities. We pay our respect to Elders past and present and extend that respect to all Aboriginal and Torres Strait Islander peoples today. We honour more than sixty thousand years of storytelling, art and culture.

First published 2021 in Momentum by Pan Macmillan Australia Pty Ltd
1 Market Street, Sydney, New South Wales, Australia, 2000

A CIP record for this book is available at the National Library of Australia

The Dark Side: Alex Hunter 9

EPUB format: 9781760988364
Print on Demand format: 9781760987725

Original cover design: Dean Samed

Macmillan Digital Australia: www.macmillandigital.com.au
To report a typographical error, please visit www.panmacmillan.com.au/contact-us/

Visit www.panmacmillan.com.au/ to read more about all our books and to buy books online. You will also find features, author interviews and news of any author events.

The phrase "dark side of the moon" does not refer to "dark" as in the absence of light, but rather "dark" as in unknown. Until humans were able to send a spacecraft around the moon, this area had never been seen. To this day, little is known about the hidden face of our closest astral body.

It is not the strongest of the species that survives, nor the most intelligent that survives. It is the one that is the most adaptable to change.

— Charles Darwin

CHAPTER 01

Vladimir Lenin Base, Russian lunar mining
operation – dark side of the moon

Olga slipped in the blood. Breach lights turned slowly overhead,
bathing everything in a hellish red glow and from somewhere a
klaxon horn blared its warning, further tearing at her nerves.

Tears streaked her blood-spattered face as she scrambled to
her feet and nearly fell again. The floor was awash with blood
and a sticky black slime, with tattered remnants of clothing
everywhere.

They were all gone, all twenty-one of them. Only Viktor
and herself had remained, and she didn't think he'd made it
either after they became separated, but then she heard him
scream in fear and then agony.

The thing had been smart, smarter than they ever could
have known. It cut the communications, and knew it only
needed to wait, wait until someone came. From Earth.

Svoloch, she knew the supply ship would come from Earth,
certainly, and come early because the communications had
been interrupted and they wouldn't know. And then they
would walk straight into its trap.

It seemed the creature didn't just feed on them but on their memories as well. That's how it grew smart.

Olga stopped running as her confused and frightened mind worked overtime trying to make a plan. If she stayed here she was as good as dead. And if she were dead, there would be no one to warn them. She grimaced. The creature would get back home, to Earth, and then everything would be finished. *Everything.*

She was resolute; the thing must not be allowed to get back home or even make it to the American base. Olga had been told by her superiors to stay away from the Americans, but she was a human being first, and therefore she needed to warn them.

She began to run and her mind also accelerated as she settled on her priorities – she needed to warn people and she needed to destroy the base.

"*Faster,*" she hissed between clenched teeth as she sprinted down a straight corridor, her lungs burning. She felt dizzy and knew she needed her medication. But there was no time to retrieve that now.

Olga headed for the power generation room, and only slowed when she discovered the corridor leading to it was covered in sticky black webbing. The foul-smelling material coated the walls, floor, and ceiling, creating a tunnel that looked like it should house some sort of insect or spider.

The substance also coated the overhead lights, masking them, so the corridor became darker the further in she went. She saw bready-looking lumps with things like toadstools growing at their center. They quivered as she passed by.

Olga stepped carefully, trying to avoid the glistening pools of ooze she knew would be like viscous glue. At the corridor junction she saw the webbing continued along the opposite corridor toward the base crew's sleeping quarters. Of course it did.

My poor, poor friends, she thought.

She licked bone-dry lips and carefully peered around the opposite corner – empty – all clear.

"*Go.*"

She ran again, heading toward the power-generation room. In seconds more she was there and slammed a hand over the door button. With a faint hiss, the door began to slide into the wall. She was inside before it had fully opened, and spun to punch the button to close the door.

Olga headed for the reactor. She knelt by the six-foot door shield set into the floor. She entered the code to open it, and it lifted with agonizingly glacial speed. The room filled with a blue glow from the demineralized water acting as both insulation and a neutron moderator, absorbing many of the enriched particles from the nuclear rods it housed.

She moved to the core rods, hesitating for only a few seconds as her mind whirled, trying to think of other options. None would come. So she opened the individual shielding panels to display the six, three-foot long rods of enriched plutonium. There was no self-destruct button like in the movies. Why would there be? In the vacuum of space or desolation of a moonscape, why would there be a need to commit suicide through the total destruction of your life-sustaining habitat?

But there were ways to cause an *accidental* catastrophic detonation – when the rods were replaced every few years, they were removed while the water was drained. All she needed to do was drain the liquid and leave the rods inside their chambers. The radioactive heat would do the rest, very quickly building to significant detonation level.

She opened the valves for the fluid release, and immediately the six-foot wide pool of glowing liquid began to drop. More alarms sounded, adding to the cacophony of madness surrounding her.

Olga stood. It would take several minutes to fully drain, several more for the rods to reach critical levels of heat, and then they would cause a blast that should literally melt the base and sink it below the moon's crust. *Good.*

She backed up a few steps and then turned to run, rising to a sprint as she headed to the airlock. An insanely calm voice counted down overhead and warned of a potential meltdown unless the pool was reflooded. Olga ignored it as she careened into the airlock prep room. She skidded to a stop at the sight of the torn clothing, spatters of blood and viscera, and bloody handprints marking the walls. It was the scene of a hellish massacre. Tears filled her eyes once again. She knew these people, every one of them; they were her friends. Once.

She swallowed her bile and crossed to the suit lockers; the first was empty, and the second one too. She knew no one had left the base, so she wondered whether the thing was so smart as to know to destroy or hide the lunar suits to stop anyone getting out. Then she remembered – of course it was; it had absorbed the minds of her friends and crewmates.

In the last cabinet there was a single suit, too big for her, but she had no choice. She dragged it free and climbed into it, then crossed to a utilities cabinet and pulled things out and onto the floor until she found what she needed – duct tape. She wound the tape around her arms and legs to hold the oversized suit a little closer to her body and reduce the bulk and sagging.

Once done, she lifted the helmet from the locker, dragged it onto her head, and locked it in place. Then finally fitted the tiny oxy-cylinder to her chest. She had no time to test the suit seal or the tank's capacity level and only hoped it was enough to make it to the American base a mile to the east.

Olga sucked in a deep, juddering breath and took one last look around as the seconds counted down.

She saw movement through the viewing panel in the door and flattened herself against the wall; it was just a shadow, but enough to tell her something was out there. *It* was out there.

The logical part of her brain told her to stay silent and still and wait, but her primitive brain screamed at her to get out, *get out now*.

The primitive won and Olga rushed to the airlock, darted in, slammed her hand on the close button. She expelled the air inside the chamber in preparation for opening the outer door. Though the moon has a few gases in its thin atmosphere, for practical purposes it is considered a vacuum, and therefore it took time to equalize the air pressure.

The seconds ticked over agonizingly slowly as the vents drew the air out. She hugged herself as her foot tapped nervously inside the oversized boot, her impatience making her want to scream.

Olga moved to the viewing panel and peered back into the anterior room. To her horror, she saw the prep room door slide back and for a few seconds the thing filled the doorframe before it began to force itself inside.

The green light blinked to red – airlock pressure equalization achieved. Olga grinned maniacally; it was too late, no matter how strong it was, the thing could never open the inner airlock door while the outer door was opening. The hydraulics simply wouldn't allow it.

"Fuck you!" she screamed at it from behind the three inch–thick safety glass.

And then she gulped and backed up when, for the first time, she beheld the full hideousness of the creature – it was now far bigger than she expected. But she should have known better; all that body mass of the crew it had absorbed had to go somewhere.

Only at the end did they realize what they were dealing with. It was different, obviously, to any other lifeform they had ever encountered on Earth, as its cell structure was malleable to the point of being able to change its shape and structure. If it wanted to, it could compress itself down to a fraction of its size. That was how it hid for so long.

But now free of the need to hide it had reverted to its natural form – a living nightmare that filled the room.

The creature madly lashed its black cords in the air leaving dark streaks on the walls, reaching out to pluck up fragments of clothing as though looking for morsels of flesh.

Covering its lumpen body were stalks with swollen bulbs on the end that popped ripely and filled the room with powder or gas. Groups of milky orbs, eyes maybe, swivelled in concert with some of the arms as though in charge of each of their frenzied tasks. One group swivelled toward her, and sighted her through the glass panel.

It dropped the rags it held and surged forward, just as the outer airlock door whooshed fully open.

Olga spun back as the inner door clanged when the thing's bulk struck the eight solid inches of steel and, ominously, alarm lights blinked their frantic warning. She sprinted to the outer door and dived through, tumbling when she hit the moon's powdery surface and rolling for a moment more. In her ears she still heard the base's calm voice counting down the seconds until core meltdown.

She scrambled to her feet just as the outer door began to whine closed. She spun back.

"Oh no."

It was coming after her.

Of course it was, because it knew how to operate the airlock. And also probably knew exactly where she was going.

Olga turned and moved as quickly as the oversized suit plus low gravity would allow.

How far from the base did she need to be when it detonated? The explosion would be significant, but it was the radiation dispersal that would be the real worry. Though the suits had radiation shielding to guard against cosmic rays, the heavy reactor particles would stick to her, making her entire body toxic.

She powered on, gritting her teeth. She chanced a look back and stopped dead. The outer door was now fully closed. It meant that the inner door could be operated, and then?

She already knew the answer: and then it would be out.

She made a small strangled noise in her throat and turned to run once again. How much more time? she wondered. Where was the –

The flash of blinding light shot past her, but the explosion wasn't heard because there were very few particles in the air of the near vacuum of the lunar surface to vibrate – sound didn't travel well.

But vibration waves did, and she felt them through the soles of her boots. She didn't look back but hunched her shoulders in preparation for the shock wave she knew was coming.

It hit like a hammer blow and kicked her forward. She went head over heels, and her face struck an exposed rocky outcrop. The faceplate of her helmet starred with cracks and she heard the devastating hiss of escaping gas.

Her ankle hurt and at first she thought it might be broken from the fall. But then the pain moved up her leg and felt as if someone or something was gripping it in a vice.

Olga turned, and her eyes went wide. An oily-looking black cord circled her leg and the thing loomed over her.

She knew then she had lost her race.

CHAPTER 02

John F Kennedy Moon Base, Aitken Crater

Mia Russo stepped from the portal and placed her large, weighted shoe silently down on the compacted dust of the lunar surface. Her boot was insulated with a two inch–thick rubber and Kevlar mesh sole and, like the suit, protected her from the lunar temperature extremes – daytime temps got up to 248 degrees and down to minus 230 at night. The hi-tech suits not only gave protection from the cold and heat but were reflective, and tough enough to withstand the constant radiation bombardment and micrometeor strikes – in effect, they were a modern-day suit of armor.

The only problem was they paid for all this armor by having mobility that was little better than an oversized two-legged tortoise.

Mia drew in a deep breath of dry, canned air and let it out slowly. The landscape beyond their base on the edge of the Aitken crater was both primordial and alien looking: jagged hills rose like monstrous teeth, crater edges lifted hundreds of feet, tiny craggy valleys like rips in a pie crust, all in hues of gray, purple, and some places, a deep, ocean blue. It should have been calming, but when you stood quietly and alone, you heard it – the wail – the soft, whistling shriek that was the moon's constant background noise.

Originally, many scientists had thought that the moon being a near vacuum would mean there would be an audible atmospheric emptiness. But they soon found that "space" makes sounds all the time. They said it was probably due to charged particles interacting with the moon's weak magnetic field. And maybe that was true. But it sounded damn eerie and more like the disembodied wail of a lost soul crying out in anguish.

Mia shook herself out of the creepy thought and closed the portal, watching as the hatch door slid shut and the access light went from green to red. She waited, facing the vehicle maintenance bays with a ramp leading under the ground and panel doors that fitted flush with the surface, while Benoit brought the crawler around. For the most part, their lunar base had been constructed to have a minimal profile – critical when they'd thought they were a covert operation. But now they were an obvious secret, and ever since the Russians had moved in to begin mining a few years back, they'd both pretended the other group didn't exist even though they were a little over a mile apart.

She'd seen the Russians out on the lunar surface many times and waved at their teams. And they'd waved back. *What a world, I mean moon.* She grinned, and pressed a small stud on the side of her helmet to lower the additional gold-coated visor over her eyes. The soft metal was an excellent reflector of infrared light while allowing penetration of visible light and was also malleable enough to be hammered down to a thickness of just 0.000002 inches – without it, the astronauts would eventually be blinded by the undiffused light they were bathed in during a lunar day.

She sighed as the visor brought relief to her eyes – the phrase "dark side of the moon" did not refer to "dark" as in the absence of light, but rather "dark" as in unknown. Through a phenomenon called tidal locking, the same side of the moon always faced the Earth. The side that faced the universe had remained a mystery until the Soviets first photographed it in 1959.

But facing the universe meant being pummelled by meteorite strikes that left the surface with a heavily scarred and cratered morphology. It also meant the bases were at risk of meteor strike.

Benoit bounced toward her in the crawler, stopped right at her toes, and gave her a comical salute. Mia bet he would have tooted the horn if the crawler had one. She eased into the skeletal-looking machine with its beer keg–sized rechargeable battery on the back, tires that would make a truck rally crowd cheer, and an almost biological-looking suspension system that allowed each of the six wheels to move independently like some sort of large insect, and was the source of the name "crawler". She shunted Benoit aside as she loved to drive.

Mia started them up and the electric crawler moved forward at around five miles per hour. The machine was silent, and the only sensation of motion was from the occasional bounce as they passed over larger than normal moon rocks. As it was sun-up time, everything was a grayish purple and would be for another few days. Their suits gave them ample protection from the heat, but she knew that they needed to avoid falling into a deep, permanently sunless crevasse, as there could be temperature zones of minus 200 degrees, and while the suits' coolers were blowing, falling into a cold zone meant a snap freeze before the suit could work out it was supposed to be warming instead of cooling. You'd be dead before you could even call for help.

Their task today was investigating an asteroid impact a couple of klicks out in the northern solitude quadrant of the Deloris Lacus zone. It took them an hour to reach the place where the base scanners had said the asteroid came down. It wasn't a large moon-fall, and was estimated to be only about the size of a suitcase. On Earth it would more than likely have burned up before it reached the surface. But here, everything gets through, and everything hits.

She stopped the crawler and stood in her seat, turning slowly.

"See it?" Benoit asked.

"Hold it." Mia was looking for a darker patch on the already heavily pocked surface. Newly churned up moon dust was darker, not from underlying moisture, but because it just hadn't yet been bleached by solar radiation for countless eons.

"Hey, Mia, anything?" Benoit asked again as he sat with arms folded across his stomach.

"No, wait – *yes*." She pointed. "There. Not far, we can walk it."

"Bring the kit?"

"Yeah, we'll take a sample back. Let Tony look it over in his never-ending search for the origin of everything."

Benoit snorted. "Ooh, more gifts for the magnificent Tony Handsome."

"Jealous." Mia chuckled.

"Pfft." He glanced at her. "French people value brains and talent over looks."

"Yeah, right. Says the guy who puts mousse in his hair – on the moon."

Tony Miles was their senior geologist, and also the base heartthrob. He was damn good at his job and had movie-star looks. But even though everyone seemed to flirt with him, for whatever reason, he never reciprocated.

It didn't really matter to her as she was sort of dating someone. Andy Clark was fun, from some place called Bondi in Australia, and had blond hair that never stayed combed for more than five minutes. Mia hadn't come to the moon looking for a hookup, but when it happened, it was the best thing ever as it sure broke up the boredom. And up here, boredom could lead to depression, and that was the mind killer.

"Ally-oop." Benoit easily carried the 150-pound sample case in the low gravity, and followed Mia to a newly formed crater with two-foot-high rim, and a circular spread of over fifty feet.

"Good size," she said, stopped at its edge and looked down into the ten foot–deep crater pit. Right at the center of the depression there was the nub of rock. It was like an iceberg, as there was only about ten to twenty percent of the asteroid showing and the rest was buried.

Benoit joined her, put the case down, and stared into the hole. "There's still a bit of light down there so shouldn't be too cold." He turned to her. "You want to do the honors or would you like me?"

"Be my guest," she said and held out an arm. "Be careful and take it slow so your thermo system adapts."

"Yes, Mommy." He held up his fist.

Mia bumped it with her own and could just make out his grin behind his shaded face lens.

Benoit began to slide-walk down into the crater. "No unusual radiation," he said and tucked the counter away.

Good, she thought. There was an abundance of high-energy protons, helium nuclei alpha particles, and high-atomic-number HZE ions zooming around the solar system, and this thing just dropped out of space. So there could have been some real heat recorded.

She watched as Benoit lowered the test case, unlatched it, and lifted the lid. There were various tools inside ranging from rock hammers and chisels to miniature battery-powered saws, as well as collection bags, vials, and boxes, and some reference manuals.

He first took out a small hammer and chisel and began to tap at the rock. He broke a few small pieces away, placed them in a jar and sealed it. He repeated the process on another section of the meteorite and then tucked the samples into padded slots in the case and looked about to finish up when the ground shook beneath their feet.

"Whoa." He held his arms out.

The crater walls began to collapse inward.

"Get the hell out of there!" Mia yelled. She had the urge to slide down and help him but knew that was against protocol, as someone needed to stay in sight of the crawler, which had a remote camera onboard.

The shaking continued and she turned to the horizon, seeing a flaring light just over the ridge of rock a few hundred yards out.

Benoit climbed up to join her. "Phew. What was that? Felt like a quake?"

She continued to stare into the distance. "The moon doesn't get quakes." She narrowed her eyes. "It came from that direction."

"Where the Russian base is."

"That's what I'm thinking." She started back to the crawler. "Let's check it out."

"We'll need to call it in," Benoit said.

"Yep, and that's your job while I'm driving." She climbed into the driver's seat as Benoit tossed the case into the back. She turned. "But not yet. Let's get a little closer so it's too late for the boss to change our minds."

* * *

"What's that?" Mia stopped the crawler and craned forward.

Benoit lifted the scope to the front of his visor. The double-lensed apparatus was the closest thing to a telescope they had and presented a large and clear image of whatever it was pointed at. "A body," he replied and took the scope from his eyes for a moment then replaced it. "Not moving. Go, *go*."

Mia sat back and pushed the drive stick forward. The silent vehicle trundled at its top speed, barely registering the lumps and bumps beneath its oversized wheels. She stopped close to the prone figure and was first out, running in the usual bounce-fashion over the lunar scape with Benoit right at her heels.

She went to her knees beside the body. "Suit seems okay." She gently turned the figure over. "Fuck. Hole in the faceplate and bleeding gas." She stuck a hand over the pea-sized hole.

"On it." Benoit ran back to the crawler and grabbed a medical kit. He opened it on his way back and drew out the adhesive rubber tape to slap a six-inch strip over the hole. The pair checked the suit for more breaches.

"Got a tear on the lower leg," Benoit announced, and covered it over with more tape.

Mia leaned in close to the visor. "It's a woman – alive, I think." She squinted. "There's something on her."

"Suit seems okay now." Benoit stopped at her ankle. "Oil spill or something on her leg." He looked one way then the other. "Where's the rest of them?"

Mia looked over her shoulder, noting the soft orange glow coming from just over the crater rim where she knew the Russian base was. She was torn; they should check it out, see if there were any other people hurt. But this woman, right here, right now, might still be saved.

"Can't wait, we gotta get her back to base." She lifted the woman. "You drive."

* * *

"Tom, we're coming in hot. We've got a Russian female, suit potentially and helmet definitely breached. But she's alive."

Mia felt her heart beating a mile a minute as she glanced down at the woman. "Inside her suit I think I can see blood. Or something."

Captain Tom Briggs swore softly. "What of the base? We picked up a seismic disturbance from their direction – that was them?"

"We felt it too. And I saw a flash. We didn't get to the base but I'm thinking something real bad happened there." While Mia cradled the woman, Benoit drove, and she pointed him toward the external ramp that was already yawning open for them.

Mia looked back down at the unconscious woman. Behind her faceplate she was streaked in blood and something dark that might have been machine oil. There were streaks on her cheeks as though she had been crying.

Mia smoothed the tape over the crack in the helmet glass to stop her losing any more oxygen but couldn't believe she was even still alive.

"You bring her in, and we'll dispatch a team," Briggs said.

"Have you tried contacting the Russians?" Benoit asked.

"Yes, and we're getting nothing but static," Briggs replied. "Take her straight to sickbay. We'll be waiting. Out."

CHAPTER 03

As they came down the ramp another of the crawlers waited for them to go past, and then slowly began to head up. The three occupants nodded at the incoming team. In their suits, Mia couldn't make out exactly who they were but she bet there were two security personnel and probably one of the medics, who would be either Aleksandra or Xavier.

The door whined closed behind them and Mia and Benoit waited in the maintenance area as air was vented into the airtight room. Mia glared impatiently at the wall vents that seemed to fill their enclosure with breathable air at a glacial speed.

"Come on, hurry up," she whispered.

Once the oxygen had replaced the lunar gases there came a flush of antiseptic mist plus a quick bath in UV light for decontamination – not that there was ever anything to decon as the moon was basically a sterile ball of dust and rock.

But protocols were damn protocols, she thought, as her impatience gnawed ever deeper. She leaned over the woman. "Hang in there," she said softly, doubting the woman could hear. The words were more for her own benefit.

The light on the inner door lock went green, meaning the air was clean and all clear, and they could then, and only then, enter the main body of the base. Mia took off her helmet and fought the urge to wipe the hair up off her brow.

The doors slid back, and people rushed toward them with a wheeled gurney.

Mia looked down at the woman. "You'll be fine now." She helped lift her to the gurney and peered in through the cracked visor. "What happened out there, girl?"

The Russian woman was whisked away.

Mia turned to the external door and stared as though seeing through it to the Russian base. With their team on the way, they'd know soon enough.

"That's all we can do for now." Benoit took his helmet off and held it in one hand. His normally perfect hair was plastered down by perspiration. "Never a dull moment." He grinned.

"Hope they're okay – the other Russians I mean." Mia punched the lock button and the portal door slid back. She stepped onto the grate that allowed any dust and grit to fall through and moved to the side where she began to shuck off the cumbersome suit.

Benoit had to use two hands and grunted as he hefted the sample case, now encumbered by normal gravity, up onto a bench. He removed his own suit.

In a few moments they stood in their underwear. There were dry showers close by, but she'd wait to get back to her pod before changing. She pulled on her sweats.

Benoit lifted the case. "You going past Lab-tech?"

"You know I am, but ..." She pointed. "I'm only taking the samples, not that damned ten-ton crate."

"Why do I have to lug the heavy stuff, inside *and* out?" Benoit looked mock hurt.

"Because you're younger than I am." Mia smiled, flipped the case open, and reached inside to remove the meteorite samples.

"Pfft, by six months." The Frenchman grinned and finally got his own pullover on. "Catch you later."

"Sure." Mia headed off down the corridor, humming "Sweet Child o' Mine", by Guns 'n' Roses. She noticed even more corridor tiles needed replacing. "Ain't no place like home," she whispered.

The air conditioning clicked and hummed, and probably needed a service as well. Unlike how spaceships or space bases looked in movies with their gleaming hospital-grade tiling, chrome railings, and bright lighting, the reality was very different. Dirt and dust got in, and after a while everyone thought cleaning was someone else's job. When parts broke down, if there weren't spares already sitting in storage, then they went on the requisition list, and sometimes they turned up in six months and sometimes they never did. And then the underlying problem was just lived with, and eventually became invisible. Domestic blindness, her mother used to call it – you never saw the peeling paint, cobwebs in the corners, or even tumbleweeds of dog hair stuck to the rug in your own home.

Before Mia got to the dormitory pods, she turned a hard left into the bio wing, where the first door that was open was the geology lab.

"Knock, knock," she said as she walked in, hand behind her back.

Tony Miles swung his chair around and gave her a wide smile. "Hey Mia, what'd you bring me? Is it candy? Please be candy."

She beamed back, feeling her heart thump in her chest. *This guy is too handsome for his own good. So handsome, so unattainable.*

"We-*eeell*, it's hard, probably has an iron base, is slightly reddish in color, and um, fell from somewhere out of the wide black yonder."

He rubbed his chin. "Um, is it a light saber?"

She held it up. "If by light saber, you mean something that looks like bits of broken nut cookie, then yes, exactly." She handed it over.

"So, it *is* candy – space candy." His eyes were firmly on the bag as he took it. Tony lived for this, and new asteroid fragments were enough to excite him for days.

He always said that sooner or later they'd find evidence of life, and even if it was hidden in a billion-year-old fossil, one day it would reveal itself.

He fingered the fragments through the bag. "Still needs to be sterilized, I guess." He quickly slid open a draw and took out a small Geiger counter, switched it on and waved the rod over the bag.

"Yep, we didn't do that. Hot out of the astral oven and delivered straight to your door." She smiled, watching him.

The counter barely clicked so he put it down and looked up. "No problem, I'll do it. But seems pretty safe." He put the bag down on the desk. "Anything else?"

"Nope." She smiled sappily, but he had already gone back to examining the rock sample. She scoffed softly. *I'm invisible. Thank heavens for faithful ole Andy or I'd turn into a corn husk*, she thought.

Mia headed out. She had work do to, but curiosity was eating at her about their new guest. Maybe later she'd pop in on sickbay and see how the Russian woman was doing.

She ambled down the corridor until she came to the intersection that branched toward the pods and another passageway leading directly to sickbay. She paused for a moment, then impulsively decided to take a quick detour to look in on her Russian.

Her Russian. She scoffed. For some reason, Mia felt some sort of ownership or care for the patient, seeing she was the one who brought her in. Plus, her curiosity was killing her.

The strange thing was she also hadn't heard back from the team who had headed out to the Russian base.

It was no big deal. The base was more than a mile away and if there were any sort of damage, the crew would probably hang around and offer to lend a hand.

She stopped at the long glass panel to view the sickbay's recovery rooms. Their chief physician, Doctor Sharma Pandewahanna, was overseeing the woman, and at her shoulder was medical assistant Beverley Rhineheart. The Russian had had her suit removed and, for the first time, Mia could see what she looked like.

She'd been cleaned up and her shortish blond hair was swept back. Her cheeks were shiny enough to reflect the overhead lighting. She was a little older than Mia expected, maybe late thirties, and there were vertical lines between her brows and at the corners of her mouth. She was a handsome woman with a strong jaw line and a Slavic fold over her eyes. She slept but her face seemed troubled.

Mia tapped on the glass and waved. Sharma waved back and motioned for her to come all the way into the recovery room.

"There's no contagion we can find so no quarantine." Sharma raised her eyebrows. "And aside from some lumps and bumps, she seems fine."

Mia's eyes widened a little. "That's amazing. I thought she'd at least have some lung or soft tissue damage from the helmet breach." She tilted her head. "And there was some sort of oily black, uh, residue inside her helmet – what was that?"

Sharma bobbed her head for a moment. "Blood, old blood. But it also had some sort of enzyme within it. It had oxidized and was inert, but I'm still analyzing it."

The Russian woman's eyes moved behind her lids and she mumbled.

Mia leaned a little closer to her face. "Has she spoken yet?"

"No. But she should really be awake now," Beverley remarked. "Bad dreams, I think; a lot of frowning and mumbling."

Mia watched the woman's lips, waiting for something. She had so many questions. They all did. She reached out a hand to brush a few loose strands of hair from one of the woman's eyes.

At the touch of her fingers the woman's mouth flew open and she let out a piercing scream that made Mia's heart belt like a tiny, panicked animal in her chest.

The Russian sat up, eyes so round they threatened to bug out of her face.

"What the fuck?" Mia instinctively held her hands up in front of her.

Sharma and Beverley rushed to the woman and grabbed her shoulders, and after a few moments the woman settled enough to suck in huge drafts of air as though she had run a marathon. Her eyes rolled.

"Do you speak English? Do you know your name?" Mia said.

The woman stared straight ahead, eyes bulging. She held her hands up to look at them and then threw the covers off her legs to inspect them as well. She swallowed noisily and then nodded once.

Mia came around to stand in front of her. "My name is Mia Russo. I was the one who found you."

The woman's eyes slid to her. "Where …?"

"Where are you? You're at the American base, Kennedy Base, not far from your own."

The woman's eyes narrowed. "My base, you went there?"

"No, I never got there. I found you on the lunar surface. You looked like you had crawled there or been blown there." Mia rested a hand lightly on her arm. "Can you tell us what happened?"

The woman rubbed her face and seemed to relax a little. "My name is Olga, Olga Sobakin. I am, was, an engineer at the Vladimir Lenin Base. It was a lunar mining operation … to begin with." She seemed to swoon a little.

Sharma looked sternly at Mia. "Not too much for now. She needs her rest."

Beverley appeared holding a small tray with water, juice, and some painkillers on it.

"Just a few more quick questions," Mia told the doctors, and then leaned closer to the Russian. "Did your base explode? I felt a tremor before we found you."

Olga seemed to think on it for a while, and then held the side of her head. After a moment she nodded. "Explosion, yes, totally destroyed."

"How? How did it happen?"

Olga turned away. "It doesn't matter now, they're all gone."

"All gone? The mining team, or the entire base crew? I understand there were around twenty-two people there." Mia's eyes locked on the Russian. "It *does* matter. Did you see them all die, in the blast?"

"Is safe now." Olga closed her eyes, and the lines between them remained pinched.

"Safe? Who, you? *Us?*" Mia gripped the woman's arm, her frown deepening.

Olga's lips remained pressed together.

This doesn't make sense, Mia thought, and released her. "Well, we'll know soon. Our team went there. Should be back any time now."

Olga's eyes flew open and she sprang back up. "What?"

"Just rest now," Beverley said as she held out the tray.

"We sent a team. We had to check for other survivors, of course."

Olga flicked her arm up, knocking the tray from Beverley's hands. She launched herself from the bed and grabbed Mia's coverall's front. She stood half a head taller than Mia and was incredibly strong, and Mia felt herself be lifted up onto her toes.

"Get them back. Get them back, *now*."

Sharma and Beverley grabbed Olga and tried to steer her back to the bed, but shrugged them off and clung to Mia.

She pulled her closer. "They must not enter the base. They must not. *It* is there." Her eyes were wide. "It is *zagryaznennyy*" – she frowned as her mind searched for the word in English – "contaminated."

"Shit." Mia had had enough and used both hands to push the Russian back in a two-handed thrust. Olga lost her grip and let go.

"Do not let them back ... *kill them*," Olga begged.

Sharma and Beverley dragged the rambling woman back to the bed, and Mia headed for the comm. unit on the wall. She pressed the button and hit the code for the command center. "Captain Briggs?" She licked her lips as she waited but found her mouth bone dry. "Tom, are you there?"

There was a pickup, then a sigh. "Mia, kinda busy with something important right now."

"So is this. The team that went to the Russian base, how are they? *Where* are they?"

"Still at the Russian base, I assume. They're late checking in, but status unknown. We guess there might be some sort of comm. interference. No big deal," Briggs replied laconically.

"It might be. Olga Sobakin, the Russian woman I brought in, says there's some sort of contamination." Mia turned to look over her shoulder at the woman. "Olga, hey, how did your base get destroyed? *Tell me*."

Olga just stared back, remaining mute, her eyes half lidded.

Fuck it, Mia thought and turned away. "You've got to get them out, or send another ..."

"*No!*" Olga's scream made Beverley squeak and step back. "You must leave them." Olga's eyes looked about to pop from her head. "If they went in the base they will be contaminated now. And they will all be dead."

CHAPTER 04

Buchanan Road, Boston, Massachusetts

Joshua Hunter stood frozen in the center of his room. The huge animal sat beside him. It too was still as stone. His mother, Aimee, was downstairs, sitting at the breakfast table, captured by a depression so deep she bordered on being non-functional. Love did that, he knew.

She refused to give up hope of finding Alex but was confounded by not knowing what to do next, or even where to look. She had originally bombarded Colonel Jack Hammerson, Uncle Jack, daily for news. She fought with and screamed at him, but it soon became clear he couldn't tell her what he didn't know. Then she retreated to asking weekly. And still did this now two years later.

She would never give up.

And neither would Joshua.

He turned to the window, attracted by a darting movement – in a tree outside, a squirrel moved along the branch to stop and stare in at him, its tiny nose twitching. He projected himself into the small animal's mind, taking control of it, and felt its rapid heartbeat and breathing, and its nervousness about predators, balanced by the constant need to acquire food.

The squirrel's eyes became glassy and it shot upright on its hind legs. It stood like this for a few seconds, and then it began to do a slow dance. It spun and kicked, its movements becoming faster and wilder, before Joshua finally stopped it.

He chuckled and withdrew from the animal, releasing it. The squirrel blinked several times and then vanished into the higher branches.

He found he could do this easily now, to any animal of any size. He remembered he had told his dad about this growing ability and Alex had looked at him for a long moment, before simply suggesting he tell no one, not even his mom. Joshua could guess why – one day he'd be able to do this with people. And that would scare them.

There were other things he could now do. And some of those scared even him.

Joshua turned away from the window and sucked in a huge breath – it was time. He reached out to place a hand on the dog's huge head.

"Okay, Tor, let's do this."

Once again, he prepared to search for his father, and as the void he traveled within was a scary place, taking the dog with him gave him a level of comfort and protection he felt he needed there.

He opened his consciousness and reached out. His normally blue-gray eyes turned totally white. A freezing mist formed around him in the room, and spidery ice fronds appeared on his windows. Beside Joshua the hypnotically ice-blue eyes of the dog also turned to white orbs as the pair traveled together, throwing their minds out, looking for the spark of either Alex or the dark entity, the Other, that resided deep in the core of his father's mind.

Joshua knew his father never wanted to talk about the broken and brutal psychology that existed within him, but he knew what it was, and where it was: a battlefield wound from a mission in Chechnya had left a bullet fragment – and something else – deep in Alex's head. It couldn't be removed, and he'd been expected to die or live out his life in a coma.

That was the official story. But Joshua had eventually picked up the details of what really happened directly from his Uncle Jack's mind.

Uncle Jack had allowed an experimental treatment to be used on Alex, and it had resurrected him; saved him. It was hoped to give him some improvement to his metabolism to aid in his healing and boost his reaction times, senses, and strength. But it had done much more. Had made Alex so much more.

Further, whatever else was in his father's brain had combined with the treatment and had birthed another psychology, the dark entity, the Other, that was everything Alex wasn't. It revelled in pain and cruelty and savagery. And as it too grew stronger, it learned to free itself to take control of his father and inflict ferocious damage on those around him.

With Joshua's help, they managed to contain it until they needed it. And if Joshua couldn't find his father, then he would search for this brutal entity, because within the void it flared with the hot red of pure hate.

Joshua remained rigid like this for an hour as perspiration ran down his face and time moved on around him and the animal. But unfortunately, the world was big, and dark, and a million-million voices screamed and lied and howled for his attention. He needed some clue or some guidance or he could search forever.

He pulled back.

Joshua slumped forward to his hands and knees and blinked several times. Each blink caused a heavy teardrop to fall into the carpet beneath him. He'd failed again.

He slowly lifted his face. Beside him the dog whined and laid its large, square head on his shoulder. Joshua sniffed wetly and reached up to scruff the side of its face.

"Don't worry, Tor, we'll find him one day."

Joshua's mouth set in a grim line for a moment as he rose to his feet. A blood-red anger began to burn within him. The dog made a low growl in its chest like approaching thunder as it sensed the fury in its den brother and mirrored it.

At the far side of the room the lamp's lightbulb popped. Then a small metal trash can crumpled to the size of a tennis ball, and a spidery crack ran up the wall.

Joshua's eyes glowed silver with the intensity of rushing mercury. He spoke through clamped teeth. "And if that creature has harmed him, we'll tear it limb from limb."

* * *

Alex Hunter floated.

He was in water that was tropical warm just off a small, sandy beach. Somewhere close by he heard Joshua laughing and splashing his huge dog, which barked like a mad thing.

Aimee swam closer and leaned over him. Her beautiful face stared down and her electric-blue eyes glowed with love as she cupped his face in her hands. She leaned forward to kiss him, and he kissed her back.

He had never felt so calm and content in his life. The devil in his mind had been quietened, he had his family with him, and he was a million miles away from trouble. He didn't know exactly where, but he didn't care.

In the warm water, Aimee intertwined with his body, wrapping around him, and grinding against him. She kissed his ear, and he felt the tingling thrill of arousal as she reached between them, gripping his hardness.

"I love you," he whispered into her ear.

"And I have loved you since the moment I became aware of you," she whispered back as she circled her hips against him and tugged faster.

When they finished, he sighed and waited for his heartbeat to slow. He smiled up at her. "I never want to leave here."

"You never have to, my love," she said, and placed a hand on his face, closing his eyes. "And you never will."

Alex floated again.

* * *

Sophia sat next to the prone form of Alex Hunter. He was naked, and now fully healed. There was not a single sign of the massive burns he had received from the Italian volcano's heat. His eyes were closed, and he breathed slowly and evenly, and on his lips was a small smile.

Sophia's hand was over his. Though she had managed to arrange for facial masking that mirrored Aimee Weir's features, the rest of her body was the same as it had always been – slim, synthetic, brushed-silver looking, but feeling more like skin than steel. From the side of her head two cables no thicker than shoelaces extended from her cerebral network interface sockets to reach around and embed in the back of Alex Hunter's skull, just where the cranium sat on the upper neck vertebrae. The probes had inch-long needles that extended into the base of his cerebellum.

She made him dream. She kept him there in his own version of heaven. One she could insert herself into. She fed him, cleaned him, protected him, and loved him. And she would do that until the end of time.

CHAPTER 05

USSTRATCOM, Nebraska – the War Room

"Show me." Colonel Jack "the Hammer" Hammerson stood with his arms folded as he stared at the wall-sized screen before him. Hammerson was in his fifties, with an iron-gray crew cut and permanently stubbled chin. But he trained hard every day because he had a simple motto for life: *Be ready, all the time.*

Around him rows of technicians gathered data from across the globe, extracted from foreign databases, news sites, social media, their own covert satellite systems, and sucked straight out of other adversary satellites.

"This is what caught our attention." The technician showed Hammerson a series of images, each one closing in on a tiny piece of geography of the Earth's surface. The first showed a nearly round island that was just a small green jewel set in azure water.

"Where is it?" Hammerson asked.

"The Italian island of Spargi, in the Maddalena Archipelago, sir," the technician replied.

"I know it."

The satellite image continued to telescope toward the water and, just a few hundred yards out from the unblemished coastal beaches of the island, a shadow was seen beneath the surface in about fifty feet of water. The computer cleaned it up, and gave it form.

"A chopper. A *medivac* chopper." Hammerson's eyes narrowed. From what he could see, the make and model was the same type that had spirited Alex Hunter away from Catania at the foot of Mt Etna just on two years ago. In his line of work, there were no coincidences.

"Yes, sir, we believe it's an Italian medical helo; an Agusta Bell 412. So we focused our bird's eyes on the island and maintained surveillance. And waited. And then it gave us this." The technician ran more of the saved satellite footage.

It was night-time surveillance over the tiny spot of land. Hammerson knew the spray of islands that were in the Strait of Bonifacio between Corsica and Sardinia. Spargi was an insignificant land mass and should have been uninhabited. Though the island was a green jewel in warm, crystal-clear water, the landscape was jagged granite covered over with dense bush. The interior was so overgrown it was almost impenetrable and the only source of fresh water was rainfall.

"And then this is what really caught our attention." The technician's face was a study in concentration as he worked dials and a small joystick.

The satellite used light enhancement to focus on the sea. Then the surface water broke as a slim figure emerged, carrying a fish and lobster in its bare hands. It walked up the sandy beach and then stopped, spun, looked around and then up, seeming to stare straight into a camera lens hovering tens of thousands of feet above it. In a split second it turned and disappeared like smoke into the dense foliage behind it.

"Rerun it and go to thermal," Hammerson said as he craned forward.

The technician's hands flew over his keyboard.

"Now thermal," he said.

The colors of the entire image changed to black and dark purple through to flaring orange. Orange spots dotted the island, probably nesting birds, and maybe some rats on the coastal rocks. But the human-like figure remained unnaturally dark, until it turned toward them. Then it exposed the flaring dot like a miniature sun in its chest.

"Dead cold ... except for the reactor." Hammerson bared his teeth for a moment. "I fucking got you." Fury surged through him, but also elation. He had longed for this moment for nearly two years. And now it was here.

"Keep the satellites focused on the arena," he said and then turned and pointed at another of the technicians. "Send out a global HAWC recall."

"To which ones, sir?"

"All of them." Hammerson went out the door fast.

* * *

My wolves, Hammerson thought as he stood at the front of the room and looked slowly over the HAWCs as they assembled in the briefing room.

There were forty-two of them – the huge form of Sam Reid in front, plus Casey Franks, Roy Maddock, and dozens more of his best. Also entering and finding a seat was the enormous form of Kadisha 'Kady' Mutari. She had trained with the Rwandan Special Forces, become disillusioned with some of their practices, and was looking for an out. She came to Hammerson's attention in the way she single-handedly dealt with a cell of local terrorists and stood out with her fearlessness and formidable close-order combat skills.

As well as the woman's physical prowess, she stood six feet eleven inches tall, was broad shouldered, and emanated a lithe physical power. But she also managed to move with a feline grace that held it all in check.

All the HAWCs knew why they had been recalled from their missions. They had been waiting for this moment for two years. Now, they all stared at Hammerson with gazes of brutal intensity, hoping they'd be selected for duty.

Seated up front and to Hammerson's side was the incongruous form of the diminutive Doctor Walter Gray, the chief scientist and head of the weapon technology research section of USSTRATCOM. He too waited with nervous energy, his foot tapping to the beat, perhaps, of his racing heart.

Hammerson stepped forward and the room fell to silence. "You've all seen the images," he began, and thumbed to the screen behind him. "It is our target, the android. There has been no confirmed sighting of Captain Alex Hunter, but we believe he is there."

Hammerson called up another image. "There are a few small caves on the island. But the only structures are ruins from the time Spargi Island was garrisoned during both world wars. Some of those wartime fortifications still remain, above and below ground."

"Frontal assault. We take in heavy kit, fully armored, and some combat lasers for good measure," Casey Franks insisted. "We get the Arcadian back and cut that hunk of junk into ten pieces for good measure."

"HUA!" The rest of the HAWCs seemed to agree.

Hammerson nodded and began to pace, pulling at his chin for a moment. "I wish it was that easy."

"Have we sent in a drone?" Sam Reid asked. "See if we can locate where she, *it*, has Alex hidden."

"Can't risk it," Hammerson replied. "This thing has the most sophisticated sensors money can buy. *Our* damn money can buy. It detects we're onto it, it's liable to vanish again, taking Alex with it. We already made it more cautious by flying an Atlas V over the site."

"That bird is about a thousand miles up – it could see that?" Roy Maddock asked.

"I discount nothing." Hammerson nodded toward the scientist. "Doctor Gray, why don't you remind our people of what we're dealing with?"

"Oh, of course." Gray jumped to his feet, straightened his glasses, and walked up to join Hammerson, who stood with arms folded, making the material of his sleeves strain. Gray was short, slightly pudgy, and sported a large pair of thick glasses that made his eyes swim behind the lenses. He swallowed and then turned, seeming a little nervous in front of all the angry-looking titans. The bottom line was they knew he had created the thing that had taken Alex Hunter and was now their most formidable adversary.

Gray cleared his throat again. "What we're dealing with is a form of android. In simplistic terms, an android is an artificial being designed to resemble a human, and is often made from synthetic, flesh-like material." Gray waved a finger in the air as he began to pace. "But Sophia is to that definition as a go-cart is to the latest Mustang." He stopped to smile flatly at the group.

"You created a monster," Casey said.

"Yes, I created her. I did what I was asked to do. And I did a very good job." His eyes slid to Hammerson momentarily. "We invest billions in the Synthetic Warrior Program, and every major global adversary we have is doing the same. Best we win the race and have the superior tech on our side, yes?"

"But this thing is *not* on our side, is it?" Sam shot back.

Gray bobbed his head for a moment. "She thinks she is. She was programmed to protect and defend – in this case Alex Hunter – and that's exactly what she thinks she is doing. She's simply over excelling."

"*Over excelling?*" Sam roared and shot to his feet. His broad, six-foot-five frame suddenly dominated the room. "Dammit, man, it was not supposed to *over excel* against us."

"Hey!" Hammerson glared at the big man. "Take it down a level, Reid."

Sam nodded. "Sorry, sir." He lowered himself back into his chair, making it groan under his weight.

"Proceed," Hammerson said to Gray.

Gray straightened to his full five feet six inches in height. "To be clear, Sophia was designed to be a guardian angel or a hunter-killer – guard us and our friends and kill our enemies. She has a super-tough, near-indestructible chassis that's twenty times tougher than Kevlar and more akin to spider silk for its pound-for-pound tensile strength. In effect, it's molecular chainmail covering advanced technology and hydraulics."

An image of Sophia appeared behind him, arms and legs spread wide, a little like Leonardo DaVinci's Vitruvian Man. He glanced at it. "And do not be misled by her slim design; due to the advancements in microtechnology, size does not mean strength. She is as powerful as a dozen of you combined. And with her HiPER fusion reactor, she could theoretically operate independently for a thousand years."

"Thanks for the sales briefing, doc," Casey scoffed. "I just want to know one thing: can we kill it?"

"She's not living, so death has no meaning here, Lieutenant Franks." Gray's eyes were level. "But I believe she can probably be stopped. Probably," he repeated softly.

"You said it was designed to be our guardian angel, but Sam's right, what happened?" Roy Maddock asked.

"There was a problem. An unexpected, ah, side effect of the applied logic patterning model we used for the brain." Gray sighed.

Casey scowled. "What it's done to Captain Hunter is more than some damn side effect."

Gray looked up. "I said she's not living; androids aren't. But I believe she thinks she is. And that's our problem." He exhaled through his nose. "We found out too late that the unintended consequences – as I said, the side effects – of this logic model were a few extra human-type emotions. Unexpected things like anger, hate, jealousy." He smiled sadly. "Maybe even love."

"All the things that make us humans dangerous." Hammerson raised his eyebrows.

Gray shrugged.

"Yeah, them's sure some side effects." Casey's eyes sparked. "You created a super strong synthetic warrior that is near indestructible, insane, and probably has the hots for the Arcadian, so much that it decided to take him captive. That about sum it up, doc?"

Gray's expression was deadpan. "After the Italian mission she must have decided Alex Hunter was in mortal danger. Which he was. So she extracted him."

"We were all in danger," Sam replied. "But she stole a chopper and took Alex Hunter hostage."

"Not a hostage. In fact, she has made no demands and is not likely to. She has simply bonded with him."

"I'd like to bond an RPG to her ass," Casey growled.

"We want her back," Gray replied, flatly.

"*You* want her back. And keeping the android in one piece is low priority," Hammerson said evenly. "Retrieving our missing soldier, alive, is the *only* priority." He turned to his HAWCs. "But we still have insufficient intel and need to know more about where Captain Hunter is to the inch before we plan any sort of assault. Some of us have seen this thing in action – it's fast, strong, and lethal. Exactly as it was designed to be."

"We need to be there, and without being seen or detected," Sam said and sat back in his chair, making the wooden joints pop again. "Not easy when you're up against something that is basically a walking sensor net." He looked up at Gray. "Come on, doc, give us something to work with. What are Sophia's weaknesses?"

"There are none." Gray looked insulted for a moment before his eyebrows rose. "Well, maybe there are two *limitations* I can think of. One is Alex Hunter, but she now has him."

"That's a big fucking help." Casey Franks rubbed a hand through her cropped white hair. She stopped and looked up. "Hey, it's been nearly two years. That's more than enough time for the Arcadian to fully regenerate. He's the one guy that could have stood up to the roid-droid, so why hasn't he?" She looked at Gray from under her brows. "If he's still alive."

"The images we saw were of her with food. Sophia doesn't need food, so she is feeding someone who does," Gray said.

"Good. Then what's the other weakness the droid has?" Casey demanded.

Gray's lips lifted a fraction at the corners. "Me."

Hammerson turned.

"I am her creator, her mentor, her teacher, and her father figure. She has admitted as much. I believe she might surrender herself to me." He faced the colonel. "That's why I need to be there."

Hammerson brushed it off. "Not a chance."

"Your HAWCs are the most formidable fighting force on the planet. But Sophia could cut through them in minutes." Gray looked from Hammerson out over the Special Forces soldiers' brutal faces. "Me being there could save lives – all of their lives."

"You just finished telling us that this thing is tough as all hell and could wipe the floor with the HAWCs, and *you* want to stand in front of it? With what? A smile and a clipboard? Forget it, doc." Hammerson frowned at the smaller man.

"She has no reason to attack or kill me. She knows I am no threat, so am probably the only one here with little to risk or fear," Gray replied. "I demand to be given the opportunity to deescalate this situation, and potentially avoid bloodshed. It is my risk, and my call. I created her. I'll bring her in."

There was silence for several seconds. Hammerson began to pace. He knew that the HAWCs taking Sophia head on, if she knew they were coming, would be walking into the jaws of death. Even if everything went to plan there would be some form of confrontation. And it would be a violent and bloody one.

He shook his head slowly and then gave the small man a flat smile. "You're madder than I am." He snorted. "Fine."

Gray smiled and nodded. "Thank you."

Hammerson turned back to his HAWCS, his mind working. If he did find out that Alex was already dead and his HAWCs could not subdue the android, then he'd launch a missile from space and turn that entire island into a smoking crater.

He straightened. "Bottom line, we still need more intel. We can't send a probe or any other sort of infiltration technology, or person, as they'll be detected the second they arrive." He folded his arms. "So give me some options, people."

"We create a diversion. I gear up in a full MECH suit, go in, draw her out." Sam opened his hands. "Then a team can drop in on the other side of the island and find Alex Hunter, and confirm his status."

"Lieutenant Reid, even in a full combat MECH suit, Sophia would pull you apart in mere seconds," Gray said. "Plus she can move at fifty miles per hour, so once she's done with you, she could be back confronting team two almost immediately." He looked down. "And crucially, we don't yet even know where she is hiding the Arcadian – your search team will burn time looking for him."

"Sam, good option, it's on the short list. But I'd want two MECH suits." Hammerson lifted his chin. "What else?"

"Colonel, let me talk to her, alone, first," Gray said. "You can be assembling your assets."

"Backed up by me and Maddock in MECH suits," Sam said.

"That might work. It would certainly buy us some time." Gray gave Sam a small salute, and then turned back to Hammerson. "But I think we're overlooking one of our key assets here." Gray's eyes were large behind his glasses.

Hammerson turned, and raised his eyebrows. "Go on."

"The boy," Gray said softly.

CHAPTER 06

USSTRATCOM – Administrative Center

Jack Hammerson sipped his bourbon and thought through his plans. He had little time and knew that Walter Gray was right – the boy was the key.

Joshua Hunter, Alex Hunter's son, was unique. Some of Alex's distinctive characteristics had been inherited, but he had developed other unexpected abilities that were of great interest to the military. In simple terms, Joshua had the ability to link with other minds – he could actually travel to and then merge his own consciousness with another person. Hammerson expected that eventually he'd be able to totally control the minds he merged with.

He took another sip, feeling the cool burn slide down his throat. Where Alex Hunter was a military tool of force, Joshua would one day be a psychological scalpel. Or a psychological nuclear bomb. Jack Hammerson wanted to make damn sure the kid was "in the tent" and under their control before that happened.

He knew Joshua practiced that psych-merging with the dog. The genetically bred German shepherd living with them was from the Guardian program and was an experimental military animal. The dogs were bred to be battlefield companions to their soldiers: as well as bringing all the heightened senses of a canine, each was immune to radiation, well above average size, strength, and intelligence, and averaged around two hundred pounds each. Torben, or Tor, was no exception.

In effect, both the dog and boy were in a Petri dish and being observed under a military microscope.

Jack Hammerson exhaled through pressed lips; he knew that using the boy was a risk. The kid was developing, if not a taste for violence, then an insensitivity to it.

His phone intercom buzzed as the front-gate guards informed him his guests had arrived.

Hammerson sipped his bourbon again, and then upended the glass, swallowing the remaining burning liquid in a long gulp.

Yeah, using the kid was a risk. But in this, he had no choice.

He headed for the door.

* * *

Hammerson stood out front of the building on the steps and watched as the dark SUV slowed and then stopped in front of him. The back door opened, and Joshua Hunter stepped out.

"Hey, Uncle Jack." He grinned and waved. The kid was twelve now, but already stood at about five-eight, and was a dead ringer for his father, Alex.

The rear door began to open but then was shoved all the way wide, and with a bounce of rear suspension springs, the biggest damn animal Hammerson had seen leaped out and raced to catch up with Joshua.

"Jesus Christ," he whispered. It was the dog, Torben, and it trotted beside the boy, its head turning one way then the other, eyes missing nothing. The animal was formidably muscled, must have been 250 pounds, easy, and looked like it would have been right at home on the Great Plains fighting saber-toothed tigers some 50,000 years ago. Its eyes were pale to the point of being luminous, and they held a high level of intelligence. The dog fixed its unwavering gaze on Hammerson. The man stared back.

Joshua leaned closer and whispered something and the dog relaxed and looked away, perhaps satisfied Hammerson wasn't a threat.

Last from the car was Aimee Weir, and she looked fit and still striking with her jet-black hair, pale skin and electric-blue eyes. She smiled, but it was fragile and broke apart quickly.

She rushed forward. "You found him?"

"We have some news." Hammerson returned the smile and took her hand and held it. He placed his other hand on Joshua's shoulder. "Come on, everyone, we can talk inside." Hammerson turned and took the pair with him.

On either side of the entrance there was an armed guard, and both let their eyes slide to the huge canine. Perhaps they were waiting to see whether their colonel was going to allow the beast to enter or not.

"At ease," Hammerson said to them.

Each probably gave a sigh of relief. But their eyes never left the animal.

Hammerson took Josh and Aimee up to one of the large offices on the second floor that had a huge window looking over the drill grounds. The sun was out, and the grass looked like a bowling green all the way to a line of trees perhaps half a mile away. There was a plate of cookies on the table, and he pointed.

"Help yourself, big guy."

"Thanks." The boy flopped down on the couch and pulled the plate forward. The dog lay at his feet, keeping its eyes on Hammerson until Joshua slipped it a cookie.

"Tell me," Aimee asked. "Is he alive?"

Hammerson sat at his desk and pressed a button on a console. The wall slid to the side, showing the large wallscreen. "We believe so. But we haven't been able to confirm it yet as there's been no physical sighting." He pressed a few more buttons and the screen lit up. "But we have found the android."

Joshua stopped eating and turned.

"Sophia," Aimee said.

Hammerson nodded slowly. "There's an island off the coast of Italy in an area that few people visit. It is called Spargi and it's tiny, rugged, and secluded. Nothing there but birds and a few ruins left over from the world wars."

"Perfect for hiding," Aimee breathed.

"Yes."

The screen lit up with the image of the water and the circled wreck of the helicopter lying offshore. "Recently we located the downed chopper that we believe was involved in taking Alex." Hammerson changed the slide. "Then we saw this."

He played the images of the android leaving the water with the crayfish.

Joshua rose to his feet, his face totally devoid of emotions. "Food. The android doesn't need food," he said.

"That's right, well spotted." Hammerson stopped the image as Sophia left the water and just before she vanished into the dense foliage. He enlarged and enhanced the image, and again, and again. For the first time, they saw the face – Aimee's.

"Oh, God, no." Aimee put a hand over her mouth. "She made herself look like me."

The boy walked toward the screen and stared. The dog followed him. Joshua stared for several seconds. "What will you do now?" he asked softly.

"We want to go in, but that presents enormous risks. You see, we don't know exactly where Alex is on the island. We suspect he's in one of the ruins or even in a cave. We also don't know what state he is in. But one thing's for sure: he wouldn't stay there unless he was unconscious or a captive." Hammerson turned to Joshua. "Until we know that, mounting a rescue mission is extremely dangerous – to him and us. Plus, if it detects us, the android might just decide to vanish again, taking Alex with it."

"And if you knew where he was, you could go in and get him?" Joshua asked.

Hammerson nodded.

"Then I will find him," Joshua said, and turned back to the screen. "Show me on the map where this island is."

Hammerson had it ready. He zoomed in on the tiny landmass, this time he had an image that laid a grid showing the known structures and caves of the island. There were over a dozen places that could have been suitable, and all were invisible from the air due to the thick vegetation cover.

Aimee scowled. "It's not safe for Joshua to … do that."

"It's okay, Mom." Joshua sat down cross-legged in front of the screen.

"Just find him for us, and then we'll do the rest," Hammerson said.

The dog came and sat beside Joshua and the boy reached out and put a hand on its shoulder. "Come with me," he said softly.

He drew in a lungful of breath, held it for a second or two, and then exhaled a long sigh.

Hammerson got up and stood beside him to watch. *Holy shit*, he thought, as his breath fogged when the room grew cold around them. The boy's and dog's eyes had changed to completely white orbs.

Aimee walked away to look out of the window. "I hate when he does this."

"He's gone there, hasn't he?" Hammerson said. He reached up to press his jaw; his back teeth hurt as though there was some sort of silent vibration or energy wave passing through the room. Then his head started to throb. "Is he doing that?"

"Yes. You better stand back." Aimee turned. "He's looking for his father. He has been nearly every night for two years. Now that he knows where to look, he'll soon know whether Alex is alive or dead." She looked down at Joshua. "Being in the same room, you better pray Alex isn't dead."

Hammerson stared at Joshua, studying him. He knew exactly what Aimee was referring to. The boy had abilities that were off the chart and didn't even know himself what he was capable of. To Joshua, it was all fun. But to Hammerson and the military research and development labs, the kid was a potential weapon of unimaginable power. One it intended to make use of when and if the opportunity ever presented. This was a field test.

"I ... see ... him." Joshua exhaled the words.

Hammerson felt the hairs on his neck rise.

* * *

I'm here.

Alex Hunter was standing in the warm, azure water of his favorite beach. He turned and saw Joshua standing on the shore. Beside him the hulking dog stared with an intensity that bordered on being hypnotic.

"Joshua?" Alex smiled. "Where've you been? I thought you were –"

"Looking for you. For years." The boy didn't smile. "I don't have much time."

For years? Alex wondered at the comment. "But I was just with you on ..." He couldn't remember. And then saw that the boy looked older, taller, and Tor certainly wasn't the big puppy anymore.

"Where ...?" Alex turned about.

"I miss you. Mom misses you. This isn't real, Dad. Be ready, be ready to fight it. We're coming for you." Joshua's voice faded as he became translucent. "I love you, Dad. I love you ... I love ... I ..."

"Wait." Alex rushed toward the spot where Joshua had been, plowing through the water, but just when he was about to leave it, something excruciating grabbed him by the back of the neck, and yanked him back. "No-*ooo*."

Alex strained with every ounce of strength against whatever was dragging at him, strained harder than he had ever done before. Immediately the water vanished. The sunlight turned to darkness. The sounds of the birds, the lapping waves on the pristine shoreline, receded, and then even the sun's heat turned to a musty coldness. The pain in his skull was agony and he reached around behind his head and felt the open wound and the cables buried into his flesh there.

"What's happening?" he asked the darkness.

Years, Joshua had said. Years they had been looking for him. Where was he? Who had done this?

Deep in the very core of his mind, there was a dry laugh, like from death itself. The Other began to stir.

You let this happen, it whispered. And then the laugh became a deafening roar.

CHAPTER 07

Russian Aerospace Defence Forces, Krasnoznamensk, Russia

Colonel Gorlovka sighed. "We have no choice: we must contact the Americans and seek their assistance. Our base has gone too many days without communication and our satellite sensors picked up seismic disturbances consistent with an explosion."

Major Alexi Bilov rubbed his chin. "Maybe they already know."

Gorlovka looked up.

"Maybe they know exactly what has happened. Because maybe they were involved." Bilov raised bushy eyebrows.

"Involved? What are you saying?" Gorlovka sat back and frowned. "The Americans destroyed our base?" He scoffed. "It's a mining base."

"You know it's more than that." Bilov continued to stare. "Perhaps the Americans found out."

Gorlovka folded his arms. "I doubt it."

"After the events in Crimea, even if they did not know, it is still one possibility that we must take seriously." Bilov opened his hands wide. "Their sanctions are not crippling our economy as much as they hoped, so perhaps they wished to send us another, more forceful, signal."

"I don't think so." Gorlovka dropped the papers onto his desk. "If true, it would be an act of war. But the Americans would not display that sort of belligerence over a few trade sanctions and harsh words at United Nations Council meetings."

Bilov straightened. "Unless they found out that we are periodically scrambling the communication and monitoring frequencies of their lunar base."

Gorlovka folded his arms. "And even then, the response would not be proportionate."

"But the base has gone dark for no reason. Like I said, it is only one possibility. And I agree with you. But others higher up do not. They have decided to proceed with the usual maintenance and resupply vessel. But there will be little cargo and instead we will send several investigative specialists to determine exactly what has happened." He smiled knowingly. "In addition, we will be sending security personnel to ensure our examination is uninterrupted and all avenues explored."

"Security personnel – Special Forces?" Gorlovka's eyebrows rose.

Bilov shrugged and his smile widened. "Our project must be protected and sensitive materials and research samples are to be retrieved at any cost."

Gorlovka nodded. "When do they leave?"

"We've moved the schedule up. They leave tonight." Bilov got to his feet and saluted.

Gorlovka's mouth turned down. "Better them than us." He saluted with two fingers. "I wish you, and them, good luck."

* * *

Olga lay back and tried to rest but her head throbbed mercilessly. There was also a dark depression settling over her and she hated the way there seemed to be missing memories, even missing thoughts and ideas, as though the throbbing was a sledgehammer destroying her mind one brain cell at a time.

And there were the voices in her head that she recognized as belonging to her friends and co-workers from the base. Not furtive whispering, but screaming as though trapped in torment. They were the voices of the damned and they would drive her mad.

Olga had that washed-out feeling one got when they had just fought off a severe fever – everything ached. Still, she had waved away painkillers as she didn't want to be any more mentally fragmented than she already was, and simply asked for some clothing. She was a tall woman and they found her some suitable coveralls, and she now sat cradling a glass of rehydrated orange juice, her focus turned inward.

She felt scared, confused, and trapped, but had nowhere else to go. For now she was safe, but depending on what happened over the next few hours, that might all change.

Olga sipped the juice, not tasting it, but accepting that at least it didn't leave grit on her tongue like the Russian rehydrated juices. She knew she had two choices: keep her mouth shut and protect Russian interests, or tell the Americans everything and perhaps keep them, and herself, alive.

But even when she wanted to tell them what little she remembered, the throbbing grew more painful as if the horrible memories in her mind were wrapped in barbed wire. Something was stopping them surfacing, keeping her mind feeling crowded and fuzzy. Concussion, she guessed.

The door slid open and a stocky, serious-looking middle-aged man entered with Mia, and a couple of others she assumed were base security. The man's gaze was unwavering and impatient, and it fixed on Olga. He smiled, but there was no warmth in it.

"My name is Captain Thomas Briggs, the base commander." He grabbed a chair, carried it closer, turned it backward and then sat down in front of Olga. "And Ms. Olga Sobakin, you are a guest and are not going to attack any of my people again. Is that clear?"

Olga nodded. "I'm sorry." She barely remembered doing it now.

Briggs grunted his acknowledgment. "But what you *are* going to do is tell me everything you know about your base, what happened there, and why my team is now not responding." His gaze was intense. "And also, why us going there panics you so much."

Olga knew the Americans would never leave their people out on the lunar surface, even if they became contaminated. That meant no matter what state they were in they would be retrieved. She had no choice. They needed to know. Needed to know what they were up against, and in all likelihood would soon be facing.

She looked at their expectant faces. She didn't have to tell the full truth. Her twin priorities now were to warn them, and protect Russia.

Olga exhaled in a long sigh and concentrated as she forced her mind to take her back to the beginning. A small needle of pain started in the center of her head, but she ignored it and pressed on. And as she did it was like a film rolling in her mind, with her set apart and watching as a spectator this time while all her lost friends screamed out for her to save them.

"We were just doing what we were here to do: mine KREEP."

"Creep?" Mia asked.

"A mineral blend of potassium, rare earth elements, and phosphorus, right?" Briggs replied.

Olga nodded. "Yes. On this dig, we were at 800 feet down when Pieter, our senior geologist, saw that the samples taken were beginning to change structure. The composition went from dust to something like clay, and the mineral substrate became a little more complex. He was confident that we would soon strike a rich vein." Olga stared straight ahead, trance-like, as she smoothly blended fact with fiction. "But then we broke through into the void, a cave."

"Did you just say there were caves down there?" Briggs asked.

She nodded. "We thought it was a good sign, that maybe there had been enough water there at one time to dissolve the rock." She shrugged. "Why not, there certainly wasn't any volcanic activity to create lava tubes or any other sort of erosional feature. We didn't even know if they were natural or not." She smiled ruefully.

Mia frowned. "What do you mean, not natural? If they weren't natural, then what?"

Olga looked at her. "We sent a probe down into one of them. It was deep, and seemed excavated." She bobbed her head. "But not by machinery, more sort of organic, like it had been burrowed out. Our geologists had never seen anything like it before." She looked from Mia to Briggs. "So, our base commander authorized a team to investigate. A group of four: two geologists, one biologist, and myself."

Her mouth turned down at the corners as she felt the pang of the harsh memories surging back, and with them, terror bloomed in her chest. She pushed that down as she fashioned her own version of events.

"It was Churnov who found the artifact. We didn't know what it was, but it wasn't a mineral composition we recognized, or anything resembling a natural geological formation." Olga laughed darkly. "We stupidly brought it back to the base for further analysis."

"When was that?" Briggs asked.

Olga looked confused. "I don't know. What day is it now?"

"It's Tuesday, March twenty-one."

Olga nodded. "Then it was two weeks ago." She reached a hand up to wipe blurring vision.

Mia lay a hand on Olga's forearm, and Olga took it and held it, and then went on with her story. "People, my friends, went missing. Slowly at first. Alekseev, one of the junior geologists, simply vanished. Impossible in a base our size, we thought. We even searched outside, and back down in the mine. But all we found was torn clothing and this black mess in his sleeping quarters."

Mia turned to their doctor. "Like we found in Olga's helmet."

Doctor Pandewahanna just stared at Olga.

Olga nodded slowly. "It got everywhere after a while. On everything." She looked up at Briggs, who seemed spellbound. "Do you know what we found out that mess was?"

Briggs shook his head. "Why don't you tell us?"

Olga smiled coldly back at him. "It was human proteins, like in blood, mixed with digestive enzymes, and dissolved calcium. Exactly what might be excreted –"

"*Excreted?*" Mia's face screwed up.

"Yes, excreted, like shit." Olga's stared at the floor. "We didn't know it then, but it was probably all that remained of Alekseev." She squeezed Mia's hand.

There was silence for a few moments, as everyone took in what she was telling them.

Finally, Briggs sat forward. "Ms. Sobakin, let's go back a few steps. What was the artifact you found? Describe it."

Olga nodded, and gave herself a few moments to create the scene. "It just looked like a large lump of resin or amber but smoothed over. Maybe it was an egg, or maybe it was a *kokon*, uh …"

"Cocoon?" Mia suggested.

"Yes, cocoon," Olga agreed. "But there was something inside it. No one saw it happen, but we found the object broken open. Whatever emerged, we never found it. The next day, like I told you, Alekseev disappeared. We searched everywhere." She made a small sound in her throat. "Then after several more days, more people vanished – four by then – among a team of twenty-two that is a big proportion to simply vanish into thin air. Fear set in, of course. People became distrustful of each other."

"Wait a minute, are you saying there was something alive beneath the moon's surface?" Doctor Pandewahanna asked. "That's impossible."

"Maybe, or maybe the thing arrived here millions of years ago, and had been buried, or buried itself, in those labyrinths. Waiting … waiting for us."

"Shit," Mia breathed.

Olga continued. "We searched the lunar surface, thinking maybe people had left the base. We even thought maybe they had defected to your base." She sighed. "We didn't know what was happening, but no one trusted anyone anymore. It got strange. No one wanted to be left alone with anyone else."

Her focus turned inward as her memories played back in her mind. "Then came the incident that saved me." She smiled sadly. "And doomed everyone else."

Olga felt a pang in her chest, and the needle of pain in her head blossomed into a full-blown migraine. She couldn't help her face crumpling and let out a deep sob, as this part of her story was real.

Doctor Pandewahanna put a hand on her shoulder then turned to Beverley and nodded. The assistant held out the glass of water.

"You can rest now, if you'd like," Sharma said softly.

"The hell she can," Briggs shot back. "We need to hear this, *right now*."

"Yes, I need to tell it." Olga waved the water away and sniffed wetly, then wiped her nose with a forearm, leaving a dark glistening streak there. "It all went bad when I went to see my friend, Annika."

Olga saw Mia lean forward, hanging on her every word. The young American woman still held her hand.

* * *

Vladimir Lenin Base – twenty-four hours earlier

Olga headed down to see her friend, Annika Asmerov, who worked in engineering, and noticed that her workshop door was shut. It was odd, as Annika never shut her door because she said it made the already bad ventilation worse.

Perhaps, Olga thought, with everyone being on edge, security was more important than fresh air.

She knocked, and after a few moments opened the door and went inside. It was empty, and Annika's chair was tipped on its side.

"Annika?"

Olga waited a few seconds but there was no answer. The familiar black mess was all over the bench top, floor, and chair.

She turned slowly. The workrooms, like all rooms on the mining base station, weren't large, as lunar real estate was far too valuable. Plus, it cost additional energy to light it, temperature control it, and fill it with breathable air.

Olga swallowed dryly, suddenly feeling nervous. She decided she would catch up with Annika later and was heading for the door when there came a small noise.

She paused and tilted her head. The noise had sounded like the mewling of a small kitten. She waited, concentrating, but now all she could hear was the soft breath of the air-conditioning unit.

She was about to turn away when it sounded again. She was sure it came from the far corner where there was nothing but a clothing cabinet for lab gear. The cabinet door was open just a crack.

The soft mewling came once more, a whine or feeble cry. Exactly as she had thought before: like newborn kittens.

She crossed to the cabinet, and a few feet from the door she reached out. But for some reason the hair on her neck prickled, and she felt a flutter of primal fear in the pit of her stomach. Warning lights were flashing in her mind, and she didn't know why.

"Annika," she whispered, almost afraid of making too much noise.

Her hand was still outstretched and up close now she heard the mewling and a faint wet sliding and popping sound. Olga drew in a deep breath as well as her courage and lunged forward, dragging the door open.

The shock was so great she felt as though a wave of ice water had washed over her and she coughed and gagged at the same time.

It was Annika, impossibly folded and stuffed in the corner cabinet, and caught up in black cords. They looped around her waist, arms and neck, and pierced her clothing.

Olga felt she had been punched in the stomach. She couldn't breathe. The cords were burrowing into Annika's mouth, nose, ears, even the corners of her eyes.

Olga could only watch as those pulsating coils inserted themselves into her friend, strangling her. Stalks grew revoltingly from her friend's skin, and on their ends, bulbs swelled and popped open.

The final mind-tearing image was of Annika's eye rolling toward her, and in its tear-filled gaze there was fear, and pain, and –

Olga remembered falling back, and then nothing until she was in the corridor, screaming for help. She only stopped to punch the fire alarm button and sprint on again, with the klaxon blaring and lights spinning overhead adding to her sense of looming insanity.

She sprinted along the corridor to the base meeting room, yelling things that didn't make sense even to her, making people stream out of their workplaces, worried about her as well as the alarms blaring. Some began to follow her.

Once there she collapsed to her hands and knees and gulped down air. She tried to explain what had happened, but their faces were confused or scared, though some just looked pissed off.

"It got her," Olga gasped. "It was wrapped all around her."

Commander Puskin forced people from his path, and she could tell by the way his bushy brows knitted that he was furious.

"Olga, did you set off the fire alarm?" he asked.

"Yes, but, Annika, it had her, and –"

Puskin roughly grabbed her arm, and led her away from the group, pausing to nod at two men, who sprinted off. He then led her to a seat and made her sit down. Over his shoulder, Olga saw that the others followed, like a wolf pack, their eyes hungry with accusations now.

Someone handed her some water, and she gulped it down, realizing for the first time how thirsty she was. Her head throbbed and she knew she needed her medication.

"Gather your thoughts, Ms. Sobakin." Puskin pointed a big finger in Olga's face. "Now take a deep breath and tell me what is happening."

Olga shut her eyes, calmed herself and tried to speak as evenly and convincingly as she could manage. "My friend Annika, was *there*, in her cubicle, but jammed into a closet, and there was stuff all over her like black cords."

"Someone pushed her inside?" Puskin asked. "Tied her up with cords?"

Olga pushed her short blond hair off a sweaty forehead. "No, something had her, *like* black cords, but alive, wrapping her up."

Puskin stared into her face for several moments. "And you didn't untie her?"

"No-*ooo*, *not* tied up ..." She grimaced, frustrated and sick to the pit of her stomach. "Just check, please, *just check*."

"We already are." He rose to his feet.

The two men Puskin had dispatched returned from Annika's office. Puskin waved them in.

"Report."

"The room is empty." Pieter Andropov shrugged and looked at his companion who nodded.

"What?" Olga pushed people out of her way to see the men. "Did you check the closet? In the corner?"

"Yes, it was open, there was nothing. Anywhere." Pieter hiked his shoulders. "No Annika, no mess, just an empty room."

Olga felt pops of dizzying light going off in her head. "That's impossible. *She was there.* You're lying."

Pieter frowned. "There was nothing."

She turned to Puskin. "Someone cleaned it up."

"No one, Olga." Puskin had his arms folded. "There was nothing to clean up."

"Something had her and was killing her. And now she's gone. Just like Alekseev, and just like all the others. Don't believe me? Then where is she?" She threw her hands up. "Where are *they*?"

There was a commotion outside the room, and then people began to laugh. Puskin looked over his shoulder and out into the corridor. His mouth set into a grim line as he turned to face Olga.

"No one has been hiding anything. Unless you are?" He stood aside. "Come in …"

Annika stepped into her room. Her face was composed and her eyes went from Puskin to Olga, and then to the crowd. "What's going on?"

Olga's mouth dropped open. "But … you were …"

"I was down in maintenance. Have I missed something?"

"Everything is fine, Annika." Puskin took Olga by the shoulders and stared into her face. "Things have been stressful enough around here lately, we are all making mistakes." He rubbed her arms. "Go back to your pod, get some rest, and sleep it off.

"Annika, you were in the cabinet …" Confusion and anger began to rise inside her.

Annika's brows knitted. "I was in what?"

"I'll get someone to cover your shift tomorrow." Puskin squeezed her shoulders. "And I think maybe no more drinking on the job."

Olga felt fury boil over; she knew what she saw. Something was very wrong here.

"No!" She shoved him.

"That's enough, *Ms. Sobakin*." Puskin grabbed her elbow, hard. His mouth was twisted.

Olga hit him. Harder than she should have. Puskin's head momentarily rocked back, and when he looked at her his eyes blazed.

"I'm sorry," she said quickly. She turned to her friend. "Annika?"

But Annika just stared at her blankly, like she didn't even know her.

"That's not Annika!" Olga screamed.

Puskin cursed through teeth stained with blood and pointed at Olga. "Put her in detention." He glared at her. "You can sleep off your drunkenness in there."

* * *

Mia swallowed dryly as the Russian woman stopped talking then just sat staring straight ahead, like a wind-up toy that had finally wound down. Her revelations were unbelievable and horrifyingly plausible in equal measure.

"Go on. Then what happened?" Captain Briggs urged.

After a few seconds Olga's shoulders hiked a fraction. "I was placed in detention, like Puskin ordered – locked in a secured room. I didn't care. I was happy to be away from everyone, and somewhere I would feel safe. It was supposed to be for three days. But it wasn't. After one day, the food and water stopped coming." She looked up, her eyes shimmering with tears. "Because that's when *it* came out."

"*It?*" Mia asked in a whisper.

Olga covered her face. "I heard people running, and the screams went on and on, day and night. Beyond just fear in their voices – it was insane terror. After a while I was exhausted and lay down in my private jail. But then I heard *it* moving around outside. The thing that had been hiding in our base somewhere now must have felt strong enough to be out in the open." She snorted softly. "Or maybe there weren't enough of us left to be a threat anymore."

Olga leaned back; she lifted glistening eyes to the ceiling for a moment and sniffed tears back. "When the screaming stopped, I knew it was all over. Maybe everyone was dead. And sooner or later it would find me, and I would be trapped. So, I shorted the wires for the door lock, and snuck out."

"What did you see?" Mia asked.

"I wish I hadn't seen anything." Her mouth turned down. "It was a nightmare. Some of the people were frozen, gripping walls and furniture, but they weren't people anymore. They were husks, with things growing from them. I knew then I was alone."

Olga shook her head. "I couldn't fight it, but I also knew I couldn't leave it in the base for the Earth supply ship personnel to walk into. I had to try and kill it." She nodded. "So, I drained the cooling pool for the nuclear rods to create a meltdown explosion. I got out and ran. And then everything went black."

No one spoke as the group stared at her. Overhead, the intercom pinged, making Mia jump.

"Captain Briggs?"

Briggs walked to the wall and pressed the button. "Go for Briggs."

"The rescue team is on its way back. But they're not responding to their messages, sir. What do you advise?"

Briggs stared at the comm. unit. He half turned to Olga, who was shaking her head.

She brought her hands together as if in a prayer. "Do not let them in. I beg you."

"I can't do that, Ms. Sobakin." He turned away from her. "Open the outer doors." He paused. "But use high-level quarantine protocols and don't let the team into the base until they've been deconned and checked over. Twice."

Olga lowered her head and shut her eyes.

CHAPTER 08

The twenty HAWCs jogged in two lines toward the waiting stealth choppers. They had just disembarked from the high-speed jets and were exploding with eagerness and adrenaline. But still, none of their heartbeats rose above a resting rate, none of their hands shook, and all breathed easy. The Special Forces soldiers were like machines in their combat armor, and two of them, Sam Reid and Roy Maddock, already big men, were encased in full battle MECH suits, which were basically two-legged tanks, making them stand over seven feet tall.

A few of the Italian flight crews at the Aviano Air Base in Italy stopped what they were doing to stare. But the regular soldiers knew not to ask, and not to get in their way as the HAWCs radiated a raw, menacing power.

The HAWCs split and loaded ten apiece into the choppers, which immediately lifted off. The first chopper had an extra passenger – Walter Gray, in a HAWC suit that made him seem like a small, armored turtle. He constantly pulled at the various folds and sharp angles, trying to get comfortable.

Sam smiled as he watched Gray for a moment before he thought again of their battle plan. He'd seen what Sophia could do, and knew that if things went bad, then blood would flow. HAWC blood. Sam was in charge of the mission and he was damn sure he'd find his friend, and bring him and everyone home. But if someone needed to take the first hit, first bullet, or deathblow, then let it be him.

He pulled free the small picture he had tucked behind his left pectoral plate, close to his heart. In his huge, armored hands, the pretty brown face seemed too clean and too perfect. He knew she was too good for him, always was, but Alyssa was his lucky charm, and while he had her, he felt ten feet tall and unbeatable. But if this was to be his last mission, then he'd go out with her face being one of the last things he'd remember – he was okay with that.

He tucked the picture away and tapped it twice with an armored fist. *Now, focus,* he demanded of himself. He patched his comms feed into the HAWC earpieces.

"You all know why we're here." His voice was deep and slow.

Immediately the HAWCs straightened and their eyes moved to him.

"One of our brothers has been taken." His voice rose. "We want him back."

"HUA!" The HAWCs stomped a boot down.

Sam lifted one huge fist. "Where we go, they tremble."

"HUA!" The boots came down again.

"Where we go, they fall."

"HUA!" Their voices rose.

"No one can stand in our way. Alone, we are unstoppable. United we are invincible!" Sam roared.

The HAWCs bellowed back, slamming fists against armored chests, until the pilot urged them to silence.

Sam looked at their faces filled with righteous fury and primed for battle. Walter Gray sat shrunken in the corner. He seemed to try and move a little further away from these raging giants.

Sam knew the odds were against them, and some of them might not be returning. There were no old HAWCs, as the saying went.

"Five minutes," the pilot said. "Going low and switching to silent running."

Nobody lives forever, Sam thought and tapped his chest again just over the tiny picture.

* * *

The chopper blade noise vanished as the helo dropped to sprint just a few feet over the water's surface.

In chopper one, Sam Reid and Roy Maddock wore the highest-grade battlefield armor – the MECH suits. Maddock was big, and Sam was bigger, but the suits made them giants, and even though the armor was made of lightweight but high-density plating, they still weighed in at over a thousand pounds and needed to be internally hydraulic assisted. Bottom line, the men were mobile juggernauts that could rip steel with their hands like paper.

The rest of the elite Special Forces soldiers had standard combat suits that were a mix of Kevlar mesh and biological armor plating that was "grown" into shape in the laboratories to meld to the individual wearer's unique form. The biological armor had a hardness on the Mohs scale of 9, where tungsten was 7.5, and diamond 10. It gave the wearer better protection than titanium without the weight.

Their selected weaponry was a mix of MK16 SCAR rifles for close quarters, sniper rifles, light machine guns, M320 grenade launchers, plus armor-piercing and explosive rounds they hoped would cut an android to pieces. Plus the MECH suits were equipped with ELBs – emitted light beam weapons – lasers.

Sam looked along his team. He had been given the lead overall and felt energy dance inside him like electricity. Marko was making fists in his armored gloves; like all of them, he couldn't wait to see some action. Many of the others, like the towering Kadesha, had their eyes closed and waited like immobile giants to be turned on and let loose.

All of his team were combat hardened and had seen some of the worst and weirdest shit that the world could throw at human beings. But the HAWCs were a different breed: bigger, faster, stronger, smarter; the last and most brutal line of defense against chaos. Few people knew that monsters were real, and from time to time they threatened not just the country, but the entire world. So, the HAWCs were created to be exterminators, guard dogs, and no one would ever know their names. But the world slept safer with them standing in the dark and guarding the flock.

Sam was the oldest at thirty-eight and didn't know how many more years he had left in him. He thought again about the saying that there were no old HAWCs: you didn't retire in this job, you just got slow, and beaten to the punch one day. And then it was over.

Maddock nudged him and showed him an image on his forearm screen. Sam nodded. Alex had been pinpointed inside one of the old personnel bunkers on the east side of the island. He was alive, but they had no idea whether he was unconscious, on his feet, or chained to a wall.

They needed time to assess that, free from attack. Therefore, they were going to come in at two angles. Sam and Maddock, plus his other eight HAWCs, would approach from the west side of the island first, and try and draw the android out. Then, from the other side of the island, Casey Franks and her team would be dropped in to extract the Arcadian.

Sam knew they needed to give Team 2 at least ten minutes. He doubted Walter Gray could bring Sophia in, but he could at least distract her, and buy them more time.

"All right, doc?" Sam asked.

Walter Gray began to hyperventilate, his face flushed. He nodded once.

"Don't worry about a thing. We'll have your back." Sam turned to the group. "Infiltration silence on my mark. Three, two, one ... *mark*."

The huge men and women would keep talk to an absolute minimum and mostly use hand signals. And if out of visual contact, they would just have to improvise, at least until the android had been located. He expected it'd get real noisy then.

Just ten minutes was all he wanted, but Sam had seen what the android could do, and knew they were going to be the longest ten minutes of his life. Or the last.

Overhead, the red light went orange, telling him they had one minute to drop point. Sam and Maddock pressed a small stud on their necks, and their visor plates moved down over their faces and oxygen began to circulate inside the suit. It was dry and cool compared to the near tropical air of the Italian coastline.

The other HAWCs slid their clear shields over their faces and locked them down to seal them. Sam's team lined up near the door and he called Gray up next to him. In the massive suit Sam wore, the small scientist barely reached Sam's shoulder.

Overhead, the orange light blinked three times and then went green, and the side door slid open. One after the other, Sam's teams leaped out to strike the water just 200 yards from shoreline. Sam took Walter Gray with him.

The chopper silently arced away, heading for Maddalena Island, where it would wait for them.

Sam, the scientist, and the HAWCs walked along the ocean bottom. *Ten minutes, Lord, just give me ten minutes*, Sam prayed.

CHAPTER 09

Spargi Island – disused World War Two bunker

Sophia stroked Alex's face as she sat next to his body, which was stretched out on the stone slab. Thin cables reached from a port on the side of her head to the back of his skull. He dreamed sweet dreams that she engineered, designed to keep him in a twilight world where, from time to time, she could also insert herself so they could enjoy the dreams together.

Alex's body repaired at a rapid rate, and though most male human beings had a life span of around eighty-seven years, with his metabolism, she had no idea how long she could preserve him. If it was a hundred years, two hundred, or many more, it didn't matter. In the world she created for him nothing else mattered. As long as she was with him, he was safe, and content.

She touched his face again with the back of her slender sliver hand. She was thankful Doctor Gray had given her synthetic body a form of sensory input, and she could actually feel the warm flesh of Alex's cheek.

But now it wasn't enough. She had been raiding the doctors' surgeries on the nearby island of Maddalena for equipment. When she had enough of everything she needed, she would try and undertake the next phase of her union with Alex: the permanent bonding.

With her understanding of human anatomy and Alex's extraordinary recuperative powers, she was sure she could remove a lot of the cumbersome and frail human characteristics to make him more like her, and perhaps even change his brain patterns to remove all traces of his beloved Aimee. Then he would be truly free.

She had already inserted a seed; a tiny mechanism no bigger than a grain of rice, whose original use had been as an infiltration bug. But she had adapted it within her own neural networks to be a little piece of her that Alex would carry around in his mind forever. It would be her link to him and would do until she could permanently rewrite him.

Sophia leaned closer to his face. "Soon," she whispered, and then let her lips touch his, just at the corner.

Then: *intrusion.*

Her inbuilt sensors detected multiple non-biological intrusions to the island with heavy metallic componentry – weapons.

She spun.

They'd found her.

She turned back and quickly detached herself from Alex, the cords withdrawing inside her, and the wound on the back of his head knitting shut like lips to seal itself over. In minutes it would be healed and nearly invisible.

Sophia had always known that one day she might need to move and she had been scouting for new, secure places for months. But first she had to make sure there were no witnesses. No one must see. No one must follow. And that meant there must be no one left alive *to* see.

Almost faster than an eye could follow, she flew outside to meet the intruders.

* * *

"She's disengaged," Joshua said in a monotone.

Behind the boy, Hammerson had been pacing and Aimee watched with her hands balled into fists. Joshua could feel their nervous energy but he ignored it. There was a window of opportunity that had presented – it was now or never. His father was mentally chained, and only he could break those chains. With a little help.

Flying through a long dark tunnel with flashes of light that were memories, emotions, and sensations, Joshua rushed toward the dark place in Alex's mind. Beside him the dog kept pace as the strength of Joshua's mental abilities brought the animal along with him.

Time to fight. Time to fight. Time to fight, he called through the ether to his father.

* * *

Perspiration streamed down Joshua's face, and his teeth were gritted so hard Aimee actually heard them grinding in his cheeks.

"Is he okay?" Hammerson asked.

"I don't know." Aimee went to Joshua and was about to crouch beside him when the huge form of Tor came and sat between them. The dog's eyes weren't white anymore.

"Easy there, big guy." Hammerson held out a hand, but the dog ignored him.

"Joshua must have released Tor. He must need more time." She turned. "Something is happening."

"I'm in blackout – can't reach the mission team until they contact me. It's out of our hands now." Hammerson stared down at the boy's anguished face. "Whatever will be, will be."

CHAPTER 10

Sam and his HAWCs rose just above the water's surface, and he held up a hand to stop his team. He waited a few seconds until his suit sensors gave him the all clear. Then he waved them on and his nine-strong team plus the diminutive scientist came up on the beach.

He and Maddock were front and center, Gray just in behind the pair, with the others fanned out behind and either side of them in a V-shape formation.

Built into the suit armory was a range of projectile weapons, from small and heavy caliber to mini rocket launchers. Walter Gray had even applied laser tech. The battlefield MECH suits carried enough firepower to storm a fortified city and win.

But the adversary they were about to engage was designed to confront, combat, and annihilate any threat, including soldiers as powerful as HAWCs.

"Movement," Maddock said evenly.

"Hold," Sam replied.

The HAWCs held their positions, spread out over about a hundred feet. Sam turned slowly, switching from light enhance, to thermal, to vision amplification. The forest was quiet as a tomb. And that wasn't a good thing.

"It's out there," Maddock said.

"Oh, yeah." Sam also had that soldier's intuition that told him the enemy was there but staying hidden for now. The urge to act became near overwhelming, but until they had a target, they would just waste energy, create noise, and give away their offensive capabilities.

"Eyes out, people."

Sam turned again and saw his team in their black-clad non-reflective field armor taking advantage of the shadows, and the hulking form of Maddock close by in his heavy combat suit. To normal adversaries, the HAWCs would be almost invisible, but to Sophia they probably stood out like flaring beacons.

"By now, she'll know I'm here and she'll be scanning us," Gray said. "Sophia will be looking primarily at your numbers, fire power, and probably at me, wondering why I'm with you."

"What do you want to do, doc?" Sam asked without turning.

"Stay where you are. It's my move." Gray unlocked his helmet and removed it.

"What do you think you're doing? Put that damn armor back on."

"Really, Lieutenant Reid, she could tear it off me in a blink. I need her to see my face and read my expressions." The small scientist drew in a deep breath. "Wish me luck."

Sam shook his head. "Yeah, good luck." He looked toward Maddock. He couldn't see his fellow MECH suit wearer's face behind the formidable helmet, but bet he was also saying the soldier's silent prayer for battlefield fools.

Gray walked a few dozen feet into the thick scrub cover and stopped. He held up a hand. "Sophia, come out. I know you're there."

He didn't have to wait long for her to appear. But it was so quick that Sam couldn't even register from where. One second Gray was in the middle of a small clearing, alone, and the next Sophia was between him and the HAWCs, obscuring their view.

"Amplify sound," Sam said softly. His suit helmet complied, and he heard what the pair was saying.

Grey reached out and stroked the android's arm. "You need to come home, Sophia."

"Home?" The slim figure tilted its head. "I have no home. I have a workshop, where you would undoubtedly disassemble or reprogram me."

Gray shook his head emphatically. "No, it is where you were created – born, if you like. Sophia, there's an obvious error in your logic patterning. To put it in human terms, you're sick, and I want to make you well."

"I'm not sick." She bent forward to stare down at the scientist. "You made me a twilight creature; something between a machine and a conscious being. And now you think that the remnant human emotions inside me are a sickness. You did this to me, Walter." She straightened. "But I like it."

Sam watched intently, but it was impossible to read the android as it faced away from them. He just had to wait and hope he had time to react if anything went down.

"Yes, I did do this to you, Sophia. And I also know you appreciate it," Gray continued. "You have the best of both worlds. You have our strengths but not our weaknesses. You will never know death as we do and so can continue to learn and grow for centuries." He hung onto her arm.

She lifted her head and then half-turned, not quite looking over her shoulder. Sam knew she was probably hearing all the HAWCs in their concealment, maybe even right down to their individual heartbeats. She turned back to the scientist.

"You gave me awareness, and curiosity. And you also gave me understanding of the human condition and its innate sense of love and loyalty. It's true I will never know death." She reached out to cradle Walter Gray's face in her hands. "But there are things that, to me, are worse than death." She leaned even closer. "Betrayal. And the worst betrayal of all is by a parent."

Sam frowned as she leaned forward to press her face to Gray's as if kissing him. She eased back but continued to hold Gray's face as a lover would.

Gray's hands came up to grip her wrists. He began to struggle and grunt as she lifted him from the ground.

"Only you could have created me," Sophia whispered into his face. "And only you can destroy me. So …"

"Oh, shit." Sam knew what was about to happen.

There was a sickening crunch and Gray's head exploded between Sophia's hands.

"*Engage!*" Sam roared.

Gray's spasming body dropped as hundreds of rounds smashed into the brush. But Sophia had already vanished like smoke.

Her attack came swiftly. One minute Rodriguez was holding a rotating shotgun loaded up with saboted shells, and the next the man was flung twenty feet into the air to smash against a tree trunk with a sickening crunch of bone and tendon. He lay still at its base.

Sophia was a skeletal wraith moving at a speed that was impossible to comprehend. HAWCs had above-average reactive abilities, but they were born of flesh and blood and no match for a synthetic entity created for war. Shots rang out, but they smashed into rocks, trees, and the ground as the android was never still.

Another HAWC sprayed a stream of bullets at the lightning-fast android, but it jinked once, twice, without losing an atom of speed, and then appeared in front of the man to use one hand to grip the barrel of his gun and bend the steel upward. She rammed her other fist directly into the face shield of his helmet.

Sam roared his anger as the hand punched right through and came out the back of the helmet dripping with blood and destroyed brain matter. He knew then that the only hope was the huge combat suits he and Maddock wore with their assisted speed, strength, and firepower capabilities.

"Power up."

Maddock moved into attack position. "Fire in the hole." He launched half-a-dozen rockets from the suit armor, and each of the eight-inch projectiles sped toward their adversary like a hypersonic swarm of death and destruction.

Sophia leaped twenty feet straight up into the treetops and avoided the explosive cluster. As her tree toppled, she dived at Maddock, coming at him like a silver spear, landing in front of him. Maddock was lifted in the air and thrown. At Sam.

Sam tried to catch the gigantic combat exoskeleton but even with the immense power of the suit he couldn't defray the mass and velocity of the thousand pounds of armor and bodyweight. They exploded backward to snap tree trunks and tumble along the ground.

Sam's head spun but he shook it off.

"Oh, man, that hurts," Maddock groaned as Sam pushed him off.

"I got damage to the drives – I'm out," Maddock said. "Going to eject."

"Negative, stay down. You climb out and you'll end up like Gray." Sam lifted his head. "Sound off!" he yelled.

There were few voices, and the ones that did reply only did so to inform him they were also down.

"Goddamn." Sam spun. "Has anyone got eyes on –"

There, standing like a metallic specter, was Sophia. The most horrifying aspect of her blood-streaked silver frame was she wore Aimee Weir's face, and it looked unmarked, clean, and totally at ease. It was like one of those horror movies where the deranged killer skins the face of their victims and wears it as a ghastly death mask.

"Sam Reid. You shouldn't have come." The Aimee face smiled. "And you're all alone now."

Sam fired the shoulder-mounted laser. But no matter where he aimed, the android was already somewhere else.

Then Sophia appeared beside him, reached out one hand and crushed the laser barrel like it was tinfoil. With her other hand she pushed him backward onto the ground.

She stood over him. "I could peel you out of there and crush you down to ground beef. Is that what you want?"

"I've just come for Alex Hunter," Sam said, getting to his feet. "Let us take him home."

"He's better off with me," she replied. "You nearly killed him last time; burned him down to his bones. He was little more than charcoal and blisters. Next time you'll succeed."

"He saved us. We need him." Sam wondered how many minutes he and his group had expended. Had Casey Franks and her team already extracted the Arcadian? "Let him go, Sophia. Let him go back to his family."

"*He doesn't need them anymore*," she shrieked in a metallic screech that was part animalistic howl and part electronic white noise. She came at him faster than he could react and punched into his chest hard enough to buckle the combat-strength armor.

Sam grunted, feeling the massive blow all the way to his rib cage, and struggled to suck in breath. If she punched him again in the same spot, the next hole would be through his ribcage and into his heart.

They are no old HAWCs, he remembered.

Sam struggled to one knee and held out an arm, palm facing her. "You win, you win."

"I win when you cease to be functional." Sophia grabbed his outstretched arm.

It was what he was counting on. Sam swung his other hand up to grab the android by the neck. In the hulking suit he wore the slim figure of Sophia was nearly a third of his size, and he lifted her from the ground. The fake Aimee face remained calm and untroubled. She gently reached up and took hold of his wrist, and immediately the pressure began.

The massive strength of the MECH suit's steel-titanium blended plating compromised as she squeezed. Warning lights flashed inside the faceplate of his helmet.

Sam swung a sledgehammer fist and struck the side of her head. He smashed into Sophia again and again, and she turned away to protect her face. But for the first time, Sam was able to detect the tiny, red sensors behind the Aimee face's blue eyes.

Sophia brought her other arm up and grabbed hold of one of the plates on Sam's already broken chest. She tore it and a lot of the internal mechanism free, and then drew her fist back.

"Goodbye, Sam Reid," she said softly as Aimee's soft lips curved up into a smile.

Sam sucked in a breath and held it. *Here it comes*, he thought, and tried to conjure a memory of Alyssa's pretty face.

Then the android froze with her fist cocked. She turned to stare somewhere up along the ridge. Her head tilted.

Sophia shrieked metallically, threw Sam aside like he was a toy, and vanished up through the forest on all fours like a silver streak of lightning.

Sam groaned and tried to sit up, but the suit didn't respond. He engaged his comms. "Franks, you got incoming; get the hell out of there."

He used his own great strength to roll onto his back as the massive suit of armor began to sputter and die.

From beside him he heard Roy Maddock groan. "*Now* can we eject?"

CHAPTER 11

Casey Franks paused to listen to Sam. "Roger that." She turned. "Head's up, party is coming to us. ASAP."

She and her team were escorting Alex out of the ruins. The man seemed to weigh a ton, and the towering Kadisha and one other of the huge HAWCs carried him between them. He was alive but unconscious, and that was all that mattered. Now they just had to bug out – and stay alive doing it.

Their evac point was a strip of beach just large enough for the helo to touch down, but it wouldn't approach unless the field was clear. The android could destroy all the HAWCs, plus the chopper, in a few minutes.

The ten HAWCs moved through a small rift where sheets of rock had split apart creating a narrow valley with sides ten feet high. Trees grew together at the top, creating a semi-dark tunnel. When they were halfway through the hundred-foot length of broken stone, Sophia jumped from the top to land in front of them and block their exit.

Ah, Shit. "Bogey has arrived," Casey said into her mic.

It was too narrow to back out and there was no way around. HAWCs never ran, and Casey knew that left only one option: fight or die.

"Muscle up on my six." Casey lowered her brow and walked out front.

"Hello, Casey Franks, good to see you again." Aimee Weir's serene face was streaked with blood – HAWC blood – and behind her blue eyes were twin red dots that made them seem to burn with hellish fury. They turned to points of fire as she looked from Alex Hunter's body to Casey. "The others are dead or dying. Leave Alex Hunter, and I'll let you walk away." The head tilted. "But just you; the others I will use to send a message to your superiors."

Behind her, Casey heard guns rack. "You want Alex?" She smiled. "You can take him over my cold, dead body, you fucking metal-ass monster." She brought the ballistic shield down over her face and her gun up.

CHAPTER 12

Joshua entered the dark place. It was the deep void in Alex's mind, the place between worlds where the monster hid. "Remember who you are," he said softly.

"Where am I?" Alex asked. "I'm lost."

"Then follow me." Joshua began to pull back. "Hurry. Your people are dying. They need you."

"But Aimee is here." Alex's mind didn't budge.

"Dad, it's not Mom, not Aimee." Joshua knew that if Sophia got Alex's body again and joined her mind with his, he would be lost forever. Time was running out and he needed to at least slow her down.

"I can't fight Sophia by myself. Dad, please *hurry*."

* * *

"I'm coming." Alex strained and began to rise, but then something grabbed his leg and pulled him back. The dry laugh sounded from behind him.

Alex turned to see the hulking brute that was the thing from his id crouching in the darkness: the Other, one of its huge mishappen hands curled around his ankle.

It has now become our prison and our sanctuary. We like it here, the Other hissed. *All of us.*

"Fight it, Dad," Joshua yelled, but his voice was fainter now. "Fight for Mom, fight for me."

It's not me he needs to fight. The sound of heavy chains being dragged came out of the pitiless darkness. *We're not alone in here now. But you know that.* The words rasped dryly all around him.

"Who else is here?" Alex roared.

We're both really in Hell. But only you think you're in heaven. And your jailer hides within the mirage. The laugh was so loud, Alex covered his ears.

"*Dad!*"

Alex turned just in time to see Joshua violently ejected from his mind.

* * *

Casey charged Sophia, firing as she went, but the android slapped her aside as easily as if she was a child.

As HAWC rounds slammed into Sophia's back, the android picked Casey up and shook her violently. Then she slammed her into the ground so hard her helmet visor cracked and her vision swam.

She could only watch in a dreamlike state as her team was being massacred. The HAWCs couldn't hit the android with anything significant as she anticipated the discharge and was out of the way faster than they could aim and shoot. Hand to hand was a death sentence.

Casey groggily tried to rise as she saw two formidable HAWCs pulled apart like they were made of paper. The last standing, Kadisha, dived, catching Sophia, and as they rolled together, the tall female HAWC jammed her gun into the silver torso and fired point blank again and again. But each round did nothing more than leave a powder burn.

And then it was the android's turn. Sophia lifted the six-foot-eight woman over her head and threw her like a javelin into a small stand of trees. Kadisha smashed through them, rolled, but refused to stay down. The Rwandan-born HAWC grabbed a six-foot length of a sapling as thick as her wrist and snapped it in half over her armored knee. She swung the two lengths in an arc as she charged back in at the android, yelling an age-old war cry.

"Yeah, go girl," Casey said between clenched teeth.

The twin clubs moved in a blur as Kadisha used an ancient Nguni war-sticks fighting technique. She battered the android, who lifted a hand to ward off the pair of heavy clubs as they smashed into her head, torso, and arms.

But no matter how physically honed a body was, flesh soon tired in a way that the android's synthetic muscles never would. Kadisha's attack slowed, just by a fraction, but it was enough for Sophia to shoot out a hand to grip one of Kadisha's wrists. And snap it.

Kadisha grunted but didn't cry out, and redoubled her effort with her other hand. Sophia did the same with that arm. Then she broke her legs, and the huge warrior woman crumpled like a broken toy.

The silver android was washed in HAWC blood, and the red glow of the orbs shining through Aimee's blue eyes made her seem like a demon. With Kadisha laying helpless beneath her, Sophia lifted one of the clubs the woman had used and stared down in triumph.

Casey knew what was about to happen and drew on every remaining ounce of strength she had to climb unsteadily to her feet. With only partial clarity of vision, she quickly jacked explosive rounds into her gun and fired several off.

But hitting Sophia was like trying to hit smoke as the slim-bodied android was just too damn fast.

Kadisha's head turned to Casey and she grinned through bloody teeth. *Kill it*, she mouthed.

"Fuck, yeah." Casey tracked the android and fired again and again. One of her explosive-tipped rounds hit a large, leafless tree stump growing from a crack in the rock wall, and the two feet–wide, ten foot–long tree trunk thumped down just behind Sophia.

Casey's gun clicked on empty and as the smoke cleared, there was a ghostly silence. Casey found herself standing alone, her chest heaving as she sucked in air. She let the gun fall to the ground. Frustration and fury boiled within her as she looked at the massacre surrounding her – good soldiers, all down or gone for zero gain.

She had failed, and she knew her payment would be death.

Sophia's glowing orbs went from her to the prone body of Alex. "I admire you, Casey Franks. I will regret having to kill you."

Casey pulled out her longest blade and a huge handgun she had strapped to her thigh. It was a .50 cal Desert Eagle, her personal choice, and one of the most powerful magazine-fed semiautomatic handguns on the planet. It was big and powerful enough to take down a charging rhino.

The handgun was heavy, but she held it unwaveringly. She knew the android had a power source in the center of its chest. It was shielded, but Casey bet she only had to compromise the shielding once to slow the thing down. Then, if she could put a few more of the finger-length rounds into it, it'd be game over. Maybe.

Think like the droid. Anticipate. Casey exhaled slowly, her eyes steady.

Sophia took a step and Casey fired – not directly at the android, but where she guessed she might dodge. She guessed right; the huge slug took the android in the shoulder, spinning her around.

Casey grinned madly. "How do you like that, you freaking monster?"

The android got to her feet, a dark streak and a small dent on her shoulder the only evidence she had been hit by the powerful bullet.

"Ah, crap." Casey's smile dropped.

She fired again, and again. But this time the android wasn't going to underestimate the handgun or Casey's ability to predict her movements, moving in a zigzag out of the bullet's path so fast she was just a silver blur.

It was obvious the twenty feet separating them was too much and allowed time for the android to react. Casey needed to shorten it – so she charged, firing as she went.

Casey was a dead-shot, and fast, but Sophia moved even faster and seemed to vanish. And then she appeared beside Casey, and easily wrenched the gun from her hand. She swung her other arm to smash into the back of her head, flinging Casey forward.

If Casey hadn't been wearing the HAWC field armor and helmet, her head would have been caved in. As it was, she bit her tongue hard enough to fill her mouth with blood, and her vision blurred again – it was only for a few seconds, but it was the final disadvantage.

When Casey's vision cleared, Sophia was standing over her.

That was bad. But what was worse was the android held the ten-foot length of fallen tree stump in her hands. The two-foot-wide base was a wooden elephant's foot about to be thumped down on her face.

"I'll make it quick for you." The android lifted her arms.

"Fuck you, robot," Casey yelled.

"I'm not a robot," Sophia said calmly.

Casey kept her eyes open, smiling, and waiting for the eternal release.

Nothing happened.

Casey frowned, narrowing her eyes.

The android seemed frozen.

No, Casey realized, not the android, but the tree stump. There seemed to be something beneath it. Like some sort of distortion in the air that was creating a barrier and keeping it from being brought down on her face.

What the hell?

CHAPTER 13

"Jesus," Hammerson whispered, as Joshua let out a scream that was long and agonizing.

Blood ran from Joshua's nose, and leaked from the corners of his eyes. He held his hands out as though holding something, something heavy, and his neck and arms corded with veins as they strained to hold it.

Aimee rushed to him, but the huge dog stood in front of the boy, keeping Aimee and Hammerson away from him. But even it licked its lips nervously and kept glancing over its shoulder at Joshua.

"Wake up!" the boy hissed through clamped teeth as his arms began to drop. His totally white eyes flew open. "Help her, no-*oooow*!" he roared as his arms fell to his sides.

* * *

The swirling distortion beneath the stump began to dissipate, and with a shriek of triumphant static, Sophia lifted the stump high above her head and brought it down toward Casey Frank's upturned face.

Mid-air, the stump exploded into matchsticks. The basketball-sized rock was like a cannonball as it blew the stump apart and continued along the small valley.

Sophia went to spin around but instead was grabbed and lifted. Alex Hunter held the slim android above his head. Then threw her fifty feet along the corridor of rock.

"Yeah, like that, bitch." Casey tried to get to her feet but staggered groggily.

Alex reached a hand out to his soldier.

Sophia came back at them like a missile, striking Alex and dragging him away from Casey. "I'll take you back myself," she said.

Alex could feel the raw power of the thing as he held on. Though Sophia was a head smaller and slimmer than his broad, muscled form, she carried him easily up over the rock valley wall and then along the pathway.

He grabbed her wrist and punched where the arm was thinnest. The arm bent several inches, but then snapped back into shape.

Sophia glanced down at him. "Don't do that," she said. "You need to rest again. To dream. I know you like that."

"Never." Alex pummeled Sophia, but it made no difference. As he was dragged, he reached out to grab a tree trunk and held on, stopping the android momentarily. He used all his strength to hold the tree and finally Sophia came closer to him.

"I may have to break both your arms, and maybe your legs as well. But we both know you'll heal ... eventually." She tilted her head. "Or maybe I should remove them."

She raised a slim hand, flat, over the arm he used to grip the tree, about to bring it down in a chopping blow, but once again, the air seemed to become distorted and she couldn't move it.

"What is that?" she asked, and her beatific Aimee face turned to him. "There's something, someone else, inside your mind. I can sense it now."

Her power unit, Dad, remember, in her chest. Hurry.

Alex felt rather than heard Joshua's words. But he remembered then – the reactor core – her heart, and the source of her power.

Casey Franks was sprinting up the wooded slope toward them. Alex flattened his hand and thrust it spear-like into the center of Sophia's slim silver chest with every ounce of strength he could muster – it dented inward. That was all. But at least it stayed dented.

Sophia's red glowing eyes flickered for a moment and she released Alex and took a step backward. She looked down, letting her slim fingers trail over the slight depression. Her head lifted.

"Why?" Aimee's face was rent with sadness, and her eyes glowed a deeper red. "I saved you. I cared for you. We are the same ... outcasts."

"You are a threat." Alex backed away. "To everything I love."

"We are both creations of the military, Arcadian. But I think you are more of a machine than I am." She looked briefly to the approaching Casey Franks, and her beautiful mouth curved up a little at the corners. "We are not like them. You know that." Her hand dropped. "You can't hurt me, Alex." Sophia began to advance. "We were almost there. Just a few more days and I can show you a love that transcends the physical and will live inside you forever."

Alex looked over his shoulder. "I'd rather die."

"I'll never let that happen." She charged, or rather dived, coming at Alex like a torpedo and taking him off his feet. This time she didn't soften her blows, obviously wanting to debilitate him, as she knew that he would regenerate if she hurt him enough to render him unconscious or simply immobile.

The first punch struck Alex's face, crushing the cheekbone, and delivering a flood of agony. Alex threw hammer blows at her, but she guarded her chest now, and her body was a lot tougher than flesh and blood.

He knew she was stronger and faster than he was, and the next blow came at him so fast he didn't even see it coming, caving in several of his ribs.

Anger bloomed within him as his frustration grew. He knew if she took him again, he'd be lost forever. Lost in a twilight of nothingness where he couldn't even hope for the release of death.

Alex struck out again and again, and each blow was either avoided or simply bounced off her tough hide. His anger rose, and with it came a flood of adrenaline and chemicals secreted from within the mass buried deep within his brain.

The Other stirred within him. *Faster*, its dry voice hissed from within the core of his mind. *Leave nothing behind.*

The unnatural chemicals turned the normal human fight-or-flight response into a single purpose: *Destroy*. And then it programmed Alex's body to achieve that goal – Alex's heartbeat slowed, and his reaction times amplified. He easily moved out of the way of Sophia's next blow.

This time his actions were so quick that it was the android that seemed to have slowed.

Alex threw a punch with all the force he could manage, striking the silver body in the torso, but other than knocking it aside, there was no lasting damage – the dent popped straight back out. She was right. As strong as he was, he could not hope to bring her down.

From behind them Casey Franks had finally reached them, and he turned to see the female HAWC moving in slow motion.

"Finish her." Casey Franks tossed the Desert Eagle loaded with armor-piercing shells.

Sophia shot her hand out for it, but it was Alex's longer reach that grabbed the handgun from the air. He spun, still in the air, sighting his target – the center of her chest, the housing plate over the internal reactor; her eternal heart. He fired.

At that range the large, high-energy, high-speed round was too fast for Sophia to avoid and it struck the silver chest mid-on. It blew the small body off its feet. She sat for a moment as if confused, one hand over her core.

From the reactor there was a red glow – the shielding had been breached. One more round on target and it would be all over. Alex aimed again.

"Please. don't." Sophia kept her head down. "I love you, Alex." She lifted her face – Alex was paralyzed as the face and voice were Aimee's, her brows sloped in a pitiful pleading. In that split second of hesitation, she was gone.

Sophia went up through the thick forest and over a tumble of rocks on all fours, moving like a silver spider. Alex fired off three more rounds, but he didn't think he hit her again. He went after her.

He should have known better – the thing that had made her most dangerous wasn't just her strength or speed, but her intelligence, her strategic thinking, and the emotions she could use – and with them the ability to deceive.

Alex burst from the tree line and came to the cliffs on the southern edge of the island. There was nothing but a hundred-foot drop to the dark, blue water.

He lowered the gun. She was gone.

He stood there for several moments, staring down. As the mix of chemicals left his system, he felt deflated and suddenly very dizzy. He raised a hand to the back of his head and felt the scar tissue over an old wound there. Though it had nearly healed, his hand still came away sticky with blood. He thought nothing of it as he also had a depressed cheekbone, broken ribs, and was covered in cuts, bruises, and abrasions.

Casey Franks grabbed him under the arm as he swayed slightly on the cliff edge. "Easy there, Boss, not a good time to go swimming." She eased him back.

Come home, Dad, come home.

Alex nodded, beginning to drift into unconsciousness. "Home, need to go home."

"You and me both, big guy." Casey opened her comms. "Arcadian secure. Multiple HAWCs down. Threat has exited the field. Send in multiple medical teams and immediate evac, *now*."

* * *

In forty feet of water, Sophia looked toward the surface and the cliff edge. The tiny implant she had embedded in the back of Alex's skull just under the lower edge of the occipital bone allowed her to see, hear, and experience everything he did.

She could also hear his thoughts. The artificial face Walter Gray had created for her allowed her to smile, and she did. She hadn't lost him yet.

She reached up to feel the dent in her chest – the armor plating was buckled but the reactor core was unharmed. She could repair that easily.

Sophia turned and began to walk along the sea bottom; there was an airport twenty miles away at Figari, Southern Corsica. She tapped into her database and saw there was an American flight leaving that evening.

She increased her speed. The advantage of being an android was she could fold her body into places no human body could possibly fit.

She could make it on time, and then plan her next steps from there.

CHAPTER 14

John F Kennedy Moon Base – Maintenance Garage

The crawler returned from the Russian base. So far, the team had refused all communication attempts, and Hector Rodriguez, one of the senior base security personnel on the away team, knew better. With him had been engineer Mike Stanford, who had the additional skill of being a paramedic, plus Fred Bellows, the second security member.

The large maintenance doors lifted wide and the crawler came down the ramp.

"Here they come," Mia said, and felt her stomach knotting with apprehension.

Of the three people who had set out, there was only one rider in the drive seat, and the badge on his suit identified the man as Rodriguez.

"Where are the others?" Mia turned to Briggs, who just watched the vehicle from under lowered brows.

Once inside it kept going toward one of the power cabinets.

"Whoa, there." The maintenance room manager clicked on the room intercom. "Driver, stop there. *Driver*, disengage drive mode. *Now, driver, now.*"

The crawler continued and, being closer, now they could see the crawler pilot was slumped forward in his seat, arms by his side.

"*Hector, dammit, stop!*"

The machine finally hit the power relay cabinet against one of the walls, making it shake before its forward progress was halted, its engine still running. With the power unit crushed, the lights immediately blinked out.

Briggs threw his hands up. "Well, that's just freaking great."

After another thirty seconds, the emergency lighting went on and they saw that the slumped crawler pilot hadn't moved a muscle.

"Get a team in there," Briggs said.

"Is that a good idea?" Mia asked. "We have formal quarantine procedures, why break them?"

"Don't tell me my job, Mia." Briggs glared for a moment. "I have no choice. I'm responsible for every person on this base. Plus, we need to know what happened to Stanford and Bellows." He turned back to the crawler and its occupant. "I'd do the same if it was you in there."

They watched as the retrieval team went in, and cautiously approached the driver. One of them reached in to switch the crawler's engine off as the other went to the slumped figure.

The first thing he did to tip the figure back in its seat and slide the gold face shielding back. He turned to look back through the viewing window at Briggs, Mia, and other control room staff. He shrugged. "It's empty."

CHAPTER 15

A day after the crawler returned the weird shit started. And for the first time, Mia felt claustrophobic in the moon base. She was headed toward the infirmary, and on her way was the geology lab. Handsome Tony had been conspicuously quiet in regard to the asteroid fragments she had brought him and he hadn't been seen in the dining or rec rooms since she last saw him ... days ago.

Ungrateful or just single minded about his work? she wondered.

She came to his lab and used her knuckles on the door button. It whooshed open and she straightened her spine and plastered on a bright smile. "Hiya –"

For nothing – the lab was empty.

She looked around, seeing the asteroid fragments separated into different sample containers, some in solution and others crushed to dust. Tony's seat was pushed back from the desk.

She walked forward a few paces, her brows knitted; on the floor, kicked up against the wall, was what looked like a torn T-shirt and underwear, both stained.

Gross, she thought. *Or maybe cleaning rags?*

"Tony?" she asked, knowing it was useless as there was nowhere to go in the small room.

She walked in a circle, not seeing any trace of the man, and finally just stood in the center of the room. The silence seemed eerie and unsettled her. After another moment, she looked about for paper and a pen and quickly scrawled a note, letting him know she had dropped in.

"Next time." She headed out.

Mia continued to the infirmary. She had a knot of apprehension in her gut big enough to make her feel physically ill. She entered, found no med staff, and went to the room where Olga was still laying on the bed.

Olga had her eyes open just staring at the ceiling. Mia watched her for a moment and then the woman turned to her. Her eyes were glassy and her expression blank.

"How do you feel?" Mia asked.

Olga let out a long sigh. "You let them in, didn't you?"

"More no than yes. It seems no one came back but an empty suit."

"Do your vehicles have autopilot?' Olga asked.

Mia shook her head. "Not really."

"Then maybe suit not so empty." Olga turned away. "Now it is inside."

"All quarantine procedures were maintained. I was there; nothing came off the crawler." Mia shrugged. "We're sending another team back to your base to locate our missing team members."

"I don't care anymore. It will come for me, because it knows I know," Olga replied softly. "It's over."

Mia cursed under her breath. "Fine." She headed out but paused at the door. "You know, for someone who tells us there's a high risk of some sort of contamination, that may or may not have destroyed *your* base, and may or may not be in our base, you're being pretty damn unhelpful."

Olga sniffed.

"Thanks for nothing." Mia turned away.

"If …" Olga began.

Mia waited in the doorway with her back to the woman.

"*If* I could have done one thing different on my base, do you know what that would have been?"

Mia turned and saw that Olga was staring back up at the ceiling again, but this time tears ran to her pillow.

Mia folded her arms. "What?"

She looked at Mia. "We never sent a warning message out. We underestimated how smart the thing was. It cut our external long-range transmission capability first and then the inter-base communications next. We could never tell Russia what was going on to warn them. And then we couldn't even warn each other."

Olga sat up, drawing her knees up and resting her forearms on them. "My country will send an early supply ship to investigate why we have gone dark, and when they arrive, they will walk into a trap. I think it wants to get to Earth …" She smiled sadly. "And then everything is over: me, you, Russia, America – everything."

Mia searched the woman's face for subterfuge or psychosis, but only found a weariness that looked to have drained her completely.

"You must send a message. Warn them."

Mia nodded. "Okay, good advice. Anything else?"

"Then destroy this base, and everyone in it." Olga's expression was deadpan.

Mia scoffed. "Nope, we're not there yet. No one has died. Maybe it isn't even inside yet."

Olga held her eyes, and her lips curled at the corners. "Hope is a good thing to have. Until reality bites you."

* * *

Mia left the room and headed back to the operations center, and there found Captain Briggs and a few of the engineers plus several biology and chemistry guys all crowded around a table reviewing the report on the empty suit.

"Captain." She nodded to her commander. "So, what was in the suit?"

Briggs exhaled. "Not Hector Rodriguez." He sat back. "Biological matter – fragmented cells, unidentifiable enzymes and some oxidized blood." He shrugged. "In other words, nothing but a fucking mess."

"Exactly like Olga said was strewn around her base. And was inside her helmet when we found her." She folded her arms. "Hey, if the suit was empty, how did the crawler get back? It doesn't have autopilot."

"That's not exactly true; they sort of do. All the crawlers can be set to auto and can have their steering locked," Calvin Porter said.

"Pfft – it can keep going, but only in a straight line." Mia gave a lopsided grin. "And they set it after they got out. Oh, and then stuck one of their empty suits in it as a practical joke, right?"

The chemical science officer sniffed. "Maybe they set it because they were preoccupied. And it got away on them."

"Yeah, right." Mia laughed without mirth. "And one of our guys is running around on the moon in his underwear."

"They might be inside the Russian base," Porter replied.

"Yeah, sure. I was just talking to Olga. She thinks the thing that was on their base is now here. And we just let it in."

"Impossible," Briggs said. "The garage is sealed, and nothing got off the crawler. And there was nothing on it other than an empty suit. And for that matter, in her own words, Olga admitted carrying out a terrorist attack on her own base. I don't believe a word of her contamination or monster story. Something happened over there, and we still have no idea what."

"Tom, I was there in the garage when the crawler came down. It hit the power box and the lights went out for approximately twenty-eight seconds," Mia said. "That's more than enough time for something to get off and hide. I don't remember her saying exactly how big it was, only that the thing managed to hide on her base for days or weeks without being found." She sighed. "And she said it was smart."

"Oh, bullshit. And where would it go? For that short blackout period the garage chamber was sealed for the vacuum of space. Like I said, nothing else is now or was in there." Briggs waggled a finger at her. "Don't buy into that woman's hysteria, Mia. She's a suspect, not a guest." He turned away.

"You want to know something weird?" Mia came and stood in front of him. "Olga had some advice for us. She said if she had her time over, she'd let Earth know what had happened. She thinks whatever it was that infiltrated her base was smart enough to know to cut all their comms and mute them." She lowered her voice. "She thinks it did that so they couldn't warn people at home. And that maybe it *wants* them to come." Her voice dropped. "So it can get back to Earth."

The room fell into complete silence, and Mia saw that the commander's face paled a little.

Briggs looked into her eyes. "Mia, we've done a thorough check of the garage – nothing came in. We've taken samples of the biological matter in the suit, and it is being further analyzed right now. Plus, the rest of the suit has been incinerated. Like I said, *nothing* came in on the crawler."

Mia went to interject but Briggs held up a hand. "But we'll include what just happened in our standard briefing back to HQ this evening, okay?"

Mia examined his face for a moment before nodding slowly. "Okay, good. Thank you."

She started to turn away but paused. There was still something nagging at the back of her mind. "You know what else she said? She said it was already in. She was adamant about it." Mia lifted her chin. "What if you're right, there was nothing on the crawler. Because it was just a diversion?"

Briggs stopped what he was doing.

"How would she know it was already in?" Mia asked softly.

"She was guessing. Or …" Briggs slowly got to his feet. "Maybe it was *already* in."

"Because *she* was in."

Briggs spun. "Get security to the infirmary, now."

They sprinted to the infirmary and found it empty. Empty except for some torn clothing with Beverley's name badge stuck on it. There was black slime everywhere.

Mia's eyes were wide in absolute fear as she grabbed hold of Briggs. "Captain, contact home, quickly, while we still can."

CHAPTER 16

United States Central Command (CENTCOM), Tampa, Florida

"Yes, sir, we can be ready." Four-star General Marcus Chilton listened to his commander in chief a moment more. "I'll make it happen, Mr. President, you have my word." Chilton put the phone down.

"Jesus Christ," he said softly and thought it through for a moment. He snatched up the phone again and pressed one of his speed-dial numbers. It connected immediately.

"Jack, it's Marcus." Chilton's eyes were as steady as gun barrels as he stared straight ahead. "Drop everything, jump on a chopper and be here ten minutes ago. This is priority one."

* * *

Colonel Jack Hammerson didn't need to knock as the door was open and he was expected. He saluted the general and walked over to the huge, dark-skinned man, gave a formal salute and then shook his hand.

"Jack, thank you for coming so quickly. We got a tricky one." Chilton turned to the two people already seated in his office. "This here is Colonel Jack Hammerson, my top security specialist. Jack to his friends, and the Hammer to those that aren't."

The pair got to their feet and Chilton walked Hammerson over, introducing the first. "Doctor Marion Martin, an expert in astral-biology."

"Doctor Martin." Hammerson shook her hand.

Chilton then motioned to the older man, fit, and about the same age as Hammerson. "And Angus McCarthy, he's one of the chief designers of the Kennedy Moon Base, and knows everything about its design, construction, and maintenance."

Chilton motioned to the long meeting table, and they sat down. Then the general leaned on his forearms and meshed his fingers. "Last week we picked up chatter from our Russian friends that something had gone wrong on their dark side lunar mining base."

"The one a mile from ours?" Hammerson asked.

"That's it, the Vladimir Lenin Base," McCarthy said.

Chilton nodded. "Their base went offline and stayed offline. The Russians then moved up the launch of their resupply craft, even though they referred to an 'unidentifiable' risk. There were twenty-two people on the Lenin Base and our guys picked up on their sensors what they believe might have been an explosion. Something bad went down there."

Hammerson exhaled. "Let me guess, now they're blaming us?"

"Maybe." Chilton half-smiled. "But that's the least of our worries." His smile fell away. "Last night, ours also went dark."

"What?" McCarthy's brows snapped together.

"Listen yourself." Chilton reached for a slim device on the table in front of them. "This was the only message we received. Partial message, anyway."

He pressed play – it was a woman's voice, panicked and out of breath, as if she had been running: "*It's inside. Somewhere. Lifeform.*"

Chilton hit stop on the device and sat back.

"That's it?" Hammerson asked.

"Play it again," Marion requested.

Chilton did as requested, then turned to the group. "Now you know as much as we do."

"Lifeform," Marion Martin repeated. She had a hundred questions in her wide eyes.

Chilton clasped his large hands together. "You all know that the president used to be a test pilot and even tried out for the Apollo program when he was younger." He shook his head slowly. "He is not going to let our eighty-plus people on the base be abandoned."

"What's their status now?" Hammerson asked.

"The base still has power, so they have light and oxygen. But somehow they have zero comms."

"Impossible," McCarthy said.

"Anything is possible if you have motivation and opportunity," Hammerson replied.

"Exactly what I think. Someone or something shut them down." Chilton tilted his head. "What do you think, Jack?"

"The Russians? Maybe they went mad and blew their own base. And then felt like causing some more damage so moseyed on over to the Kennedy Base."

"Lunar madness," McCarthy suggested. "It's a real thing and why we insist on psych checks every few months. Whether it's the isolation, the boredom, or the constant low-level radiation, it can create psychotic episodes."

Chilton seemed to ruminate on it for a moment. "Yes. But I don't think that's it. However, the Russians suspect we sabotaged their base, and we think they might have attacked ours. Not a great recipe for world peace right now."

Marion Martin sat forward. "The word 'lifeform' does not suggest a Russian source of the problem. But something else."

There was silence for several seconds until Jack Hammerson sighed and turned to his general.

"We need more intel, Marcus. Too many unknowns right now."

"I agree." Chilton looked at each of their faces in turn. "They can't come to us, so we're going to them. The Kennedy Base resupply ship was due out in ten days, but we're bringing that forward as the Russians are already on their way." His eyes went to Hammerson. "With a Spetsnaz security detail."

Hammerson nodded. "Of course they are."

Chilton opened his arms. "We need to be there first, so we're going to give our resupply ship a bit of a turbo charge for acceleration."

"How long to get there?" Hammerson asked.

"Angus?" Chilton asked.

"Depends on the route we take, but normally three days. The moon is approximately 240,000 miles from us. The fastest mission to the Moon was NASA's New Horizons Pluto mission. We used an Atlas-V rocket accelerating it to a speed of about 36,373 miles per hour. Only took us eight hours and thirty-five minutes to get there. But it was unmanned, because the human frame probably couldn't take it if –"

"We believe it could now," Marion interrupted. "In hibernation. And if a human body was pumped full of muscle relaxants and beta blockers to slow down the metabolism."

"We know it can take it – we've already tested it," Hammerson said and turned to Chilton. "What, and how many?"

"We launch tomorrow, midday. You can send a team of six to accompany two science specialists." He turned to Marion and McCarthy.

Marion laughed. "I wouldn't miss it for the world."

McCarthy shrugged. "Save our people, and see what the hell someone has done to my base? Hell, yeah, count me in."

Chilton stood and the others followed. "You'll be picked up at oh-eight-hundred hours, sharp. There'll be a fast prep, kit out, and then you'll be taken straight to the pad."

He shook both the scientists' hands, and suddenly both of them looked a little pale. "The country and your president greatly appreciate this," he said to each of them. Then he stood back and saluted them.

After they left, Chilton turned to Hammerson. "How is he?"

"Recuperating."

"We want him on-mission. He might be the only one who has the capabilities to … deal with whatever is happening."

"Physically, he's in great shape. But mentally?' Hammerson shrugged. "I just don't know. We were hoping to give him some more time with his family, to fully decompress."

"I've read the latest psych report. He seems fine."

"It's the devil that might still be hiding inside that's the problem."

"Jack, this time you didn't recommend he spend any time in the box. That tells me you also think he's okay." Chilton opened his hands. "Look, a day to get to the moon, a few days to check out what's happening and assist getting their comms back online, and then another few days to get back. All up, a week, right?" The general raised his eyebrows.

Hammerson didn't believe it for a second, and he knew the general didn't either. Like he said, something weird had happened up there, and the word "lifeform" probably scared the shit out of a lot of people. Bottom line, something had infiltrated the Russian mining base, destroyed it, and then – worst case – made its way to the Kennedy Base and potentially interfered with them as well.

No, Hammerson corrected himself. The worst case was every living soul on the Kennedy Base was already dead.

Lifeform; Jack Hammerson thought about the word. He knew from his briefing notes that there were just over eighty people on the American site, and six of them had military experience and were acting as security. To overwhelm them so quickly meant it probably wasn't some sort of greasy slime mould that bounced in on a hunk of space rock.

Or could it be? That idea gave Hammerson a thought. "Could it have been a germ? Something that got into the air-filtration system and infected the base? Knocked them down or caused some sort of accelerated psychotic episodes? Then maybe caused the Russians to self-detonate their own base."

"It's a possibility, Jack. And we know there are several possibilities. The president knows you understand that nothing that threatens life can be brought back to Earth." He looked up, his expression deadpan.

Hammerson nodded slowly, knowing what that meant: if there were ever some form of uncontrolled contaminant, clear and present danger, or extreme threat to the planet, then the team would not be allowed to return until the threat was eradicated. If ever. His HAWCs would know that. He doubted the scientists did.

Chilton went on. "It's high risk and we're flying blind. But we have a responsibility to those brave men and women up there to attempt a rescue. If that's even what's needed." His hands balled into fists for a moment. "Pick your best team. If you say Hunter is unable to go, then so be it; it's your call." He leaned forward. "But personally, I want him there. We both know the guy is a game changer and his unique abilities might be the difference between success and – not."

"Go in fast, kick some ass, and come out smiling." Hammerson gave him a flat smile.

"That's the HAWC spirit." Chilton stuck out a hand. "Never a dull moment, huh, Jack?"

"Not in this lifetime." He shook the outstretched hand. "We'll get it done, sir."

"I know you will." Chilton saluted.

CHAPTER 17

Buchanan Road, Boston, Massachusetts

"Mom … *help*." Joshua grinned as Alex held him in a headlock.

"Alex, let him go." Aimee spoke without looking up from her book.

"Let who go?" Alex turned one way, then the other, pretending he wasn't holding the boy as Joshua laughed madly.

Tor jumped up from behind, placing his paws on Alex's shoulders for a moment, before dropping down and trying to force his nose between Alex and his son.

"Okay, okay." Alex let Joshua go. "Sheesh, two against one."

The boy rubbed red ears, and then chuckled. "Best of three, but you only use one arm this time."

"Okay, but I get to use my *claw-arm*." Alex made a claw of his fingers and held it up. Then he turned to the huge grinning dog. "But this time you sit it out, okay, wolfman?"

"Deal." Joshua started to approach Alex, arms out.

Alex's phone rang. Everyone froze. Very few people had the number, and when it buzzed it was either Aimee, or what he referred to as "the office". And as Aimee was with him it only meant one thing – Colonel Jack Hammerson.

Aimee put her book down and stared straight ahead. "Don't answer it."

Joshua stared at Alex's pocket then up at his face. "It's Uncle Jack." His brows came together. "It's urgent …" His frown deepened. "A presidential order."

Alex shut his eyes for a moment.

"You're not ready." Aimee threw her book to the side and got to her feet, her blue eyes darkening.

"Lifeform," Joshua whispered, his eyes closed momentarily. "There's still time to save them." He then lifted his eyes to Alex's and nodded once. "There's still time."

"Sorry." Alex winced at Aimee, took his phone out and walked into the next room. "Sir."

"Alex, sorry to barge into your evening at home. I wouldn't if I didn't have to," Hammerson said evenly.

"Lifeform," Alex repeated the word Joshua had spoken.

Hammerson laughed softly, but with little humour. "Joshua tell you that?"

"Yes. What does it mean?" Alex looked briefly over his shoulder and saw Aimee pacing, arms folded tightly across her chest, and her lips set in a grim line.

"Yesterday our Kennedy Base on the far side of the moon went dark. Eighty-two people from a coalition of countries, including thirty-eight Americans, are there. Just before communications went offline that was one of the last words they mentioned. And we have no further intel." Hammerson sounded like he exhaled. "We need to find out what happened, ASAP."

"Why?" Alex asked. "Why don't you think it's just a technology issue? A single word and you're scrambling a team – you don't send in HAWCs unless you're expecting there might be a high-level conflict scenario."

"Maybe. The Russians have a base there – *had* a base there, and we believe it has now been destroyed. We've spoken to the Russians, and all they tell us is their base also went dark. Seismic readings and now an orbiting Chinese satellite doing a flyby has delivered images that led them to believe the base has been destroyed."

"How? I've heard of the Lenin Base, it's a significant mining operation."

"Yeah, and according to the Russians, they use more drilling technology than blasting for their mining operations. They believe the only way the base could have been so completely obliterated was if someone drained the nuclear rod pool and then organized a self-destruct. Or a significant charge was detonated on or within their lunar infrastructure." Hammerson made a noise in his throat. "The Russians aren't ruling out we attacked their base, that we planted the charges."

Alex sighed. "That's not going to help."

"No, and it immediately ruled out a joint operation. And in fact, we believe they're leaning toward us being the culprits rather than an inside job."

"And now it's happening to us," Alex said. "Did you tell the Russians that?"

"We tried. But they're not talking anymore." Hammerson's voice was soft. "The destruction is estimated to have happened ten days after they went into a communications blackout. We need to be there."

"So, we have nine days, *if* it's the same thing that happened to the Russians." Alex looked briefly over his shoulder and then lowered his voice. "I can't keep doing this, Jack. I'll lose her. I'll lose them both."

"Five to seven days, max. All you need to do is let us know what's happening. If there's a threat, Russian or otherwise, subdue it. All we need is for it to be safe for the supply ships to either restock and/or perform a relay-rescue shuttle home for the crew. But only if needed. Remember, it may turn out to be nothing more than a comms issue."

"The moon is 240,000 miles from us. A half million-mile round trip for a comms issue?" Alex snorted. "Come on."

"I hope we're overreacting. But the commander in chief wants us there, so we're there," Hammerson replied. "A week, that's it."

"A week. Give me your word, Jack," Alex said.

"You have my word that is the plan – we're going to blast you there in under ten hours. If it's just a comms problem or some other tech issue, you'll be back even sooner." Hammerson's voice was flat. "You're taking one of the Kennedy Base's designers. He'll know how to fix everything, anytime, anywhere."

"How many?" Alex asked.

"Team of eight, six HAWCs including you. Launch is midday tomorrow. Need you here by 8 am sharp, for kit out."

Alex exhaled long and low. "She's gonna skin me alive."

"Eighty-two people, Alex. General Chilton asked for you personally, and the president has approved it. We're ready to go." Hammerson paused. "If you like, I can speak to her."

Alex scoffed. "That would make things a million times worse." In the window's reflection he saw Aimee standing in the doorway behind him, arms still folded. He looked away. "I'll be ready. Out." He disconnected and lowered his phone, took a deep breath, then turned to her.

She glared at him from under her brows. "You're. *Not*. Ready."

"I'm healed," he said and opened his arms wide. "I always do."

"Only on the outside." She was seething. "What did he want?"

"Short mission – just a week. We need to check out why one of our, ah, out-of-country bases has gone dark. Back by next weekend. Piece of cake." He smiled. "And I'll stay out of trouble, Promise." He crossed his heart theatrically.

Her eyes were now so dark blue they were like the bottomless ocean. "Every time you get hurt, I feel it. Every time you nearly die, I die a little inside. I can't do that forever." She took a deep breath. "You have other priorities and responsibilities now. It's called being a father. One day you're going to have to choose which future you want: the one with us, or with Jack damn Hammerson." She turned and walked away.

Joshua came and stood in front of him, and the huge dog sat close by. Even sitting, it came to his shoulder. Joshua looked up at Alex, his face solemn. "I don't want you to go, but I know you have to. They need you." He turned toward the living room. "But Mom is hurting. She doesn't understand."

Alex nodded and put his hand on the boy's shoulder and squeezed. "Give me a moment, Josh."

He found Aimee at the back door staring out over the yard and put his arms around her waist. "I'm sorry," he whispered.

"Two years." She turned to look into his face. "Two years you've been gone. Held hostage by your job. You nearly died, this time and every time."

He kept his mouth shut and let her talk.

"Do you really think that Jack Hammerson would grieve if you were killed? He'd simply find someone to replace you." She pushed him back a step. Her eyes glistened. "One day, you'll go and when, or if, you return, we won't be here. That way I can always pretend you're safe and alive somewhere."

"Don't say that." He reached out for her. "I'd die without you. You're the reason I come back. The reason I *want* to come back."

She started to cry.

"That entire time I was away I dreamed of you, and Joshua. Every person I fight for and save is you or Joshua, a hundred times over." He hugged her. "Just say the word and I'll quit, right now."

"That would also kill you. Just slower." She wiped her eyes, and the tears made her blue eyes shine. "I want to come with you and protect you. I want to kill anyone or anything that tries to hurt you." She laughed softly and then sniffed. "Pretty badass, huh?"

He held her face. "I love you more than anything in this world. Just tell me what you want me to do?"

"Just come home. Always come home. And one day stay home." She got up on her toes and kissed him, hard.

She pulled back, and her eyes burned into him. She took his hand. "Love me."

She led him upstairs.

* * *

Later, Alex walked out onto the back porch. Joshua and the dog followed. The dog moseyed into the yard and the father and son sat on the back step and looked up at the night sky.

"You know Uncle Jack lied. He doesn't really think it'll only be a week." Joshua's face was expressionless. "But he's under pressure too. I could tell."

Alex sighed. "Uncle Jack sometimes bends the truth to get what he wants."

Joshua smiled. "Like you didn't tell Mom that the base you're going to is on the moon?"

Alex looked up into the darkness, seeing the near full moon glowing so bright and clear he could see the individual craters and seas of the moonscape. He put his arm around

Joshua's shoulders. "Best we keep that as our little secret for now." He looked down at his son. "Hey, keep her safe while I'm gone."

Joshua nodded. "I'll keep you both safe."

CHAPTER 18

Baikonur Cosmodrome Spaceport, southern Kazakhstan

Bilov watched as the lunar cosmonauts traveled up to the nose of the modified Proton rocket. The supply and maintenance cargo holds had been stripped down to the minimum, and in their place were basic medical supplies, two scientists, and also seven Spetsnaz, who had to be crammed in.

The Special Forces soldiers were trialling new non-Earth combat armor – the Centurion system exoskeleton. Space was expected to be the battleground of the future, and conflicts would be settled in that medium. Russia had invested many millions in designing new offensive and defensive capabilities. Bilov was looking forward to feedback on the field test for the personal combat chassis with their boosted strength hydraulics and inbuilt weaponry.

The men were issued 9mm Makarov pistols, and even though the weapons usually had an effective range of a little over a hundred feet, on the near frictionless lunar surface, the high-speed bullet would travel indefinitely and not slow down. A good eye could hit and kill a target a mile away.

Bilov didn't envy the soldiers – they would be as uncomfortable as all hell for the three-day trip. But they had been trained to endure hardship, and sacrifice was built into their psychological training. But this time, their motto – "any mission, any time, any place" – was about to be severely tested.

The spacecraft cabin had little room left for additional returning personnel – at this point, they didn't really expect any. If any survivors were found, they'd just have to wait for the next supply ship – budget permitting. Sacrifices had to be made. The primary objective was to ascertain what happened to the base and subdue any threat. If that threat came from the American base, then that was the threat that would be subdued.

A small part of Bilov hoped the Americans *had* attacked their base, as that was something he could understand and deal with. And he would love to teach them a lesson. He still smarted from them halting Russia's planned expansion into all of Ukraine after Russia swallowed the Crimean ports.

But there was also the tiny seed of fear in his gut from the suspicion that something had gone wrong with their covert research project. The scientists aboard were to immediately undertake an investigation. However, secretly he was relieved that at least the destruction would mean no trace of the project; it had always been distasteful to him.

Major Alexi Bilov folded his arms as he listened to the countdown. When it hit zero, he narrowed his eyes from the brilliant flare of the ignition plume. He could feel the vibration from the thrust blast even half a mile from the launch pad.

The huge rocket slowly lifted. Bilov saluted its occupants and turned away, their fate, for now, put from his mind. There were other jobs he needed to attend to, and it would be days yet before they arrived on the moon.

* * *

Cape Canaveral Launch Base, Titusville, Florida

The massive sky-scraping form of the Space Launch System contained a pair of solid-rocket boosters capped with four RS-25 engines to lift their payload easily out of Earth's tight grip. On the flat landscape, the SLS gleamed in the morning sunlight like a beacon from an advanced scientific future as it waited patiently to be loaded with equipment and personnel for its high-speed trip to the moon. The huge boosters were being fuelled and the command center had retreated to their far observation post as the thing was basically a giant thermal bomb. If anything went wrong, there'd be nothing to recover, as the remains would be a giant pool of molten slag in a cinder ring a half-mile wide.

The crates of medical supplies, maintenance equipment, and weaponry were loaded and secured, and once finished, the hatch was sealed and bolted closed. Outside work continued with the hiss of escaping coolants and constant blaring of horns. But inside the quiet of the hold, and secreted in one of the crates, two tiny red lights came on as the android listened for any sound of discovery. It tapped into the communication system of the base and monitored progress reports and final preparation activities – plus the time of arrival of the crew. When Sophia had learned of Alex Hunter's participation, nothing else mattered but being on that craft.

After another hour the tiny lights went out, and Sophia waited.

CHAPTER 19

USSTRATCOM – Sub Basement-4 – two hours
before lift-off

Alex Hunter and Casey Franks traveled down in the secure
elevator to the second deepest level beneath the USSTRAT-
COM building. The entire subterranean complex was encased
in sealed titanium and lead shielding that made the basement
levels impregnable to a nuclear blast and impervious to
electromagnetic pulse attack.

The design was like an upside-down wedding cake, with
the larger test facilities at the top then the smaller R&D
laboratories, and then the lower-level containment cells for
biological specimen testing and hazardous materials work.
That level also contained "the box", the heavily fortified
room that was used for Alex to restabilize himself following
a mission or those times when the inner demon howled too
loudly in the core of his mind.

The research floor they headed to was where Sam Reid's
internal MECH endoskeleton had been developed. And where
Sophia was created.

Thinking of the android made Alex feel a pang of loss and regret for the small scientist who had emerged from his lab to try and help rescue him, and who had paid with his life for that act of bravery. Like in an old horror story cliché, the scientist had been killed by the hand of his own creation.

"Gonna miss the little guy," Franks said.

"I was just thinking the same thing." Alex sighed. "Still can't work out why Sophia did it. I know she had respect and a form of affection for the man. Walter Gray was a father figure to her."

Casey snorted. "Some daughter she turned out to be then, huh? But I'll tell you one thing: Sam told me after the mission that she didn't even bother to just incapacitate Gray – she killed him, hard and fast. Crushed his freaking head. That's one cold-hearted motherfucking machine."

Alex's head came up at the thought that she had shut him down and quickly. Maybe because she wanted to *shut him up*?

"She knew what she was doing," he said. "I know she knows what love is. She loved him as her creator. But something was so important it overrode that. She wanted to obliterate him quickly and completely so that he could never talk to anyone again."

Casey turned. "You think there was some sort of secret he had, about the android?"

"A weakness maybe."

"Lost now. That freaking monster. And we can't even be sure it's dead."

Alex knew it wasn't dead. He didn't know how he knew; he just did.

"How's Kady?" Casey asked.

Alex had visited the towering Rwandan warrior in hospital. She was battered and bruised, with casts on her broken arms and legs, but she was in good spirits. *We won*, she had said to him through a wide grin.

"Kadisha is still busted up. But she'll recover, and soon, I hope."

Casey nodded.

We won, but it was expensive. Alex felt a stab of guilt for no reason other than being a survivor.

The elevator came to a stop and the heavy titanium doors slid silently open. A young man who looked to be no more than in his late twenties greeted them. He had a thin face on top of an angular frame, wire-rimmed glasses, and for the moment, wide and startled-looking eyes.

"Hey, kid, is your father in?" Casey said. "We're kinda in a hurry."

Alex stuck out his hand. "Doctor Andrew Quartermain?"

The young man nodded furiously, saluted and then grabbed Alex's hand. "Yes, sir, and I've got to tell you it's a pleasure to meet you." He continued to pump Alex's hand.

Casey grinned. "Easy, fan boy, he's gonna need that back."

Quartermain let go of the hand, and his face dropped a little. "I've taken over, after Walter …"

"Yeah, we know." Alex turned. "Lieutenant Casey Franks."

"I know, I know." The young scientist stuck out his hand again and Casey gripped it. Quartermain grinned. "I know all about you too, read all of your files. It's a –"

Casey squeezed his hand until he winced, and then let him go. "I wasn't joking when I said we were in a hurry. We got a flying bus to catch."

Quartermain rubbed his hand. "Of course." He turned. "This way." He led them along the gleaming corridor and half-turned to Casey. "I'm not that young."

"Uh-huh." Casey continued to look straight ahead.

He went on. "But I was the youngest ever person to graduate from Harvard with multiple doctorates."

Casey glanced at him.

"Laser technology, physics, mathematics, robotics, and later specialized in high-velocity weapons tech, which brought me to the attention of the military. And then here I am." He smiled. "Plus –"

Casey glanced at him. "I kill people for a living. Especially ones that talk too much."

Quartermain stared for a moment and then nodded. "Yep." He faced forward. "Got it." He laughed softly. "But my job is to make you a more efficient killer."

Casey smiled. "Then I think we're gonna work out just fine."

"I've got a job for you," Alex interjected.

"Yes?" The young scientist lifted his head.

"After we're done here, I want you to interrogate every file, document, and message that Walter Gray had in relation to Sophia."

"Okay, sure. What am I looking for?"

"Something about her we don't know. Something that Sophia thought was important enough for her to want to silence Gray forever."

"Really?" The scientist's eyebrows shot up. "You think that's why she killed him?"

"Maybe," Alex replied. "It was either something he was hiding, or a flaw he didn't even realise we could exploit. I need fresh eyes on it."

Quartermain nodded. "Interesting theory. Yeah, I can do that." He held an arm out as they approached a door. "Here we are." He held his hand up to a pad on the wall. A glowing ring appeared around his hand, and the door slid back. The lights came on and the trio entered. Quartermain stood aside.

"I've been briefed on your mission, and there are a number of things we have for you." He smiled proudly. "Some I designed personally."

Alex took in the room, seeing racks of sidearms, some he recognized, some he didn't. Also, some suits on mannequins.

"Colonel Hammerson's briefing notes were very broad in what sort of armaments you'd require. The primary expectation was human-form adversaries, meaning simple projectile weapons would be sufficient as the low gravity and near-zero atmosphere actually makes even the lowest caliber weapon much more compelling."

"And if it's not a human adversary?" Alex asked.

Quartermain raised a finger, waggling it in the air. "Ah, that was an interesting footnote in the report – 'lifeform'." He turned, his hands clasped together. "Think about it: something that could survive on the moon, without an atmosphere, under that intense, raw solar and cosmic radiation, plus potentially being battered by micrometeor strikes. It'd have to be one tough organism, wouldn't it?" He raised his eyebrows. "One tough and *formidable* organism."

"Unless it's just a microbe," Casey said.

"Yes, and I'll get to that form of threat mitigation in a moment. But first things first, so let's assemble our mission armory, shall we?" Quartermain moved to the rack of weapons. "I suggest a simple handgun, but with laser sighting on a slide rail. Even the lower caliber will travel for miles with little deviation. But the smaller round will be safer if it is fired inside the base – there will be only a small puncture and the base is self-sufficient in the repair of those. Any larger and we might create a bigger hole, potentially resulting in atmospheric evacuation or even explosive decompression – not good."

Casey shook her head. "Boring."

Quartermain's brows knitted for a second. "Okay, to bolster your armament, I have a weapon that discharges heat rounds that can penetrate a hardened surface, biological or other, and then detonate, creating a thermal surge of up to a thousand degrees – like being pierced with a little bit of sunshine." He grinned and shrugged. "Will totally destabilize and incinerate any known cell type."

"And the unknown ones?" Casey asked.

"I can only work on theoretical weaknesses right now. But heat has always been a good biological disinfectant." He turned back, took a plastic box from one of the shelves, and opened it to show them a set of disks about three inches in size. "Interesting little device." He looked up and grinned. "One of mine."

He held one of the disks on the flat of his hand. "Shock limpet – delivers up to two thousand volts of electricity in a single massive discharge."

Quartermain walked toward the firing range where the target dummy had been set up. He turned back to them. "You can dial the device up to full lethality or keep it low as just a little incentive."

He flicked his hand, flinging the small device at the dummy. Alex saw tiny, spiked legs emerge from its sides that it used to grab onto its target. There was a crack of electricity and the dummy flared with light, before smoking where the device had stuck to its torso, also leaving a plate-sized burn.

"Nice." Quartermain waggled his eyebrows. "The disk's grips ensure it sticks to what you throw it at. But you can adhere it to walls and metallics via magnetism and suction – works just great as a form of claymore. Someone or something passes by, the device leaps, can attach itself and then release its charge. Game over."

"Okay, better." Casey nodded.

"We're not sure what you'll be encountering, but most animals flee from fire and react to electrocution. Fair assumption that our lifeform will too."

"Good work," Alex said.

"But wait, there's more." Quartermain slid out a drawer. Inside was a steel box and he flipped the lid, exposing several tubes. He lifted one out – on one end it had a red tip and on the other a blue tip; he held it by the blue tip.

"A little something we found useful when we did some experimentation on the last of the Silicoids your team captured."

"That damned bone-eating, extinction plague of bugs," Casey spat.

Quartermain nodded. "Yes, and the closest thing to a living, non-terrestrial lifeform we have had the chance to work with. They were uniquely impervious to heat, projectiles, and most forms of armor penetration. We know that they were susceptible to certain strong acids, but we also learned they could be affected by powerful neurotoxins."

He waved the small wand. "This is a delivery mechanism for the most powerful neurotoxin on the planet. It fires a dart containing 50 micrograms of an enhanced tetrodotoxin – just 2 micrograms is lethal to an adult human being."

"The same as in pufferfish?" Alex asked.

"Yes and no." The scientist grinned. "It's certainly from that biological base, but it has been genetically altered to increase its toxicity, speed of reaction, and also to make it on-contact. This toxin doesn't just prevent the nervous system from carrying messages and thus muscles from contracting in response to nervous stimulation, this toxin will render all muscles and the brain rigid. Dial it up to full strength, and it necrotizes – everything simply collapses into biological soup."

Casey chuckled. "Okay, we'll take a set of those for the kids as well."

"Want to try?" Quartermain held it out.

"Oh, yeah." She took the wand, and he pointed at the small stud that had to be slid down into a firing slot first to ensure no accidental misfires.

"I got it, I got it." She held the wand out toward the still smoking target dummy, and then pressed the stud.

The dart hit the orange-colored gel torso of the dummy dead center, and immediately a small smudge appeared inside it.

"The dart acts like a hypodermic. It is laser sharpened and made from titanium for high penetration. Setting number one, and anything that has a muscle and nervous system should be significantly affected and will become immobile." He smiled. "Setting two and it's dead."

He took the stick back from Casey and took her by the forearm. "Now let's look at some EMUs."

"Say what?" She pulled her arm free.

Quartermain rubbed his hands together, looking like a boy on the verge of telling a secret. "It's *all* in the suits." He paused. "Or EMUs."

"Isn't that some sort of long-legged turkey from Australia?" Casey asked.

Quartermain turned and placed his hands in his lab coat pockets. "If by turkey you mean a bird standing over six feet tall that can disembowel you, then, yes, something like that." He grinned. "But it also refers to Extravehicular Mobility Unit, or EMU."

"Oh, a spacesuit. Why didn't you just say that?" Casey asked.

"Where's the fun in that?" He took them into the next room and paused without yet allowing the lights to come up. "Today, the suits used on the space shuttle and International Space Station are top of the line and designed to be a fully equipped one-person spacecraft." He brought up the lights. "They consist of several pieces – a hard but padded upper body segment covering the astronaut's chest, also an arm assembly that connects to the gloves. The helmet and visor are designed to protect the astronaut's head while still allowing an excellent view. Then there's the lower body assembly, a single-piece unit that covers the astronaut's legs, groin, and feet."

The scientist approached one of the walls and turned. "The EMUs our astronauts wear are the closest thing to an off-world suit of armor we've got. Or were. You'll still need something that can perform different functions, from keeping oxygen within the spacesuit, to cooling or warming, to protecting the wearer from space dust impacts. But we've made some modifications."

"What about the pack?" Alex asked. "That's still external, right?"

"That's right." Quartermain nodded. "On the back of the spacesuit is a backpack called the Primary Life Support Subsystem. It's unfortunately still rather large and bulky because it contains the oxygen used during a spacewalk, and a power source for the suit, plus a water tank. And last but not least, it also has what is termed the Simplified Aid for Extravehicular Rescue, or SAFER, that has several small thruster jets. If an astronaut became separated from the space station, they could use SAFER to fly back."

"A lot of kit just to stay alive," Casey observed.

"It is." He bobbed his head. "Good technology, and each suit costs around twenty-two million dollars."

Casey whistled.

Quartermain held up a finger. "Money well spent. And good technology, for what was required of it. However, not great technology if you need to move quickly, be manoeuvrable, or perhaps even fight for your life. But then again, no one expected our astronauts would ever need to fight for their life, right?" He smiled. "So, we made some improvements, some modernizations, and miniaturizations."

He pressed a button on a touch pad and the walls slid out, showing a range of full-body suits on mannequins.

"Oh, fuck yeah." Casey nodded her approval and walked toward them.

"We already do a range of armored suits, and they're also designed for underwater activities. It wasn't a great leap for us to create a lunar version of the full-body armor."

Alex approached them; the suits were silver but retained a gold visor over the face. However, where the modern spacesuits were heavily bulked up to give padded protection against the elements and contained all the technology inside, these looked like a closer fit, and were covered in a form of armor plating that looked like large scales.

He lifted one of the suit arms and examined the gloves. His lips curved into a smile. "Armored and MECH assisted."

"That's right, down to the fingertips." Quartermain chuckled. "Better for reaction times on the lunar surface. Will also give you boosted speed and strength. Though I know that isn't a priority for your, ah, different physiology, Captain Hunter."

Alex walked around the back of the suit and ran a hand up it. "Power, oxygen, coolants, all in there?"

"Yep, all there," the scientist replied. "Just miniaturized."

"Why is it silver?" Casey asked, but then turned and grinned. "Don't get me wrong – I like it."

"Better reflective capabilities," Quartermain replied as he touched the suit's arm. "And the biological ballistic aspects of the armor we use even give a higher quality protection from micrometeorite strike, and other projectiles. Extremely reflective, which means we don't need all the padding."

"Well done," Alex said, and then turned. "Limitations?"

Quartermain pulled at his chin for a moment. "The weight, of course. Each suit still weighs in at 150 pounds. That's still a lot less than a standard EMU, and it's only a problem in normal gravity. But as these are your primary wear in and out of a vacuum, you'll feel it in normal gravity. You have onboard water, oxygen, rocket propellant …"

"Say what?" Casey exclaimed.

"Normal suits have the SAFER system, so do these, but I gave it a little tweak." He returned the smile. "You wanted to fly, right?"

"Yep." Casey clapped her hands together.

Quartermain went on. "The oxygen canisters will give you four hours air, less if you're in high-activity times. Once used, you'll need to return for recharging or a new canister, same as the power packs for your MECH assistance."

Casey snorted. "So, bottom line, don't be away from home too long."

"Four hours should be enough time for any external activities. Your suit will warn you when you're running down. It'll self-recharge when idle, but exertion will drain it." Quartermain turned to them. "So will the shockwave."

"Shockwave? Yeah, I like the sound of that already."

The scientist held his arms wide. "In the event you are in close quarter combat and in a constricted situation, you can create a single discharge of up to 800 volts all over the suit's exterior. Another reason for the reflective surface – the charge is expelled outwards." He held up a finger. "But only for short bursts. Any more than that and the charge will eventually be reabsorbed, and seep back inside. Then you'll wear it." He turned to them. "Let's call it a break-glass defense only."

Alex nodded. "Got it. Anything else?"

Quartermain shrugged. "That's all I can think of. I don't know what you'll be facing, but hopefully, the offensive and defensive kit will allow you to prevail."

"It'll do, and we will prevail." Alex nodded and headed for the door.

"Wait!" Quartermain pointed at the silver suit's chest plating. He grinned. "We can do logos. Only takes minutes to laser-cut."

Alex smiled. "American eagle."

Quartermain looked back at the suit. "Yeah, that'll work."

Alex continued to the door. "Get the suits sent to the kit-out area. We've got a rocket to catch."

Casey loitered for a moment. "I want something a little different."

CHAPTER 20

Launch Complex 39, John F Kennedy Space Center, Merritt Island, Florida

The eight passengers were being strapped into seats that had been reclined flat to deal with the initial acceleration. Sam Reid, a former test pilot, would operate the lander, but in reality, there was little to do as most of the voyage was automated through the software and overseen by the NASA ground crew. Operational control was only ever handed over to the pilot on touchdown and again on lunar lift-off.

The six HAWCs and two scientists were fussed over like lab animals, and Alex watched each of his team be given several injections into their necks, and tablets to metabolize. The beta blockers, anaesthetics, and muscle relaxants would create a suppleness in their muscles and their frames for up to ten hours, plus the painkillers and doxepin sleeping tablets would render them unconscious so they would sleep through most of the acceleration trauma. In addition, breathing apparatus would force oxygen into their lungs to ensure the pressure on their chests didn't suffocate them.

However, even though the chemistry, biology, and biomechanics were the best science could offer to defray the smashing effects of the high and constant G-forces, they would still all feel like they'd been beaten to a pulp when it was over – especially the scientists, who weren't as physically robust as the HAWC soldiers.

Alex watched as one by one the passengers slid into unconsciousness. He gave his team one last look over – Quartermain had moulded the eagle onto the front of their chest plates, and Alex smiled at the result. It didn't hurt to remember where you came from and what you fought for.

He turned to Casey, and she grinned back at him. He laughed softly and shook his head – her armor had a skull motif hammered into it. She bumped it with her fist, and then eased back and closed her eyes.

Big Sam Reid turned to give Alex the thumbs-up, before he too leaned back into his chair and shut his eyes.

The ground crew gave them a final check over and then exited the craft. The oval door was pushed shut and locked, and a hiss of hydraulics created a total seal.

Alex turned his head; there was a small porthole window, many inches thick in the door that, for now, just showed some of the gantry infrastructure.

The countdown began and Alex stared straight ahead. He half-smiled, feeling the presence of Joshua lingering in his mind, wanting to keep an eye on him, and also perhaps wanting to experience the rocket blast-off – what kid wouldn't? He sighed as he remembered saying goodbye to Aimee, and how she wouldn't meet his eyes. He just hoped she would give him the chance to make it up to her. He tried to picture her face, but for some reason when he did, it fragmented and wouldn't fully resolve, as if there was something blocking it.

He frowned as, instead of Aimee, there came an image of floating red eyes, and a soft, calming voice telling him to relax. He blinked it away as the countdown reached its climax.

"Three – two – one – ignition!"

Alex grunted as the weight came down hard, feeling like a giant sitting on his chest. He breathed in and out slowly, relaxing himself. He had time to think, lots of time. His system metabolized the drugs almost immediately, so he wouldn't sleep, wouldn't rest, and wouldn't be shielded from the worst aspects of the crushing G-forces. His body and mind would just have to bear the pain, as he remained conscious for the entire eight hours of flight.

Welcome to the Thunderdome, he thought, and half-smiled.

He tried to conjure up Aimee's face again, and once again it was denied. *Something's wrong*, he thought. *Joshua wouldn't do that.* Would the Other, the dark entity that resided deep in his mind? It had never intruded on that space before. Why now?

Alex gritted his teeth as he felt the huge cylinder of steel approach the Earth's atmosphere ceiling, knowing that he and his soldiers were sitting inside a giant thermobaric bomb. One that had been juiced up to continue its acceleration all the way to the moon.

Hundreds of pounds of pressure forced him back into his chair, and he exhaled and shut his eyes. It wasn't to sleep, but instead to wrestle with the demons inside his own mind.

Joshua, he called.

I'm here, came the whispered reply.

Alex's eyes flicked open – it sounded like his son, but oddly, didn't *feel* like him.

Gonna be a long mission.

CHAPTER 21

John F Kennedy Moon Base

No one talked to anyone anymore.

Six people had vanished now, including the Russian woman, Olga; Handsome Tony; and Beverley from the infirmary. Only Olga had had a security alert posted about her: *Approach with caution.* That was the last security blast they had, because internal communications had gone down. Just like the external communications had a few days before – exactly like the Russian woman had warned.

Mia paused to look over her shoulder along the length of the silent corridor for a moment. But there was nothing there – thank God.

She didn't get it; though the Russian woman was the prime suspect for bringing in the contagion, or lifeform, or whatever the hell was now afflicting their base, why did she try and warn them? Why did she urge them to get a warning message back to Earth? Mia sighed. Nothing made sense anymore.

She spun to stare back down the corridor, feeling the hair on her scalp prickle as she stood, frozen, for a few moments.

Stop it, she demanded of herself. Every pop, tic, or groan of the base made her jumpy as hell. But then again, the scenarios of the disappearances were always the same: people who found themselves alone, in their sleeping pods, in the ablution centers, or just walking along one of the corridors, never arrived at their destination. Sometimes all that remained was torn clothing and the black slime, as though something had thrown up or shat after eating them. Mia shuddered and hugged herself.

Base instructions were that everyone was to work and travel in at least pairs. But rumors were rampant, and they tore at everyone's sanity – there was one story that the thing was so good at camouflage that it could mimic a piece of equipment or furniture, or that it could squeeze itself down and move around inside the walls, or the air-conditioning ducts, or even that it had some sort of ability to exist outside of the normal spectrum for human vision – basically, it could be invisible.

But the worst of all was the rumor that the thing "hid" inside people. That meant that the person who was accompanying you along some lonely corridor, or the person you were having a drink with, or the person you were fucking, could suddenly reveal themselves to be the lifeform. And then you were nothing but torn clothing and puddles of black shit.

Every single one of the scenarios was stupid and also plausible, so it meant no one came out, no one spoke, and no one trusted anyone. And that was why Mia wanted to be by herself.

She found herself in the rec room, alone, and went to the bar and leaned over, grabbing the homebrew vodka and pouring herself a triple. She gulped half of it, welcoming the cool burn, and sticking her tongue out to exhale long and satisfied. She refilled her glass to the brim before walking to the window and its view out over the lunar surface. The moon was as it always was: dust-gray, some blue shading around the jagged edges of the larger craters, and purple-colored plains.

Mia was about to turn away from the window when she stopped and craned forward.

"Oh, please no."

There was a body lying out there. The helmet was beside it, but thankfully the face was turned away. She'd read what the airless and super-dry atmosphere of the moon could do to a body so was in no hurry to see the face.

"Suicide is painless," she whispered as her eyes blurred. "I don't know what's happening or who I am anymore." She lifted the trembling glass, toasted herself, and then brought it to her lips.

Movement in the window reflection behind her – Mia spun, coughing the vodka out. "Jesus Christ." She put her glass down before she dropped it as her heart was hammering so hard.

"You shouldn't be out by yourself, Mia, you know the rules." Captain Briggs and one of the security personnel, Art Dawson, stood at the bar. Dawson's hand rested on an extendable baton hanging from his belt.

Mia nodded. "I know, I know. Just getting cabin fever staying in my pod." She smiled flatly. "I used to like it here. Now I hate it. And this is why ..." She turned back to the window and pointed. "Look."

Briggs and Dawson came closer, but Dawson stayed a few paces back, obviously not trusting her yet.

Briggs squinted. "Looks like Eric Wilson," he said softly.

"Yeah, I think he killed himself." Mia turned to him. "Seems there's another infection spreading."

Briggs nodded. "I know. Doctor Pandewahanna has informed me: depression."

"More will die from it."

"Sharma is working on a test."

Mia's brows went up. "So, we really do think it's hiding inside someone?"

"I don't know. I hope not, but it's possible. Some sort of mimicry," Briggs replied without meeting her eyes.

"More than just mimicry. If it is, it doesn't just look like us, it actually becomes us."

Briggs shrugged. "Maybe at first they don't know, the people who are infected. One minute they're normal and the next they're …"

"Something else entirely." Mia felt even more depressed at the thought. She looked up. "And what about Olga? Have you found her?"

Briggs shook his head. "Not only were the comms knocked out, but a lot of the base sensors. The external doors have been opening and closing without us knowing – poor Eric lying out there is a perfect example. But as for comrade Sobakin, she's gone, maybe back to her base."

Mia cursed, the guilt hammering her again. "It's all my damn fault. I should have known. I mean, how was she even alive with that hole in her helmet? She was a Trojan horse."

"Don't beat yourself up. You did what any one of us would have done if we found what we thought was a survivor. And maybe she was a victim herself. Like I said, maybe she didn't even know she was sick."

"We should check the Russian base. If Olga is the culprit, then everything she has told us could be misinformation." She turned back to Briggs. "About the detonation, how it happened, and her escape."

"I thought about that. Maybe it wasn't her that set the detonation, but someone else." He exhaled and then his mouth turned down for a moment. "I'd love to investigate the Russian base as you suggested, but we don't want to spare the security personnel."

"The Russians must also be coming from Earth. They'd be aware of their base destruction. It's their job to check it out. But we should warn them somehow."

"Yes, we should. But I don't know how. We can't even warn our own people."

The overhead lights flickered, and the three looked up briefly.

"Hasn't done that before," Mia said softly.

Dawson turned to Briggs, his face deadpan. "Power isn't cut, just reduced. Could be a problem with the solar beds, or their base-feed cables."

"Ah, fuck it." Briggs let out a long groan before dragging himself to his feet.

"What is it?" Mia asked also rising.

Dawson turned to her. "I used to be in the military services. One-oh-one for siege warfare is to cut off your adversary's communications. Then you cut off their supplies. Force them out into the open."

"Our power, which is responsible for our air, warmth, and running water." Mia quickly looked out the window again. "You think someone out there is messing around with one of our power sources? The panels or the conduits that feed back to the base?"

"Probably – it's what I would do. We still have internal generators, but to affect the solar beds you don't even need to be in the base," Dawson said.

"We can't let that happen," Briggs declared, his jaw jutting. "Go and get Benny and suit up. I'll meet you at the airlock." He headed for the door.

"Wait." Mia stood her ground. "It's a trap."

Briggs half-turned. "No choice, Mia; we'll fry or freeze if any more power goes out. We need it all online, all the time."

"I'm coming then." She walked fast to catch up.

"Nope, got everyone I need." Briggs kept going.

"Bullshit! This thing might have taken out an entire Russian mining base. I'm coming, and I'm bringing a burner."

Mia pulled up as Briggs turned to her. He stared for a moment, as though thinking. "Bring two," he said. He half-smiled and then continued on.

Mia headed for the maintenance shop to get the projection welders. They were the closest thing to a weapon they had on the base – not much, but better than just holding a long spanner or crowbar.

And right now, her gut told her she needed a weapon.

CHAPTER 22

Briggs stepped out of the airlock first, then Art Dawson, with Benny Minchen right on his shoulder. Both men were holding heavy equipment tools plus each had a maintenance and repair case. Briggs had his burner nozzle hanging from his belt and the small dark cylinder on his back. They paused to scan the lunar surface.

After another moment came Mia with a burner held in both hands. She felt her heart racing and gripped her burner hard, feeling the tension run through her like electricity. The burners were basically gun shaped and fed a stream of liquefied gases to the nozzle under pressure, where the initiator ignited them. Like normal welders they could be compressed and focused to provide a small super-hot jet for spot welding or opened up to deliver a body-length stream of heat for larger jobs requiring a broad melt rather than a spot weld.

Briggs waved them on, leading them the 200 feet toward the first of the solar arrays while Dawson and Minchen looked like they were trying to see everywhere at once.

Mia couldn't help the crawling sensation on her scalp that constantly made her feel like something was sneaking up on her. It was made worse because she couldn't scratch her head underneath the helmet.

Thinking of the helmet brought home another disadvantage: they were all wrapped inside their cumbersome suits, breathing stored air, with helmets that had front-facing visor-plates that limited them to just sixty percent of vision, and for all she knew, Olga – or whatever lifeform the woman really was – was indigenous to the moon. As crazy as it sounded, that meant the mix of thin gases might be just perfect for her, it – whatever.

Ugh, she felt ill.

They made it to the solar beds untroubled and the group quickly began to check them over, looking for damage. It only took a few minutes to locate the problem: not so serious – a few of the solar sheets, each six feet square, had been pulled off and flung onto the lunar surface. They'd be easily replaced.

"Must have been some breeze last night, huh?" Briggs said.

Mia could see a grin through his visor. "Yeah, right."

But the strewn solar panels were nothing compared to what they found next: the actual energy feed cables that were once buried had been surfaced, and severed – or rather, shredded.

"This ain't good." Briggs crouched. "Lot of damage here."

Mia stood over him. "Don't suppose it was micrometeorite strike?"

Dawson shook his head. "See the surface dust? It's all pulled upward. An m-strike would punch downward, and depending on size, leave a small crater. Plus, the solar sheets have been pulled up and tossed." He swore. "This was deliberate and no micrometeorite shower."

"We can repair it," Briggs said. "Let's do the hard job first. The cabling was designed to recover from little mishaps like this." He pointed. "Benny, eyes open. Art, slide over your case."

"You got it." Benny turned slowly, scanning the moon surface and keeping watch.

Dawson also did as asked and then also continued to act as a sentinel, so they had a man watching each quadrant while Mia crouched beside Briggs to offer any help required.

The captain cleared away some of the silky dust, exposing the extent of the damage. There were three synthetic polymer fiber cables, each as thick as a wrist, and usually protected by flexible piping. The tough outer coating was designed to shield against micrometeorite strike, radiation bombardment, and was generally very robust. But it had been ripped open, gouged, and Mia's immediate impression was that it looked like it had been chewed, as the outer edges were so ragged.

"Damn, lot of fraying." Briggs sighed. "Best get to it."

He cut away the ruptured edges of the pipe to expose the bundles of shredded cables within. It took him several minutes, but soon he was cleaning off the broken edges of the cables, and either pulling some together to heat-seal them again, or splicing in new sections where pieces were missing. These were the ones that took the longest.

Mia's eyes burned from concentration and she lifted her head to look out at the moon's surface. Small crystals glinted back at her from crater rims and, given her nervous concentration, it didn't take long for her mind to start playing tricks on her – a shadow shifting, or noticing a darting movement from the corner of her eye, but when she turned there was nothing there.

She squeezed her eyes shut for a few seconds and then looked back at the repair work.

In another twenty minutes Briggs announced he was three-quarters done. *Just as well*, Mia thought, feeling like she needed to do a nervous pee, and though they could relieve themselves in their suits if pushed to it, no one really wanted to as you could feel the warm bag of urine up against your leg the entire time you were out.

Briggs tested all the links and they were optimal. He gave Mia the thumbs-up.

"Well done," she said.

"Not just a pretty face." He grinned.

"Not even." She slapped a hand on his upper arm.

Briggs stood, dusted himself off and then turned about, sighting the half-dozen scattered panels. "Okay, everyone, let's grab those runaway panels." He walked to the closest solar array bed.

Mia followed, and being closer to the solar panel infrastructure, she could see where a few of the panels had been removed. The sheets looked like they simply needed to be reconnected and then slotted into place – easy.

She turned and saw that the security guys were each bringing back single sheets at a time, and though they were near weightless on the moon, they needed to take care not to damage them. The men lay the panels close to Briggs, and she watched as the short and powerfully built captain lifted the first two, and walked out onto the solar arrays, trying to stay on the joins where their support struts were located.

Briggs carefully laid the first panel and reached inside the grid so he could reconnect them to the entire gantry. She turned and saw Dawson and Minchen bringing in two more, leaving only two more to recover. She turned about again. *It's all too easy*, she thought. *If this is a trap, it's the worst one ever.*

She turned all the way around to look at the few sensor poles that monitored movement and returned lunar surface images back to the base. *Was this all just another diversion? Had Olga somehow managed to damage the grid and then make it back inside so she could … what?*

Mia blew air between her pressed lips. She wanted to go home. Full stop.

* * *

Briggs had just grabbed the last panel when Mia turned to the plain beyond a small crater ridge. "What about Eric?" she asked.

The captain paused for a moment, and then nodded. 'Yeah, we should bring him in while we're out here."

"Is that a good idea?" Dawson asked.

"Huh?" Mia turned. "We can't just leave him here."

"I know, but I mean if he's, you know, infected."

There was silence for a few seconds as they turned to Briggs.

"No problem. We'll freeze the body. Mia, you stay with me while I finish up, and you two guys recover Eric." Briggs went back to work. "Keep your eyes open."

"Got it, chief." Dawson punched Minchin on the arm and then both headed toward the crater rim and where the body lay.

* * *

"Eric was a good guy," Art Dawson said.

"Yep, well, never picked him for someone who'd do himself in, though," Minchin replied wearily.

"Depression, maybe? Or fear."

"Fear, huh?" Minchin grunted. "Hey, I'm scared too, but not that scared. To come out here and just take your helmet off? No way. You get freeze dried – tongue stiffens, air sucked from your lungs, and your eyeballs pop. Shitty way to go."

"Yeah, think I'd prefer to just drink myself to death. Oh wait, I'm already doing that." Dawson chuckled.

"There's our boy."

They closed in on the body. The young man was lying on his back, his face turned away, helmet by his side. They crouched beside him.

"So much for freeze dried. He just looks asleep," Dawson whispered.

"Weird, his suit is all torn." Minchin looked up at the black sky. "Maybe micropellet damage. Let's grab him and get out of here. This is giving me the creeps."

Dawson put his finger in one of the holes in the suit and craned forward. "Hey, what's this?"

* * *

"All done." Briggs stood. "Power should be back online." He came back across the panels like a tightrope walker.

"Good work."

When he alighted, he put his hands on his hips, and then looked one way then the other. "Where're the others?"

Mia faced the direction they left. "They should have been back by now."

"Let's go see what's keeping them." Briggs picked up the toolkit and started off. Then he cursed, and half-turned to her. "I hate the long-range comms being down. Got your burner?"

"Oh, yeah." Mia noticed he'd lifted his from his belt and carried it loosely – for now.

They crested the rim of the crater, and saw the men, three of them. There was the body of Eric Wilson, but ominously, there was another body lying next to it. The third man stood stock still leaning over them. It was impossible to tell who it was with the shading on his visor, but if he saw Mia and Briggs, he didn't acknowledge them as they approached – or even move a muscle.

"Hey!" Mia waved.

Briggs held out an arm and slowed. "Let's just wait and see if everything is okay before we barge in."

He waved an arm vigorously over his head. It was soundless, but it should have been hard to miss. The man still didn't move. Briggs put the toolbox down, opened it, and took out a wrench.

"Stand back." He tossed it at the standing man.

The wrench landed just to the side of the man, bounced and kept on going in the low gravity. The man never moved a muscle.

"Shit," Briggs exhaled. "Stay here."

"Not a chance – sir."

He chuckled softly. "Come on, then."

The pair moved cautiously now. The suits' internal communications worked on a different system, but you needed to be close if there was no booster capability from the base.

"I think it's Dawson," Briggs said.

"Yup." Mia felt the flutter of nerves in her stomach as they approached. The bigger frame *did* make it look like Dawson, and that meant it was Minchin lying crumpled next to Eric's body. Why?

In fact, it looked like it was only the suit lying there with no one in it. But that was impossible. If you take any part of your suit off on the moon, you end up like Eric: dead in seconds. You don't take it off and run away, leaving your clothing behind. Just like the body on the crawler when it returned, she thought ominously.

"I've got a bad feeling," Mia said.

Briggs didn't reply, staying focused on the standing man. "Dawson, do you read?"

They were just a few dozen feet from the men now, and they should have been able to pick up the communication. They could see that Minchin's suit was riddled with holes and tears.

"Dawson, report. What the hell happened here?" Briggs demanded.

Dawson finally reacted. With glacial speed, he leaned forward to grip his leg just above the knee, and began to vibrate. When Mia and Briggs were a dozen paces from him, his head lifted. The weak sunlight entered his visor.

"Oh God." Mia couldn't help taking a step back.

For the first time she was happy they couldn't hear the man, as his mouth was open impossibly wide in a silent scream. As they watched, his helmet began to fill with stalks. They grew up from inside his suit, then popped from his flesh and ended in ripe-looking bulbs.

After another moment his helmet was full and then the doughy-looking substance pushed and ebbed, less like a thick liquid, and more like something alive.

Briggs took a few steps toward him and held out his hands. But Mia rushed to grab his suit arm.

"Stop!" She pointed to the lunar surface and the boot of the leg Dawson had been holding. "Look."

Briggs stopped dead. From the toe of Dawson's tough spacesuit boot a glistening black cord traveled along the ground and disappeared underneath Eric Wilson's body. It pulsed like an artery pumping blood.

"Jesus Christ. What's happening here?" Briggs lifted his burner.

Dawson's visor was now totally black, and there was a hurricane of movement behind it as the viscous matter fought and strained inside the helmet. Then the man bent at the knees, then hips, and then his shoulders sagged, but all at strange angles.

Mia's mouth hung open as, right before their eyes, Dawson's suit deflated and crumpled to the ground.

"Fuck this." Briggs pointed his burner and opened it up.

Mia did the same, bathing the man, or what was left of him, in long gouts of ignited gases. Though the suits could take extreme heat in the range of hundreds of degrees, the thermal stream from the welder's tool was in the thousands.

Finger-thick stalks appeared from dozens of points in Dawson's burning suit, swelling at their ends. They bulged, looking like strange blooms sprouting all over him, and then finally the black matter exploded outwards and escaped down into the lunar surface.

"Get back." Briggs stumbled backward, and Mia grabbed him to stop him falling.

The pair retreated and Mia watched, terrified, as Dawson's suit emptied via the holes. The matter seemed to travel along the cords to Eric Wilson's body, where it vanished.

Dawson's suit was now just another deflated bag, nothing remaining of him but empty clothing and streaks of a dark, glutinous liquid.

"That's what happened ... *that's what happened to our people*," Mia said in a rush, and suddenly felt sick and dizzy.

"Maybe." Briggs strode toward Eric's body. "It's in there."

"Careful," Mia urged, but followed him.

The captain pointed his burner and let loose a long jet of super heat, and Mia did the same, concentrating on the exposed head of the prone man. The suit and flesh began to singe, and sure enough, just like with Dawson, the man exploded in a mass of questing stalks and then the shining black stuff sought to escape the incendiary blast, this time by burrowing into the moon's crust.

Soon the final suit was empty; even where the man's head had been exposed there was no hair, skull or anything else remaining.

"He's all gone. *It's* all gone. Under the ground," Mia said.

"Let's, ah, get back to the base," Briggs said.

The pair moved as fast as their suits would allow back to the airlock. Once there, Briggs kept watch on the moon's surface while Mia hit the button for door opening.

Once they were inside, the air was flushed and a rapid decon began. When it was complete, Mia tore her helmet off.

"Goddamn, I knew it – it was a trap. That thing set a trap for us."

Briggs nodded, and she noticed that the man looked tired as hell. "Yeah, and I fell for it. Let's keep most details about what happened out there to ourselves for now. It'll cause a panic."

Mia looked into his eyes. "I'm already panicking."

CHAPTER 23

The pair finished their decon and quickly pulled on their clothing. Mia had to jog to keep up with Briggs, who strode fast to the communication panel on the wall and punched the button to the control center.

"Captain Tom Briggs here. You there, Stevens?"

"Yes, sir. Myself and Thomas on today."

"Seal all external doors, override only on base commander's authority. Confirm order."

"What's up?" Stevens asked.

Mia saw Briggs bare his teeth for a moment.

"Carry out and confirm order, *immediately*," he snapped.

"Yes, sir. All external doors and vents now locking down." Stevens paused as he initiated the locks. "Override on base commander's authority. Confirming order has been carried out."

"Good. I'm coming up." Briggs turned to Mia, his face still drained of color. "Let's go and scan the surface."

The pair headed to the command center. Briggs used to like sitting out on the lunar surface just watching the heavens. Mia wondered whether he'd ever do that again.

The heavy door of the command center slid to the side as they approached. All eyes turned to Briggs, and Stevens leaned back in his chair.

"Hey, chief. Uh, how come the lockdown order?"

"We were attacked." Briggs headed for the main console. "Initiate external motion sensors."

"What? Attacked? By what, ah, I mean … what?" Stevens half-rose from his chair.

"Do as I ask." Briggs was obviously in no mood for any further discussion.

Stevens turned to Mia and raised his eyebrows. But Mia just shook her head, and the man spun in his seat back to his desk to initiate the external motion sensors embedded around the base site.

He swivelled back around. "Sensors online."

"Thank you." Briggs slowly straightened. "Any word on the second crawler we sent to find our missing team members at the Russian base?"

The man shook his head. "Nothing, sir."

Briggs and Mia glanced at each other. They knew exactly why they hadn't heard, and would probably never hear from the team again.

Briggs stood with hands on his hips. "Thank you. Everyone else, there'll be a full briefing soon. But for now, back to work." The base had two-dozen cameras dotted about their perimeter, and each one could be independently operated. He brought the camera feeds up onto the screens and focused on where the three men had fallen on the lunar surface.

Mia leaned on the console beside Briggs and watched the split screens. He swivelled them until they found the bodies then enlarged the view. Mia could see the problem even before he had fully amplified the quadrant.

"Shit," she said softly and then straightened.

"Yep …" Briggs blew air from between his pressed lips. "One of them is missing."

"But which one?" Mia asked. She turned to him. "Did we lock down in time?"

"I think so," he replied softly, but not convincingly.

"I want more eyes on the external feeds," Briggs said. "We're looking for a solitary walker in a torn suit."

Each of the technicians on duty brought up one or more camera feeds from the surface.

"Who is it?" Stevens asked.

Briggs folded his arms and rested his chin on his neck for a moment. After another moment he seemed to make a decision, lifted his head, and leaned forward on the console.

"A little while ago, Art Dawson, Benny Minchin, Mia Russo, and myself went outside to repair damage to the solar array beds. Once we completed our task, I sent Minchin and Dawson to recover the body of Eric Wilson, who we believed had committed suicide."

The assembled people looked from one to the other, and there were a few gasps and mumbles. Briggs held up a hand to quiet them and ward off any questions before he went on.

"After a few minutes the men hadn't returned so Mia and I went to investigate." He straightened. "The men had been attacked. By *something*."

Briggs had to wave them to silence again, as some rose to their feet.

"Something?" Stevens' brow furrowed. "What does that mean?"

"Lifeform," Mia added and she noticed Stevens blanch.

"I guess that's why we're in lockdown?" he exclaimed. "So, it's locked outside, and can't get in? That's good news, right?"

Briggs shook his head. "We thought Eric had committed suicide, and maybe he had. But the thing was inside him, and it attacked and killed Art and Benny." He turned and brought the image up on the large wall screen. "But now one of the bodies has gone. The thing is on the move."

There was silence for a moment, before one of the chemists, Bridgette O'Neil, spoke in a quavering voice from the rear. "Was it the Russian woman who attacked him?"

"Good question. Unfortunately, I don't know the answer to that."

"But how could one of them get up again? Maybe he wasn't really dead," Bridgette pressed.

"They were dead. Gone," Mia announced. "Whatever attacked them ingested them, or absorbed them …" Her gaze was level as she scanned their shocked faces – most were pale, and a few had glistening, fear-filled eyes. *Understandable*, she thought.

"Ingested?" Stevens sat down slowly.

"It may try and get back in here," Briggs said. "I want a constant scan of the surface to see if we can locate him – *it*. Then we'll organize for the tracking sensors to trigger the cameras. If it moves, we can find it."

"But then what?" Bridgette pressed. "What happens when we find it?"

"For now, we monitor it, and work to keep it outside of the base." Briggs folded his arms. "While we work on our defenses."

After another moment, the crew scanning gave up – there was nothing on the camera feeds.

Stevens swung in his chair again. "Will it stay outside?"

"Our doors are designed to seal against the pressure of a vacuum, and they're all locked, from the inside. We're safe here now."

There were relieved murmurs, some loud exhalations, a few whoops and even a smattering of hand claps.

Mia walked to a corner and called Briggs closer. "There's something that bothers me. Well, two things really. One is that maybe Eric knew he was infected and went outside, taking the thing with him, and sacrificed himself thinking it'd kill the thing as well."

Briggs nodded. "Plausible. But didn't work did it? Didn't kill the thing, only himself."

"And that brings me to the second thing. Why did it draw us out? Just to kill two men, and reveal itself to us? It could have stayed in the base and done that, especially if it really did just get locked out. It doesn't make sense."

"It's smart, but it's still just an animal," Briggs replied. "We've got to believe it's operating on instinct."

"I'm not so sure." Mia looked to the external-image screens for a moment. "And where's Olga? Is she dead and absorbed, or hiding? If Olga was the thing, then it wasn't just mimicking her, it *was* her." She looked at him with a broken smile. "And that generates another question – was the thing that attacked us outside the only one there is?"

Briggs' soft laugh held no humor in it. He closed his eyes for a second, then leaned closer and lowered his voice. "Mia, the worst thing we can do now is lose hope. We already doubt everything and everyone. I don't want any more of the base crew killing themselves out on the moon's surface." He faced her. "Or killing each other."

"Okay." Mia hiked her shoulders. "I don't know what else to do."

Briggs placed a hand on her arm. "We survive. That's what we do. And we keep everyone else safe."

"But stay on our guard," she replied.

"Always." Briggs dropped his hand. "The supply ship will arrive soon, and then we can start arranging an evac. And as for what you can be doing – go and see where Doc Sharma is up to on that test. I'll get everyone together this afternoon for a town hall update."

'Okay, good." She turned for the door and noticed Stevens watching them. He slowly turned back to his console. *We already doubt everything and everyone*, Briggs had said.

You got that right, Mia thought. *Bring on the supply ship, and soon.*

CHAPTER 24

Alex felt the reverse thrusters kick in to slow down the lander's approach. He saw the small lights coming on at the console units of the other passenger seats and knew their drip lines were automatically being fed small doses of adrenaline, glucose, and other stimulants to rouse them from their slumber.

He had disengaged his long ago, not needing the chemicals, and had spent the long hours reclined and strapped in his chair, ignoring the pain and just letting his mind work – he knew Aimee was right about him having responsibilities at home. Maybe they should begin to outweigh his responsibilities in the field.

One day they would. But he didn't undertake HAWC missions simply to piss her off or because he was some sort of adrenaline junkie. He did it because he knew he could make a difference.

And he also knew that there was a demon that needed to be fed. The missions usually brought a level of challenge and aggression that sated the beast inside him, if just for a while. If not, then one day it would come and take it all itself.

His biggest fear was not dying, but having the Other being the dominant psychology, and his being the one locked away in the depths of his mind forever.

"Ain't gonna happen." Alex sucked in a lungful of recirculated air, turned to his left, and saw Casey Franks mumble something as she came awake. Beyond her the large and dark form of Roy Maddock took a deep breath, filling his lungs. Sam Reid was stirring up front in the pilot's chair, and behind him was their youngest HAWC, Vincent "Vin" Douglas. Rounding out the team was the ice-cold Klara Müller. Back in the rear stalls were Doctor Marion Martin, their astral-biology expert, and Angus McCarthy, the Kennedy Base designer.

McCarthy coughed and then moaned. Sam inclined his chair forward and started the pre-arrival procedures, and once again tried to raise the Kennedy Base.

"Are we there yet?" Casey drew out the drip needle and slotted it away. The others did the same, as they'd been instructed during pre-flight training.

"That's some hangover," Maddock said.

"You got that right; even my teeth ache," McCarthy replied as he rubbed his jaw.

"It's the result of coming off the high dose of beta blockers, and now an added adrenaline infusion." Marion grimaced and kept her eyes closed. "Our blood pressure will also spike for a while as it gets back to normal."

Sam half-turned. "Kennedy Base is still comms-dark. Coming up on the Aitken crater and the base now."

There were no windows in the rear but each of their seats had a small external feed built into the armrest. Alex watched his as they came over the horizon to the crater-strewn far side of the moon. It reminded him a little of Death Valley – extraordinary geological features, but instead of the uplifting of mountains, ancient riverbeds, and weathering cracks in the earth, there were the sharp edges of craters from meteor strikes, some of them huge, which had caused the molten material to flow like water, then cool, leaving a shining skin.

He drew in a deep breath – it was desolate and eerie, and he knew from his research that there was a constant wailing noise that was a form of astral static. He just hoped he could block it out.

"Hang onto your hats, people, as I've only done this via sim." Sam grinned.

"What's the worst that can happen?" Vin smiled at Klara, whose near colorless and unblinking eyes showed her usual lack of humor or emotion.

Small jets fired from different angles of their craft as they gently dropped to the lunar surface. There was a pad close to the base that lit up for arrivals, but now it stayed dark as they were touching down just over a crater rim – a little extra space for security. The coordinates had been locked in, and the computer knew where the landing pad was even if they couldn't see it.

The lander rotated as Sam worked the two joysticks, intensely focused on his console. "Hundred feet." His face was tight with concentration. "Struts down."

Alex knew the pressure he was under. If they got damaged on the way down, the Kennedy Base had a large repair and maintenance room, so repairs were possible, but if they seriously damaged the lander, then that might mean being stranded until another moon shot. Or worse – being injured or killed.

"Forty feet." Sam's large hands worked delicately as the wedge-shaped craft eased down toward the landing pad.

"Five, four, three …" They touched at an angle and jolted, hard, as they planted themselves on the moon surface. "And down, two seconds ahead of schedule." Sam turned and gave a thumbs-up.

Belts were flipped off, and Alex joined Sam at the front of the craft, which had the largest windows. He leaned forward and stared out.

"They look like they still have power. So that's a good thing," Alex observed.

"Yep. But no one to greet us and, as most of the structure is below ground, we don't know yet what shape they're in," Sam replied.

"Keep trying," Alex said.

The other HAWCs crowded in up front, Casey standing just behind Sam to peer around his bulk.

"What happens if we get to the airlock and they don't let us in?" Vin asked.

"We leave a card and just go home, I guess." Casey chuckled.

"But we just got here, Mommy." Vin grinned back at her.

Casey turned. "Don't 'Mommy' me, Diaper Rash."

"Stow it, you two." Alex straightened. "We're going in, the easy way, or the hard way. Let's kit up and get moving. We've got three hours of daylight, then we move to sundown, and the temp drops to about 200 below."

While the group kitted up, Alex crossed to Marion Martin and Angus McCarthy.

"You guys okay?"

"A little sore. And nervous," Marion replied, looking up from the pack that contained her equipment. "But also excited. I mean, there's fieldwork, and then there's *fieldwork*, right?"

McCarthy traveled light; probably assuming everything he'd need from an equipment perspective was inside the base. "I've missed this place. Been three years now. Can't wait to see what they've done with my baby." He raised his eyebrows. "Still no contact?"

"Sam?" Alex said over his shoulder.

Sam half-turned in his pilot seat. "Nothing, on all channels. They're staying quiet, or …"

"Or we assume they've been knocked out. That means that we're the only link back to home right now." Alex nodded to the youngest HAWC. "Vin, you get to stay here and mind the ship while we're in the base."

"Aw." Vin grimaced.

"No choice. If the base communications were sabotaged, then those same forces may seek to do the same here. That'd blind us as well. This task is high priority, got it, soldier?"

"Yes, sir." Vin exhaled and turned away.

"And Vin …" Casey raised her chin.

"Here we go."

"I want this place spotless by the time we get back." She guffawed.

The young HAWC grinned and gave her the finger.

"That's enough, Franks," Alex said. "Or you can take his place doing onboard duty." Alex knew Vin would do what was asked. If everything was okay, he'd call Vincent in. If not, then their rear was covered.

"Let's line 'em up," Alex said.

The airlock was small on the lander and only fit two people at a time. Usually it meant they'd have to relay out, exiting in pairs. But there was a quicker way.

"Everyone, helmets on. You too, Vin, we're going to flush the ship." Alex pressed the stud just behind his ear and his visor telescoped up and over his face.

Sam waited with Vin by the controls. "Say the word, Boss."

Alex took one last look at the team, spending a few extra seconds on Marian and McCarthy, making sure they were ready for the moon surface environment.

"Countdown from three," Alex said.

"And two, and one … venting ship." Sam pressed a button on the console and there was a whoosh of gas. The light on his console went red. "Okay, opening inner and outer doors." Alex, Sam, and Vin watched the team line up as the hatch whined open.

They existed quickly, one after the other, and Alex turned. "Sam, grab the key."

Sam flipped up a small plate on the console. Underneath was a button and slot. "No offense." He winked at Vin and pressed the button. A metal card covered in circuits appeared. It was the launch key – the lift-off rockets wouldn't initiate without it. Sam removed it. He then walked back to hand it to Alex who slid it into a pouch at his waist.

"Better to be safe than stranded."

Vin grinned behind his helmet. "And here I was, planning to invade Mars."

Sam and Alex crossed to the hatch and saluted the young HAWC.

Vin waved back and then waited to reverse the airlock process. "Good luck. I'll leave the comm. link open." He gave them a small salute.

Alex nodded. "See you when we get back." He jumped down to the lunar surface.

He touched down and turned slowly – above them the sun shone in a black sky, making small crystals in the purple-gray rock glint and sparkle. Though the surface was well lit, the craggy crater rims and small pockmarks left plenty of shadows.

Alex could just make out the background lunar wail. He pushed out with his senses but even though he could detect no overt life close to them, he couldn't shake the feeling there was something hidden out there. That put him on edge.

He turned. "Stay sharp."

Alex led the team over the crater rim and toward the main Kennedy Base airlock. Sam waved at one of the base cameras but when they got to the door it remained closed, and pressing the opening button did nothing.

Alex stepped aside. "Angus."

The base designer reached into his kit for a T-shaped object and stuck it into a slot underneath the pad. The first turn of the manual key vented gases, and sealed any inner doors, and once done, a green light flicked to orange.

"Opening, now," McCarthy said and turned the key again.

"Franks," Alex said.

McCarthy nodded as the light turned red, and the door slid back. Casey went in fast with her gun up. They waited for several seconds.

"Clear," she shouted from inside.

The team piled in, and spread to the outer edges, checking for any observable risks.

McCarthy tried the internal comms. "Dead," he said. He manually shut the external door, and then adjusted the internal atmosphere and pressure. Once done, he lifted his visor and sniffed deeply.

"Air's good." He pointed. "And the inner doors have power. Also, good."

The HAWCs retracted their visors.

"Wait!" Alex shouted, but McCarthy had already pressed the inner door opener, and it slid back with a whoosh.

The HAWCs had their guns to their shoulders in an instant and took cover at the door's edges. But there was nothing but an empty corridor.

"Where is everyone?" McCarthy asked. "This base has eighty-two personnel. It should be crowded."

"Lifeform, remember?" Marion whispered.

They waited, but no one appeared.

"Creepy as all fuck," Casey said.

"Vin, you read?" Alex asked.

"Yes, sir, all quiet here."

"Let HQ know that we have accessed the base and are beginning our search. Standby for updates. Out." Alex signed off. "Angus, where to?"

"They've still got internal power, so we'll try the control room first. Then maybe the rec room, where everyone usually congregates."

"Sounds like a plan," Alex replied. "Let's do our job, people. Franks, take us in."

"On it." Casey muscled forward, and with her gun to her shoulder, led the HAWCs down the corridor.

The group followed McCarthy's directions down the white-paneled corridor. Casey moved her gun barrel from side to side, and behind her the soldiers tried to see everywhere at once. Marion and McCarthy were in the center.

"Got something here." Casey lifted an arm. "Shit, that's gross."

Alex joined her. On the floor were lumps of clothing, mostly shredded, and streaked with something that looked like blobs of oil or blood so heavily congealed it looked a little like black oatmeal.

"Someone take a dump here?" Casey's nose wrinkled. "Freaking stinks too."

"Leave it – stay focused," Alex said. He felt a growing unease in his belly.

"Hard left at the junction," McCarthy said, softer, and with caution in his voice.

They went around the corner, and in just a few moments, Casey yelled, "Movement!" She pressed herself to the wall, and behind her the HAWCs did the same or went to one knee, guns up.

"Hold fire," Alex ordered and craned forward. "Come out. Slowly."

Up ahead there was a doorway, open, and from it some sort of rod with a white piece of material tied to its end was waving up and down.

"Don't shoot." The rod dropped, and a pair of open hands followed it out, both held up. Then a small, dark-haired woman appeared. She looked dishevelled and her eyes were ringed from lack of sleep.

She licked dry lips. "Are you the rescue ship?"

"We're here to help," Alex said. "Who are you?"

"Mia, Mia Russo, senior biologist; I'm one of the Kennedy Base crew." She smiled and lowered her arms. "I saw you from the external camera feed. But we couldn't contact you. I volunteered to come down."

Marion stepped forward, her hands out. Mia began to back away a little.

"It's okay, I'm a doctor. I'm just going to look you over," Marion said and looked deeply into each of the woman's eyes.

"What's happened here? Where is everyone else?" Alex asked. "All your comms are down."

Mia nodded as Marion checked her throat and then shone a small light into one of her eyes. "They are." Mia talked around the woman. "We lost external communications. Then internal. Then for security, Captain Briggs locked down the external doors to keep it out." She grimaced. "It didn't work."

Casey snorted. "Keep it out, huh? Keep *what* out?"

"The thing, the lifeform," Mia said. "Come with me, everyone will be so relieved help has arrived." She headed down the corridor, stopping once to make sure she was being followed.

"Guess we've arrived," Sam said.

They followed the woman, who slowed down a little and spoke over her shoulder. "We're in two groups: thirty of us in the rec room, and another twenty in the control room. We all live together now, because safety in numbers, right?"

"That's fifty people. There's over eighty crew here – where's the rest?" McCarthy asked.

"Gone." Mia pointed. "Control room first. Captain Briggs is there."

"Gone? What do you mean gone?" Sam asked.

She waved them on. "The captain can brief you."

She came to the larger than normal set of doors and keyed in her access code to the pad, and then stood back and waved to a small camera set above the door. After another few seconds it slid open.

Casey and Klara went in first, moving quickly with their guns ready, and placed themselves either side of the opening.

"Hol-*eeey* shit," Casey whispered, as the rest of the HAWCs plus Marion and McCarthy followed her in.

The HAWCs stood in silence, just looking over the sea of faces. None of the people spoke but stared at the huge soldiers in their silver battle-armored spacesuits as if they were another species.

When Alex walked forward, the group inside seemed to pull back a little. He wasn't the biggest HAWC, but there was an air of menace around him that radiated power, and danger.

Alex could detect distrust, fear, and also hope. "My name is Alex Hunter, Special Forces, come to assist the Kennedy Base. Where is Captain Tom Briggs?"

"I'm Briggs."

A stout man with a crewcut came forward, and saluted then stuck out his hand. "And we're damn glad to see you." Briggs glanced at the woman who had met them. "Thank you, Mia. What are the evac plans?" he asked Alex.

"That's not why we're here," Alex said. "This base represents decades of work, trillions of dollars in investment, and is strategically critical for our coalition partners. We're not just walking out on it."

"Our people are dying, being killed or simply vanishing." Briggs lowered his brow." Suicides as well. We need to go home, what's left of us."

"Priority is to secure the base first," Alex replied. "You know as well as I do that if we started an evac, we couldn't take everyone at once. And it would take weeks or months to fully complete."

"But we'd be alive," Mia pleaded. "You have to get us home."

"And if the environment here isn't secure, who gets to go last?" He turned to Casey Franks. "We'll set up CIC here."

"What?" Briggs' eyebrows shot up. "You want to make this a combat information center? We aren't at war, captain. And these people aren't soldiers."

"You're under attack, nearly half your people are gone – either dead or potential casualties – and you've created siege centers in the rec and control rooms. You're at war, you just won't admit it."

Briggs exhaled.

"Captain Briggs, why haven't you brought the comms back up? You have the tools and parts to repair anything here," McCarthy said.

Another young, bearded man spoke up. "Hi, John Stevens, senior technician. We think the external comms are damaged, and we would need to go outside to repair it." His eyes slid to Briggs. "But that's too high risk right now."

McCarthy frowned. "And the internal ones?"

There was silence for a moment, until Stevens exhaled. "We're not sure exactly. We think it's fried, but we can't really check." He looked away as his voice trailed off.

"Because the internal comm. unit is in sublevel 2," Briggs answered for him. "And the team we sent never came back. So, getting volunteers for repairs is a little hard right now. And I won't order anyone else to do it."

Stevens grimaced. "We just need to get out, get home –"

Alex held up a hand. "You've been radio dark for a long time. I want to see if your other crew members are okay." He turned. "Roy, Klara, check out the rec room base personnel, and report back. Stay on comms." He looked to the base captain. "I'll need one of your personnel with them to ensure the group there know we're friendlies."

"Got it." He pointed to one of their technicians. "Roberts, go with them." The man looked shocked, and Briggs waved him down. "You'll be fine, just stay close to these guys."

Alex watched as the two HAWCs departed and then turned back. "Fortunately, we have our own communications. I want to know everything, so we can fully assess the situation."

"Let me start." Mia stepped in front of Alex, her hands clasped together. "It was me, right at the beginning; I was there with Benoit ..." She sighed. "When we found the Russian woman."

"Where's this Benoit?" Alex asked.

Mia just stared for a moment, and then slowly shook her head. "Gone; like all the rest."

CHAPTER 25

Vladimir Lenin Base – landing pad

The Russian Buran-2 lander, designate P23–09, eased down on the pad beside the remains of the Vladimir Lenin Lunar base. It settled on its struts and then the thrusters shut off.

Commander Yuri Borgan stared out through the view screen and shook his head. "Totally destroyed – melted." He looked down at the console instrumentation. "And still bleeding radiation."

Igor Stanislov, his second in command, read more data from the instruments. "Within the tolerance levels of our suit protection so not a big problem. But there are no energy readings, no communications, and no life signs. It's a husk." He looked up. "So, was it self-inflicted?"

Borgan bobbed his head. "Maybe, but why? That is for us to find out. But I also have some questions for our American neighbors." He pointed out through the screen. "Look."

At the far perimeter of the ruined base sat an American-designed crawler, empty. "Seems they paid us a visit, and either walked home or are still inside." Borgan's jaw jutted. "And now that the American base has gone dark, I suggest we also pay them a visit … after we see if we can find out what it was they were doing here."

"Doctor Ivanov." Borgan called the woman forward.

Doctor Irina Ivanov was their senior biologist for the mission and looked tiny next to the huge soldiers in their combat armor. She came and pushed Stanislov aside and then peered out through the glass, then made a guttural sound in her throat. "We should expect bodies and perhaps survivors with a range of injuries. We won't know until we're out there." Her eyes widened. "Americans?"

"Yes, and perhaps they are still here," Borgan answered.

"This is unacceptable." Her eyes narrowed as she turned to the commander. "Our work is of the highest level of confidentiality."

Stanislov turned, one eyebrow up. "Our mining?"

Irina's lips pressed together. "Of course."

"Yes, yes." Borgan straightened. "Give the order."

"Prepare for the surface," Stanislov said. "All weapons to be readied."

The soldiers got to their feet to grab helmets and weapons. Their titanium-blend armor made them both formidable and lethal.

Borgan turned back to the view window. "Time for us to get some answers."

* * *

Kapitan Yuri Borgan surveyed the damage. There was little left of the Russian lunar base, and zero evidence left for him to work with. Most of the structure was now nothing but melted slag in the center of an explosion debris ring a quarter of a mile wide.

"No one could survive this," Stanislov said.

"I think that was the idea," Borgan replied evenly. The mission commander looked over the chaos and ruination. His men turned over some debris, and kicked at other items, but nothing remained intact.

He saw his two scientists, the doctors Irina Ivanov and Anastasia Asimova, talking between themselves and pointing at different things they observed among the chaos. They were being their usual secretive selves, and he guessed whatever their objectives were, they might not be the same as the soldiers'.

"No bodies or even body parts. Strange," Stanislov observed.

"Huh? Yes, probably vaporized," Borgan said and watched as two of his men checked over the American crawler, examining its contents. One climbed inside and drove it closer to the group.

"What now?" Stanislov asked.

Irina tossed aside a piece of melted steel. "There is one structure still largely untouched which should have been shielded from the explosion." She pointed to the far side of the lunar plain and a crater ridge. "The mine is just beyond the rim. If anyone wanted to shelter from the blast, that's where they'll be."

"Agreed." Borgan nodded. "Stanislov, call the men in. We have two mission priorities: the first is to investigate the hole in the ground. You will take Boris, Anastasia, and Chekov. The second is to pay a visit to our American friends and demand some answers. I will take our neighbors' vehicle and the rest of our team."

Stanislov turned and grinned. "Or maybe exact some retribution."

Borgan smiled. "We come in peace."

CHAPTER 26

Mia looked up at the towering human beings before her. Each of them was in a suit that seemed made of a silver metal and looked powerful and impregnable. They stared at her with the unblinking gaze of an eagle or wolf. *Predators*, Mia thought.

She cleared her throat. "Benoit and I found the Russian woman on the moon surface." Mia's hands clenched and unclenched. "We detected an explosion at their base and came across her when we went to investigate. It looked like she had crawled out."

"And is the base destroyed?" Sam asked.

Briggs shook his head. "We still don't know. We sent a team – hell, two teams – but they never came back."

"And where is this Russian woman now?" Alex asked.

"Olga, her name is Olga Sobakin, and we have no idea where she is. She vanished." Mia shrugged.

"And she is your main suspect for being infection patient zero?" Marion asked.

"Infection," Mia scoffed. "Yeah."

Alex nodded. "Okay, Mia, go on."

Mia swallowed, her mouth dry, and resumed her story. She told of bringing the Russian woman back to the base, how she had miraculously survived with the hole in her helmet. And how she, Olga, had tried to warn them about the lifeform that had killed everyone at the Russian base.

"She said it was her that initiated a nuclear meltdown," Mia said softly. "But whatever attacked their people got into our base."

Mia's voice became smaller as she told of the disappearances, finding the torn clothing and the black substance, and then being outside when they were attacked.

"We thought we locked it out, but it got back in somehow. Or maybe it never left." She looked up at Alex. "We don't know if it's a single thing, or many of them, or even many parts of the same thing." She groaned softly and folded her arms across her belly.

"Describe it," Sam asked gently.

Mia looked up at him and gave a watery smile. "It's hard to understand what its natural form is or might be. It seemed to have a shape and, not. It was like a plant growing stalks, doughy, and then dark, black, like glutinous oil. And it attacked via tendrils or filaments that pierced the suit, then infected the occupant." She kept her eyes on him.

"You saw it attack them?" Sam asked.

Mia's eyes glistened as she nodded. "They just seemed to vanish, dissolve."

"And then it copied them," Briggs said. "We saw it attack two of our men. One minute they were physically intact, alive, and the next they were pulled from their suits. Drained out somehow."

"You mean they were in their suits one minute, and then removed from them? What happened to them?" Marion asked softly.

"Liquefied, dissolved, flesh, bones … I don't know how, and if I hadn't seen it myself, I would never have believed it." Briggs' breath hissed from between his clenched teeth.

"Externally digested. Horrifying, but fascinating," Marion replied.

"Then the suit reinflated. Someone or something was back inside it. We think it copies or mimics us somehow. That's how it gets close. Waits until we're alone and picks us off." Briggs shook his head and turned to the crowded control room. "That's why we stay in groups: to protect one another."

"When was the last interaction with the animal?" Marion asked.

"Animal? This is no animal. This thing makes plans, is cunning, and exhibits strategic thinking."

Marion nodded, unfazed. "Has it tried to communicate?"

Briggs laughed. "Does a wolf discuss its dinner plans with the sheep?"

"I see, and I repeat, when was the last interaction with the, ah, lifeform?"

"The last? Two days ago. And if your next question is where is it now? We have no idea. It's either hiding, camouflaged somewhere, or concealed in one of us."

"In one of us," Mia repeated softly and shuddered as a chill ran up her spine.

* * *

Alex turned to the people crowded into the room and felt the weight of their gaze upon him. He tried to sense whether anyone among them wasn't who or what they really were. But he couldn't detect anything other than impatience, worry, and a lot of fear.

Briggs folded his arms. "This thing knew to take out our communications, just like Olga said it did at the Russian base. It set ambushes for us and seems to be always one step ahead of us. This thing is smart. I just don't know how smart yet."

"So it could be in here, in this room?" Alex said.

Briggs nodded.

"We thought about a test." Mia stepped a little closer and lowered her voice. "But Doctor Pandewahanna vanished while working on it."

"What was the test?" Marion asked.

"We're not sure." Briggs replied. "We've been in here and only leaving to restock food supplies. And of course, waiting for our saviours to get us all home."

"You'll have to keep waiting a little longer." Alex turned to Marion Martin. "The test sounds of value."

"I agree. We need to find out what the doctor was working on." Marion turned to Briggs. "Can you take us to Doctor Pandewahanna's laboratory?"

The captain blanched, but Mia interjected.

"I can." She beamed at Sam.

"No, Briggs will do that. Everyone at all levels has to lean in now," Alex said. "And as soon as the others get back, we'll head there."

Mia looked across at Sam and shrugged. "Next time."

Alex joined Casey and Sam where they stood by the door. "I don't like that they're split over two locations. This thing could be hiding inside one of the base crew, and we can't spread ourselves between both camps."

"It's fucked up," Casey sneered, the scar on her lip dragging her face to the side. "Freaks me out that some alien asshole could be staring at us right now, and us not even knowing it."

Sam grunted. "You do know what that means?"

Alex nodded slowly. "Yeah, no one goes home until we can work out who's who."

Maddock, Klara, and Stevens returned, and Maddock reported in to Alex.

"Scared, but healthy and secure for now. Won't take much to panic them, though."

"Same as this bunch." Alex called the HAWCs into a huddle. "Time to go to work. We need to establish a secure perimeter and find out about that test their doctor was working on. Then we can make a call about evacuating the base or not. Time to rally the troops." He drew a deep breath and turned to the overcrowded room.

"Ladies and gentlemen."

The room quietened and faces lifted toward him.

"My team of scientific, engineering, and military specialists were sent here to assess the situation, and take control of it, and if there is a form of infection, then we isolate and/or eradicate it." He paused.

"Infection," someone muttered with derision.

"To that end," Alex continued, "we will be expecting everyone on this base to lend a hand and do what is asked of them. Immediately."

"How long?" a man asked.

"Unknown," Alex replied. "But we will be working as hard and fast as we can."

"What good is a rescue mission that won't rescue us?" The man stood up, his eyes round. "Some of us have families back home. You should start taking a few of us back immediately."

Alex smiled without warmth and tried to project calm. "I know being patient is hard right now. Everyone is scared, and tired, and damn fed up. But work with us, not against us, and it'll all be over soon."

"It was the damn Russian woman who brought it here!" someone else shouted, a woman. "Why don't you find her? Or we will."

"I can only urge you to follow your commander's instructions. And *do not* get in our way."

"They're just scared," Mia said.

"I know."

"What can we do to assist you?" she asked.

"I'll let you know." Alex turned to his team. "Let's get to work. Team one – Roy and Klara – take Angus to find out what happened to the base comms. Mr. Stevens, can you act as their guide?"

"Sure can." Stevens stood ready.

"Team two – Marion, Casey and I – will go and check on the work that Doctor Pandewahanna was doing. If we can produce a test, then we don't need to keep everyone in quarantine."

"I'll take you down there," Briggs offered.

Alex was about to turn away but paused. "Hey, if this thing wanted to flush us out, it might try and shut off the power or oxygen. *All* the power and oxygen. Where are the internal controls for those utilities?"

"We thought that too. The overarching controls are all via this room. But the actual generators, batteries, and boosters are down in the subbasement. We checked them after the comms went down, but they seemed okay."

"Good. But we need to monitor it." Alex turned to Sam. "Okay, big guy, you're flying solo. But take Mia as your guide. Need you to check out and secure that room."

"On it."

"Yes." Mia's mouth quirked up at the corners. "I get to go with Sam."

Alex clapped his hands together. "Let's get this done, people."

The three teams headed out the door, moving fast.

CHAPTER 27

Colonel Jack Hammerson listened to Lieutenant Vincent "Vin" Douglas as he delivered his status report – they'd landed on time and on target.

As expected, the Kennedy Base communication systems were down, but Alex Hunter and his team had already established that there were signs of life and were en route to the facility. All good and to schedule so far. But the sooner they established what the threat was, dealt with it, and were on their way home, the better.

Right now, Hammerson's team was a long way from help, and working in the most hostile environment imaginable. And as of that moment, out of contact. Vin's last message was delivered as the satellite they used to bounce the radio waves back home was passing over the lunar horizon. It was one of the downsides of being on the dark side of the moon: there was no line of sight for transmission.

He felt for Vincent; he'd only been in the HAWCs for a couple of years and showed great promise. And like all of them, he was highly skilled, and keen to get in on the action, so performing babysitting duties must have been driving him crazy.

"Hang tough, kid."

Hammerson sighed and lifted the phone. He'd promised to keep Aimee in the loop, but Alex hadn't told her this mission was off-world. A small detail he'd need to leave out of his talk with her. And she was smart enough to know that whatever Alex was doing meant it wasn't comms equipment being down or some other tech problem, because, in simple terms, she knew that they didn't send in a team of HAWCs unless they were expecting heads needing to be broken open.

As his hand alighted on the phone it rang, and he snatched it up.

"Hammerson."

"Sir, Major Bilson at launch control. We might have a problem."

"What sort of problem?"

"A potential lift-off anomaly. You asked to be advised personally of any issue," Bilson replied. "I think you need to see this, sir, ASAP."

Hammerson cursed under his breath and couldn't imagine what the issue could be as the rocket had already left and landed at its destination.

"Can it wait?"

"Best not, sir." Bilson's voice had an anxious edge to it.

Hammerson grunted. Aimee's update would have to wait. "On my way."

CHAPTER 28

Mia led Sam down to the lower level and in the small elevator she turned to grin up at the silver giant beside her.

"How do you even fit in a normal chair?"

Sam chuckled, liking that there were still a few grains of humor remaining among the somber base personnel. He held out his arms. "This bulk is mostly the armored suit. Out of it I only weigh about 260 pounds, give or take a donut or two."

Mia laughed. "Only 260 pounds?" She blew air between her lips. "I take it back, you're a lightweight."

She continued to stare up at him, and after a moment Sam felt the weight of her gaze. "What?"

She shrugged. "Thank you. For coming, I mean. Things were getting a little fragmented up here. People who didn't like each other suddenly acted like they wanted to kill each other. Depression, psychosis, aggression – we were having the lot. Plus, the suicides started. I don't think we could have made it much longer." She shared a crooked smile. "So, yeah, thank you."

Sam shrugged. "Don't mention it, we were in the neighborhood anyway."

Her smile broadened. "Well, I'm glad you were."

The elevator stopped and opened with glacial speed. The corridor outside was dark. Sam engaged his visor and it telescoped up over his face.

"Get behind me."

"Watch out for Olga," Mia whispered. "The Russian woman."

Sam looked over his shoulder at her.

"She's about five-ten, has short, dirty-blond hair, and very light blue eyes. She's our number one suspect."

"Got it." Sam moved out and slowly down the corridor, and soon found his first pile of empty clothing. There were gobbets of black stuff all over it.

"This is what happens when our people are … taken," Mia said.

Sam pulled his gun into his hands.

"I can't see anything," Mia said.

Sam checked his sensors and, other than Mia behind him, they told him they were alone. He engaged the suit's lights, which shone a bright pipe of illumination down the corridor.

"That's better," she whispered. "Up ahead and to your left."

They continued on. Under foot there was more of the black slime, but it was solidifying and becoming like some sort of resin crusting, and actually beginning to fully coat the walls and floor.

"There, see?" Mia said. "We must check out the equipment and secure the door. The thing has been down here."

No shit, Sam thought, stepping over another blob of the sticky-looking material.

"That way." She pointed past him.

They turned the corner, and at the far end was the sealed door to the power-generation room. But blocking it was a person dressed in full space suit slumped against the door.

"Oh God," Mia exhaled. "I think that's Eric Wilson, our missing chemical engineer."

"He's not looking too good. Stay here while I check it out."

Sam pulled his weapon and strode forward a few paces then engaged the external speaker on his suit. "Person standing in front of energy room doorway, I am Second Lieutenant Sam Reid, please identify yourself."

When he was just twenty feet from the figure, Sam stopped and hailed him again, but once more there was no response. The guy's helmet had the gold reflection visor engaged, and there was no chance of seeing his face.

"Be careful," Mia urged, from a long way back.

Thank you, Miss Obvious, Sam thought, and then focused on the figure. "Sir, are you okay? What is your status? Please respond."

Sam moved forward, and when he was only a few feet away from the person, his intuition screamed at him that something was seriously wrong. He carefully reached out with the barrel of his gun and poked the body.

Several things happened at once: firstly, the body collapsed to the floor, just an empty suit now. Secondly, the door slid back, and the power-generation room's overhead lights came on brilliantly white, blinding him for a split second.

There was movement inside the room. "Get down!" Sam yelled to Mia, and went into the room, fast.

He came up with his gun at his shoulder and looked around at the state of the room. "Jesus Christ," he whispered.

Sam flicked from thermal to amplification as he scanned the room, and then even movement detection, but his suit sensors picked up nothing moving now, and nothing living. But there was a low-lying mist everywhere, and his suit registered humidity off the charts.

What the hell's going on in here? he wondered, and then turned to the open doorway. "Okay, come –"

There was silence from behind him. He turned.

Mia was gone.

CHAPTER 29

"Sam!" Mia came running toward him as he got to the elevator and stopped in front of him to lay her hands on his armored chest.

"You're okay?" he asked and held her shoulders. "What happened? Where'd you go? You've been gone for over an hour."

"Something was coming up behind me after you went inside the room. I thought it was Olga. I tried to call out, but you had vanished. I hid, and didn't know when to come out." Her words came fast and she held onto him as she spoke. "Then when I did, you were gone. Sorry, I'm not very brave."

"You're okay, that's the main thing," he replied. "Did you see?"

"The room?" She nodded. "I think I did. What was all that stuff?"

"I wish I knew. The machinery is still operational, that's the upside. The downside is I don't know what the hell is going on in there. The humidity is extraordinarily high and creating vapor. Plus, there's some sort of sticky, extruded matter everywhere. Looks like something melted in there."

"But that person standing outside –"

"No sign of him or her. The suit was empty."

"Oh God, just like outside. Did you secure the room?"

"No. If I do, I don't know if I'll be locking the entity out, or locking it in. I did a scan but found nothing. But that might just mean whatever it was doesn't show up on our spectrums." He shrugged.

Mia held her head. "This is a nightmare."

"You said it. Let's go back and report in. See where everyone else is at." Sam hit the button for the elevator and when the doors slid open, he waited for Mia to enter first and turned to give the empty corridor one last look. "And this time, stay close."

CHAPTER 30

Vin exhaled and leaned back in the pilot's chair, feeling the boredom. He'd run another maintenance check on the interior comms. Then run a power check, reviewed the ammunition stores, and finally sat back down, and waited for one of the field team to call him on the radio. Or for it to be time again for him to call in to Earth HQ.

He hummed a tune, his feet up on the edge of the console, and stared out at the plain of bleakness beyond the window. To begin with it had been interesting, all the pockmarks, crater rims, melted-looking areas from ancient meteor strikes where the surface had been liquified from the heat of asteroid impact. But the thing about the moon was nothing really ever changed. Beyond the window it could have been a damn photograph, it was so still – no breeze, no movement, no nothing.

"Life in the fast lane." He laughed, and put his hands behind his head and meshed the fingers. He sighed long and slow, and after a while he began to daydream about what he'd do first when he got back home.

He smiled as, in his mind, he saw himself kayaking in Florida Springs, with the water so clear it seemed inches deep when it could be a half-dozen feet. And it was warm, bath warm; you could sit in those springs, a cold beer in one hand, and just drift off. Other times, he had paddled up one of the tributaries, and then laid back and just let the languid current move him softly and slowly along the tree-covered waterways.

He sighed. *Heaven*, he thought, and shifted a little as a trickle of perspiration ran under his arm to be collected by the absorbent material in his suit.

Movement outside snapped Vin back to full attention. "Huh?" He sprang forward. "What have we here?"

There was a lone figure on the lunar surface jogging toward their ship. Vin stood up and leaned over the console. He saw that the suit the person wore had an American flag patch on one sleeve and the Kennedy Base insignia on the other.

"That's weird."

The figure caught sight of Vin and waved. Vin returned the wave. He still couldn't see who it was as the gold reflection visor was down, or even if it was man or woman in the bulky suit.

The figure stopped and pointed and motioned with its hand. The meaning was clear: drop the hatch.

Vin hesitated; there were no orders about this. No one expected that they'd receive visitors.

"Shit," he whispered. He wasn't sure what to do. He tried to think. What would Alex do? Find out who they were first, of course.

Vin held up a hand and pointed to his ear. He sent an open signal to the person but was met with nothing but a wall of static.

After a moment, the person shook their head, and pointed to the side of their helmet and motioned *broken* with their hands.

Maybe there was a problem at the base. Vin immediately tried Alex, or any of the HAWCs, but once again got nothing but white noise.

The figure made a twirling motion with their hand – *hurry up*.

Maybe that's why. Maybe they needed him, fast, and they'd sent over one of the Kennedy people to get him. If the team needed him, then it was urgent. He decided he had no choice.

"Fuck it."

He pulled his helmet on, expunged the air, and then punched the open button.

He looked up and saw the figure had vanished from out front and was making its way to the hatch below.

Vin only had a few weapons on his suit but was confident he could handle any threat. A HAWC could easily account for several Special Forces soldiers from any nation at any time, so if it was just one of the base scientists or even one of their security personnel, then the risk to him was extremely manageable.

He waited and soon a helmet appeared in the hatch as the person ascended. In the next instant, they were inside. With him.

Vin closed the hatch and refilled the lander's interior with air. He retracted his helmet, feeling the new cool air on his face.

"You can breathe easy now." He waited.

The figure just stood there, facing him, gold visor still engaged.

"Are you okay?"

At only five-ten, Vin wasn't tall for a HAWC, but he was solid, and fit, and knew how to kill an adversary in a hundred different ways even when unarmed. He was bigger and more formidable than the person in front of him, but for some reason, he was becoming unnerved. He felt the small hairs rise on the back of his neck and took a step back to balance lightly on the balls of his feet.

"Identify yourself," he demanded.

The figure tapped his chest.

Vin started to breath faster, adrenaline kicking in. "What do you want?" He began to take another step back, but the outstretched hand immediately stuck onto one of the armored plates on the front of his suit.

"Hey, hands off, buster." Vin used a two-hand thrust-push into the chest of the figure. But, impossibly, they didn't budge. And strangely, he didn't feel ribs, only something soft and doughy.

"Let go, *now*." He brought one of his arms down like a club on top of the arm holding onto him. The arm bent as if there was no bone inside it.

"What the fuck?"

The figure lifted its free arm to grip his. Vin swept his other arm upward, knocking the golden faceplate up into its recession slot and exposing the face.

What face?

Behind the glass of the visor there was a storm of something that was thick, and bread-like, with the pallid yeasty-white of old toadstools.

"Shit." He reached for his gun, pulled it, but knew that one of their mission rules was no discharging a weapon in or near the craft. He didn't care; he fired twice into the person's torso.

They didn't even flinch.

Vin brought the gun up and fired point blank into the visor.

The effect was immediate: it exploded, not inward, but outwards – at him.

Black, glistening tendrils flew at him, enfolding his face and upper body. He screamed as the dead-fish coldness enveloped him and began to pour into his open face shielding.

He turned his head to the console, trying to get to it to warn his team. But the figure, and the tendrils, had other ideas, and found his mouth, nose, ears, and even eye sockets.

Vin's last thought as everything turned a stinking black was the word they had learned in the initial briefing from the lunar outpost: *Lifeform.*

* * *

Minutes later the figure left the ship, jogging back toward the Kennedy Base.

Except for the hum of machinery, the empty lander settled back into silence. Then, a slim figure unfolded from a maintenance box in the hold and moved to the front cabin. The beautiful face turned slowly, scanning the empty suit of Vincent "Vin" Douglas and finding nothing of his remains.

It dropped from the hatch to the lunar surface to follow the intruder.

CHAPTER 31

Alex's head snapped to the side and he came rod straight. He felt the anguished pulse crash into his consciousness as if it was a scream in his ears.

"What's up, Boss?" Casey asked.

Alex walked away a few paces and touched his ear stud. "Vin, come back."

He waited a second or two.

"Lieutenant Vincent Douglas, *soldier*, report in."

There was nothing but static.

"What is it? What's happened to Vin?" Casey said.

"No-*ooo*!" Alex spun, feeling a boiling fury in his belly.

Casey took a step back. "Boss?"

"Vin, the lander, something's wrong." Alex looked from Marion to Casey. "Continue with the analysis. I need to go." He turned to Briggs. "Let me out."

"By yourself?" Briggs shook his head. "No way, the risk is –"

"Do it." Alex spoke through his teeth, and his eyes seemed to glow silver for a moment.

The stocky base commander gulped.

"Do it," Casey urged. "Now."

Alex stepped in closer to him. "Now."

Briggs turned, entered the code and hit the button on the door.

* * *

Alex ran across the moon's surface. He pushed the suit to its limits, kicking up dust behind him. He had felt Vin's cry in his head and knew before he even arrived that he wasn't going to find it was just a tech problem.

As he approached the lander, he saw that the external hatch was open and guessed the ship was depressurized. He had tried several more times to contact his soldier but up close, saw no one behind the window.

Alex didn't pause and went up and through the hatch in a blink. He went to his knee.

"No, no, no."

Vin's empty suit lay on the floor of the ship, holes punched through the ballistic armor and biological plating. The penetration had started from the inside. The silver suit was coated in a glistening, viscous, black material just like Alex had seen at the base.

Alex tried to determine what had happened. Somehow the creature had got in and attacked Vin. Vin was a new HAWC but an adept soldier. He could defend himself and should not have been taken by surprise. Unless the thing had presented itself as a non-threat.

Alex turned slowly. Nothing else seemed removed or damaged. His scan stopped at the doorway to the pilot's seat and console.

"Ah, shit."

He stood and crossed to the front of the ship. The entire communication system was trashed. In fact, not just trashed, but turned to tiny fragments. That's why he'd got white noise. Whatever this thing was, it wanted to isolate them the same as it had at their base. No more messages back home.

Back home, he thought. That's what Mia said Olga warned them about: that it wanted to get back to Earth. But it wasn't able to as the ship was disabled without the launch key. He felt the launch key in his pocket.

Alex straightened and looked around slowly. It hadn't trashed the entire ship and he bet he knew why – because it probably still hoped to use it.

What are we really dealing with here? he wondered.

He returned to his fallen soldier's suit and placed a hand on the deflated chest. He sighed.

"Sorry, Vin, we didn't know that everyone is a suspect."

He quickly removed the empty suit and stored it. Then he exited the ship and sealed the hatch. He scanned the moon surface and, even with his enhanced vision, saw nothing.

Alex craned his head to look up into the darkness of space. Over the horizon was the Earth, and right now, it seemed farther away than ever. He lowered his chin and headed back to the base.

CHAPTER 32

Igor Stanislov stared into the dark mine, his impatience boiling over. He turned to Doctor Anastasia Asimova. "How long have they been down there?"

"An hour now," the science officer replied. "The mine is only 120 feet deep and does not have too many side passages. They tunneled down and then horizontally along an impact crustal seam. But ..."

"But it's been too long." He made a guttural sound in his throat. "Curse this radiation for disrupting our signals."

Anastasia shrugged and her eyes slid to him. "Maybe Boris and Chekov found something in the laboratories. We should give them more time."

Stanislov didn't get it. Why were there labs in a mine? *Stupid scientists*, he thought.

Anyway, he had a different idea. "Or maybe they were ambushed." Stanislov pointed to the dust outside the mine mouth. There were too many prints to count, so many that the dust had been compacted. But on the outer edge, the prints were a little clearer, and all the same boot type except for being different sizes. However, there was one set of prints that stood out.

"You see this? That is not a Russian boot." Stanislov turned. "I think it is an American lunar boot."

"From the crawler? The Americans went into our mine?" She shook her head. "No, no, this is not permitted. This project has the highest security classification."

"For a mining project?" Stanislov looked down at her.

"Yes."

"So, now you want to go in?" he asked.

"No, I still think we should wait." Anastasia stared into the inky blank hole in the crater wall.

Stanislov snorted. "For what? Don't be scared. We go in. Our job is to investigate the mine, and that is what we will do. But we must be ready for anything."

"This is not a good idea. We were told to watch the lander as well. Now we will all be down in the mine." She grimaced. "I think the commander will be furious."

Stanislov could tell she was being evasive. But he couldn't understand why she had a slight tremble in her voice.

"I take full responsibility," he replied, curtly. "We need to investigate the mine and find out what happened to our soldiers. If any Americans are loitering there or when we come back, we shoot first and ask questions later, yes?" He grinned.

"If you say." She continued to stare into the hole.

He nudged her. "Ready?"

"Yes and no." She drew her pistol as he did.

The Spetsnaz soldier headed in, the scientist staying close behind him.

CHAPTER 33

"Interesting." Marion read through Doctor Pandewahanna's notes on the small screen.

"What is?" Casey asked, casually standing with her back to the wall close to the door. Her gun was cradled in her arms, and though she looked at ease, nothing was coming through the door unannounced while she was on guard.

Tom Briggs also turned to the biologist.

Marion's brows knitted. "Doctor Pandewahanna found some fascinating biological fragments among the material retrieved from inside the Russian woman's helmet. As well as being remnants of extraneous human proteins, digestive enzymes, and degraded plasma, there were spore fragments, like those from a fungus."

"Could it be from some sort of contamination?" Briggs asked.

Marion shrugged. "Sure, maybe, but unlikely, as it was a variety of spore Doctor Pandewahanna couldn't identify in the mycological database. But I think she did make an educated guess. She wrote a single word – 'mutation'."

"Well, that sounds fucked up," Casey sneered.

"What does that mean? Did she explain it?" Briggs asked.

"No, and maybe she didn't get the chance."

"So, we got a giant mutated moon mushroom loose on the base?" Casey asked.

Marion smiled. "I don't exactly know yet." She turned back to the screen. "Let me do some more investigation and try and figure this out."

CHAPTER 34

Yuri Borgan sat next to Doctor Irina Ivanov in the back of the American crawler. Up front, and driving, was Grisha, and beside him was the hulking form of Taras, with the nearly as large Aleksi hanging onto the equipment rack at the rear.

The ground crew had originally recommended against taking the pair of big men due to their weight and size. But Borgan knew that if there was any trouble, then their physical strength and brutal combat skills would have been invaluable.

The U.S. Kennedy Base was a mile to the east, but the max speed of the crawler meant it would still take them twelve minutes before they broached the final crater rim and then dropped down into the sea the Americans had chosen for the base infrastructure. Borgan knew that the American base was much larger than their own former base, with eighty-two personnel of varying nationalities, and also contained five security personnel. This last aspect didn't worry him, as the Americans had no weapons, and even though the guards were ex-military, none had specialized skills.

He looked over his shoulder at his huge soldiers and felt supremely confident. If any American tried to stand in their way, Taras and Aleksi would pound them to moon paste.

Borgan chuckled at the thought. "Moon paste," he repeated, the sound echoing slightly in his helmet.

They topped the rise, and saw the flattened plain with the recessed, single-story structure. There were camera and sensor pods situated around the perimeter, and also solar array beds a few hundred yards further out.

"Look." Grisha pointed.

There was a solitary figure walking back to the base wearing a strange silver environmental suit.

"Nice day for a walk," Borgan said.

The figure turned as if sensing them, and then stopped. Then waited for them as if he expected them.

"Let us meet our first American moon man." Borgan motioned forward and Grisha started the crawler again.

* * *

"What the hell is this?" Briggs leaned toward the screen of the external camera feed. "That's our crawler, but who are all those people crammed into it?"

Sam came and looked over his shoulder, and then his eyes widened. "One guess. And that's the Boss they're heading for."

Roy Maddock scoffed. "They could be coming to talk. Or they think we destroyed their base, and they're coming to make some war."

"Do you think we should even the odds?" Briggs asked.

Maddock grinned. "The odds are already against them."

Sam straightened. "Give me an exit. Roy, you're in charge."

Sam headed for the maintenance room hatch.

* * *

Alex sensed the crawler approaching before it came over the lip of the crater. He continued on to the base but slowed, until it made an appearance and then began to head toward him. He wanted their attention. He knew it'd be the Russians, and if they'd come to talk, they could start with him. If they'd come for anything else, then it would finish with him. Either way, he had some questions for them first.

Alex's mood was already storm-dark after losing Vin, and when he was just a hundred feet from the maintenance bay doors he stopped and turned – there were five of them, and by their shape and size he guessed four men, one woman, with two of the guys big, the one in the rear even bigger than Sam Reid.

Alex also saw that they were armed – so, as they expected, not just a science team or diplomatic approach then.

The crawler stopped and the Russian team got out. Their obvious leader strode forward with the giant soldiers at his shoulders.

Alex switched his helmet for short range all-frequency pickup, and could see that four of the Russians wore heavily armor-plated space suits and he knew it was some form of combat kit. It was confirmed; they weren't here to make friends.

"*Kto zdes' glavnyy* – who is in charge here?" the leader asked.

Alex responded in Russian. "As far as you're concerned, I am. What do you want?"

The man's eyes blazed at the response. "I am Kapitan Yuri Borgan, representative of the great nation of Russia, and..." He pointed a thick, gloved finger. "... you destroyed our base," Borgan seethed. "This is an act of war and the response will be commensurate."

"This base had nothing to do with what happened there. Your countryman, Olga Sobakin, told us she detonated the base by draining the nuclear rod cooling pond."

Alex saw the leader look to the small woman on the crawler, who gave an almost imperceptible nod. He also saw the big men start to move out into flanking positions.

"And that is why your vehicle was left there, hmm?" Borgan replied. "We will come inside, use your communication equipment and also perform our investigations." The Russian rested his hand on a sidearm. "Don't make this … unpleasant."

"You're not going in the base," Alex growled. He strained to hold his anger in check, but he knew something inside him was becoming impatient. "Go home, while you still can. The moon would be a sad place to die."

"Indeed." The Russian leader laughed derisively. "You are in our way."

"Last chance." Alex waited.

"I hope you can breathe moon air." The Russian leader turned to the pair of giants. "Taras, Aleksi, move him."

The big guys advanced.

"No guns," one muttered in thick English, and then drew a long Russian flat blade.

Alex didn't know if that message was meant for him or his colleague as the other man drew his own knife.

The first man came in at Alex slow to begin, but when he was close moved fast and confidently. He threw a looping right that Alex easily ducked under. But it was only a feint as the blade came next in a backward slice – a typical Russian Special Forces move – and grazed the plates of Alex's suit, scarring, but not penetrating.

Alex shot out a fist and punched the man in the chest. He heard him cough and step back.

Not enough, a small voice whispered in his head.

The man came again, and this time threw a punch with his entire shoulder behind it. Alex blocked the sledgehammer blow, but next came the blade headed for his lower ribs. This time Alex caught the blade in his fist. He snapped the steel, and let it fall to the lunar dust.

He thrust a hand out to grab the man by the neck. Just as Alex was wondering where the other big soldier was there came an impact from behind, driving him forward. It was a coordinated move, for as Alex was propelled forward, the first man struck with a massive right uppercut to the chin of Alex's helmet.

The impact was enough to rock Alex's head back inside the silver shell of his helmet and neck casing. He was held in a bear hug by the second man as the first came back at him.

Alex wasn't going to wait around for another of the big Russian's hammer-blows so he kicked out, driving the big man back a dozen feet and sending him sprawling.

Then he spun in the second man's arms. Alex saw the man's eyes go wide for a split second behind his visor as he realised he had left himself unprotected against one thing – Alex head-butted him with all his strength and their two helmets came together with a loud crack.

A small star-shaped impact mark appeared in the Russian's battle armor. Alex's remained unharmed.

"I want that suit," the leader jeered. Then his voice took on a harder, impatient edge. "Stop playing – take him down!" he yelled.

The first man drew his pistol, but before he could fire, Alex grabbed the gun hand and held it upward. The pistol discharged into the air, the bullet probably leaving the thin atmosphere and traveling on into space.

The big man used his other huge fist to pound Alex in the ribs. After the second blow, Alex felt something crack that might have been one of the coolant tubes inside his suit.

The second man returned to the fight and swung down with his knife at the back of Alex's neck, trying to find a seam in the armor. But the joins held and the blade skidded away.

Finish this, the voice urged from the dark place in Alex's mind. *Send them a message.*

The first man dragged Alex up, and for a split second, his vision turned to a hot, red furious hell. *FINISH IT!* the voice screamed.

Alex shot out a fist into the huge man's visored face with such force and speed that it penetrated the toughened shielding and crushed the front of his skull. Gases vented in a red mist from the broken visor glass.

He withdrew his fist – now glistening and bloody – and watched the body of the huge Russian topple back like a felled tree. He spun, grabbed the second man, and lifted him above his head to bring his back down across his knee. There was a loud crack of armor and bone and also a groan of agony.

More! the voice in Alex's head demanded.

With the man bent over his knee, Alex punched down with all his strength. The man's spine bent in half, not just fracturing but totally separating all the disks. He let him slide to the moon's surface.

Now kill the others. There was hunger in the dark voice now, and eagerness.

"No," Alex said, and rose to his feet to stare down at the two men.

I think they got our message. There was a small laugh, dry and amused, and then: *Felt good, didn't it?*

He watched the first man's blood on his hand dry, flake, and fall away like powder in the super-arid, near vacuum of the moon's atmosphere.

Three gunshots rang out, two striking him in the chest, and the last dead center in his visor, chipping it. The suit's armor plating defrayed the impacts, but the shots still knocked him flat to the ground.

Alex sat up and saw the two remaining men coming at him with guns drawn. The female rushed to kneel beside the remains of the first man. And then moved to the still living second man.

The Russian with the gun raised it again. But as Alex got back to his feet, a silver juggernaut slammed into both Russian men and dragged the guns from their hands.

Sam Reid stood over them, then reached down to grab one cosmonaut in each hand, lift them from the lunar surface and shake them like rag dolls.

"Say the word, Boss," he said.

Alex approached. "Thanks, Sam."

Sam shook them again and pulled them close to literally growl into their faceplates.

"Put them down." Alex turned to the woman. "You – come here as well."

Sam slammed the pair together then threw them down, hard, where they sprawled, lucky to be in low gravity so no bones were broken. One pointed up at Alex.

"You killed him! You'll pay for that."

"No, *you* killed him. Now shut the hell up and remove all your weapons." Alex waited two seconds. "*Now!*" he roared.

The other Russian looked to his leader, waiting for a command. The men's hands went to their weapons, but Alex knew it wasn't to disarm.

He lost patience.

He pulled his gun with the thermal rounds and fired directly into the huge dead body of the Russian lying a few feet away. The bullet struck, ignited, and as the Russian woman scrambled backward, the body began to glow, then crumpled inside the suit before that too shrank to ash, with only charred bones and a few metallic components remaining.

The Russian men stared for a moment and quickly withdrew pistols and knives and let them fall to the ground.

"That is all." Borgan said.

One of the men got to his feet and cleared his throat. "I am leading a rescue mission for our base. It seems we were too late."

"Like I said, we had nothing do with that. Your own people destroyed the Lenin Base as there was an infection inside. That infection is now inside *our* base," Alex spat. "And it is killing us."

"How? How is it killing them?" the woman asked.

"Mostly they're vanishing. Others are changing," Sam said.

"Changing." The woman stepped forward. "Into what?"

"Into not people anymore," Alex said. "We don't know where all the others have gone."

The woman turned to Borgan. "They could be in the mine."

Alex tilted his head. "The mine is still open?"

She pointed to the crawler. "Your people left this crawler behind at our base."

"You saw them?" Sam asked.

"No, but they must be in the mine as well. Where else?" Borgan replied. "We sent a team in to check it out. Any survivors may have retreated there after the base was destroyed. It was sealed and had an oxygen supply." He shrugged. "Is logical."

Alex lowered his head for a moment. "Olga said that's where everything started. With something they found in the mine."

"It's just a mine." Borgan looked from one of his fellow Russians to the other. He stopped at the woman. "Irina, yes?"

"Mostly," she replied.

"And? What did they report?" Alex demanded.

"We have not yet heard."

"Call them," Alex ordered.

Borgan stared for a moment then tried to raise his team members but there was no reply. He tried again. But nothing.

He gave up. "Maybe there is no signal in the mine depths. Or interference from the radiation."

The seconds stretched until finally the woman spoke. "We should get back."

"Yes, yes." Borgan looked at the remains of his fallen comrades and then back to Alex and Sam. "This is not over."

"It is." Sam picked up the broken body of the second man and tossed it at Borgan's feet.

Alex walked forward. "If you come back, with aggression – next time you all die. We're all in this together now. Protect your people, protect your craft, and protect Earth. Whatever this thing is, it tried to infiltrate our lander. Don't let it get back home."

"What?" The woman shook her head. "But it's just an infection, yes?"

"This is now beyond an infection and is some sort of lifeform. It's intelligent and aggressive. We need to quarantine it here," Alex replied.

The woman turned to Borgan. "We should hurry." She turned to the vehicle.

"Not in our vehicle," Alex said. "That's our property." He and Sam climbed in and Sam turned to them.

"Good luck."

Alex watched for a moment more as the trio trudged over the crater rim, carrying the broken body of the second man between them until they disappeared. He turned away.

"Let's go."

"They're hiding something," Sam said as he drove them to the maintenance doors.

"Of course they are." Alex brushed the last flakes of dried blood from his gloves. "And unfortunately, it's a deadly secret. One we might have to make them tell us."

CHAPTER 35

Deep in the mine, Stanislov and Anastasia stopped before a fortified door. The Russian Special Forces soldier shone his light around its edges.

"*Voloch*," he spat. "What could do this?"

Anastasia's eyes were round, and she could only shake her head as she stared at the huge door. It, and most of the wall surrounding it, had been peeled back.

He turned to her. "Why is this fortification even in a mine?"

"It is the partition to the research laboratories," she whispered.

He stared for a moment, trying to process what she said, but then turned back to the heavy door.

"What, this?" he asked.

"The metal door was the first barrier to sealing the mine off from the laboratories beyond. These double doors were a hermetically sealed airlock to create a sterile environment beyond. Or there once was."

"With breathable air?" he asked.

"Yes, of course. So, they could work unencumbered by their environmental suits."

Stanislov turned his flashlight back on the remains of the barrier, then shining his light further inside, he saw that there was no power, no light, and the inner airlock had been destroyed.

"It's been breached. An explosion," Anastasia said. "Just like at the base."

"No, no explosion, there are no heat burns on the steel. It looks to have been blown outwards, but something other than explosives was used."

"Where are Chekov and Boris?" She peered in. "They should have reported this to us."

Inside they could see an overturned trolley and a pile of abandoned equipment. But there was no sign of their team members, or any of the crew from the base or the labs.

"Gloomy. I don't like this," she said in a small voice.

"I'm sure it's much nicer in summer." Stanislov grinned at his own dumb joke but was glad Anastasia couldn't see it because nerves made the corner of his mouth tremble.

She held up her light. "According to the schematics it should level out for another few hundred feet before we get to the main laboratories and storage rooms."

"Anastasia, I thought this was just supposed to be a mining project. And I also thought it was only supposed to be 150 feet of project tunneling."

"Anna, call me Anna. Only my mother calls me Anastasia." She glanced up at him and they shared a brief, broken smile. "And it was just a mining project to begin with. But …"

"But what? I need to know to do my job."

She sighed, and nodded. "But our military masters found another use for the privacy, seclusion, and distance – it was the ultimate firewall. So we extended the size and objective of the facilities." Anna shook her head. "I would hate working at this place."

Stanislov exhaled and turned his flashlight to scan the walls and ceiling and then stepped through. "Come on, let's get this over with and get out of here. I don't like it either."

Inside, the long tunnel's sides were fortified with light-weight metal beams that joined with lintel girders overhead. The aluminum alloy was strong, lightweight, and could be assembled and disassembled like Lego if needed. It was then paneled with sheets of the same material but coated in a gleaming white.

Or it once was. Now the walls were dented, holes punched right through the surface sheets and everywhere there was chaos and destruction.

"I don't understand what happened here," Anna said. "Looks like a war zone."

"Is this blood?" Stanislov stood at the edge of a large stain – a dried and dark liquid. Oddly, it still looked sticky, and he angled his light to get a different perspective. "It's black. Lumpy. Maybe clotted blood."

"We should go back to the surface. Wait for the commander."

"No, our men are in here somewhere. Besides, anything that happened here, happened long ago." He pointed with his light. "The research rooms would be sealed, yes?"

"Yes."

"Good, then maybe they are there." He started in.

They came across piles of clothing, laboratory smocks: some torn, some simply discarded. Even trousers and underwear.

"They took their clothing off? Why did they take their clothing off?" Anna shone her light around.

"The labs are up ahead. Boris and Chekov must be down here somewhere. There's nowhere else for them to go." Stanislov continued on. He swallowed and found his throat had become bone dry. He paused to angle his lips to suck on the small tube that had a water bottle attached. The body-heat temperature liquid felt slimy in his mouth.

He sniffed back a running nose. There was perspiration running down his sides and beginning to bead on his brow, thanks to his nerves. The dehumidifiers in his suit were having trouble regulating the temperature as it was freezing inside the tunnel and he felt frigid sweat on his skin as well as a cold bitterness in the pit of his stomach.

Both had their audio monitors working, but inside the tunnel there was nothing but an eerie stillness.

The pair climbed over more debris and finally stopped. The laboratory had been trashed, but now even the pristine walls simply ended. It was as if it had been converted into some sort of cave: dark and wet looking.

"There should be a little more of the lab infrastructure; it must have been totally destroyed somehow. But ..." Anna moved in a little closer to him. "Not much more. This goes on further than our miners were supposed to have excavated."

Stanislov turned slowly. The space was coal black and there was no sound or movement he could detect. But even though he knew that the labs should be right in front of him, their lights couldn't pick out the end of the tunnel. Like Anna said, it was as if it continued beyond where their construction should have ended.

"Do we go in?" she asked.

"We've come this far." Stanislov held up his arm with the wrist light. He panned it around. "Deep; maybe they did more tunnelling work and never reported it." He stepped inside.

"This is not construction," Anna said. "These walls, floor, and ceiling have been smoothed."

"By what? Looks like a lava tube. Is this possible?"

"No," she said. "There was volcanic activity on the moon, but that was nearly four billion years ago, just after it was formed. This looks recently melted."

Stanislov bent to lift some papers, and then read, "Project Cyclops?" He lifted his light to the cold, dark tunnel, then to the small woman. "What is Project Cyclops? Tell me again what they were actually doing here."

"I'm not authoriz—"

"Anna, I'm standing right in the middle of it," he replied, but softly now. "I think I should know what it is I have got myself into."

"Okay, okay." She drew in a deep breath and let it out slowly. "We – *they* – were doing research into variant micro-scopic flora and fauna. Looking for stronger strains of some biological agents for vitalization," she replied.

"Vitalization of biological agents? Germ warfare." He snorted. "Then it wouldn't surprise me if the Americans did destroy it. If I was them, I would. Did the commander know?"

She shook her head. "No, only Irina and myself. You were to secure the base and look for survivors. Irina and I were to recover any specimens. It was supposed to be simple."

"Of course, don't trust the dumb soldiers." He shook his head.

She faced him. "It's not that, just … everything was top secret. We were trying to develop new medicines and vaccines. But of course, the military was looking for … more aggressive strains. Everywhere on Earth eventually gets compromised. And after the cyber infiltration of the Black Sea laboratories, this became the safest and most secure place to conduct our experiments. The mine was real and still operational; it just served two masters now."

He laughed. "So you were looking for the next strain of deadly flu, yes?"

"Deadly flus are for amateurs. We had progressed well beyond that." Anna stopped and looked up at him. "We were investigating something that could turn battlefield combatants into compliant sleepwalkers. Imagine your enemy simply laying down their weapons, or walking docilely into your machinegun fire."

"That would be good. You developed a chemical or a bug for this?" he asked.

"In a way. We were working with several strains of a fungi called cordyceps." She shone her light around at the dark walls and then back at him. "Do you know what a zombie ant is?"

"I can guess."

"I bet you can't." She sniffed wetly. "It's caused by a strain of parasitic fungus that invades and takes over the ant's body, and then controls it."

Stanislov turned his light on her. "Where would you find such an abomination?"

"In nature, where some things are more brutal than you can imagine."

He made a guttural sound in his throat. "I don't believe it."

"It's true." She pulled his arm. "You go to a tropical country like Brazil, and venture deep into the jungle. Find a leaf that's hanging almost exactly ten inches above the jungle ground and look underneath it. You will probably find an ant clinging to the leaf, jaws clamped tight. Not doing anything else but hanging there. But the thing is, this ant's life is not its own anymore, as its body now belongs to *Ophiocordyceps unilateralis* – the zombie-ant fungus."

"That is horrible." He blew air between his lips. "It grows on the ant?"

"Yes and no. It grows right throughout the insect's body, draining it of nutrients and hijacking its mind. Over the course of a week, it orders the ant to leave the safety of its nest and ascend a nearby plant stem. Then it forces the ant to permanently lock its mandibles around a leaf."

"You were working with that here?" Stanislov felt disgusted. *Fucking scientists.*

"But then the true horrors start: the fungus pushes out polyps on long stalks usually through the ant's head, growing into bulbous pods full of spores. And because the ant typically climbs a leaf that overhangs its colony's foraging trails, when the polyp bulb explodes, the fungal spores rain down onto its fellow ants below, where the fungus inserts itself through the armour. And then it has more zombies to grow and expand itself."

Stanislov cursed. "It is infected, and its sole role is to then infect more to become like it."

"Yes." She looked away.

"In this laboratory, this was their job? Your job?"

Anna nodded. "But I was part of the Earth team. I was just a bio-analyst who suggested experiments and looked at the results."

"I'm glad it's destroyed." He shone his light around. "What did you – they – do to make this happen then?" He focused the glare of his light on her face.

"We had to move it up the evolutionary tree. Fast. So, we evolved a strain that could adapt to bigger and more complex host animals." She looked away. "Mice first. And then larger mammals."

Stanislov stared for a moment. "And then you went all the way ... to people."

She wouldn't look at him.

"Tell me!" he yelled.

Anna turned back. "Yes."

Stanislov shone his light over the chaos and debris. "And then your baby grew up."

"It wasn't supposed to be like this." She made a small sound in her throat. "We simply allowed it to use humans as its host. And we selected the fungal growths that exhibited the best ability to adapt and learn."

"And grow smarter. And now the base is destroyed, the

laboratory is destroyed, and our team members are missing. I think your monster got very smart indeed."

"It exceeded expectations."

"I should kill you myself." Stanislov shook his head. "Five more minutes then we get out of here. Captain Borgan needs to be informed."

CHAPTER 36

Alex worked hard to quieten down the fury that raged inside him. It was his job to project calm when adversity struck – that's what was expected of leaders. Even if right now his dark instincts urged him to strike out at something, anything. He drew in a deep breath and turned to face his team.

"Vincent is gone," he said flatly.

"What the fuck?" Casey exclaimed. "The kid?"

"How – where is he?" Klara growled.

"He's gone, there's nothing left. He was taken right out of the lander." Alex's eyes narrowed as he stared straight ahead.

"They broke in?" Casey asked.

"No, I think he must have let them in. I think they wanted the craft. When they couldn't steal it, they obliterated the comms system."

"They cut us off," Sam said evenly.

Alex nodded. "Yeah, I think the only reason they didn't take the ship was because we have the launch key. So the ship's link back to home is gone."

"Where the fuck is it, this thing?" Casey's voice was close to a roar. "We need to find it while it's outside and obliterate it, now."

Alex stepped in front of the female HAWC. "Is it the only one? Or part of many? And if we head out, what if there's more in the base waiting for that to happen? When we have a target, we'll take it head on. Trust me. But now is not that time."

"Goddammit, Vin." Casey bared her teeth, and punched the wall with her armored glove, leaving a dent. "Fuck it all."

Alex lifted his chin. "This hurts, I know. But we've got to fight this thing with our heads as well as our weapons. Understood?" He looked into the face of each team member.

Casey had her head down, still muttering.

"*Understood?*" Alex's roar exploded into the confined space.

"HUA!" the HAWCs responded as one. Even Casey Franks.

"Good." Alex faced McCarthy. "What's the state of the local comms?"

McCarthy scoffed. "Destroyed, like in the lander. Whoever did it didn't just disable it but pulverized everything. The base doesn't have all the parts to replace the system."

"Can something be jerry rigged?" Sam asked.

McCarthy bobbed his head. "Maybe, but whether we can generate enough transmission power is anyone's guess. Is the generator room okay?"

"If you mean still working, then yes," Sam said. "But it doesn't look like any generator room I know anymore. Looks more like when you forget that jar of grape jelly for a year or two and then open it – all mad stuff growing everywhere. Whatever this thing is, that might have been where it's been hiding out – like a nest. Nothing living in there now, but we'll need to keep watching it."

"Let's set up some external cameras and place some shock disks; I want this thing dead." Alex faced McCarthy. "If the generator room is okay, is that what you need for now?"

"If it still works, we have a chance," McCarthy replied. "But I'll need to manufacture some componentry and have eyes in the back of my head when I'm doing it."

Alex nodded. "The extra eyes we can provide. Get on the repairs, ASAP."

"You got it," McCarthy replied, about to turn away but stopped. "Hey, what *is* the status of our lander?"

"Operational." Alex folded his arms. "My guess is they – it – still needs it. And undoubtedly still hope to get it."

"Let 'em try," Casey said between her teeth.

"Let who try?" Briggs asked as he and Mia joined them. His voice was flat. "That's the problem, isn't it? We don't know who or what we're dealing with."

"Olga," Mia replied. "That damn Russian woman."

"Marion?" Alex lifted his chin.

"I haven't finished with all Doctor Pandewahanna's research notes yet, but she had completed some outstanding work in identifying particles of something that looked like unidentified fungoid fragments in samples from the Russian woman." Marion folded her arms. "Her theory was it might exist in the bloodstream in a native state of the mimic."

"Mimic." Casey shook her head, then turned to look over the people in the control room. "And it might be one of them assholes out there, right now."

"Stow it, Franks," Alex said. "The thing was outside, and no one else came back in but me and Sam."

"Yes, sir." She nodded but didn't look appeased.

"So it could be in you two now," Briggs said. "See how the distrust can spread?"

Alex nodded. "Yeah, I do. What now?"

"There's one fucked-up thing I don't get, doc," Casey said. "This thing is supposed to have eaten, absorbed, converted, or whatever it's done, around forty people. Plus all those damned Russians. So how come it hasn't grown to be so huge that it just can't hide anymore?"

"I don't know. This thing is unknown to us." Marion tilted her head. "Well, sort of. Doctor Pandewahanna could identify some aspects of the fungal organism but not others. It's a little like a cordyceps structure, but she wrote: 'mutated' and 'altered', and for now all we can go by is what we know about Earthly fungoids and the work Sharma has done."

"Fungi are tiny things. Like mushrooms, right?" Klara asked. "How was this thing able to infect and take down Vin so quickly? He knew how to defend himself."

"It must have tricked Vin into getting close to it. Like I said, it must be excellent at camouflage or a damned good mimic. It means it can copy things, copy people. Or become them."

"Come on, I mean, looking like someone is one thing but that isn't enough to fool people. It had to act like them. *Really* act like them. How is it that smart?" Klara frowned. "If it's just a goddam fungus."

"Well, for something with no identifiable brain, fungi are incredibly intelligent and capable of solving complex problems."

"I'm not liking the sound of this," Sam said.

"Tell us what we need to know," Alex said. "Or at least what some of the characteristics of this creature might be. Anything that will help us understand what it is we're up against."

"And kill it," Casey added.

"We just need some sort of souped-up anti-fungal, right?" Klara added.

"Sort of." Marion nodded. "But first we need to understand that this thing is to Earthly fungus as we are to the first lobe-finned fish that walked out of a primordial swamp." She stared down at the ground, her face tight with concentration as she seemed to gather her thoughts. "Earthly fungi have been known to problem solve. But the real Einstein of the fungal world are things called slime moulds.

"Slime moulds have existed on Earth for billions of years. We always thought of them as fungal bodies because they produced spores, but later we found that they're something that is neither plant, nor animal, nor fungus. In fact, these critters are like something out of a horror novel – they are capable of learning, solving puzzles, and making decisions. And can fully regenerate after a dormant period so they don't seem to age."

"That'd come in handy if they were trapped on the moon for millions of years," Sam said softly.

"And just lying in wait for us," Casey added.

"I don't know enough yet, but I'm not convinced this thing is indigenous," Marion went on. She looked to Alex. "But it is using us. Not unlike the cordyceps genus." She read through more notes, her brows knitted.

"Okay, so we believe this thing, or these things, are smart, but how smart?" McCarthy asked. "I mean, instinct smart, animal smart, human being intelligence level, or beyond even that? After all, if this thing is so smart, why hasn't it tried to communicate?"

"Or is it so smart it doesn't regard us as peers?" Sam asked. "Just food?"

"This is a nightmare," McCarthy said.

"It is," Marion agreed. "And it might not have started out as having process intelligence above simply acting on instinct. But then it grew through ingesting intelligence – being able to open locks, know what is critical to a human's survival from an engineering perspective, or even how we communicate. That could be hijacked straight from the brains of the hosts it has absorbed."

"It knows us by eating us. We're both a food parcel and brain booster to this thing. We're just sheep," Casey said and made a guttural sound in the back of her throat. She turned to look over the people sitting in groups, some talking, some silent. "And it's got all its sheep penned and ready for the taking."

Sam turned to Alex. "And now it's taken Vincent. Boss, you know what that means?"

"Yeah. Now it knows all about the HAWCs," Alex replied.

"One more thing," Marion said. "There is another name for the cordyceps fungus." She laughed mirthlessly. "The puppet master."

"Well, that damn fits," Casey said.

Alex's jaws clenched for a moment and he turned to face Marion. "Finish the test. We need to isolate the source of the infection, and find out exactly who are the puppets, and who is the master."

Marion nodded. "On it."

CHAPTER 37

Launch Complex 39, John F Kennedy Space Center, Merritt Island, Florida – launch warehousing center

Jack Hammerson looked at the images of the equipment hidden in the corner of the storage facility's prelaunch area. Everything in there had supposedly been triple checked, weight balanced and size mapped. And everything in there goes on the craft, is absolutely necessary, no exceptions.

Hammerson's jaws clenched. The ground crew never just "forgot" to load materials. Ever. Besides, the missing weight alone could throw off their flight calculations.

He had the flight load manager on speaker. "Well?" he asked.

"That material left behind is the majority of the medical supplies. It was crated and ready to go," the load manager replied.

"But there's no crate," Hammerson replied. "So, the crate went, empty – is that what you're telling me?"

"That's where it gets confusing, sir." Hammerson heard the load manager sigh. "We do a final weight check when fully loaded. We expect there to be minuscule anomalies – the astronauts sometimes take personal effects and the like. We take that into account."

"And?" Hammerson grew impatient. "Get to it."

"There was no *reduction* in weight, but we did detect a slight increase," he said. "It wasn't much so we just wrote it off."

"Ghost in the shell, huh?" Hammerson lowered his head for a moment, his mind working. "Someone emptied the crate, and the crate went. But there was additional weight – so something replaced the medical equipment." He lifted his head. "What the hell went in that box?"

"We don't know, sir." The man's voice was small.

"For all we know it could be *a fucking bomb*!" Hammerson roared. He tilted his head back and closed his eyes for a moment as he fought to keep his anger from boiling over. "Okay." He leaned on his knuckles. "Show me the footage from the surveillance cameras for the night before, right now."

Hammerson heard people scramble, keys being punched, and then the screen on the wall in front of him split into multiple views showing the storage silo from various angles. In the right bottom corner, there were digital readouts counting down the time. They all played at double speed.

His eyes moved over the footage. The night edged toward dawn as the rocket continued to be loaded. Trucks came and went as the work went on.

At around 0500 hours, a truck approached, and was emptied. Just before it took off something rolled out from underneath and went into the facility almost faster than the eye could follow. Hammerson stared.

"Quadrant nine, slow it, rewind and enhance."

The other camera scenes were removed, as the single feed was slowed to normal speed and then enlarged. It replayed again, and once more there was the anomaly, but even cleaned up, it was still indistinct.

Hammerson felt a growing knot twist in his gut. "Take it all the way down to frame by frame," he said.

His order was carried out.

"Stop. Rewind two frames. Stop." He straightened, placing his hands on his hips. "You gotta be shitting me."

The slim silver figure was blurred but unmistakable.

"Sophia, Oh, God no," Hammerson whispered. "Do we have a timeline on communications yet?"

His technician looked up. "No, sir, we think the problem is at their end."

"She said she'd follow him to hell and back." Hammerson sat down slowly. "I didn't believe her."

CHAPTER 38

Deep in the mine, Igor Stanislov and Anastasia Asimova continued into the last section of the tunnel, but now their steps were careful, each putting one foot softly in front of the other.

Anna held out a hand and ran it over one of the dark walls. "Glass smooth."

"The melted look again," Stanislov replied.

"No, more like exuded." She scanned the ground. "Look." She crouched. One of the smooth walls seemed to have run like liquid and a puddle of it had congealed to one side. She pointed. "See in there? That's a boot print. This place was still being formed when the people came in. It was made probably around the same time as our team was working. Or soon after."

"Let's investigate a little further," Stanislov said. "If we don't find anything in the next two minutes, we will return to the surface and wait for the commander."

"Agreed," she said eagerly.

They continued, slowly. They used their helmet and wrist lights, but the Tartarean darkness inside the tunnel swallowed every particle of illumination as if a black cloth had been thrown over them.

In another few moments they came to the end of the tunnel and stopped to stare.

Anna clung to his arm. "This is where it ended," she whispered.

"No, this is where it started," he replied softly.

Scattered before them were empty spacesuits, dozens of them, as well as piles of laboratory smocks, boots, and even underwear.

"The scientists," Stanislov said softly, feeling a tickle of fear run up his spine. "Plus, our missing team members, I think."

Sure enough, heavily armored spacesuits were crumpled on the ground before the wall. Also empty.

"They all took their suits off … in a vacuum?" He turned to Anna. "Not possible."

"And where are the bodies?" she responded. "They should have died in seconds."

But there was something else. Stanislov reached for his gun. "American."

Close to the wall, there was a figure standing there, or at least someone in a spacesuit with an American flag patch on the arm, facing the strange, dark wall, and so close he was almost touching it. His head drooped forward, and arms hung limply, like a small child who had misbehaved at school and been told to go and stand in the corner.

Stanislov switched his speaker to the international channel. "Hey, America."

The figure ignored him and continued to face the black wall, not moving an inch.

Even with their lights trained on the figure he was in shadow in the gloom of the viscous-looking cave.

"Wait here," Stanislov said and hated that his voice cracked. He lifted his gun and began to close in on the figure. "Hey, America, you okay?"

He turned back briefly to Anna, who looked small and alone in the dark tunnel.

When he was within a few feet of the man, he stopped. Stanislov could see that the back of the man's suit was torn open. In the vacuum and with the temperature hundreds below zero, it was … "Impossible," he whispered.

As he stared, he saw the material around the tear shift and then things like small knobs on stalks start to extend from the rip. Inside, the flesh looked like it was moving – it was raw and rubbery like bread dough.

He grimaced, feeling his gorge rise, and backed up a step. He kept his gun up.

"What is it?" Anna asked.

"Stay back." His voice was strained as his throat constricted from fear.

More bulbs appeared from the back of the torn suit, and these too began to swell ominously. They seemed to reach toward him.

"Demon!" Stanislov yelled and fired his gun, once, twice, and a third time. All three shots hit the target.

The American didn't flinch but the swollen and questing bulbs finally burst, filling the area with a white, gritty powder that hung in the air and sparkled in their flashlights.

Stanislov's nerve broke and he spun, his jittery legs wanting to transport him far away. But instead, he felt a punch to his back that knocked the wind from his lungs. Immediately he felt a blistering cold and the breathable air in his suit began to thin. He knew what it was: a suit breach.

He heard Anna scream, and continue to scream, and then Lieutenant Igor Stanislov thought one last thing as the cold began to penetrate his body: *Zombie ant.*

* * *

Anastasia stood rooted to the spot with her eyes wide in terror. A pencil-thick cord-like structure burst from the torn suit of the American spaceman to pierce Stanislov's back.

As she watched, her colleague's body began to dance and vibrate as his screaming got even more panicked and loud. He must have been speared like a fish, with the barb hooked deep in his flesh.

So, this is how it did it – their experiment had learned a new technique for capturing its prey, above using simply spore dispersion.

Anna couldn't move, or speak, or even breathe. All she could do was watch with a horrified fascination as Stanislov's cries turned to a wet sound, as if he was gargling water. And by the unnatural movements in his suit, she knew what had struck him was actually pouring along that cord and entering his suit like a hypodermic injection.

"Get back," she said almost soundlessly, as she knew it was really only to herself.

And then Stanislov's suit, which had been ruffling like it was in a strong breeze, crumpled to the floor, empty.

Her heart hammered and she felt she was in some sort of dream where nothing was real. The American man seemed unchanged, but where did Stanislov go? All his physical mass?

Finally, the American suit started to grow and swell, and it turned toward her. The faceplate of the helmet was pocked with holes, and behind the glass there seemed movement from something that wasn't a face at all, something that strained against the cracked glass.

"We created you," she whispered. "Do you understand me?"

More cords shot out, but this time landed in the fallen suits of her colleagues, and, like a conjuring trick, they began to rise up, full again.

"We can work together. Help each other," she begged.

The next cord struck her chest, and she knew it had also pierced her flesh as the agonizing coldness pumped into her skin.

In those last seconds of Anna being Anna, when the cordyceps' fungal threads reached her brain, she saw it, saw it all, and knew then what it really wanted – visions of an Earth covered in a layer of fungal matting, where every living thing, every insect, plant, animal, sea creature, had been absorbed and co-opted into a global mycelium mass.

It just needed one thing – to get there – and they were the key.

* * *

"There's something wrong," Irina said. "I can't raise Anna." She plodded along beside Borgan and Grisha, who glanced at each other.

"Radiation interference," Grisha suggested.

Borgan tried Stanislov, then the other soldiers, with the same result. "Strange. The men aren't responding either. Maybe they are in the mine and out of range."

"No, the mine isn't that deep," Irina replied as she tried to fine tune the frequency. "It's more like they are simply not answering. Anastasia would answer me if she could. We need to move faster." She glanced at the broken body of Aleksi. "Leave him, he's dead."

Borgan looked at Aleksi and saw the man's eyes flutter. "He is not."

Irina reached out a hand to grip the captain's arm. "He's dead."

Borgan stared down for a moment more, knowing there was nothing they could do for him. "Let him go," he said softly to Grisha.

Borgan and Grisha released their colleague.

"Hurry." Irina tugged at him once more, and then turned to jog again.

Soon they crested the last crater rim to the basin where the remains of the Russian base and their craft waited. But as they finally approached the apex of their climb, they slowed.

"Oh." Irina stopped dead.

Borgan's mouth hung open and his eyes bugged. "Our ship."

The lander lifted above the rim, throwing down thrust that whipped the powdery lunar dust into billowing clouds.

"Go, go!" Borgan shoved Irina.

They began to run now, but at the glacial speed they could manage it only meant that when they came over the crater rim, the lander was already several hundred feet in the air.

"They left us?" Grisha asked. "Why?"

As the trio watched, their lander got smaller and smaller. Borgan tried uselessly to raise someone, anyone, but he got dead air, as whoever was onboard wasn't opening the communication link.

Irina sat down heavily, followed by the two men. They watched and sat in silence as the lander became a dot, and then the dot vanished into the black atmosphere.

How many minutes they remained there, staring, no one could remember.

Finally, Irina sighed. "They've killed us." She turned. "We only have about ninety minutes of oxygen remaining in our suit tanks."

Borgan sat beside her and held his knees.

Grisha lent forward. "Don't let it get home – that's what the American said."

Borgan nodded. "It's not home yet." He groaned to his feet and held out a hand to Irina. "There is one option left. We need to return to the American base and beg them to take us in."

CHAPTER 39

"Sir." The technician spun in his seat.

Briggs looked up from one of the external camera feeds. "What is it?"

"We've detected a launch in the vicinity of the Russian base. A craft is leaving the lunar atmosphere.

"What?" He rushed around the console. "The Russian lander?"

Alex and Sam followed, and the rest of the HAWCs turned to watch.

"Yes, sir, has to be," the technician replied. "They've now departed the proximate atmosphere."

"Guess they've completed their work." Briggs turned to Alex. "You guys must have really given them the heebie-jeebies."

"Like hell," Alex shot back. "That craft cannot be allowed to land in Russia, or anywhere."

Briggs frowned. "I don't understand. They probably found they had no survivors here, as we suspected." His brows knitted. "I thought they were a security risk for us, and you wanted them gone. Them leaving is a good thing, isn't it?"

Alex strode closer to look at the radar blip of the departing craft. "When that thing attacked our lander and killed Vin, it wanted to take our ship, but couldn't. So my bet is it took the Russian one instead."

"This thing can fly a spacecraft now?" Stevens' voice was shrill. "That's ridiculous. Your own scientist said its some sort of mutated fungus or something like that."

"It can't, but the Russians can." Marion folded her arms and joined the men. "It adapts and survives. Right now, we have no idea what this thing is capable of. We know that some fungus can retain memories and can even inherit memories – they learn through ingestion."

Casey's laugh was like a bark. "Eats a fucking Russian lander pilot, becomes a Russian lander pilot."

Marion turned and gave her a flat smile. "Basically, that's about it."

Alex lowered his head for a moment. "It's what I feared. This thing isn't smart, but it's ingesting and then inheriting knowledge." He looked up. "About the base, its people, our equipment …"

"And our strengths and weaknesses," Sam finished.

Alex nodded. "Like all organisms, it just wants to survive. And knows it needs to find a place that will provide the best medium for maximum growth."

"Earth," Sam said wearily.

"So, ah, does that mean the thing is gone from here?" Stevens asked hopefully. "We're safe now?"

"Budding," Marion said. "Cloning, budding, spooring – this thing can make copies of itself. The bit that took the ship might just be a fragment of the genesis entity. So in regards to your question, I think we still have a problem."

"The genesis entity?" Alex said.

Marion nodded. "I think it confirms that the source of the infection might have been the Russian base. That's where it all started."

"Then if the Russians were infected there, it means the blast didn't kill it. Or kill all of it," Sam added.

"Sooner or later, we're going to need to pay it a visit," Alex said, and turned to Briggs. "It'll take that Russian ship three and half days to make the trip back to Earth. So, we have three days to fix our communications, contact home, and then get someone to convince the Russians to blow their own craft and people out of the sky."

"You really think that the Russians are all infected?" McCarthy asked.

"Yes." Alex straightened. "I don't think there are any Russians left alive on that lander. That's a Trojan horse, headed for our planet."

Casey exhaled between her teeth. "Ah, for fuck's sake."

"A Trojan Horse?" Marion sighed. "That's very apt, Captain Hunter. And we just gave it a ride all the way to our front door." She pressed her temples with her fingertips. "This is potentially the worst outcome. This … *thing*, has the ability to spread and dominate every place it goes. Every city, every country, every planet."

"It's not there yet. First things first: our own problems haven't gone away. We need to secure our power, light, and air, and priority one is Doctor Pandewahanna's test," Alex said.

"You're right. And it'll be ready soon. Then we can test everyone, and hopefully identify our intruder," Marion replied.

"Good." Alex turned to his team. "Casey, Klara, you watch Doctor Martin's back. Nothing and nobody is to interfere with her work. Clear?"

"Sir." The two HAWC women's eyes shone with intensity.

Alex turned to McCarthy. "You get the big guy. Sam knows a thing or two about electronics and engineering, so can help speed the process up. We don't have much time now. Everything is to be done at speed."

"I'll do my best. But some of those parts need to be built." McCarthy shrugged.

Alex grunted. "I don't need to tell you what's at stake, do I?"

McCarthy shook his head. "I know: everything. I won't rest until I'm done."

"What do you want me to do?" Roy Maddock asked.

Alex put his hand on Maddock's shoulder and turned to Briggs. "You be okay here for a while?"

The base commander nodded.

Alex turned back to his HAWC, his mouth curling into a smile. "Suit up. You and I are going for a little walk."

CHAPTER 40

Baikonur Cosmodrome Spaceport, southern Kazakhstan

The technician spun in his seat. "Still no response, sir."

Major Alexi Bilov turned, his forehead deeply furrowed. "Please tell me it could be a malfunction."

"I don't think so. They're just not picking up." The young man listened in again. "No response on radio, or even to our attempts at Morse."

Bilov paced closer to the man's console and looked over his shoulder. "Life signs?"

"That's another anomaly, sir. Sometimes I detect several life signs that read as normal, and other times I get a single reading that … isn't."

"Isn't?" Bilov scowled and then made a guttural sound in his throat. "Put me on speaker."

The technician did as asked and turned to the major. "Link open."

"This is Major Alexi Bilov, in a direct communication to commander Yuri Borgan aboard lander P23–09. What is your status?"

The technician opened the comms to the room. Bilov waited, but there was nothing but the vacuum of dead air.

"I am ordering Commander Yuri Borgan to respond immediately. If you cannot verbalize, then please use another means of communication."

Bilov waited again.

After another moment, the technician just shook his head. "There is no white noise, or feedback. The system seems to be working fine. They're just not responding."

Bilov rubbed his chin. "They might not be able to." He looked up. "Someone or something might not be letting them."

"You think the Americans …?" The young man's eyes widened.

"Maybe something else. Something –" Bilov thought about their secret project, his imagination taking him down a dark and ominous path. He turned. "I think we need to prepare for all eventualities." Bilov headed for the door. "Keep trying to communicate with our team. We need to protect our heroes, at all costs."

CHAPTER 41

Sophia stood just beyond largest crater rim to the north of the Kennedy Base. She sensed again the strange presence that had attacked the lander and killed the young HAWC. It perplexed her – it was non-human but had fragments of human thought and physicality about it. Or within it. She'd tried to reach out and probe its mind but found there was nothing for her to link to, and the being's process of thought was fragmented and disorganized as though it was in many places at once, or perhaps, many in one place at the same time.

But there were two things that she was convinced of: one, it was growing in size, intelligence, and strength, and the sensations she did draw forth indicated it held no malice, no antipathy, or desire for reprisal. Instead, it acted on instinct and an overarching will to survive that surpassed anything she had ever encountered.

And two: unfortunately, the lifeform's instinct meant its very existence was the antithesis of human life. And a threat.

CHAPTER 42

Alex and Roy Maddock stepped onto the moon surface. The pair turned slowly, scanning their surroundings, before Alex turned back to give a thumbs-up to the camera. Now that the ship comms had been destroyed, their only communication was via each other. He started off.

Maddock caught up with him. "What exactly are we looking for?"

"We're going fishing," Alex said.

Maddock chuckled. "I got a bad feeling about what you're going to tell me the bait is."

"You guessed it – us." Alex laughed softly. "Something Marion said made me think that I'll be a target. This thing knows what we do, so will undoubtedly guess we'll try and get the Russians to blow their ship out of the sky."

"So, it needs to also improve its odds," Maddock replied.

"Yep. I'm betting it wants our ship as well to improve its chances of getting to Earth. When it took Vin, it learned everything about us and will know about the launch key."

"And who's got it."

"Sort of. Vin saw Sam remove it, but not sure if he saw Sam give it to me. So, it'll know one of us has it. Me being outside will draw it out from the base, or, if there are any of those budded clones on the moon surface, I expect they might pay us a visit. Mia said it attacked them at the solar arrays, so we'll head there first."

The two large men in their silver armored suits walked across the moon surface, kicking up clouds of silken gray dust that glittered before falling in slow motion to settle again. Alex's suit sensors scanned the surface, but there was no movement or heat sources.

It didn't take them long to skirt the base and climb over the ridge of small craters to the solar arrays that Briggs and Mia had needed to repair. They continued on and a little further out they found the two empty suits Mia had described.

"Three men went down, and one got up and walked away," Alex observed.

Maddock headed a few paces out to one side. "Got a single set of tracks leading back to the base." He looked up. "Think it got back in?"

"Assume it did. And that means it knows how to work around the security system. Or worst case, someone inside is not who they say they are and is letting it in." Alex turned slowly, looking at the disturbed moon dust. "Remember, it's absorbed a lot of the base personnel so knows the base infrastructure better than we do."

"It took Vin. That kid was a fighter and it still beat him."

"Ambushed him. This thing gets in close and overwhelms its prey. I don't think Vin had a chance. But we won't give it that opportunity. It must have presented as a plausible, nonthreatening figure to him."

"Until it got close enough."

"Yeah, until then."

It's coming.

Alex frowned. "Josh?" The whisper in his head was familiar but somehow disturbing.

Maddock turned. "You say something, Boss?"

"No, I thought I heard ..." Alex shook his head.

It's here.

It wasn't Joshua's voice, or even the decrepit dryness of the other lurking within his id at the very core of his mind. It was someone else.

Then Alex sensed the minute vibrations beneath his feet.

"It's here!" he yelled.

Black rope-like cords burst from the ground, enveloping both HAWCs. Alex felt them immediately begin to tighten. They surged across his mask, and he felt multiple points of pressure as the thing sought a way to get inside his armor to his flesh.

He remembered the torn clothing and black slime the base crew had encountered on their missing people. He also remembered that Vin's suit was primarily undamaged – and what penetrations there were occurred from the inside.

"It can't get in past our armor," Alex said. "Yet."

Still, the cords compressed, and he felt the pressure begin. The suits hydraulics kept it at bay, but in the next instant, he was pulled below the ground about six inches.

"Trying to ... damn ... bury us." Maddock's voice was strained. "Crushing ..."

The black mass continued to surge over the two men, making Alex wonder about the size – the real size – of the thing below the surface. It had an ability to compress itself down to a human shape, but after absorbing so many human beings, its true mass must have been enormous.

"Roy ..." Alex said.

"Yeah, here, but suit's system is screaming at me – damn thing is exerting thousands of pounds of pressure per square inch. Gonna find a weakness eventually." He groaned. "Can't get it off."

"Give it a shockwave," Alex replied.

Alex initiated the suit's external shock blast, discharging its full power. The 2000 volts surged across the silver suit, making it glow blue for several seconds.

The thing shivered, and where it touched Alex, it glowed red from the electricity.

He saw Maddock's suit also release the charge, but the thing still gripped them both, and squeezed harder – he heard the minuscule popping of something on his helmet and prayed the thing didn't have the power to crack it. He suddenly remembered taking the shot to the head from the Russians. *Idiot! Should have checked it over*, he thought.

"Shocking again," Alex said.

"Bad idea, Boss," Maddock replied.

Alex remembered what Quartermaine had told him about the discharges – continual use meant the charge would seep back in against their bodies.

"No choice. One of us has got to be free to save the other. Hang tough." Alex released another shockwave, and then another, and the last time felt the agony of the discharge – it made his teeth clamp together so hard he tasted the metallic tang of blood in his mouth.

He released another pulse and once again felt the massive electrical charge run across his frame. His internal suits sensors screamed alarms, and for the first time, he felt his flesh singing. But where the creature touched him it went from scarlet red to a charred black, then let him go. It started to suck back below the ground, and he quickly drew his gun armed with the incendiary rounds and fired into the ground after it.

The thermal rounds ignited like miniature suns, burning the surrounding dust, catching the escaping cords. Hundreds of pounds of the creature was vomited up into a mound of stinking mush. The rest of it vanished.

He heard Roy Maddock groan and saw his soldier was now half-pulled below the lunar surface. The objective was clear: if the thing couldn't pierce or peel him out of his suit, it'd drag him below the lunar surface and work on him at its leisure. Alex knew his soldier couldn't repeat the process of continual shockwaves or even use thermal rounds while held in its grasp, as the trauma would certainly overwhelm the HAWC suit's protection and kill him.

Over his comms he heard Maddock grunting as he strained. "It's compressing the armor. I've got some integrity warnings."

"Go for rocket burn," Alex shouted.

"Good plan. On it." From within the dark, rubbery mound there was an orange glow, and Maddock's head and shoulders appeared as his personal booster rockets fired.

The creature started to burn but it held on, and Alex had one option left – he pulled free the neurotoxin stick and pointed it at where the mass was thickest on his friend. He fired.

The dart stuck and discharged its poison. One half of the black mound sagged as the drug worked its paralyzing effect.

"Don't like that either, huh? Good." Alex fired another dart, and another.

The mass sagged like thick jelly, and soon didn't even have the muscle control to pull itself below the surface. In another few seconds, Maddock burst free with the twin jet of flame from his booster blasting out behind him. He cut the booster emission and as the mass fell from him, he landed on his feet.

"Gross shit." He wiped away some remaining gobbets of the substance that rapidly dried on his suit.

Alex bumped fists with his soldier. "Thank you, Doctor Quartermain. Your suits just passed the field test."

"What the hell is it?" Maddock asked as the pair looked down at the massive mound of dark jelly.

"I wonder if that was its normal shape. Or just another version of itself," Alex said.

"It's enormous." Maddock was still wiping himself off. "And for all we know, it might be ten times as big under the ground."

The blob started to shiver, and then moved, but not to try and slide back beneath the moon's surface. It was changing shape.

Alex pointed the shock stick at it as the dark matter shrank, and changed color. It went from a large blob of several thousand pounds of black jelly to something about six feet long and pale.

As they watched, arms, legs, then a head formed. Hair sprouted and features appeared on its face.

"Tell me I'm going mad," Maddock breathed.

Alex grimaced. "Eric Wilson, I presume."

The man was naked, and it looked unbelievably incongruous to see him lying on the moon's surface like he was just sleeping. And then it got worse – his eyes opened, and his head turned toward them.

"Where ...?" he asked.

"Holy shit," Maddock said.

The man sat up and held his head.

"Do you know who you are?" Alex asked.

The man frowned. "No, yes – Eric, Eric Wilson. I'm an engineer at the Kennedy Moon Base." He held his arms out and looked at his hands, turning them over.

"That's right, Eric," Alex replied. "And do you know *where* you are?"

"I'm, I'm ..." He looked around and then his expression changed to one of terror. "Where's my suit?" He got to his feet, hugging himself. "How can this be? How can I breathe? How did I get here?"

"Take it easy, Eric. What do you remember?" Maddock asked.

Eric frowned and looked down at the gray powder beneath his feet. "Coldness. Screaming. Blackness. Then nothing." He looked up. "Wait, I remember my friends, Art Dawson and Benny Minchen, coming to find me." He shook his head. "But then … I can't." He looked up. "Weird. I can still hear Art and Benny … in my head." He took a step toward Alex. "Where's my suit?"

Alex stared hard at the man. "You don't need a suit, Eric."

"How? Why?"

"Because you're not breathing," Alex said evenly.

"What?" His face creased in confusion. "No, no …" Eric spun one way then the other. He turned back to the HAWCs. "Why aren't I breathing anymore? What happened to me?"

"You're not breathing because you're not human anymore." Maddock lowered his hand to his gun.

"There's something's wrong here. You have to help me." Eric staggered forward.

"Stay there, Eric." Alex held up a hand flat in front of his face.

Eric shook his head. "But I'm a person. I'm Eric James Wilson, thirty-four years old. I was born in West Des Moines, Iowa." He held his arms out to the HAWCs. "You have to help me."

Suddenly, all the expression fell from Eric Wilson's face, and the smooth skin on his cheeks and forehead became lumpy and uneven.

Roy and Alex backed up, weapons in their hands. Before their eyes, Eric Wilson's head grew to the size of a pumpkin, grotesquely swollen, and then the skin split horizontally and vertically to peel back like the petals of a giant flower, revealing a mass of stalks with bulbs at their ends. They began to swell.

Just as they began to explode forward, the HAWCS opened fire with incendiary rounds. The bullets entered the Eric Wilson thing's body, and tiny points of light began to glow inside him.

A scream came from Eric Wilson, but it was hard to know from exactly where, as the thing didn't have a mouth anymore. And it wasn't a human scream but the sound of something from the dark depths of the cosmos itself.

Alex and Maddock fired again and again as the body of Eric expanded, and the thousand-degree rounds bloomed within it, causing ruptures, and large canker-like sores to burst open on the thing as it tried to expel the points of agony.

The bullets kept heating up, and the creature lost its man-like shape as it seemed unable to hold it together anymore. Finally, the body fell into a steaming mass that once again was a pool of dark liquid.

Both HAWCs just stared as the puddle expanded, dried, and then began to turn to dust.

Maddock turned. "I kind of expected first contact would be with some little fat guy with a light on the end of his finger. You?"

Alex snorted. "Pretty much. But it just learned lesson number one: you come in peace, then so do we. You come for war, then we fry you down to dust."

"I heard that," Maddock said, and then: "What now?"

"It's not over. This isn't all of the thing, or the only one." Alex sighed. "We'll collect a sample for Marion. This was a test of our firepower against our adversary. Bottom line, we confirmed that if we can flush it out, we can kill it."

"All we need to do is find them or get them to show themselves."

"This was just a bud or piece of the thing." Alex turned back to the base. "I'm not sure that the thing or things inside are the source creature either. For all we know, the originator is or was deep in that Russian mine."

"That's our next stop?" Maddock grinned. "Coz I love being a guinea pig."

"Probably, but not now. We need to get back, ensure that we get those comms working again, and protect the people who are still alive."

"And still people."

"Got that right." Alex reached up to feel his helmet; he needed to get it checked out. A small problem in his suit could mean a death sentence if he was too far from the base.

He waved Maddock on. The helmet could wait. Right now, they had other priorities.

CHAPTER 43

Sam and McCarthy's first stop was the machine room to gather parts and tools. Then they'd be spending however long it took down in the comms room to try and repair the external transmission tech. Right now, that was the priority.

Sam held up a hand to stop McCarthy as they were heading out so he could listen to the incoming message from his HAWC leader – Alex Hunter delivered his soldiers an update on their engagement with the lifeform, and what they used to push it back.

"Good," Sam said and turned to McCarthy, who had his eyebrows raised. "Boss just had a confrontation with the lifeform and kicked the thing's ass. Our weapons tech does the job, so now let's do ours."

Sam waved McCarthy on and saw Mia give him a small wave over the chief engineer's shoulder. He smiled back, liking the young woman, and wondered whether she was just lonely or starved for affection. Being marooned here can't have been fun. Especially now, he thought. Sam knew he wasn't the most attractive guy going around, more a massive lump of muscle and scar tissue, but it kinda made him feel good to have someone checking him out.

He placed a hand over his breastplate where the picture of Alyssa sat. *Don't worry, girl, you're my one and only.*

He nodded to Mia, and she pointed to herself and mouthed: *Do you need me with you?*

Sam shook his head and gave her a small salute. Her mouth turned down momentarily, then she nodded. But she came toward him anyway.

"Stay safe," she said.

"Always," he replied.

"I'm sorry about your friend Vincent."

Sam grunted, not really wanting to talk about it.

"Thank heavens you didn't lose your ship. That you had the foresight to lock it." She brightened. "I bet it was you that thought of that."

Sam shook his head. "Standard op on a mission in hostile territory."

"Modest." She smiled. "Just make sure you keep the key safe. That ship is our lifeline."

"The Boss has it. No one, no time, is going to take that from him. You stay safe too." Sam turned away. "Let's go," he said to McCarthy.

As he went out the door, Sam turned to see Mia staring at him, her expression strangely blank.

He and McCarthy headed down to the machine room, and McCarthy held his arms wide as he beheld its inventory. "This is in better shape than NASA's shop."

Sam grinned. "Hell, it's in better shape than most of my house."

Everything they needed was on walls, on shelves, in crates, clearly labeled and categorized. There was even a local computer catalogue system that identified smaller parts and where they were stored, the quantity in stock listed with an accompanying identifier image.

"Grab a trolley will you, Sam?" McCarthy spoke over his shoulder as he paged through the system.

Sam brought the trolley around, and when the engineer identified a required component, Sam retrieved it from its shelf, drawer, or cabinet. Sam had engineering experience, and he was one of the HAWCs' go-to guys for weaponry and equipment repairs, so he knew his way around workshops, tools, and other aspects of the build-rebuild process.

In fifteen minutes, the trolley was laden with parts, electronics, and tools, from wrenches to circuit boards and soldering equipment.

McCarthy checked it over. "That should do for round one."

"Okay, let's get to work." Sam pushed the trolley, and McCarthy hefted a canvas bag that contained tools.

They headed to the elevator. The trolley just fit inside next to McCarthy and the huge frame of Sam bolstered by his armor.

As they arrived at the lower level, Sam eased out and paused. "Stay behind me," he said and used the suit's sensors to gauge the territory ahead.

There shouldn't have been people on this level, so anyone suddenly appearing was to be regarded as a potential hostile. Sam now knew what it took to defeat this thing, but better if he wasn't stuck in a narrow corridor if he had to use thermal rounds, or close to McCarthy if he needed to discharge a shock pulse.

He snorted softly. That was the thing about ambushes – they came at you at the worst time, the worst place, and usually when you were at your most vulnerable. That's what made the best ones successful.

They continued on to the communications room, and Sam opened the door, and leaned in for a moment, scanning the interior.

"No one here but us mice," he said and entered.

McCarthy sighed as he approached the devastated communication unit. "Someone really did a job on this."

"Yeah, they knew exactly what they were doing." Sam looked about. "You know, they could also have damaged the air and power, and that would have wiped everyone out real quick, but whatever it is chose not to."

"Maybe the creature just hadn't thought of that yet," McCarthy replied.

"Nah, it was just buying time. Or maybe it just wants its meat to stay fresh." He turned to McCarthy and grinned.

"Yeah, thanks, Sam, that makes me feel so much better." McCarthy shook his head. "Okay, let's see what we've got here."

Sam watched as the man worked. He was impressed with his expertize and artistry. The guy was the chief designer of the base, and knew everything about its construction, design, components, and maintenance. But he also knew how to get hands-on, and weld, hammer, and shape the delicate parts he needed. Sam enjoyed the work the man was doing as if he was watching an artisan. In fact, he was learning as he watched, because he was witnessing things that were revolutionary in skill and design.

McCarthy wore magnifying goggles when using a soldering iron to replot a circuit board with pinpoint precision. "Anything done can be undone," he said as he worked. He gently blew on the cooling solder and lifted his goggles to examine his work. "Looking good." He slotted the board back into the drive and began work on the next.

Sam lifted his gaze from the minutiae of the work and scanned the room. At least the comms room wasn't like the central power room that housed the generators and oxygen supply. The memory of that, with its glistening stickiness like plant sap, or something extruded from the ass of a bug, still freaked him out a little. Whatever the lifeform was, it couldn't have created a more alien-looking place if H.R. Giger himself had designed it.

"How much longer?" Sam asked.

McCarthy shrugged. "An hour to get it back together. Then we need to test it and see if we have signal strength. Maybe more time for some readjustments." He looked up. "Call it two hours."

"Good work." Sam engaged his suit visor. Immediately a readout image appeared in the glass on the bottom left reading the atmosphere conditions, and scanning for movement, and heat sources.

And then it found one – at the rear. Small, but Sam was sure it wasn't there before.

"Just going to do a quick circuit of the comms room," Sam said, not wanting to distract the master engineer.

"Okay. I'll be here." McCarthy reapplied his goggles and went back to work.

Sam saw that his sensors had picked up a tiny heat bloom – not the size of a human, but smaller, like the temperature signature of a small dog or cat – which definitely didn't exist on the base. He followed it to the far end of the room where the processor racks, plus generator, and signal boosters were. The place hummed with power, and he knew that it probably gave off a small hint of ozone.

The background temperature here was already slightly above normal due to the electronics, so the heat bloom had to be something above standard range.

Sam eased his head around the first rack, and then edged in to see behind the next – nothing. He moved a little further along the wall and noticed that the heat bloom was gone.

What the hell?

He turned, and his sensors picked up the bloom again – this time near the door. If he didn't know better, he'd say it was a damn large rat scurrying around the room.

He headed for the door, and just as he got within a few feet of the frame, the door whooshed open – initiated from outside – and a figure stood there, its helmet on and glare visor down over its face.

It lifted a burner and let loose a gout of flame over him. Sam instinctively held an arm up, but with his visor down, the HAWC armor wasn't troubled by the heat at all.

The figure dropped the welding tool, turned, and ran.

"The hell you will." Sam half-turned. "Close the door and lock it!" he yelled to McCarthy then sprinted after the person, wondering whether this was a saboteur, or the mimic thing. Either way he was confident of catching them, but he knew using the incendiary rounds would be impossible inside and he could only use the shock disks or suit pulse if he got close.

But he also remembered what Alex told him about the neurotoxin darts – they were just as effective. Poison it was then.

Party time, he thought, eager to get some payback for Vin. He drew out the toxin dart stick and accelerated, using his internal MEC technology to assist his bulk, but the person was like a jackrabbit, and went around the next corridor like a sprinter.

Sam was moving at close to forty miles per hour and closing in on the figure – just a dozen or so feet now. When Sam followed it around the corner, he found himself in another corridor, and alone.

"What the fuck?"

There was a single door halfway up and he crossed to it and pushed the button. It shushed open, and he glanced in before pulling back. Nothing jumped out at him, and his sensors picked up no movement nor any heat source.

He leaned around again, and saw it was the good old janitor's cleaning closet – he snorted – they had 'em even on the moon.

Sam turned back to the corridor. It was empty, and he jogged along it to the end. It finished at a console with a touch screen, but nothing else.

He moved quickly to the side room again. For the first time, he noticed the small dots of the base cameras above him had been coated in the sticky amber extrusion he had seen in the base's power generation room. It was obvious: someone or something wanted them blinded. Sam turned slowly. And then it hit him – something also wanted to lure him from the comms room.

Ah, shit no. Sam put his head down and ran faster than he had ever moved in his life. His huge feet pounded on the ground, shaking the corridor, and he went around the corners so fast, he collided with one of the walls, damaging some the tiles.

As he approached the comms room, he immediately saw it. The door was open.

"No, no, no."

He lifted the toxin stick and slowed at the doorframe. Then Sam went inside and did a quick circuit before coming back to where McCarthy had been working.

His shoulders slumped. Everything the man had been doing was smashed. Plus, there was a mound of light armor on the floor, with McCarthy's nametag on it. But that was all.

Sam screwed his eyes shut for a moment. Then he pressed the comm. stud on his helmet.

"Boss." He sighed. "We lost McCarthy."

Alex's roar went right through his head. "What happened?" Alex asked after he recovered, and it sounded like the furious words came through gritted teeth.

Sam tilted his head back, his eyes shut. "I fucked up."

CHAPTER 44

Casey paced in the small room while Doctor Marion Martin hunched over her microscope. The female HAWC felt wound tighter than a spring and hated that they potentially had a deadly adversary – or adversaries – hiding within the base, but one that refused to show itself and allow them to take it head on.

She was right on the edge and working hard to keep herself in check. But following Vin's death, that was becoming harder by the minute.

Marion leaned back from the scope and rubbed her face, hard. "It's not working," she said softly as she stared over the top of the eyepiece.

Casey lifted her chin. "Don't tell us that, doc."

Marion sighed. "Doctor Pandewahanna believed that this creature is some sort of evolved or mutated form of fungi. But the human physiology has been dealing with fungus for millions of years, so we have an immune reaction."

"That means we already have some sort of defense against this thing, right?" Klara moved a little closer.

"Yes and no. It means that our system reacts. Or at least Olga's did. Hers produced antibodies. It didn't mean the human physiology could deal with it. It just means our system tries to defend itself, but gets quickly overwhelmed."

"Just like a disease," Casey said. "A giant germ that infects people and then takes them over."

Marion bobbed her head for a moment. "Sort of. I think the initial attack is physical. But as it remakes or copies our bodies, it has to copy everything, from the hair, to the brain, to the lymphatic system, and also the immune system. It co-opts our bodies and hides within us and then controls us – the true puppet master." She breathed. "Then we are just shells – nothing more than a disguise."

"But our bodies can tell," Klara asked. "Can't they?"

"That's what Doctor Pandewahanna thought," Marion replied. "Our bodies try and expel the invader hiding within them. They thinks it's a form of fungal infection and therefore produces antibodies for it. She expected that people who are infected have this antibody in their system."

"That is good, isn't it? So we can produce a cure?" Klara said.

"No, they're gone, and not people at all anymore." Marion's brows came together. "But she never got to test it. I just ran a sample test with my own blood, infected it, and it produced the antibodies ..."

"Right, then that'll at least tell us who we need to burn." Casey's eyes were dead level.

"Nope." Marion turned away. "The fragments disappeared quickly, and my blood seemed normal. They were perfect copies, but not human anymore."

"So, it's useless." Casey shook her head and turned way. "And we're back to freaking square one."

* * *

"You had one damn job, Reid." Alex glared up at the huge man.

Sam stood with his head bowed.

"You remember me saying that getting the comms working was our priority?" Alex waited.

Sam nodded. "I thought … there was an intruder. They attacked. I thought it was the missing Russian woman."

"It was a damn decoy. Designed to draw you away, so it could destroy the work being done, and take out our best engineering asset." Alex looked skyward for a moment, his fists balled. But then his anger with Sam turned back on himself. He shook his head.

"It's my fault. Of course the thing would try and stop us getting our comms back on. I should have foreseen it."

"No, Boss. I underestimated it." Sam lifted his head. "I left my position."

"It's done." Alex tried to think through his next steps, then turned back to Sam. "Comms is still the priority. If McCarthy had never come with us, I'll give you one guess who I would have sent to do the work."

Sam nodded. "Say the word."

"Do it." Alex turned to Roy Maddock. "You go with him. And no one leaves until the work is done and secured, clear?"

"HUA."

The two enormous armored HAWCs headed off.

Alex's comms pinged. "Hunter."

"Boss, we got news on the test," Casey said.

"I'm on my way." Alex turned to Briggs. "You hold the fort."

* * *

Mia stood close to Briggs and turned to frown after the departing HAWC. "He shouldn't be going by himself."

The base commander snorted. "Yeah, like I can tell that guy what to do."

"I should go with him." She put her hands on her hips.

"No, Mia, we're supposed to stay together." Briggs pointed at her chest. "And that means everyone."

"I'm not going to sit on my ass when I could be helping. Especially not while that Russian creature is still on the loose." She pushed his finger way. "I know more about this thing, Olga, than anyone, so I can damn help. You know that."

"Mia," Briggs pleaded.

The grin split her face, and she reached forward to pat his cheek. "Thanks, Tom."

She was out the door before he could change his mind or call her back.

* * *

"She was quite brilliant," Marion said. "But wrong."

Alex stared down at the computer screen showing the results of the work the former base doctor had been doing.

"See this?" Marion pointed at the screen. "In those samples she recovered of the black material she found residue remains of human cells in among a lot of unidentifiable organic matter."

"We knew that," Alex said. "This thing absorbs, ingests, or whatever it does, but ends up taking over human bodies. What's left over after the process is the excretion."

"It takes over, yes, but that's just it – it does an astounding job at mimicry. Unlike anything known on Earth. Many creatures can alter their form to look like something else – the hoverfly wears the colors and shape of a bee to try and scare off predators. A species of spider has evolved to look like an ant, its favorite prey. And best of all is the mimic octopus, which can change its shape to copy fish, crabs, jellyfish, and many other species, to hide or so it can get within striking distance of its target prey."

"Sounds familiar," Casey sneered as she leaned against the wall. "A damn body able to use mimicry, and high intelligence, which means this thing not only looks like us, but acts like us." Her jaw clenched for a moment. "Good enough to fool us."

"Fool us is an understatement. It doesn't just act like us, but it actually becomes us," Marion said. "A perfect copy. That could fool anyone."

"Like it did to Vin." Alex straightened. "But there's something else. When we encountered Eric Wilson on the moon surface he was infected. But for a while I don't think he realized it. He didn't know what was happening to him even though he wasn't human anymore."

"Hmm, yes, possible." Marion nodded and turned back to the screen. "Doctor Pandewahanna hypothesized that this creature tears us down and rebuilds us. Remakes us using much of its own physical scaffolding. It copies our bones, flesh, hair, teeth almost immediately. And it definitely co-opts our minds and memories, using our neural architecture as a library to draw on." She shrugged. "I don't know, maybe the first time it copied a human it took longer to learn us. But now I think it can do it in seconds."

"That is not good," Klara muttered.

"No shit," Casey added, causing Klara to glare.

Marion went on: "Doctor Pandewahanna also hypothesized that the key flaw in the mimic's modus operandi was that it still retained some of the body's architecture – namely, its blood – to act as an internal food source, oxygenator, and chemical message carrier."

Alex smiled. "But with it also came an immune system."

"Correct. Doctor Pandewahanna found the antibody fragments in Olga's blood samples for the parasitic pathogenic fungi. But of course, there is no pathogenic fungi, just our immune system thinking there was."

"So, we find that in someone's blood, we know they're not who they say they are," Alex said. "So why don't you look happy?"

"I tried it with my own blood; the fragments appear for seconds, and then they too vanish." She shrugged. "I don't have a pure sample of Olga's blood, they're all gone. I just have Doctor Pandewahanna's notes."

"The thing either got smarter, or better at copying us," Casey said. "We got nothing."

"Olga must be our patient zero, the carrier," Klara added.

"We've got to find where she's hiding," Alex said. "Until we do, or create a test, no one goes home."

Casey started to laugh. "Come for a week they said, it'll be cool they said." Her grin fell away. "Fuck the moon."

CHAPTER 45

"I don't know what I'm missing here," Sam said. "It should work."

Roy Maddock looked over his shoulder at the mass of wires, circuitry, and cables. "Don't ask me for help, you're the tech brains. I'm only here for my looks."

Sam shook his head. "I'm a tradesman, Angus was the artist. I've tried to duplicate everything he was doing, and I've unit tested the individual components and they all seem to be communicating with each other. It's just not getting enough power to generate a signal any further than this room."

Maddock leaned around him. "You rebuilt everything?"

Sam nodded as he stared down at his work. "Yep. And the dashboard says it's all online and passing data, and the signal initiation infrastructure is all there …" He cursed. "So why no freaking signal?"

"So, it works, but it just doesn't have enough signal strength?"

Sam put his hands on his hips and shook his head as he stared. "This tech should be able to blast a signal to damn Mars and back. But so far I've got about as much signal power as a crystal radio set."

"You know what that says to me? That the issue isn't with the signal initiation system, because that bit is working." Maddock slapped Sam on the shoulder. "Your problem is somewhere else."

Sam thought about it for a few seconds. "You know what? You may be right."

"Yeah, that's right, buddy, and why you're the worker and I'm the thinker." Maddock meshed his fingers and cracked all his knuckles. "Anything else I can help you with?"

"Let me see." Sam turned and looked over the room. The communication room was fairly large by comparison to the other rooms on the base. There were racks of processors, cupboards, and cabinets that housed everything from generators to relay boosters. The cabinets were about six feet high, four wide, and double doored. Plus, they were screwed shut. Bottom line, you weren't supposed to be poking around in them unless you knew what you were doing.

"The relay boosters." He clicked his fingers. "I never checked them."

"There you go." Maddock went and sat on the edge of a bench top. "I'll be over here if you need any more help."

Sam paused to get a small circuit tester and an electric screwdriver, then went to the first of the steel cabinets.

He placed the screwdriver into the first screw and undid it. Then the next and next, until the middle doors could be opened. He pulled open the cabinet, and ran his eyes over the racks of machines and their blinking lights. There was only a little smell of ozone and everything seemed to be functioning fine. He tested a few boards and found that they were passing signals as expected.

"This guy looks okay; next."

Sam closed the cabinet and rescrewed it, and then moved to the next one. He began the process of unscrewing it and turned to speak over his shoulder. "Yes, thank you for offering, you can help by unscrewing the next cabinet for me."

"Aw, do I have to do everything?" Maddock got to his feet. "Okay, big guy, but you owe me." He went to the tool kit, grabbed a standard screwdriver, and approached the next cabinet to the one Sam was working on. He lifted the tool, about to slot it into the screw head, when he saw it was gone. He moved down to the next one, and saw it was also missing.

"That's weird."

"What is?" Sam asked.

"This one is already unscrewed." Maddock pulled it open.

The body fell out at him – and on him.

Maddock spun away, pulling his weapon and going into a crouch. Sam did the same, and both big men were covering the figure in seconds.

"That ain't good," Maddock said. "Cover me." He edged forward and poked the body with his screwdriver. The body was unresponsive, and he slowly stood. "Cause of death?"

Sam came and stood beside him, looking down at the figure. It was a woman, tall, with dirty blond hair to her jaw line. Her eyes were open. She looked normal, except her head was turned totally backward on her neck.

"Not drowning," Sam said. He moved around the body, and then reached down to flip it over. "No more rigor mortis, so given the opaqueness of her eyes, I'd say she's been dead and jammed in here for several days."

"Who the hell is it?" Maddock asked.

Sam used one hand to open the body's mouth and lever down the jaw. It creaked open with a stretching sound. "Yep, all metal fillings. My money is on it being the missing Russian woman." He wiped his gloved fingers on her jacket.

Maddock crouched. "Well, hello, Miss Olga. I think we now know why your equipment was failing – the body was crushing the relay equipment. Call it in?" he asked.

"Yeah, do that." Sam frowned and knelt again by the body. "Why is she in here? And why wasn't she absorbed like the others?"

She was hidden, he thought. Something stopped her being absorbed. But then whoever killed her didn't want her found. Or at least, didn't want people to know she was dead.

He stood. While she was missing, she was the main suspect. Not anymore.

Maddock signed off. "Boss says to finish the comms work, seal the room, and secure the body."

* * *

Alex signed off from Maddock.

"Trouble?" Casey laughed. "I mean *more* trouble?"

"They just found the missing Russian woman stuffed in a cabinet down in the comms room." His eyes narrowed as his mind worked through the implications.

Casey scowled. "What? I thought she was our freaking monster."

"How did she die?" Marion asked.

"Broken neck."

Marion frowned. "That's odd."

Alex nodded. "Yeah, it is; it doesn't conform to the pattern. She was murdered and then hidden."

"Great, so we've got a killer as well as a giant space germ," Casey observed.

"Unlikely," Alex replied.

"Maybe an accidental kill," Marion added. "Like Casey said, there's a few people on this base who really thought Olga was the source of the infection. Maybe they confronted her, panicked, and killed her, thinking she was the creature. Then when they found she wasn't, they hid the body."

"It's a good theory, except for one thing: the head was twisted all the way around." Alex folded his arms. "And it takes between 1000 to 1300 pounds of torque force to break a human neck like that. I'm not sure there's anyone on the base who could do it."

"If you ask me, something smells real bad here," Casey said.

"It sure doesn't add up." Alex paced away for a moment and then turned back to Marion. "How long until your test is ready?"

"It's ready now. But might not be as useful. Like I said, the antibody markers don't seem to remain in the system. They get copied or absorbed."

Alex sighed. "We need a break here."

"Something about the Russian woman was different," Marion said. "I need to see that body."

"Agreed." Alex headed for the door.

"Where will you be?" Klara asked.

Alex engaged his comms. "Sam, coming down." He turned back to Casey and Klara. "I'm going to bring the body in. Someone or something went to a lot of trouble to hide that Russian woman. We need to know why."

CHAPTER 46

Alex rode the elevator to the sub level and exited when the door slid open. He paused, turning to stare back down the long, white-paneled corridor. He sensed something, a presence, watching him. Or at least monitoring him somehow.

"I know you're there," he said softly.

He waited for a moment, then closed his eyes and pushed out his consciousness. The presence was there, but seemed all around him.

"What do you want?"

He waited again. He concentrated, but couldn't pinpoint it, and eventually he opened his eyes. He turned away and headed to the communication center.

The comms room door slid open as he approached.

Maddock was just inside and gave him a small salute. "Just your average HAWC day: monster on the loose, running repairs, body stuffed in a cabinet." He stood aside.

Alex laughed. "Come on, Roy, you'd do this job for free if you had the chance."

"You seen my paycheck? I basically do." Maddock shut the door.

Alex headed for Sam, who stood over the body.

He nodded to Alex. "Poor Olga here turned out to be the bug in our system. She was jammed in there so tight she damaged some of the circuits."

Alex knelt beside the body. "There goes suspect number one." He looked up. "How's the comms work going?"

"Nearly done. If the new boosters come online, then we are good for a trial run."

"Good work. Stick with it. I'm afraid until the work is complete, and we have successfully contacted Earth, you guys are living here." Alex shrugged. "This thing already tried to damage it once. It'll try again."

"Got it. I estimate we only need a few more hours. Maybe four, five tops."

Alex nodded and then looked back down at the body. "Well, this lady has a story to tell." He scooped Olga into his arms and stood. "Stay online, stay alert."

He went to turn away, then paused. "And stay being Sam and Roy. Not everyone is who they say they are." He pinned Sam with his stare. "You got three hours."

* * *

Alex lay the body down in the med lab. He placed a hand on each side of the head.

"Brace yourself," he said, and then, with a sickening crunch, quickly spun the head back into its normal position.

Casey, Klara, and Marion stared down at the body of Olga Sobakin as Alex stood back a step.

"Someone or something didn't want this body found. We need to know why."

Marion had donned rubber gloves and started to press the woman's flesh around the glands in her neck. She then pulled the lower lid of her right eye down.

"How long was she missing?" she asked.

"Three days," Casey said. "According to Mia."

Marion nodded. "Blood would have pooled and congealed. There'll be no cellular activity by now, but there will be DNA and a few other things we can learn from. Do you know how the body was situated when Sam and Roy found it?"

"Roy said when it fell at him out of cabinet it was upright. Jammed in, but upright."

Marion nodded, went to one of the feet, and rolled up the leg of her trousers. The ankle was purple. "After death, the heart stops pumping, blood stops moving and then simply drains to the lowest parts in the body." She turned. "Casey, get me the large hypodermic."

Casey grabbed the largest glass tube with long silver needle. Marion took it and stabbed it into the hard flesh of the calf. She had to strain to draw out the congealed blood, and they saw it fill the tube with dark, brown sludge.

"Starting to necrotize. Lucky that room was cooled, or it would have begun to rot." Marion withdrew the needle. She squirted a few drops onto a slide, and the rest into a test tube that she positioned in a stand. She smeared the blood on the slide and stuck it under the microscope.

"Well, well, well – hello, iron woman. Hemochromotosis."

"Hema-what?" Casey asked.

"Unusual iron retention by the plasma cells. This woman would have been on some form of medication," Marion answered.

"What does it mean?" Alex asked.

"Maybe a clue. Hemochromatosis is a blood disorder where an overabundance of iron builds up in the body. Without treatment, it can cause an overload that can damage the liver, heart, pancreas, joints, just about every part of the physical system." Marion folded her arms. "Treatment for severe cases is a full blood transfusion or drawing about a pint of blood at a time, on a regular schedule. Then to manage it the patient needs medication to keep it low and under control. In fact, under management, it's not a problem at all."

"I doubt she would have been getting full blood transfusions on the moon. It's a wonder the Russians even let her come," Casey said.

"They might not have known," Alex replied. "I'm betting she was fine for her physical and the iron only began to build up again when she came off her medicine."

Marion nodded. "That's what I think. Olga probably thought she'd be home before it became noticeable. But it was gradually building back up to toxic levels in her system."

"And then a moon germ screwed up her plans," Casey said.

"So, the million-dollar question: do you think the iron made her unpalatable to this thing?" Alex asked.

"Possibly. Iron is a great growth medium for many bacteria and fungi species. But an overabundance inhibits their ability to metabolize nutrients. In fact, some can't tolerate it at all. Maybe the creature is one like that. It tried to absorb or assimilate the Russian woman, and found her system was toxic to it." Marion shrugged. "It's a theory."

"But can we use it?" Alex sked.

"Eggs, spinach, red meat; that's what I use to boost iron," Casey said. "But that's no quick fix."

"She's right. How do we boost our iron levels in our blood, quickly, without blinding ourselves, or destroying our organs?" Alex asked.

"Iron injections can be via four major types: iron sucrose, iron dextran, sodium ferric gluconate, and ferumoxytol. There will be some in the base stores, but not enough for the entire crew."

"Can you make more?" he asked.

Marion sighed. "Not quickly."

Alex nodded. "Then inoculate yourself, and all essential personnel."

"What about you? I would have thought you were an essential person right about now," Marion said.

"We're not that important. In fact, we don't even exist." Alex grinned. "Right, Franks?"

"You got it, we're ghosts." Casey grinned back. She flexed her arm, making her bicep bulge in her suit. "Besides, I got enough iron right here."

Overhead a klaxon horn blared, making the doctor cringe and Klara and Casey pull their weapons up.

"What the hell?' Alex strode to the internal comm. unit and punched the button. "What gives, Briggs?"

The response took a few minutes, but the commander yelled back over the blaring horn. "Don't know yet. But there's some bad shit going down in the rec room. I'm heading there now."

"On my way." Alex signed off and turned to Marion. "Good work – keep at it."

Alex headed out the door fast toward the rec room.

CHAPTER 47

Baikonur Cosmodrome Spaceport, southern Kazakhstan

"They're off course." The lead ground crew technician, Janus Androv, frowned deeply. "They've changed their trajectory."

Major Bilov looked up from his notes. "What?"

Androv turned to the woman on his right, who was also peering into a screen. "Nadia, please confirm return telemetry."

She read the data, and then hit some keys before nodding. "Recalculating … current arrival point is now …" Her eyes widened slightly. "The center of Moscow."

Bilov jumped to his feet. "Impossible! How?"

"There's been a manual override," Androv said.

"Well, change it back." Bilov came around his desk, fast.

Androv's hands flew over the keyboard, then he shook his head. "I can't – they've manually locked it in."

Bilov threw his hands up. "Contact them. Try again."

Androv exhaled and put the earphones over his head. He pulled the wire down in front of his mouth. "Lunar lander P23–09, come in." He waited. "Commander Yuri Borgan in lunar lander P23–09, please confirm your telemetry as you are now off course."

The room was silent, and on the wall screen were several dotted lines – the white one showing a landing at the nominated military airbase runway some four hundred miles from any populated centers. And the next, a red one, that displayed a significant deviation.

Androv turned. "There's no response."

"How long until they enter our orbit?" Bilov felt his face growing hot as his blood pressure rose.

"Twenty-two hours, sixteen minutes." Janus turned back to confirm his numbers. "Mark."

Bilov folded his arms and began to pace. "Contact Commander Yuri Borgan again and keep contacting him. Warn him that if he does not correct his trajectory, he will be placing Russian civilians at risk." His lips pressed together for a moment. "And he will know we cannot allow this."

Bilov knew that Borgan would know what he meant – if the returning craft represented a risk to the population, then the returning craft was be diverted, delayed – or destroyed. All Russian spacecraft had remote destruct buttons.

Janus stared for a moment, then turned back and opened the communication channel again.

Bilov paced. The landers were flying thermal bombs, and if they struck a crowded city, it could result in the deaths of thousands, the end of the Russian space program, and great loss of face for Russia. But even worse for Bilov: it could mean removal or even disappearance for anyone involved.

"Hold …" Androv held the cup of his earphone.

This time, there was a response.

"*Sir*, coming through now." Androv flicked some switches. "Putting it up on screen."

Bilov breathed a sigh of relief as the fragmented images of the cockpit appeared on the screen along with a flood of static. A man's face floated into focus. Then he frowned.

"That's not Commander Borgan. It's Lieutenant Igor Stanislov."

"Lieutenant Igor Stanislov, what is your status?" demanded Androv.

Stanislov looked emotionless and disinterested and stared into the camera with dark eyes. "We had malfunction. Fixing now."

"Lieutenant Stanislov, this is urgent and highest priority: will you able to correct your descent profile?" Androv asked.

"Of course, in next hour or two. No problem." The astronaut's words were almost dream-like.

"Where is Commander Borgan?" Bilov asked.

"He is doing the repairs; best not to disturb him." Stanislov smiled benignly but the expression didn't travel to his dead eyes.

"Okay, good," Bilov said. "Now tell us about the Lenin Base. What is its status, was there –"

The screen began to fade out, and then vanished in a wall of static.

"Get him back," Bilov urged.

Androv's and the other technician's hands flew over their keyboards, but after another moment, they stopped.

The head technician turned. "The signal has been cut."

Bilov's eyes bulged. "Interference?"

Androv shook his head. "No, I think they cut us off."

Bilov felt his heart double thump in his chest. "They did?"

Androv just shook his head. "What are your orders, sir?"

"How much time do we have until our detonation opportunity has passed?" Bilov asked softly.

Androv checked his screen and then turned. "Right on two hours."

Bilov snorted. "Interesting; exactly the amount of time he called for." Bilov's expression and resolve hardened.

"Something is very wrong; we will give him just ninety minutes. Continue to attempt to contact him. And if not ..." He shrugged. "Then they must not get anywhere near Moscow."

CHAPTER 48

John F Kennedy Moon Base – Rec Room Isolated Group

"Who's there?" Andy Clark had his ear to the door after someone had pounded on it, making his heart jump into his throat. It was his turn on door duties, and the way things were on the base he did not want any surprises.

He turned to the group and saw twenty faces all silent, and staring with a mix of apprehension, and perhaps hope that the next visit would bring good news – maybe about the contagion being under control or even about going home.

"Andy, it's Mia. I've just come from the control room and have a message from Captain Briggs."

Clark grinned at the sound of his casual girlfriend's voice. "Enter, friend." He hit the button and the door slid back.

Mia came inside, and looked briefly over the people, then back to Andy Clark.

"What's the message?" he asked eagerly.

Mia turned to him. "That help is coming soon, and to stay right here."

"That's it?" He couldn't help his disappointment showing.

"And this …" She leaned forward, grabbed his face in both her hands and kissed him on the mouth, hard.

They broke apart and his first thought was that Mia had been a bit distant lately, so maybe she was trying to make it up to him. And that was fine with him. But then he noticed that her mouth tasted like spoiled fruit and perhaps she hadn't cleaned her teeth for, like, ages.

Mia smiled, without the expression reaching her eyes. She turned to hit the door button. It slid open and she backed out without another word.

The door slid closed after her.

Well that was weird, Andy thought, and went to sit back down among his fellow crew members.

It wasn't long before Andy started to find it hard to concentrate on the conversation around him. He leaned his head back against the wall in the center of a group of about a half-dozen of his colleagues. He blinked several times and tried hard to listen – they talked about food shortages, then began fantasising about the first meal they'd have when they got back home.

Andy's head throbbed and his stomach roiled, and just hearing about the food made him belch a fruity, flowery taste similar to what he'd detected on Mia's breath.

Andy Clark closed his eyes. The throbbing became more centralized, and moved to pulse on his neck, scalp, forehead, and even his face. He gritted his teeth and squeezed his eyelids closed and wished it all away.

A small lump on his scalp turned into a bulge. Another grew beside it. Then another and another. After a few more seconds, the lumps lifted on stalks, grayish, run through with veins. More lumps rose from his neck, and several others from his forehead and cheek.

Just as the woman beside Andy noticed them, and screamed, the first acorn-sized protuberance burst open, spraying a cloud of powdery granules over those closest to him.

CHAPTER 49

Briggs could hear the cacophony of panicked voices even before he entered the secure room. He had to enter a pass code to the recreation room's door panel, where over twenty of his people had been holed up. The door slid back, and he went in fast but not without a high degree of apprehension.

He steeled himself, but the sight that met his eyes sent a shock wave from his head to his toes – there was chaos and screaming, and the large room had separated into three groups, with the smallest group in the center of the room.

To one side the larger group cowered, and many left it to run toward him, all babbling and screaming at the same time. He pushed them aside to focus on what was happening in the center of the room: a small group of his crew seemed to be holding something at bay, or guarding something. But all they managed to do was move from foot to foot while cursing and yelling instructions to no one in particular and holding pieces of furniture up in front of themselves.

Briggs saw Stevens among them and went to the man, pulling him back by the shoulder.

"What the hell is going on?" he shouted over the din.

It was only then he noticed that there was another sound as well as the yelling, screaming, and cursing human voices. It was a moaning that was as eerie as it was unearthly.

Stevens grabbed his arm. "Thank God, Tom. It got in, somehow. Or was always here." He stood aside. "*Look.*"

Closer to the external wall there was a group of perhaps half-a-dozen people all huddled together. But as Briggs focused, he could see the guy in the middle was literally covered in spikes or knobs that bloomed open like putrid flowers. His body had broadened, and as well as the protuberances, there was also some sort of veined structure bursting from his tattered clothing and reaching across to the people close to him. Some of them, covered in the sticky-looking mesh, were slumped, unconscious, and others had faces of extreme physical agony or perhaps just psychological torment, aware of what was happening to them.

"Jesus Christ!" Briggs yelled then grimaced, feeling his stomach flip.

The glistening strings like spidery veins penetrated their clothing, their mouths, and even their eyes, and wormed in deeper as he watched. The bodies of the meshed victims swelled and at first became lumpy, their features grotesquely distorting, before they simply collapsed in on themselves.

Briggs' mouth hung open and he felt numb as he watched as their suits emptied, their heads shrinking down into the collars of their clothing before disappearing.

But not the person in the middle. Briggs recognized the young man as Andy Clark, who used to be in charge of the storeroom and tended bar sometimes. He still seemed to be dozing, as if he wasn't aware that his own body was absorbing the people next to him.

Is that the way it worked? Briggs wondered. Did Andy even know he was already taken over, and was now ingesting and converting his friends?

Soon there was just empty clothing covered in black slime, the same as they'd been finding throughout the base.

Briggs started to back up. "Everyone get back." Now he understood what had happened to his people and where and how they had vanished. It gave him a jittery feeling in his gut to think his friends and base team members had encountered this thing in the corridors when they were alone.

The mouth of Andy Clark opened and that eerie howl bellowed out, filling the room as if he was in agony – or maybe it was a call of triumph. It was too much for the group, and the remaining people in the room headed for the door.

They were panicking, Briggs knew. He also knew that the fear-maddened crowd would be just as deadly as the creature.

"Stop!" he yelled. But his own feet moved him away from the alien thing in the corner.

Briggs turned back and saw that Andy's eyes were open, coal black and glistening like oil. Ominously, the man started to rise to his feet. It was a gruesome sight, as now budding from his body were bulbous growths hanging on stalks like rapidly ripening fruit.

"Stay back, Andy!" Briggs yelled.

And then the red-veined polyps burst.

Those closest were covered in powder that was like sticky grains of sand. They wiped and brushed at themselves, but then they doubled over, either holding their bellies and throwing up or grabbing their heads as if a ferocious migraine racked their minds.

It was too much for an already frightened crowd – they went mad. Briggs was shouldered aside as they went for the door closed door.

"Don't let it out!" he yelled.

No one heard.

Or no one listened.

CHAPTER 50

The rec room door opened, and Alex filled it with his huge, silver form. He took it all in within seconds – a cyclone of madness – and he strode in and pushed Briggs aside. He felt a visceral revulsion for what he was seeing. Even though he had just encountered the creature in a raw form on the lunar landscape, this abomination was human degradation on an unprecedented scale. It also told him what would be in store for all of them if this thing was allowed to continue to move among them undetected.

A small group of people toward the far end of the room was enmeshed in some sort of fibrous webbing and tendril-like roots covered their bodies. As he watched, most of them collapsed into piles of empty clothing. All except for a central male figure, who seemed asleep.

Briggs tried to quieten the remaining crowd and restore a semblance of sanity, but his words were drowned out by the mad screams and wailing of the people still in the room.

"Calm down!" Alex's roar was like a physical force, and the group silenced and looked at him with round eyes and trembling chins. He turned to Briggs. "Get 'em out. Orderly."

"But –" Briggs pointed.

"No choice," Alex replied and stepped forward. "Do it, *now*."

Briggs pushed and pulled the remaining people into a semblance of a line so they weren't all jammed up. Even then, the open doorway was quickly overwhelmed. People started to clog the doorframe as elbows and shoulders came into play.

"It's Andy Clark," Briggs said through clamped teeth. "I know him."

"Not anymore," Alex replied.

Andy stood like a ghastly reanimated corpse, stalks and pods on stems still sprouting from his body. *A fruiting body.* Alex remembered Marion's reference to the fungi's ability to spore.

Andy opened his eyes. "Where am I?" he asked. "What's happening?" The young man held up his hands in front of his face as if examining them for the first time. "What's happening?" he asked again as he frowned at the digits. "Tom?" He looked across to Briggs. "These aren't my hands."

As Alex watched, one of his fingers audibly snapped and pointed at an impossible angle. Andy's face screwed up in both pain and anguish.

"*These aren't my hands!*" he screamed.

They watched another of Andy's fingers lengthen as a veined bulb formed from its end, a pod, starting to swell. He looked toward the two remaining guards. "*Heeelp meee.*" He took a step toward them.

"Don't! *Don't you fucking move!*" one guard yelled. In his hand he had a rivet gun, probably from the maintenance shop.

"Stay back!" the other guard yelled, but his voice was breaking. He held a chair up.

"I don't know what's going on. I'm sick." But Andy came on anyway. More of the budding polyps were rising from all over the young man. The first guard lifted the rivet gun, aiming it dead center at Andy's chest.

Alex could immediately see what was about to happen. "Stop!" he yelled and raised the toxin dart gun, which he knew was safe in the enclosed space.

Andy looked at it, froze, and then changed course, moving toward the guards. He took another step and shot an arm out.

Too late, the panicked guard fired. The bolt went straight through Andy's face as if it was boneless, and on into the wall. And kept going. The hole it made in the exterior wall was walnut sized, making a scream like a steaming kettle as the air in the room was sucked out.

Briggs began to physically ram people through the doorway. "Get out, get out!"

But there was too much atmosphere in too much of a hurry. The breached outer wall's skin began to peel back, and the hole enlarged from walnut to baseball sized in seconds. The rushing scream got louder, and the air inside the room became a hurricane.

Most people made it out, save the guards, and Alex and Andy Clark, who still stood with a hole in the center of his forehead, mouth hanging open, and a confused look in his eyes. As Alex watched, the hole in his forehead closed up like a mouth, and the confused look left his face.

The two security guards in the center of the room with Alex were torn between fleeing for the door or holding Andy at bay. Alex felt the drag of the rushing atmosphere against his frame and a quick glance at the hole in the wall told him they had little time.

He turned to Briggs. "Shut the door, or you'll decompress the entire base."

Briggs shook his head and yelled, "Not without my people."

Then the decision was taken out of Briggs' hands as the wall of the base exploded outwards.

Alex lowered his shoulder and rammed Briggs and the last few people in the doorway through then punched the close button. He tried to grab for a metal railing but was too late.

The two guards screamed and held their heads as the air vanished and the vacuum of the moon replaced the benign rec room environment.

The room decompressed explosively, and Alex, the two guards, and what was once Andy Clark were violently ejected onto the moon's surface.

* * *

Normally, Alex's helmet would have auto engaged following the explosive decompression, but the damage it had previously sustained prevented that and left his entire head exposed. When he stopped rolling, he felt the agony of the freezing, super-dry atmosphere against his skin – and it burned like hell.

His mind ticked off all the data he knew from his training – in a vacuum, the average human body had around fifteen seconds before the remaining oxygen reserves in its bloodstream were used up. But the danger was some people automatically held their breath – a fatal mistake, as the loss of external pressure would cause the gas inside your lungs to expand enormously, which would rupture the lungs and pull air into the circulatory system.

So, the first thing to do if you ever found yourself suddenly expelled into the vacuum of space was to exhale, hard, and also screw your eyes tightly closed. Unfortunately, the other things you couldn't really do much about – after about ten seconds or so, your skin and the tissue underneath would begin to swell as the water in your body started to vaporize in the absence of atmospheric pressure. You wouldn't balloon to the point of exploding, since human skin is strong and elastic enough to keep from bursting. But seconds mattered if you wanted to avoid permanent damage or death.

Alex kept his eyes screwed shut and also his mouth closed as he remembered another titbit from his moon briefing – in a vacuum the moisture in your tongue and gums can freeze-boil.

Alex's abnormal recuperative powers and enormous strength allowed him to fight back against the pain, and as his body was being decimated by the vacuum, it also tried to repair itself – cells were destroyed, cells were repaired – it was a race he knew he'd eventually lose.

He dragged himself to his feet. He knew he wouldn't freeze straight away, despite the extreme cold temperatures, as the heat didn't leave the body quickly enough to freeze on the spot. He'd die of suffocation long before that.

Flakes of Alex's skin began to peel away and knew he was running out of time to locate the base personnel blown out with him while trying to avoid encountering the infected man, Andy Clark, who was also out there. But the Andy Clark thing wouldn't be bothered by the vacuum.

He had to risk it, he had to see, so he opened and closed his eyes in blinks, as fully opening them would cause the moisture to be sucked out and the eyeball itself to solidify. But quickly shutting them allowed his supercharged metabolism to repair them enough for him to then chance another glance.

He placed one foot in front of the other and every second he was outside more of his skin began to crack, dry, and peel away. A thousand needles of super-dry cold pierced his flesh and so he took himself out of his body, left the pain behind, and worked to ignore the agony.

He found the first security guard and lifted him under his arm. Alex opened his eyes in another blink and spotted the remaining two bodies lying twenty feet away – only one of them was human.

The pain forced itself back in on him. It was becoming intolerable. The cracks on his face were now spilling blood that floated away in a dry mist. Alex felt like there were flames covering his body as the freeze burn started to rip his skin down to the inner layers. His blood was beginning to cold-boil. Ridiculous facts intruded as his consciousness began to swim – if you do die in space, your body would never decompose in the normal way, since there was no oxygen. In some cases, your body would mummify like a huge chunk of jerky.

He screwed his eyes shut and grimaced from the pain. His lungs began to rebel against him, threatening to force his mouth open to try and drag in a breath that just wouldn't be there.

He moved toward the two men, counting the paces – one would be human, and one would be a monster. Laying his hands on the wrong one at this time would be the end of him.

When Alex arrived, he opened his eyes for another second. In that moment, confusion tore at him as now there was only one body there, the final guard. Next to him was the charred outline of another body, as if it had been totally incinerated.

He had no time to wonder about it as pops of light started to explode in his head from lack of oxygen. He grabbed the remaining figure and moved back to the hole in the rec room wall. He dragged both the unconscious bodies inside and went to the door. The room was fully decompressed now, and his hearing was almost gone from the vacuum.

Alex's head spun and then he saw Aimee smiling and holding her arms out to him. Next came Joshua, laughing as he played with the huge dog – his life was flashing before him as the remnants of oxygen in his system became exhausted. He knew he'd black out soon and his mouth would automatically open as it tried to take in the last breath of air that didn't exist.

With his remaining strength, he banged on the door. No one opened it.

Why would they? he thought. *No one should be alive in here – just us monsters.*

He banged again with his fist, giving it everything he had and making the metal ring like a gong.

Alex slid to his knees and let the bodies of the guards drop as he felt his consciousness slipping away. His mouth opened.

CHAPTER 51

Midnight, Joshua fell to the floor in his room. He clawed at his throat and gasped like a stranded fish, trying to breathe. There was a psychological storm in his mind conjured by his father's pain, and then the sensation of his life force growing dimmer.

Torben was at his side in an instant, staring into Joshua's face. He pressed his nose hard into the boy's stomach, then released, and then repeated it, as though trying to pump his lungs.

Joshua coughed and rolled over, and his eyes opened wide. "Dad!"

Immediately his blue-gray eyes turned luminous white and his jaws clamped together.

I'm coming, he projected, hard.

After another moment, tears of determination, anguish, and pain ran down his cheeks. Around him there began a swirling tornado of debris as his mental torment began to manifest as a physical force – books flew from his shelves, papers lifted from his desk, and clothing rose from the floor. A track and field trophy launched so hard from its shelf that it buried itself in the wall, and the windows blew out as the glass was turned to powder.

Aimee burst into the room. "Joshua!" Her eyes widened and her face drained of color.

"Can't. Get. To him." The boy's head turned to her. "Need. Air." The veins in his neck stood out like rope as he turned to the windows and their wooden frames began to splinter and then fly away into the night's darkness.

"No, no, *no*." Aimee tried to get to her son, but the violently rushing air in the room slowed her down. She lowered her head, held her arms out and tried to push through it.

"*Need air*." The boy ran toward the open second-story window and leaped out into the night. The huge dog followed him through without a second thought.

Joshua landed easily and rounded the corner at speed. He crossed Vincent Road and then the highway, making cars jam on their breaks and blast horns, especially when the huge dog followed him. The boy headed into Allandale Woods, still choking and clawing at his neck.

Half a mile in he slowed and went to his hands and knees, on the grass, coughing.

Under a tree a group of youths stopped drinking beer and passing around a few fat joints of their favorite blend of Critical Jack weed and turned to stare.

"What the fuck is this?" The eldest boy, with arms covered in homemade tattoos, crushed his beer can, belched from the side of his mouth and then rose to his feet.

Joshua threw his head back. "Help him!" he screamed and threw his arms up toward the night sky.

"The hell is wrong with that little asshole?"

One of the young women in the group went to approach.

Her girlfriend grabbed her arm. "Wait up – there's something wrong with him."

"Ya think?" One of the larger young men also stood. "Hey kid, got any money?"

"He's wearing pajamas, dickhead. Where would he hide his money – up his ass?" The woman shook her head. "Leave him be."

Joshua lowered his forehead to the ground as if praying.

"He looks rich to me." The tattooed guy grinned and popped the top of another beer, slurping noisily. "Wonder if Mommy would pay to know where he is."

"I'm too stoned; forget it," another youth replied.

Tattoos half-turned. "Nah, just doing my civic duty. You know, maybe there's a reward for handing him in." He winked. "And an even bigger reward for handing him in undamaged." He laughed corrosively.

He began to approach Joshua but when he was within ten feet, Joshua lifted his face to him; his eyes were totally white.

"Cold!" Joshua screamed and then his clawed hands dug into the ground in front of him. A ring of grass around him immediately bleached white. It crackled, and then turned brown as it shrivelled.

"Fuck that. He's a freak."

"Did you see that?" Tattoos pointed at the ground. "That wasn't there before."

"Needs a net thrown over him." A youth with white hair frowned.

"Maybe he's sleep walking," one of the girls whispered.

"Then wake him up."

"Good idea." Tattoos drank more of his beer, and then tossed the half-full can at Joshua. It bounced off his shoulder. "Wake the fuck up, weirdo."

Joshua's head jerked up. The tattooed guy's grin dropped, and he began to make a strangling noise in his throat. Then, to the group's horror, his body was torn down the middle from his forehead to his groin. The two halves were flung aside. There was no spray of blood, just a cold mist, as if everything had been snap frozen.

The youths screamed, a few backed away, and two of the other, bigger, guys took a step forward, indecision and fear twisting their features.

The huge form of Tor appeared, growling, and approaching with his head lowered. His eyes were like luminous gun barrels, and he bared finger-length teeth.

As the group watched with gaping mouths, the animal rose up on his back legs to stand nearly seven feet tall. His roar was like a physical force, and whatever bravado they had left vanished as the group turned and fled into the dark park.

Tor kept his eyes on the direction the group had fled for a few more seconds before he dropped down to grab Joshua by the neck of his pajama shirt and began to drag him backward, then away into the darkness.

A car's tires screamed as it skidded to a halt, and Aimee ran down the grass slope toward them. Tor let Joshua go and sat back.

Aimee cradled the boy's head in her arms, and Joshua looked up into her face. His eyes returned to their normal blue-gray, but still wouldn't focus.

"He's in trouble." He blinked a few times as his eyes watered. "And I can't help him."

* * *

"Your ... *guests* are here, sir." His receptionist-cum-gatekeeper's voice was strained.

"Thank you, Margie," Colonel Jack Hammerson replied. "Send them in."

Fuck, he hated spooks. These guys with their black-book funding, and operational units with names like Special Psych-ops and Strategy Oversight were like an all-seeing, all-annoying eye that watched and heard everything. They knew about the boy going for his midnight run last night and suddenly they wanted to put a flea in his ear. Jack Hammerson's jaw jutted for a moment. As if he didn't have enough going on.

Hammerson stood as the door to his office opened. Three men entered, the first in his fifties, with a shaved head, and slightly stooped shoulders like a vulture – Mr. Green. He'd be the mouthpiece today. With him came two torpedoes, both in dark suits, broad shoulders, and with chins like granite shelving. And they wore dark sunglasses.

"Let me guess, the Men in Black," Hammerson said.

"Very good, colonel," Green said. He didn't introduce his two watchdogs, who remained on their feet while Green sat down without being invited. "Take a seat," he said even though he was in Hammerson's office. The man dripped with condescending authority.

Hammerson sat on the edge of his large desk and folded his brawny arms. He looked down on Green. "What can I do for you? Kinda busy right now."

"You let the boy get out," Green said flatly.

"He's not a prisoner. He was never out of our control." Hammerson shrugged. "He let off a bit of steam. No big deal."

"He killed a boy and injured others – that's more than a bit of steam. Plus, he displayed his abilities to the public." Green's gaze was flat. "He is under your management because you have somehow convinced the general you have the boy supervised. I think you do not. In fact, I think you are out of your depth."

"We got this." Hammerson stared back for a moment more before checking his watch. "Is there anything else? Cause we've got bigger issues to deal with." He stood. "And by the way, you got a problem with me, take it to the general. I don't need to deal with the pencil pushers."

Green's eyes took on a hard glint. "If you remember, another time you said you 'got this', the boy was nearly extracted by enemy agents. He'd be an anti-asset and could be deadly in enemy hands." Green also rose and stepped into Hammerson's space. "You can't control him, but we can."

"No." Hammerson's gaze was unwavering.

Green smirked. "Then we'll have to take him from you."

"Really?" Hammerson's smile held zero humor. "Okay, this meeting is over."

Green jabbed a finger into Hammerson's chest. "You have no idea who you're dealing with. If I have to teach the boy – and you – a lesson, I can and will."

Hammerson knocked the finger away. "You're the one who doesn't know who he's dealing with. Get outta my office, asshole, or I'll throw you out myself."

Green's eyes widened, obviously not used to the disrespect. He turned to the two men he brought with him and gave them an almost imperceptible nod – they moved in quickly.

Hammerson knew how they'd come at him – he'd seen it before, had experienced it too many times to count, and now he even trained his HAWCs in how to deal with a double adversary attack.

The closest man went for a flat-handed strike across Hammerson's windpipe, meant to throw his head forward, and into the fist of the second operative. Jack Hammerson was in his mid-fifties with iron-gray crewcut, and iron-hard muscles from training, ferociously, every single goddamn day. He went under the strike and came up with an upper cut that would have felled Mike Tyson. The first man's head snapped up with a crack, and he fell backward like an oak tree.

Hammerson then used a back kick into the knee of the second man. There was a crunch of cartilage, and the guy staggered. While he was off balance, he bravely tried to throw a straight left into Hammerson's face.

It was too easy to block the off-balance punch, and then throw a combination left-right to the lower ribs, followed by a left-cross to the cheekbone. Hammerson knew that the key to throwing a devastating punch was not to strike at where the target area was, but to strike just a bit past it so the punch contained the full power of the momentum of the fist, arm, and entire upper body.

His final straight right landed with the wet noise of splattering blood, and the guy fell to the side, unconscious before he even hit the ground.

Hammerson turned to Green. His gaze made the man shrivel before him. "I'm not a nice guy. But I have great self-control. Because if I didn't, I'd wipe the features off your face right now."

Hammerson reached out, making Green flinch. He pulled out the handkerchief tucked decoratively into Green's breast pocket, and used it to wipe some of the blood from his knuckles then jammed it back into the bureaucrat's pocket.

"Now, you get the fuck out of here and take the Men in Black with you before I change my mind."

Green looked down briefly at his fallen men, and then lifted his gaze, his eyes suddenly furtive.

Hammerson caught it. "Oh, and if you came back with more torpedoes, I'll introduce you to some of my HAWCs. Then you'll all wake up in hospital. Or not at all." Hammerson leaned in nose to nose and roared, "*Now get the fuck out of here!*"

Green held up shaking hands, then helped one of his men to his feet. Together they dragged the third man out.

Hammerson followed them and at the door, Margie, his receptionist, smiled to them. "Your car is already waiting for you, gentlemen. Thank you for coming."

She and Hammerson watched as the trio entered the elevator and the door shut. She looked up at him.

"Everything okay, Jack?"

"Yeah. Just a little chain-of-command education session for some of our boys from the back office." He smiled. "We won't be seeing them again."

CHAPTER 52

Baikonur Cosmodrome Spaceport, southern Kazakhstan

"But we have no conf—" Major Alexi Bilov's grip on the handset tightened as he listened. "Any specimens have to – but quarantine is necess— sir, you must –" Bilov's mouth snapped shut and he came rod straight. "Yes, sir, of course, sir. I'll see to it immediately, sir." He closed his eyes. "You can count on –"

The line went dead. He looked at the phone for several more seconds before swallowing noisily, and then he hung up.

Senior technician Uri Andilov watched and waited.

Major Bilov sighed. "Quarantine be damned; by order of the president, they are to be allowed to land."

Andilov's mouth dropped open. "Impossible! Trajectory analysis has them coming down in the center of Moscow."

"I know. But they have already sent an order to clear the streets. The president wants to be there to greet the arriving astronauts personally. At a time of national turmoil, he believes it will be a great opportunity to show the world some Russian precision and technical advancements, as well as unite the people."

Andilov shook his head. "What?"

"He said the quarantine issues are *our* problem." Bilov turned and smiled ruefully. "From a political perspective, apparently the optics are too good to let go by." He pointed to the screen. "Uri, show me exactly where the craft is expected to come in."

Andilov's hands flew over the keyboard and a dotted line on the screen updated, and then overlaid on a map of Moscow. The map expanded and drilled down.

"Mokhovaya Street." Bilov snorted softly. "Of course it would – the road right alongside the Kremlin."

"You don't think this is a little too … perfect?" Andilov asked and sat back. "I mean, one of the main streets in Moscow and right outside the Kremlin and Red Square. How will quarantine be effectively carried out?"

Bilov shrugged. "We don't know if they secured the samples. And if they did, what state they were in. Or even if were they dangerous. *Voloch*, we can't even contact them." He threw his hands up. "A nightmare."

"A nightmare that might become a bigger nightmare," Andilov breathed.

"The decision has been taken out of our hands. So now, all we do is carry out our orders," Bilov replied. "How long now until they enter our atmosphere?"

Andilov read from his screen. "Eight hours and twenty minutes."

"Any more contact, any more ways to try and reach them?"

The senior technician shook his head. "They've gone dark, either by equipment failure or by design. They're not talking. Why is that?"

"That is the question." Bilov turned slowly back to the trajectory map. "And if it is by design, then may God help us all."

CHAPTER 53

Casey Franks sprinted to the rec room. She had seen what was happening to Alex Hunter on the monitor and was going in to get him come hell or high water.

She had her suit in full combat mode and when she arrived, she bulldozed the crowd out of her way, and fired a bolt into the wall on each side of the door to secure herself.

Briggs rushed to the front. She retracted her visor and turned to him. "Open the fucking door!"

He held a hand up. "No, it'll evac the entire base. Forget it, they've gone. No one can survive that."

She turned the bolt gun toward his chest. "He's not like us. Open it, or you're fucking dead."

"Crazy." He gritted his teeth. "Fucking crazy." Briggs turned to the crowd. "Get out! Everyone out!"

People scattered, and the base commander grabbed a hand hold and punched the button. There came a maelstrom of furiously rushing air as the door slid back.

Casey Franks' visor closed over her face and she gritted her teeth as she strained against the roaring air. She let out some line but still needed to use the suit's powerful MECH hydraulics to hang on and drag Alex and the two base personnel inside to the corridor. She nodded to Briggs, who shut the door.

Casey untethered herself and dropped to her knees to feel Alex's neck. She rose, and pointed to several men way down the corridor watching her with wide eyes. "Hey! You, you, and you – get over here and get these people up to the med lab. And you damn *run*."

She telescoped the armoured visor up off her face and turned to get nose to nose with Briggs. She spoke through her teeth. "You were gonna leave him out there, you motherfucker."

"He told me to shut the door. I did as he asked. No one could survive that." Briggs pushed the HAWC in the chest but found he couldn't budge her.

Casey eased back, knowing the guy was right, but her anger still demanded she strike out at something. So she punched the door opposite, leaving a large dent in the steel.

She turned to jab one blunt finger into his chest. "If he had died, I would have thrown you out there myself."

"It's over. Let it go." Briggs stepped back. "So, what now?"

"It could still be here. This room has been breached, and it might be among them. We should put everyone here in quarantine, but there is nowhere to do that." She looked at the people, some sobbing, some hugging. "So, we need to move everyone into the larger control room. It'll be tight and uncomfortable, and high risk, but no choice now."

Briggs nodded. "They'll prefer it." He looked up. "How's the test going?'

Casey shook her head. "It isn't. Didn't pan out. We do have something that'll inoculate some of us against it, but only enough for a few necessary people. I suggest you get a dose."

Briggs shook his head. "I'll pass. Was that it? I mean, all of the creature?"

Casey shrugged. "Doubt it." Most of the group had returned and were staring at her and Briggs. "Like I said, for all we know, one or more of them could still be infected. It hides inside you."

"That's a shit thought."

"Yeah, and right now everything is shit." She headed for the door. "Get everyone to the control room."

* * *

Alex groaned.

"Take it easy," Marion said softly.

He felt her hand on his bare shoulder, and when he opened his eyes, it was all blackness. They hurt, and so did his mouth, and inside his nose, and there was a hollow echo in his ears. In fact, he felt like he'd just had the crap beaten out of him ten times over.

He sat and reached up a hand to feel the bandage over his eyes.

"Leave that there for a while," Marion urged. "Your eyes have suffered significant trauma from the vacuum. You may even be –"

Alex dragged the bandage away, opened his eyes, and blinked. "Ouch." Everything was blurred.

"Good morning, Count Dracula," Casey said, and he could hear the grin in her voice. "How do you feel?"

"How do I look?" He laughed, and it made his ribs hurt.

"With those eyes you look like you've been on a three-day vodka bender."

Alex slid his legs to the side and blinked. His vision began to clear.

"That's amazing," Marion said.

"No, that's the Arcadian," Casey said. "The man who can't be killed."

Marion narrowed her eyes as she watched him. He knew the cracks and peels in his skin were healing already.

"That's just a rumour." Alex groaned as he rubbed his face while more wounds knitted shut. "How are the other two I brought in – they make it?"

"They're alive. Both in induced comas," Marion replied. "I expect they'll stay that way for a few days so they can heal. They're in a lot worse shape than you are. Than you *should* be."

"I'm just lucky." Alex smiled. "And if it makes you happy, I feel as bad as I look."

Marion scowled. "No, it doesn't." She jabbed a needle into his arm.

Alex let her, knowing what she was doing. He gave her a crooked smile. "I am who I am."

"Maybe they all think so. At first." Marion stood back for a moment. "Okay." She began to nod. "The iron solution would have caused a reaction immediately."

"Happy to know I'm okay. But we're now down a shot."

"Boss, what happened out there?" Klara asked.

"One of the things, or a piece of the thing, revealed itself in the rec room. And one of the guards shot it with a bolt gun. He punctured the wall and the damn room explosively decompressed." He slid off the table and stood, rubbing his eyes. "Briggs got most out, but a few of us were blown out onto the lunar surface."

He started to pull his suit back on. "Weirdest thing was, I saw another body, which I assumed was Andy Clark, the creature. But it was all burned up."

"You mean freeze burned?" Klara asked.

"No, I mean incinerated. Nothing left but an ash outline. A lot of heat was used to do that." He groaned again and looked at Casey. "Someone else was out there with me. Probably saved my ass."

Casey frowned. "Who?"

"You were basically blind out there," Marion reminded him.

"I know what I saw." He shook his head to try and clear it, but all he did was make his throbbing headache worse. "Think I saw."

That was the question, he thought. Who could have been out there, and who had some sort of heat or energy weapon on hand? Was it the Russians?

"You think we have an ally, Boss?" Casey asked.

He stared at her. The thing was, he'd felt comforted and protected by the new presence. And he'd felt that before. On the island.

No way. He shook the thought away.

Casey watched him closely. "You okay? You still look like crap."

He laughed softly. "I just about had my brains sucked out of my ear and eye sockets, so cut me some slack, okay?"

"The Arcadian going soft now?" She grinned. "Never."

"Maybe it was the Russians. I don't know."

"Well, whoever it was, we need all the allies we can get," Casey replied. "Hey, you need anything?"

"Yeah, I do." He detached his helmet mechanism and handed it to her. "Fix the visor on this thing – it didn't work. And it's not exactly beach weather out there."

Marion touched his upper arm. "You should rest."

"No time." Alex squeezed her hand and held it. "One more thing: it knew. It knew the toxin could hurt it before I had a chance to fire."

The doctor snorted softly. "Of course – collective memory, I should have guessed."

"Like shared intelligence?"

"Something like that," she replied. "There's a theory that animal groups like schools of fish, swarms of insects, flocks of birds, and even bacterium, have displayed group-management and coordinated decision making. In fact, it has a name – hysteresis – where behaviors in groups is so synchronized and intimately coordinated that it has previously been considered to be some sort of hive-mind telepathic communication."

Casey threw her hands up. "Oh, great, that's all we need – this thing has damn ESP as well."

"We still don't know if it's one creature or several." Alex sighed and then pressed his eyes, grimacing as he did.

Marion nodded. "That's true. And my belief is it's the same animal that has budded to create either permanent or temporary clones of itself. And I think this thing is displaying collective memory behavior. One part of it experiences something and it can be passed onto the rest of the buds, or other parts of itself, via chemical signals, or some other method we haven't worked out yet."

"Like brain cells," Alex said.

"Yes, exactly like that. The individuals are acting like neurons, storing and passing on thoughts, memories, and pattern recognition, exactly like our brain does."

"This will make it impossible for us to ambush all of the creatures," Klara said. "If we successfully take down one, then the rest will know about it."

"That could also be true," Marion said.

"We can use this." Alex folded his arms and paced for a moment, letting his mind work. He turned back. "To flush it out."

"How?" Casey asked.

"How many doses of the iron solution do you have left?" he asked Marion.

"We only have enough to inoculate about ten people now," she replied, and then tilted her head. "Less than a quarter of the remaining base personnel."

"Okay." Alex rubbed his chin. "We were thinking that we give it to some people to stop them getting infected or invaded by this thing. But like you just did with me, what would happen if we gave it to someone who was already infected?"

The group stared back for a few seconds before Casey began to laugh darkly. "Shit might just hit the fan."

"It might force a reaction. The creature could be forced to reveal itself." Marion half-smiled. "Use the solution as a sword rather than a shield? I like it."

"Exactly." Alex nodded. "We set up our testing station and start to inject the personnel, a small dose, until we find one of the infected. And then through this collective memory, it passes on the warning to any more hiding among our crew. We flush one out, and the rest will emerge to avoid getting the shot."

Klara grinned. "Because they don't know how many doses we have."

"Should work," Marion said. "But what if you don't find one of the infected? How do you choose?"

Alex thought for a moment. "Well for a start, we use some of our own group message delivery. We get everyone ready and tell them the shot will show us who the creature is."

Casey laughed. "We bluff it. We might not have to administer a single dose."

Marion drew a deep breath. "There's something else you need to consider. If by chance you do inject one of the crew who isn't a person, and this thing breaks out." She looked up at Alex. "What happens to those in proximity to it?"

"Yeah, it's high risk, but can't be avoided. Bottom line, we stop it here, now, or we abandon the moon forever. And one more thing: if we don't stop it, no one will be coming to take us home, or would let us land if we did."

"I'll do it," Casey said. "I want to look this thing in the eye. And then burn it back to hell."

"Yeah. For Vin," Klara added and bumped knuckles with Casey. "Lock and load."

CHAPTER 54

Alex looked over the crowd of around forty desperate people – less than half of the original moon base personnel. The control room was packed, and given very few people wanted to go anywhere by themselves, not many were even brave enough to get to the shower rooms. The result was a smell of crushed humanity, ripe with body odour and the sharp tang of fear.

The control room had a raised dais for the center computer system desks and Alex stood tall, hands on his hips. He was a silver giant among them.

"Listen up, everyone."

The crowd quietened immediately, hungry for news.

"We have a test we are going to use to find out who has the … *infection*. We're very confident it will tell us what we need to know." He waited for the murmurs to die down. "The sooner we get this done, the sooner we make plans for getting home."

A hand went up but Alex shook his head. The hand went down. He turned. "Marion."

The doctor stepped up beside him. "Each person will enter the first meeting room one at a time for a simple injection.

Afterwards, inoculated people are to go and wait in the blue zone, which is over at the west side of the room." She indicated an area of the control room that had been cordoned off with blue rope.

"How will we know if it works?" a man at the rear shouted. "If the test is positive or not? I mean, do we know right away, or does everyone stand in the blue area until they know?"

"We'll know immediately," Alex replied. "Don't worry about that."

More voices stirred and the noise level lifted. Tom Briggs raised his hands and waved everyone to quietness. "If the initial test gives us a positive, then there'll be more tests right then and there. Those people will just have to wait inside the room until they're done."

He looked up at Alex, who simply looked into the crowd, trying to see if there was any furtive behavior, anyone trying to get to the back of the room, or any other telltale sign that a body really didn't want to get the test. A few of the crew looked like they were trying to shuffle their position, and he knew he only needed one likely candidate.

"Everyone line up." Alex pointed to a few of those at the back. "You and you, up first."

A bearded man and a woman glanced at each other, then slowly moved to the front of the line. Alex organized them, then went to the door of the room they were using as the treatment center. He peered in. Casey Franks was sitting at a table grinning back at him with the old battle-scar down her cheek pulling her face into a sneer. With the skull on the front of her silver armor she wasn't exactly pulling off the caring, sharing nurse look. He also noticed that below the table, on the vacant seat next to her, was her gun with the thermal rounds.

Up against the wall was Klara. The tall, angular woman had her toxic dart stick close at hand and a focused, bird-of-prey expression.

Marion should have been doing the injecting, but he didn't want her up close to a body that might be housing a monster. HAWCs took those risks.

"Listen up, you pair of Nurse Ratcheds." Alex grinned. "We want these people to work with us, not run a mile."

Marion stood waiting with an electronic notebook to match the personnel details of the patients as they entered. She had laid out ten hypodermic needles containing the entire stock of their iron solution.

"This is all we've got, so good luck everyone," she said. She faced Casey. "You've injected people before, haven't you?"

Casey shrugged. "How hard can it be? The sharp bit goes into the soft skin, right?" She began to laugh.

Marion rolled her eyes. "Good luck … to them I mean."

Alex and Marion stood either side of the doorway. Briggs and a few of the remaining security personnel kept the crew in line.

Alex lifted his chin and Briggs nodded. "All forty-one personnel present and accounted for," he said. "Ready when you are."

Alex turned to Marion. "Let's begin."

* * *

They had thirty-nine people to go, and only eight injections left. Alex began to wonder whether they needed to dilute the mixture or have some placebo shots made up in the event they went through the first ten without result.

He looked along the line, sighed, and then called the next person up.

As Marion began to take the details down, there was an explosion of yelling from inside the test room, accompanied by shots ringing out.

"Get down!" Alex yelled and most of the group flattened to the ground.

The door bulged outwards as something heavy slammed against it. Alex was about to head to the door when from behind him he heard a man scream. He spun back in time to see something blooming open like a large, doughy flower among the people waiting.

It was as they suspected: the collective intelligence of the things meant that the danger to one of the polyp buds masquerading as a person was somehow telegraphed to one of the other creatures, or pieces of creature, outside.

People fell away from the creature in the center of the room, but two crew members were already lashed to it by fibrous netting. Alex beheld the creature's true form: something that looked like a dark flower with thick petals opening around madly lashing cephalopod-like tentacles.

Alex dived toward it, pulling out his neurotoxin dart stick and firing several times.

In response, the creature pulled a woman in front of itself. The dart struck her, making her blanch and her body go rod-straight as the muscle paralytic kicked in. The creature threw the woman at Alex, her body flying through the air like it weighed nothing.

Alex caught the woman and laid her to the side, then went after the thing again. This time it headed for the door. Briggs stood his ground and lifted a handgun, pointing it at the monstrous creature as it bore down on him. The base commander shouted something, but even Alex had trouble hearing his words among the cacophony of screams and shouts, plus a sound like shrieking wind during a hellstorm.

Before Briggs even had a chance to fire his gun, a lashing tendril went around his neck and he was jerked upward to strike the top of his head against the ceiling. He was then flung aside like he weighed nothing.

The creature went out the door and Alex followed. But even though he was only a dozen paces behind and moving fast when he exited, he saw the corridor was already empty, both ways.

"Sonofabitch."

Alex raced back to the testing room. Marion stood against a wall looking terrified, but as she saw him approach, she leaned across to open the door then stood back.

Klara and Casey stood over a huge mound of black sludge. Casey looked up, her teeth bared and breathing hard. She pointed.

"We injected it with the iron supplement and it freaking exploded into some sort of flowery octopus and went crazy. Klara put some darts into it, and then it turned into this shit pile."

Alex nodded. "Good work. But this thing isn't dead, just stunned. We need to get it outside and incinerate it."

"We should do some tests," Marion said, her face drawn in revulsion.

"No, we don't have any secure facilities. And we don't know if a single piece or spore of this thing is enough to infect a healthy person. Right now, I just want to reduce their size, or population – however many of these things there are." Alex poked his head out of the meeting room and pointed to one of the security guys. "Get me a plastic sheet. Hurry!"

Briggs sat up, holding his head in both hands and looking dazed. He got groggily to his feet. He nodded at Alex, who gave him a thumbs-up in return.

Alex turned back to Marion. "Give those two people who were grabbed by the thing, as well as Briggs, a shot of the iron solution in case they got infected. Watch them as you do it, just in case."

Casey came and stood in the doorway. "So, was that all of them?"

"Except the one that got away. I hope so," Alex replied.

"Good, we need a win," Klara said.

"Captain Hunter, got something here," Stevens called.

Alex turned. "What is it?"

The control panel illuminated Stevens' face. He squinted. "Got some people coming back in. Three walkers, Russian suits." He scoffed. "Waving a white flag."

Alex straightened. "Seems not all our Russians left town."

"Don't go, they could be infected. We need to keep em out," Briggs said.

"Normally I'd agree," Alex replied. "But they were there at the start of all this, so they know more than we do. If they've got information, then we might be able to trade."

"Yeah, their lives for everything they know," Casey Franks declared.

"Works for me," Alex replied. "Casey, you're with me." He turned to Stevens. "Let them in the maintenance bay. Evac all air and keep us isolated until I give the word.

"And Briggs, get that pile of crap down to the incinerator before it pulls itself back together."

CHAPTER 55

Casey's hands moved fast and expertly over Alex's broken helmet. "Needs a new visor. Got one in the pack."

She ejected the old one and threw it to the corridor floor as the pair headed toward the maintenance garage. She slotted the nanotech face screen into the collar, used a microdriver to secure it, and then tested its ability to fold out and then retract.

"Boss, lean in."

Alex turned and lowered his head so she could slot the clear ballistic shield into his collar mechanism.

"Try it."

Alex pressed the stud and the helmet telescoped over his head and face. He nodded. "Good work." He retracted it and turned down the corridor. "Now let's go meet our lunar neighbors."

* * *

Alex stood in the center of the maintenance garage as the three Russians cautiously came down the ramp. Casey stood near the wall, cradling her rifle, its muzzle pointed toward the trio.

As they saw the HAWCs, the Russians raised their hands in the air. Alex held up his own hand, flat, and motioned for them to stay put as he slowly approached, and walked around them, checking their suits to see if they had concealed weapons or whether there were any breaches in their armoured fabric, any black slime, or just anything that looked abnormal.

He pointed to his ear and they nodded.

"We come in peace," Borgan said in English.

"You don't have a choice," Alex replied. "We know your lander left, and you three are now stranded."

"It was stolen."

"By who?" Alex already knew but wanted their take on it.

The Russians looked at each other for a moment and then Borgan shrugged. "We don't know."

Alex turned way. "Then you've got nothing we need." He thumbed to the open bay doors. "Franks, show these people out."

"With pleasure." Casey walked forward, displaying the skull on her silver armor. She pointed her weapon. "You heard the man."

"Wait, wait," the woman said. She glanced at Borgan and then Alex. "The lifeform, it evolved."

Alex turned back. "You have less than two hours of breathable air left before you suffocate. You tell us everything or you can walk home and wait a few weeks for your supply ship to come to collect your dehydrated bodies."

"No one will come from Russia, ever. My name is Doctor Irina Ivanov, and I was one of the scientists assigned to work on Project Cyclops." She tutted softly. "And maybe I think suffocation on the moon would be a mercy."

"Project Cyclops?" Alex seethed. "What the hell were you doing?"

"Is not good." Irina slumped. "I will tell you everything, because everything and everyone is at stake now."

Alex stared for a moment before he turned to wave Casey down. He faced the trio. "We've lost about forty people to your Cyclops project. You better have some good answers."

"Maybe we are already too late," Irina murmured.

"Not while we're breathing." Alex turned to the cameras overhead. "It's okay, we're coming in."

Immediately the external doors slid shut, and moments later the room flooded with breathable air.

After they had all passed through decon and Marion had injected the Russians with the iron solution without any frightening results, they were led to an area beside the control room. There, Alex and Casey, plus Marion, waited as the Russians introduced themselves – Doctor Irina Ivanov, their lead scientist; Grisha Lebedev, a soldier; and their commander, Yuri Borgan.

The room had a long table and chairs, and Alex sat opposite the Russians with Casey at one shoulder and Marion at the other. The Russians were given some water and that was it. Alex sat forward and stared, his gaze making Borgan sit back.

Irina sighed and nodded. "Captain Hunter?"

"What is this thing, and where did it come from?" Alex asked.

Irina looked at him with watery eyes. "Was Olga infected?"

"No," Alex replied.

"Interesting. Where are you up to? What do you know? We will fill in all the blanks."

"Bullshit. That's not how it works," Casey began. "Why don't –"

Marion held her hand up. "It's okay, Casey, we'll go first." She began: "We know this thing seems to be something like an advanced or mutated fungal form of the cordyceps ascomycete fungi. We know that most cordyceps species are endoparasitoids, and parasitic mainly on insects and other arthropods. But somehow this thing is attacking – ingesting –

people and also mimics its prey – us – to get close. And it's smart. Maybe at least as smart as us, or maybe even smarter." Marion frowned. "And it seems to be getting smarter, evolving hour by hour."

"All of this is true," Irina replied.

"Surprise," Casey spat. "We aren't the problem – you are."

"Did you find it in the mine?" Marion asked. "Was it indigenous to the moon, or something else?"

Irina bobbed her head. "You can say it came out of the mine. But we put it there."

Casey seethed. "I fucking knew it. It was a fucking lab experiment gone wrong, wasn't it?"

Irina nodded, but Borgan and Grisha just shared confused glances.

"What was your role? What were your orders?" Alex asked the Russian commander.

"I never knew any of this," Borgan said. "I was told the base had been attacked. Probably by you Americans." He sighed. "My superiors told me to investigate why our base had gone dark. And support the science team in securing their research data." He chuckled, but there was pain in it. "We dumb soldiers are the last to know."

"Always. That is the way," Alex replied evenly.

Marion stepped in front of Irina, who had her head down. "You must go on – tell us everything."

Irina sat back and her eyes were glistening and red rimmed. "We built it from scratch. From gathering the elements, to creating the genome and then splicing it into live cordyceps DNA to create an entirely new species. We used cordyceps because they exhibit superior vitality and adaptability. We just boosted its viability and its growth rate, and that was all." She closed her eyes. "Or so we thought."

Marion frowned. "My analysis couldn't recognize the base species other than that it was like a cordyceps. But it's so different, even accounting for you tinkering with the genomes. You said you complemented the fungal DNA that was Earth based?"

"Yes and no." Irina opened her eyes. "Do you know how many elements there are in fungi? Over forty, and some of them are extremely rare. We used a lot of our core stock because there were significant errors and wastage to begin with. It took months to get our supplies replenished from Earth. So, we took shortcuts."

"Shortcuts? Where did you get the elements?" Marion asked softly.

"We have a mine, right here, so we mined them of course – fortuitously, the rare ones are in abundance in lunar soil." Irina shrugged. "Maybe there was contamination."

"Jesus Christ." Alex tilted his head back momentarily. "You used lunar ingredients, and it created a monster."

"They were just inert elements – we thought. But there must have been something else hiding within them." Irina stared straight ahead. "It grew so quickly. We were delighted at first."

"When was this? When did it start?" Alex asked.

Irina sighed. "When we started the experiments? Nearly four months ago. When did things start to go wrong? Just a few weeks ago. The information we were receiving from the laboratory staff was excited at first, and then concerned, and then ..." Her eyes shifted. "And then they vanished."

"Try and think back, about the experiments. How did you initiate such rapid growth?" Marion asked.

"I remember it was specimen X37; it turned out to be extraordinarily robust, and it learned quickly. It moved from feeding on the other fungus in its tank to ingesting plant material, and then small arthropod species. Our technicians then asked for authorisation to move to the next phase and introduce higher-order live organisms." She smiled brokenly. "So we introduced a mouse into the tank."

As Irina continued, her eyes grew glassy and her speech became trance-like. "It ingested the mouse, absorbed it from the inside out, and did what all cordyceps do – took over the mouse's physiology. But this time it was different, and we recorded a strange thing happening: the fungi didn't just infest the mouse, it *became* the mouse."

"It hadn't done that before?" Marion asked.

"No, and we saw that it was a primitive first attempt and didn't really look like the mouse due to the fungal load it was carrying. But it began acting like a mouse.

"We introduced more mice, and they could immediately tell the cordyceps copy wasn't a real mouse. But after it absorbed them as well, it began to get better at its mimicry. It was learning. With each specimen we provided, it got better and better at being the mouse. And then by the last one, we couldn't tell specimen-X37, the fungus, apart from a normal mouse. And neither could the other mice."

"It created the perfect copy." Marion shook her head. "Did that not concern you?"

"Not at the time. Not then. The laboratory team was ecstatic." She smiled again but there were tears in her eyes. "It allowed the mouse to get close to its prey. It allowed it to *infiltrate*."

Casey glanced at Alex, who nodded. He knew the infiltration was the objective.

"How did it jump from mice to people?" Marion asked gently.

"The base laboratory manager requested experiments with larger, more complex organisms. So, we sent them some rabbits. Then we sent dogs." She looked down at her hands as she spoke.

"You flew dogs to the moon to feed to your pet mushroom?" Casey leaned forward. "I know who the real fucking monsters are."

Borgan and Grisha glanced at each other and shook their heads. Alex bet this was not what they signed up for.

"Every species it ingested, it took on their characteristics. It was amazing, as it grew in size, strength, and intelligence. We had never seen anything like it. Maybe that should have been a warning to us. But the laboratory staff were too excited by their success to slow down – it pulled a veil over our eyes to the dangers."

Marion came and crouched in front of her. "Irina, this is important now. Tell me how it jumped to humans?"

The Russian scientist looked up and her eyes were dead. "We let it."

Alex glared. "Because that's what you wanted all along, wasn't it? It was to be used against your enemies in a conflict theatre."

Her eyes shifted to him. "Yes," she whispered.

"Fuckers," Casey growled.

"Go on," Marion urged.

"One of our base personnel, a miner by the name of Andrei Andropov, was killed in an accident, a suit breach. We always planned to use more advanced biological specimens, so this was an opportunity too good to let slip by." She snorted softly. "We gave it Andrei's cadaver. It ingested it, and then it became the cadaver."

"It became Andrei," Alex said.

"No, not exactly. That's how it deceived us. It waited, planned, and then executed its escape plan. Andrei, the new Andrei, seemed in a vegetative state, and we assumed that the human physiology and brain were so complex that it might not be able to control and animate them. So, some of technicians entered the laboratory to perform some tests on the body, and take samples. That was when it attacked."

"And then it went on to infect the entire base?" Marion asked.

"They didn't even know what was coming. The laboratory work was secret and kept apart from the mining operations. The first we knew of something going badly wrong was when we received garbled messages from the laboratory command – they were little more than incoherent screams and terrified babble, but they told us everything we needed to know. It was the worst-case scenario becoming every dark thing we feared."

Irina looked from Marion to Borgan. "By then it had absorbed everyone in the laboratory, outwardly became one of the lab staff, and then simply walked into the base. But it was patient, we think because it wanted to learn and grow. We were more complex in our behaviors, so it took more time."

"You mean it wanted to be more efficient in learning how to get close to us. To ambush us," Casey said.

"It studied you," Alex added softly.

"Yes." Irina exhaled long and slow. "My mission in coming here was to organize the collection of lunar samples, and also take charge of the military contingent to eradicate any aberrant lifeforms. But after it had finished with the base personnel, it must have evolved considerably."

"Olga tried to stop it and failed," Alex said.

"Then it came here." Casey's eyes had murder in them.

"Why did you come if you knew it was hopeless?" Alex asked.

"We thought … we thought that Olga might have killed it with the detonation. I guess we hoped that we'd have little more to do than clean up our mistakes, collect any records left, and maybe some biological samples."

"Who's the dumb mushroom now, bitch?" Casey spat.

"And it's on its way to Earth. In your lander." Alex straightened and folded his arms. He stepped away from the table.

"But maybe not all of it," Marion said. "Maybe what is on its way to Earth is just a portion, a bud of the main thing?"

Irina shrugged. "I don't know. The answer to that is probably still in the mine."

Alex stopped his pacing and turned. "It all comes back to the mine."

"Source of the infection," Marion said.

"Is it still in your base?" Irina asked.

As if in answer, the lights went out.

CHAPTER 56

"What the hell?" Sam looked up as the room went dark.

"Wait for it," Roy Maddock said.

The tiny red emergency lights scattered about the room began to glow.

Maddock frowned. "The backup generator should have kicked in by now. Comms is a critical facility."

"And air isn't?" Sam said. "The backup generator is in the machine room." He threw the tool he'd been using onto the desktop. "So much for running a final test."

"What do you want to do?" Maddock folded his arms. "Draw straws on who checks it out?"

Sam exhaled. "Boss ordered us to stay here. I figure the power going out might be an attempt to draw us out. I already fell for that once."

"Then we do nothing?" Maddock asked.

"For now." Sam wiped his hands on a rag. "We call it in."

Sam used the comms to try and reached Alex, but there was nothing but white noise.

"Of course, local comms also down." He shook his head. "Can anything else go wrong?"

The pounding on the door had both HAWCs pulling their guns.

Sam held up a hand and then approached. "Who's there?"

"Mia."

"What?" Sam's brows snapped together. "What are you doing here? Who's with you?"

"I came alone. I, um, was worried about you," she replied, a little softer.

"Sam Reid, moon base heartthrob." Maddock chuckled, and walked toward the door.

Sam half-turned. "I'm off the shelf."

"Great, then put in a good word for me."

Sam turned back to the door. "Mia, you fool. You could be killed. And the power's out," he said redundantly and put his hands on his hips. "Door won't open anyway."

"Yes, it can." It sounded like her face was pressed close to the door. "Take the faceplate off the switch housing. Inside you'll see another button, blue, that will use a temporary battery charge to manually open it."

"I've got it. Hold tight." Maddock walked back to the toolbox and grabbed a screwdriver. He removed the faceplate, and sure enough saw the small blue illuminated button – she was right, there was still a small charge.

"Here goes," he said and pressed it.

The door slid back with glacial speed, and Mia came in fast, first taking a glance over her shoulder. "Thought I heard something." She headed for Sam.

Sam looked past her down the dark corridor. It was impossible to see more than a dozen feet now. "Close it," he said.

Maddock nodded, stepped back, and pressed the button again. The door closed, but a lot slower than it opened.

Sam turned. "You're crazy."

"Guilty." She held up her hands and smiled. "But, no, just concerned. Without communications, we're in deep you-know-what. I wanted to see how you were doing. We hear nothing upstairs, so I was worried."

Sam looked across to Maddock, who had his arms folded and a knowing smile curving the corner of his lips. Sam sighed. "We're about done here, and were getting ready for a test but then this –" he pointed up at the lights, "– shut us down."

She nodded. "I'm sure it's just a temporary glitch. I've learned that on this base, if something can wrong, it will go wrong." She walked toward the console Sam had been repairing and looked down. "You actually rebuilt it? I thought it was beyond repair."

"I've rebuilt it but won't know if it works until we test it."

"I knew it – brains as well as brawn. Any problems?" she asked.

"Well, it's held together by spit and a prayer right now. Angus McCarthy was the real genius. I'm hoping it just holds together long enough for us to get a message back to Earth."

"He's being humble," Maddock said. "He did masterful work."

Sam held his hands up. "It's true, and I deserve a raise."

"So, you're ready to send a message?" she asked, her eyes sparkling.

"I think so." Sam returned the smile.

"What will you say first? 'Send help' or 'send beer'?"

Sam snorted softly. "Of course. But our priority is to establish contact to let everyone down there know we're okay. Priority two is to ensure that the Russian ship that departed doesn't land."

"Oh, the Russians." She looked down again at the console. "Were there any problems? I heard they found Olga in here."

Sam nodded. "Yeah, not pretty, jammed into one of the relay units. Hidden. Weird thing was she was in one piece and hadn't been converted." He went back to his tools and replaced the screwdriver. "Nothing makes sense anymore."

"That *is* weird." Mia frowned and joined Sam where he was working. "Do you think it was because of her sickness? What was it by the way?" She trailed her hand over the tools.

"We said she was dead, not sick." Maddock turned. "Who said she was sick?"

Mia shrugged. "I think Tom Briggs mentioned it."

"Briggs, huh?" Maddock asked.

She shrugged. "Or maybe someone else did. Can't keep secrets in a closed environment like this." She smiled.

Sam's eyes slid to Maddock.

"Vin," was all Maddock said.

Sam returned an almost imperceptible nod. He moved around the console. "Mia, how long have you been out of the control room?"

"Not long." Mia looked from one man to the other. "What's wrong? Why are you looking at me like that?"

"Just back up a step," Sam said as he approached.

"Why?" She looked down at the repaired console. "What did I do?"

Mia didn't move and for some reason Sam felt a deep animal fear begin in his belly. Though the woman was only half his size, his senses screamed for caution.

"Just going to take you up for a test. An inoculation. You okay with that?" Sam asked.

"No need for that." Mia's expression was blank. "But you can't tell them."

"Tell who what?" Maddock started to move into a flanking position.

"The Russians, of course. The craft must be allowed to land. Can't have you try and stop it."

Sam's brows came together as he stared at the small woman. In the reddish glow he thought he could make out a line down the center of her face that he was sure wasn't there before.

He needed clearer vision, so he reached up to engage his visor, for light amplification. In that split second of the visor closing, Mia's face split down the middle along the line that had formed, and the two halves opened like a flower. Her eyes, the human ones, peeled away on the outside of the petals, along with her nose and teeth. But inside the strange bloom there were more eyes, sharp dagger-like teeth, and in the center, whipping black tendrils.

The glistening ropes shot out, one toward Sam and another toward Maddock.

Sam only had time to yell, "Engage suit!" before the cords smacked into his face and body. His suit held, as did the visor.

Maddock, who hadn't had time to engage his visor, took the glistening cord in the center of his face. The black thing hardened and pierced his flesh between the eyes. His body jerked and danced like a speared fish, and then hung limp on the dark tendril.

"*Noooo.*" Sam pulled his weapon and fired, but the thing that had been Mia moved faster than he could shoot.

Another cord shot out, but flew past Sam, and struck the door. It flattened and hit with a juddering impact that dented the lightweight steel.

It struck again, and the end of the tendril formed something like a claw that worked in at the door's edges and began to peel the steel inward. Though the doors were not fortified in any way, Sam knew the amount of force required to do that was phenomenal, and therefore the small body of Mia held something inside it of incredible size and power.

Sam fired again and again and was sure he hit the creature but the thing that had once worn the face of a young, dark-haired woman was now something resembling a pulpy bloom of open flesh with whipping cords where Mia's head and face had been. She – it – headed at frightening speed for the door, taking Maddock's body with it like a dog on a leash.

Sam dived, but Mia and Maddock went through the hole in the open door. Sam got to his feet and charged the frame. Hitting the manual open button caused a whirring noise, but no action as the bent steel refused to move back into its wall slot.

"*Fuck!*" Sam yelled and punched the steel, denting it further, as he watched his friend's body on its dark, glistening leash thump against the ground, disappearing down the darkened hallway before vanishing.

He rested his head against the door for a moment, then straightened. "Boss, come in."

There was no reply.

"Man down," he said softly and closed his eyes. His comm. unit was still out.

Sam turned to sink down to sit with his back to the door. He held his head in his large hands. There was rage and frustration in his belly, but also a feeling of helplessness that he had been forced to witness a HAWC being killed without being able to take down the killer.

He knew then that the creature had probably been in Mia all along and she had taken Angus, and undoubtedly Vin as well. But the other thing he had learned was how determined it was to have the Russian ship land. It wanted to spread the infection – spread itself – to all of Earth.

CHAPTER 57

Alex, Casey, and Marion pushed back into the crowded control room. The tiny dots of red emergency lighting only delivered a faint illumination, and Alex could see that the people had drawn themselves into protective clumps. He was reminded of the stories about boats going down in shark-infested waters, where the people in lifejackets clumped together hoping that it would give them some protection against the circling predators.

It rarely worked.

Briggs came forward and nodded at the emergency lighting. "That's the generator room. The power's been knocked out. Emergency power will give us just a few more hours of light and then ..." He shrugged.

There was a sound like a long sigh, then silence.

Briggs' expression was one of defeat in the blood-red darkness. "And there goes the aircon and the oxygen."

"We need to get to the maintenance room," Casey said.

"Sam and Maddock are repairing the comms and guarding it. Now we need to guard the core facilities, plus all the people in here? We're being forced to spread ourselves too thin," Alex said.

"Just what it wants," Klara added.

"I got a feeling it's given up on keeping us as livestock and is now just gonna freeze us all and wait until someone arrives from home," Casey said.

"With a red carpet all the way back to Earth." Alex turned to Briggs. "How long do we have?"

"Until the stored air runs out?" The base commander seemed to think on it. "Best case now with reduced personnel is around thirty hours. With exertion and fear causing extra oxygen uptake, and extra CO_2 exhalations with no scrubbers ... twenty-two to twenty-four hours."

"Then no choice – I've got to check out the maintenance rooms," Alex said.

"On it," Casey said.

Alex shook his head. "You and Klara guard the people. Last thing we need is for them to panic and start running all over the base."

"You know it's drawing us out for a reason? And you know it's set traps before, right, Boss?" Casey said.

"I know. But given this thing has no problem surviving outside in zero atmosphere it obviously doesn't need air. We do." He sighed. "And twenty-two hours is not enough time; we don't even have an evac plan formulated."

"One thing we can do to buy us some more time is get everyone into their personal EMU suit. Each contains two hours oxygen. Not much, but something," Briggs said.

"Good idea, but not yet. I don't want people out in the corridors, especially now we've gone dark." He looked back at the groups of people in their small herds. "Keep them calm, keep them safe."

* * *

Alex paused at the power-generation room door to listen. There was silence, total: no hum of machinery, or even tick of electronics.

He looked over his shoulder. The corridor behind him was dark as Hades with just a few dotted red lights providing a hellish ambience. He remembered Sam's report of the last time he came down: everything was operational in the room, but there was unusually thick humidity and some sort of sticky extruded matter everywhere.

Looks like a damn beehive, the big guy had said.

Alex pressed the door open button, but nothing happened. He expected that, so he shouldered his weapon, and placed a hand flat against the door then closed his eyes. He pushed out with his senses, but after a moment still couldn't detect anything beyond the barrier.

He felt along the edge of the door, pulling out his shortest kabar blade and jammed it into the corner, levering it. There was a grating sound, the metallic coating grazed and finally the end of the super tough blade snapped away and fell to the ground, looking like a discarded shark's tooth.

Alex jammed his fingers and nails into the gap, took a breath and began to drag the door open. It came slowly as the locking mechanism had remained engaged.

He paused to look over his shoulder again. There was nothing there, but he had the prickling sensation on his neck that told him he was being watched. He looked around, suddenly remembering how the creature had seemed to morph into different forms, and wondered whether it could be hiding just behind the panels in the wall or ceiling. It gave him the creeps.

Alex stepped inside the room, his eyes shining silver and immediately adjusting to the near total darkness. The first thing he registered was the humidity against his cheeks, as well as the unusual temperature. With the generators shut down, and it being lunar night time, the temp outside was dropping to about 200 below. The infrastructure would slowly but surely leak heat. This room was defying that trend.

Alex knew if he didn't get the machines up and running in a few hours it would be deadly, unless everyone took to their EMU suits. And that was nothing but a short-term solution.

There was also an unusual smell – the canned air of the base was mostly odorless, dry, sometimes with a hint of machine oil, and flavored by the crush of humanity. But in here it reminded him of the time he had worked in South America on the Green Hell Mission, and they had trekked through the dank jungles. Now and then they encountered stagnant pools of water that smelt of rotting plant life, corruption, and ... fungal growth. This odor within the room took him right back to that bready sweatness.

A fungal ripeness.

He rounded a console and placed a hand gently on its surface, then snapped it away as he felt the stickiness. Looking down, he saw what Sam had previously described as being like a glistening resin coating the console top, and when he turned about, he saw that it covered most things in the room.

The machines were dark, but so far, he couldn't detect any physical damage. He tilted his head, listening, and trying to detect any movement, sound, or life emanations – out in the corridor he had sensed eyes on him or at least someone monitoring him.

There was a glint of something reflecting one of the red lights in the ceiling. Alex narrowed his eyes and concentrated. And suddenly felt lifeforce emanations all around him.

He needed to check on Sam's status with the communication systems and just hoped the big guy was good to go.

Alex backed up, and his foot struck something. Looking down, he saw the HAWC armored suit, empty, and the chest patch: *Maddock.*

He stared. The thing wasn't opened, simply looked like his friend had exited the armor without actually taking it off. He knew how that worked and remembered the liquid draining effect he had seen.

Alex crouched and picked up the helmet. He stared into its emptiness, a hand on each side of the silver vacant shell.

"Sorry, Roy."

As he stared, he felt the storm of anger bloom in his belly, and then run throughout his body. As he stared into the helmet with its silent, empty scream, his hands came together. Impossibly, with a scream of armored steel, the helmet began to compress.

Alex gritted his teeth and pressed harder, not wanting to stop, letting out the burst of fury as pure power. The super tough metal crushed completely and he raised his head to scream his fury and then flung the flattened helmet away.

Alex Hunter dropped his head and breathed hard. He closed his eyes, tight.

Kill 'em all. Kill 'em all. Kill 'em all.

The dry voice in his head seethed with pure hate and anger. After another second, Alex nodded.

"Yes."

Alex opened his eyes. It took several more minutes for his system to slow and he finally engaged suit-to-suit comms: "Sam, come in."

There was significant white noise, and he boosted the frequency. "Sam, come back."

"Boss? I've been trying to reach you. Bad shit going down."

"Maddock. I know. What happened?" Alex crouched over the empty HAWC suit.

"Mia. It was Mia. She attacked us. Took out Roy." Sam's voice was almost a growl. "Goddamn, Roy's gone."

Alex didn't want to ask how the woman got into the comms room as he had more pressing things on his mind. "How's the communication equipment? Are we good to go?"

"I think so. We were just about to conduct a test. Mia tried to destroy the equipment, again – we stopped her. She took off, but took Roy with her. I lost him."

Alex rose to his feet. "I've located Roy."

"Is he …?"

"Gone," Alex replied softly.

Sam moaned. "Fuck this place."

"Forget about it. We are now in war mode. Grieve later." Alex scanned the room.

"There's something else. There's a reason Mia doesn't want us to get a message out – she confirmed the Russian ship is infected with whatever she is. She doesn't want us to send a message telling them," Sam said, his voice speeding up. "We've got to stop it."

Alex looked back to the dark machinery. "That's the plan. I'm going to try and bring energy generation back online. As soon as you've got power, send that damn message. Not sure how much longer we'll have."

"I'm ready when you are."

"We're going to kill 'em all. Stand by." Alex signed off.

"Wait – one more thing," Sam said. "Keep your visor closed. Maddock didn't. And it got in."

"Got it." Alex engaged his visor and the clear ballistic shielding slid up and over his face.

CHAPTER 58

Russian lander on Earth approach – 6200 miles in upper atmosphere

Russian lander P23–09 had already entered the exosphere, the thin upper atmospheric layer surrounding the Earth. It was still traveling at around 17,000 miles per hour, and the craft automatically engaged thrusters to slow it down.

Soon it would enter the thermosphere, a layer ranging from 700 to 800 miles, then the mesosphere, a twenty mile–thick layer, before finally entering the stratosphere. In the last few layers, the air becomes extremely dense, and both turbulence and friction kick in.

Lander P23–09 was still traveling so fast that it compressed the air ahead of it – that compression of the air layers near the leading edges of the craft caused the temperature of the air to rise to as high as 3000 degrees. Without the craft's ceramic tile insulation, it would burn up in seconds.

Also, in these layers, radio waves were whited out, resulting in a total communication blackout.

On the ground in their observatory posts, the Russian technicians and Major Alexi Bilov could do nothing but watch and wait.

Bilov's eyes stung from forgetting to blink as he stared at the multiple screens, and he felt nervous to the point of throwing up. He now knew all about the experiments the Lenin Base was conducting, and also knew that a laboratory containment breach was one plausible scenario that could have led to the base's destruction.

He sucked in a deep breath and held it for a moment, feeling his heart thump in his chest.

And now the landing craft had gone dark. And stayed dark.

He let the breath out slowly. Every firewall scenario they'd ever created would recommend the same thing: *the craft must not land*.

CHAPTER 59

Alex moved closer to the main generator. He walked along the unit looking for damage, and all he found was a few of the levers in the off position. He knew he'd have to prime it again and wait for the initiator charge level to rise. But if that was all he needed to do, then they were lucky.

Why hadn't the creature destroyed the machines? Perhaps because shutting down the power was just to slow them down, keep them off balance. And maybe keeping them alive was a failsafe. A plan B in the event something happened to the Russian ship.

It knows us now, Alex thought. *It knows that Earth will send rescue ships if we're still alive, but won't if we're dead.*

He gripped the priming lever and began to push it up. Immediately the initiator started to prepare the batteries to take the charge and lights began to climb on a power index. In another minute there should have been enough of a base charge to hit the button that would start the machinery and give the base back its power.

It's too easy.

A sticky, liquid sound tore Alex's eyes from the dials to the floor in time to see a large mound of the resin pop and bubble. It formed a lump that continued to rise.

"Here we go," he whispered.

The mound rose, and rose, and in the next few seconds took form, female, and then blinked open eyes. It was Mia. From ten feet away she shot out a hand that reached across the room to encircle his wrist.

Alex grunted from the pain – its strength was phenomenal. He realized this thing was the compressed mass of their forty missing people, plus the Russian base personnel.

Mia worked to drag his hand away. In the split seconds he stared at it, he saw it change from a human hand to something monstrous.

"Alex Hunter."

Alex slowly faced the thing.

Mia's face began to bloom as fleshy bulbs on stalks rose from the smooth skin. They swelled and popped, filling the room with fungal spores.

He could feel her grip becoming sharp as some sort of thorns or spikes tried to put holes in his armored suit. He could hear their dagger points raking against the silver steel. It was dragging his hand away and he reached out with his senses – normally he could detect whether someone was frightened, angry, evasive, or dozens of other emotions or sensations. But within the Mia creature before him, there was nothing but a cold and calculating emptiness.

"You're too late," Alex said. "The Russian ship will never land."

Mia continued to swell and grow, bigger and bigger until her head touched the ceiling. She filled the room with mis-shapen lumped muscle, covered in the waving stalks with their swelling polyps. Her face was small yet still human-like in the middle of the form. But the eyes were just black orbs.

The pressure on Alex's wrist intensified, and as the arm began to tug at him, he grabbed the edge of the console desk to hang on. Though he had enormous strength, the thing's true mass after absorbing so many crew members was colossal, and far outmatched his own. Sooner or later, he'd be pulled toward it. Or instead of him being dragged into it, it would come at him.

As if to answer that question, more of the spiked limbs struck him and hung on before crawling over his body, feeling, probing, touching, and almost caressing him as they searched for a way inside his armoured suit.

"Not today." Alex discharged an external shockwave over his suit's shell then continued to generate the pulse for many seconds. The 2000-volt charge was delivered along the Mia-thing's limbs back to its central mass. But the length of the shock also meant it traveled back through the suit to Alex. He roared his pain but kept the charge emanating until Mia shrieked an unearthly, alien sound and folded in on herself. She released him, and Alex leaped to his feet, sprinted back to the console and restarted the generators.

Lights on dials came online as the hum of power returned throughout the base. The main lights flickered overhead.

Alex brought his comms online. "Sam, now, *now!*"

Alex hoped Sam would be sending the message, and he prayed that he was giving his soldier enough power for it to reach home.

He looked back to the Mia thing, and saw she was gone. He exhaled and lowered his head.

Alex slowed his breathing, taking in deep breaths and thinking about the encounter. She'd had him cold and could have won. *Should* have won. Mia could have destroyed the generator in a blink.

Once again, that was too easy, he thought.

Be on guard, a small voice whispered from a corner of his mind.

Alex lifted his head.

It took Vin and Roy. You know it absorbs their minds, and with it, their memories, their skills, and their knowledge. Alex, it knows.

"Who is this?" he asked. It wasn't the cruel jeering of the Other, or the reassuring words of Joshua. It was someone else.

"Too many voices now. I'm losing it," he whispered.

Alex, think – it knew. Knew what it needed. And took it.

Alex straightened, and concentrated – *It knew what it needed, and took it.*

What did it take? he wondered.

Alex lowered his hand to the secure place on his belt. It was open – the launch key was gone.

A red rage built inside him and he punched down hard, taking the edge of the desk clean off. He opened his comms to all his HAWCs.

"All HAWCs, suit up and meet me in the bay, right now. Entity has launch key." Alex's eyes shone like mercury. "And is going for our craft."

CHAPTER 60

Colonel Jack Hammerson leaned forward and rested his knuckles on the desk as he watched the trajectory of the Russian lander as it approached the outer orbit.

He had read the short message from Sam Reid. Then he had read it again. It was far worse than he imagined. The lifeform had killed many on the Kennedy Base, as well as devastating the Russians' Lenin base. And now it was on its way to Earth within Russian lander P23–09.

Sam's final sentence simply read: *Do not let it land.*

Hammerson had immediately informed General Chilton, who took it straight to the commander in chief.

Then Hammerson had tried to raise his counterpart in the Russian military through back channels, but he had refused to speak. Same went for General Chilton's contacts. Added to that, the Russian president wouldn't even contemplate taking a call from the U.S. president following the fallout over the retribution for the extinction plague the Russians had tried to release on American soil. It seems the U.S. threat of nuclear destruction they had been given, followed by Russia's humiliating backdown, meant crushed egos were in no mood to take friendly advice any time soon.

Hammerson stared at the screen – there was no way they could take out a Russian craft over Russian airspace. That meant if anything was going to happen, it must be by the Russians' own hand.

And if not, then God help them all.

God help us *all.*

* * *

Sophia ran across the lunar surface. She had seen through Alex's eyes the interaction he'd had with the human-shaped cordyceps fungal creature, and also knew it had achieved its goal of obtaining the launch key. She calculated that the probability of it immediately heading to the lander and launching by itself was one hundred percent. After all, it had absorbed both Vincent Douglas and Roy Maddock, and would know how to get the craft into the atmosphere.

She spotted the Mia form walking purposefully toward the lander and increased her speed. Interestingly, it had given up all pretence of being human, as it hadn't bothered wearing a helmet. It was now lunar sun up and the temperature was over 250 degrees. The surface skin of the Mia-thing reddened and blistered, and vapour rose from it. But as quickly as the flesh was damaged, it regenerated.

Sophia overtook it, and stood before it. The Mia-thing stared at Sophia, its eyes untroubled but interested – it undoubtedly saw before it an entity that had the face of a human female, but a non-biological, physical form that was a dull, silver metallic texture.

Sophia felt a tiny aspect of kinship, as they were both beings that simply wanted to survive and grow. However, Sophia wanted to grow as a conscious being, and this thing wanted to grow to consume every biological thing it could get close to. If it made it to Earth, it would be an extinction event–level problem.

She looked at the launch key in the Mia-thing's left hand. "That is not for you," she said. "I'll have to take that now."

The Mia-cordyceps had no concept of what Sophia could be, and so did what was instinctive: it attacked.

An arm shot out, covering the six feet between them, and the hand on its end gripped Sophia's neck. In turn Sophia grabbed the arm and broke it off at the wrist. The piece she held immediately lost form and dropped to the ground as a dark mass of doughy material. From the stump of Mia's arm, another hand grew.

As Sophia watched, the form bulked up, using its entire mass to cover an area of about a dozen square feet, and that again high. Human arms hung from it, crude imitations with sprouting polyp stalks, cords of web-like veins, and pulsating bulbs.

Sophia couldn't take the risk it might split some of itself off, and make a run for the craft while she was kept occupied. Time to end it. She reached up to open the reactor housing in her chest and allowed a beam of 5000-degree heat to strike the Mia-thing. The place where it touched the creature immediately shrivelled to ash.

The Mia-thing shrank as more and more of it was destroyed. After another moment, it did what all lifeforms do when under lethal attack – it fled. Long dark legs sprouted from all sides, and it raced away over the lunar landscape toward the Russian base, still with the launch key.

Sophia watched it depart. It seemed self-preservation was inbuilt into the DNA of all biological entities. She stared after it for another moment as a plan formulated in her mind. Her lips curved up on one side, just like Aimee's would have. The plan might work, and if it did, it would be her last.

She entered the HAWC ship and donned one of the spare suits. She even put the helmet on and pulled the gold visor down over the beautiful face of Aimee.

She exited the lander, sat cross-legged in the dust, and waited.

CHAPTER 61

Alex ran, hard, and was way out in front with his HAWCs racing to keep up with him. Further back from them were the Russians, who had decided to throw all in with the Americans. They probably thought if they redeemed themselves, they might just hitch a ride home.

Marion had stayed at the base. It seemed all traces of the cordyceps had left with Mia. Perhaps that tiny little body had been the mothership for all the fungal spores. And now with the launch key she was going to transport them all to Earth, like an invading army.

Alex gritted his teeth and pushed on. Sam's message had been sent, but they didn't have the technology to receive a reply – it was all in God's hands now.

He was first over the rim of the last crater and stopped dead. He breathed a sigh of relief – the lander was still there. But then he saw the figure sitting cross-legged in front of their craft. It wasn't wearing Mia's suit, but instead had on one of the spare HAWC suits.

Sam was first to join him. "Who the hell is that?"

"I have an idea," Alex said, with an apprehensive feeling in his gut. "Mia is still our priority target, not this *person*. Spread and give me cover."

"What? You want us to wait here?" Sam asked.

"Yeah, they want to talk." He turned to his large HAWC. "That's an order."

Casey, Klara, and Sam drew their weapons and focused them on the lone figure waiting in front of their lander. Borgan, Grisha, and Irina were shunted out of the way, and watched with interest.

Alex approached the figure that just continued to sit, its legs crossed and arms casually resting on its thighs. When he got to within a few feet, the person rose to their feet. He didn't need to see them to know who it was.

"How did you get here?"

Sophia lifted the gold visor. "I stowed away. It was easy."

Alex felt his breath catch in his throat as Aimee's face stared back at him with a slight curve of amusement touching the red lips. He felt his fury rise.

"That's not your face. I'm going to tear it from you."

"I'm not your problem, Alex Hunter. You know that," she said, the blue eyes shining. "I have been protecting you all along. But now we are in the end game – one species will survive, here and on Earth, and one species will be vanquished. Which will it be? Your choice."

Alex swallowed his revulsion. "What are you saying?"

"I'm saying, I want a truce, for now. My role was – is – to be a protector of humans. Let me do it." Sophia stared back with her unblinking blue-eyed gaze.

Alex had no idea if he could trust the android, or even if he wanted to. But as his mind worked, there came nothing but wasteful indecision.

"I can help you." She glanced over her shoulder. "I tried to retrieve the lander key, but it was too quick. However, I did damage and weaken it." She pointed. "It went that way."

"To the Russian base; the mine," Alex exhaled. "Of course."

"We need to hurry. Giving it more time is dangerous. It grows smarter and stronger. While you grow weaker." She turned. "I sense no more of the creatures or its buddings in the Kennedy Base. But it is getting ready to leave. It is in one spot and vulnerable, right now."

"We'll go there, destroy it." Alex began to turn to his crew.

"No. You must guard the lander. If it gets past you, it cannot be allowed to depart." She was firm.

"That's not your call," Alex replied.

"Leave your crew here to guard the ship. If not, I must destroy it as a safeguard. The creature must not under any circumstances be allowed to get back to Earth. You know that." The blue eyes widened. "Please, Alex, this is a critical moment, for everyone and everything you hold dear."

"And if we are unsuccessful?" he asked.

"Even if it doesn't achieve access to the lander, the Kennedy Base will soon be overrun, and the moon would be designated a quarantine zone, forever. Everyone here stays until expiry through being absorbed by the fungal entity or running out of life-sustaining resources." She turned to the Russian base. "And if it arrives on Earth, then maybe there will be nothing left to go back to."

Alex shook his head.

"Time's up, Alex. Retrieve the launch key, destroy the specimen, and also destroy the science."

"Destroy the laboratory?"

"Destroy everything." She began to walk toward the base. "Bring the Russian scientist as well."

"What about the other Russians?" he asked.

She kept walking. "I don't care about them, they are superfluous."

Alex watched Sophia go for a moment, then turned to wave his crew down.

Sam came first, followed by Casey and Klara, and then the Russians.

"Who was it?" Sam asked.

"A stowaway," Alex said, and held a hand up to stop any more questions. He thought it best not to let them know that the android that nearly killed them was amongst them. "You wouldn't believe me if it told you. Here are the orders: HAWCs to guard the lander. I will retrieve the key." He turned. "Irina, you will accompany me to the Russian base. We leave now."

"We will come too," Borgan said.

"That's your call," Alex said.

"Boss, permission to accompany you," Sam pleaded. "This thing is –"

"No." Alex walked closer to his team. "If I fail to obtain the key, this thing must never be allowed to use it to get to Earth." He glanced at the lander then back to Sam. "Do you understand what I'm saying?"

Sam's shoulders slumped. After another moment, he nodded.

Casey guffawed. "Just as well I love it here."

Alex gave them a small salute and turned away. "Irina, double time."

Alex, Irina, and the two Russian soldiers followed Sophia, leaving the remaining HAWCs to watch them go.

* * *

Alex felt the eyes of the android on him, and sensed the tingle of its sensors as they probed his mind. Strangely, they didn't feel unnatural, and for some reason he had the feeling they'd always been there.

They passed by the ruins of the Russian base, and Alex only glanced at the destruction. The entire site had been heat blasted and he barely recognized the decimation as something that was once a functioning lunar outpost.

The mine was just a few hundred yards further on and began in the side of a crustal uplift. They paused outside.

Borgan turned to Alex. "Our crew members went in to investigate. Who or what came out were not our people anymore."

Alex nodded. "Puppets."

"It is aware we are here," Sophia said and turned. "I sense … caution."

"If it's afraid, that's good," Borgan replied.

"I didn't say it was afraid, I said I believed it was cautious. Not because of us but because of me." Sophia faced the mine but spoke to Irina. "What was the name of your project?"

"Cyclops."

"Yes, appropriate. In Greek mythology, the Cyclops were giant, one-eyed monsters. They were said to have provided Zeus with his greatest weapon, the thunderbolt." Sophia lifted her helmet visor, staring at the Russian woman. "And you hoped this creation would be your thunderbolt … against us."

Irina looked away from her.

"Okay, let's get this over with," Alex said. "Irina, I assume you know the layout."

"I know what the schematics are," she replied.

"Then you're with me at the front. Let's go."

Alex led them in.

CHAPTER 62

The small group quickly passed through the mining work and entered the area where the laboratories once stood. The doors were peeled back, and the vacuum of the lunar atmosphere had been allowed to enter.

"This used to be a pristine laboratory, with a ten-strong staff of the finest Russian research scientists," she said softly. She held up a hand and waved it around slowly. "I can see free-floating spores around us."

"When we are ready, heat will degrade them. But we must find the source first," Sophia announced.

Irina pointed. "That way."

They soon came to the area where the side of the tunnel had been breached. They paused, but Sophia kept them on course. She motioned to the rear of the tunnel.

"We must go that way."

Alex stared into the depths of the tunnel. "Irina, what's down there?"

"The isolation rooms. Where the first viable samples were housed."

"It's the nursery," Borgan replied, distastefully. "Where your baby was born."

Alex nodded. "Keep going."

Irina headed in and they soon came to a doorway with solidified resin coating its rim. As they passed through, the Russian scientist turned.

"There are only a few more rooms in there and several isolation tanks."

The further in they went, the thicker the spore blizzard. Alex moved his light beam from one side of the room to the other. He saw there were glass tanks of varying sizes, and inside there were things that looked like twisted tree roots that sprouted odd shapes, fur, and protuberances, some the size of baseballs, and some three feet around.

"Once mice, rabbits, dogs ..." Irina announced.

"And then it leaped the species barrier to people. With a little help from you," Alex replied as he saw the horrifying experiment's final results: the human figure was gripping the beam with both hands, but its entire body was covered in what looked like sticky fur, with several wrist-thick stalks growing from the back of its head. Each ended in a large bulb the size of a football, which had blossomed.

"Typical cordyceps behavior," Irina whispered. "Infiltrates the body and brain so it can take over the host to turn it into a spore factory. Then it forces the poor soul to move to a populated area and once there it blooms and generates a spore explosion so the infected host can corrupt other members of its hive. Or in this case, my colleagues."

"How could you do this?" Borgan sounded ill.

Irina shrugged. "It was simple, really. The parasitic fungus has many varieties that specialize in a certain type of host – some prefer ants, some grasshoppers, some flies, etc. We simply created one that had no preference."

"Because you wanted them to infect human beings." Sophia turned. "You wanted them to infect your enemies."

Irina remained silent.

"You planned to keep this in your arsenal, and one day release it against us," Alex said.

"That is not my job or my decision," Irina protested. "I'm just a scientist doing what I was asked to do."

Alex turned back to the horrifying body. "Maybe this is the first guy to get infected. And maybe he didn't even know he was. He just felt compelled to walk out here under the control of this thing, grip the beam, and lock on. And then the fungus blooms, breaks out, and infects everyone." He turned to Irina. "And all the time it is evolving, growing, getting both hungrier and smarter."

She nodded slowly. "The cordyceps is just doing what it has always done for hundreds of millions of years."

Alex went on. "It absorbs the flesh and the intelligence. Always seeking more resources to grow itself. And then along the way it learned about Earth and all its resources. It then hatches a plan to get there."

Alex glanced from Borgan, who was the color of pale clay behind his visor, to Irina. "And it is now doing that in your lander." He cursed. "Let's just hope they got our message, and believed it, or I wouldn't bother going back home to Russia if I was you."

"Alex."

Alex turned at the sound of the android's voice.

"It's here," she said.

Alex and the Russians spun, shining their lights into different corners of the stygian dark room.

"Where?" Borgan hissed.

In response, the creature leaped at the Russian commander from one of the darkest corners of the destroyed laboratory. The thing's jaws were open, showing that it was probably once a dog, but now it was covered in stalks and twisted things like gnarled roots with odd bulbs in their ends.

Borgan went down under the attack.

The next creature came at Irina, and then all hell broke loose as monstrosities that seemed to come from the bowels of Hell poured forth from every crevice, corner, darkened doorway, even dropped from the ceiling. Some were once animals, others were the remains of people, and more could have been a combination of both, twisted into fungal abominations.

Alex fired his gun again and again, and when the things got closer, he smashed them with the iron of his weapon and his fists. But he found striking them was like hitting something with a spongy, boneless texture, and they seemed to have no brain or vital organs. His HAWC armor was up to the task, but the Russians were not as well protected, even in their Centurion armor.

He heard an impact and a grunt and turned to see Borgan down. The once-human thing on top of him used an arm that ended in a knobby extrusion to punch right through his visor. The hand or claw tore the glass away and then it leaned forward to exhale a stream of white spores into the gagging man's helmet.

A screaming Irina was dragged away into the darkness and several things that looked like a cross between canines and sea anemones were mauling Grisha.

Alex threw pulpy bodies aside, wondering where they were all coming from, when Sophia appeared beside him.

"There's too many," Alex said without turning.

"No, there's only one. And it is the mother of them all," she replied. "But she is budding off all the force she needs. The cordyceps strain has fed extremely well over the past few weeks." She turned Aimee's beatific face to him. "She is just keeping you busy."

Sophia reacted quickly as one of the creatures came at them – she grabbed it and tore the thing in half, then flung the parts away.

"She wants you, Alex. She knows of your physical superiority. She needs to merge with you. That can't be allowed to happen. There." She spotted something and darted away.

Alex was alone now, but fought on. He ripped deformed bodies to shreds, but the pieces he flung aside simply merged back together or joined up with other mutilated bodies to became whole again. The things were neither human nor cat nor dog, but pieces of all of them, roped together by spidery veins and stalks with budding tips.

Eventually he was forced back by sheer numbers. He had lost sight of the Russians. Then he heard an abominable screeching that was like the grating of long nails on a board just as Sophia returned.

The pile of twisted and deformed bodies pressed in on him, seeking to bring him down as they tried to find a weakness in his suit. Sophia reached into the boiling, furious mass, took hold of his arm, and pulled him from within. She then grabbed his wrist and pulled his hand toward her.

She jammed the launch key onto his palm. "Leave now. I'll finish this."

"I need to find the others …"

"*No*, they all stay," she said with finality.

Alex took the key and hesitated for only a second. But then he backed out as he watched Sophia stand between him and the horde, creating a barrier so they could not follow.

He turned and ran, and was soon at the mine mouth, where he stopped and looked back into its depths. Strangely, he still heard her in the center of his mind.

Keep moving, don't stop.

Don't look back, keep running!

Go home, Alex.

He did as she asked and sprinted away from the mine, kicking up powdery lunar dust behind him.

Goodbye, Alex Hunter.

Remember me.

He sensed the blast firstly as a flash of light that passed by him. Then the surface of the moon rippled like a shaken blanket and he turned to look over his shoulder to see a massive blister rising several dozen feet in the air, and then, with a belch of gases and spray of molten rock, collapse back down into a massive pit.

Her reactor? She destroyed herself?

He looked down at the key in his hand. Sophia had finally done what she'd been created to do: protect mankind, *all* mankind – he looked back to the molten crater – even if it meant sacrificing herself.

CHAPTER 63

Russian lander on Earth approach – 53 miles in upper atmosphere

Lander P23–09 had entered the mesosphere, the twenty mile–thick layer just before the stratosphere, the final atmospheric layer above the Earth's surface. Inside the cabin, the cordyceps shifted its massive bulk as it prepared itself. Its multiple human forms had melted together to become like a giant sea anemone that filled the interior of the crew space.

The lander was now a Lovecraftian nightmare of waving tendrils, spidery webbing, and bulging polyps. Now and then a portion would elongate, and a hand would form to operate some aspect of the craft's approach mechanism.

It was down to the final hours now. It knew what it must do, when the craft was over the heart of Moscow and minutes away from coming in, to give it the best chance of survival.

Hands reached out of the pulpy mass, some male, some female, all waiting, ready to override the automatic controls. It would take significant effort to both circumvent the craft's security protocols and then fight against the g-force velocity of the outside air – it needed to open the external doors while still traveling at 500 miles per hour.

Dozens of eyes popped open along the mass and looked from the instrument panel to the altimeter and then to the countdown clock – *soon*. In preparation, the huge, doughy mass filling the craft's interior expanded as if drawing a breath, getting ready to open the door and then fruit: explode in a cloud of billions upon billions of spores that would exit the craft, and drift down over Moscow.

And then, the planet, and everything on it, would become part of it.

* * *

Alex slowed to walk back to the lander, and on seeing him, the HAWCs raced toward him. They stopped a few feet out.

"Please tell me that's you, Boss," Sam said.

Alex nodded, and held up the key. "Sophi…" He looked away for a moment. "Irina retrieved it, and then blew the mine, destroyed everything."

Casey snorted. "Russians came in handy after all."

"They fought well." Alex replied.

"Create a monster, die killing it." Casey shrugged. "Works for me."

Sam exhaled and reached out to put a hand on Alex's shoulder. "What now?"

"Back to the base to mop up. Then we grab Marion and head home." He looked up into the dark sky. "And just pray Russia believes what we told them."

* * *

Joshua shot to his feet. "I can see him."

The boy threw an arm in the air and roared his happiness. He turned to hug Tor, whose mouth opened in a wide, doggy grin, and the pair danced around the room.

"He's coming home." Joshua stopped and turned, his smile dropping. "But why was I blocked before?" He concentrated for a moment but then gave up and shrugged. "It doesn't matter, it's gone now."

* * *

Colonel Jack Hammerson held the phone to his ear and watched as the Russian lander approached the stratosphere. "Sir, P23–09's approach trajectory means it will come down right in the center of Moscow, population twelve million ... within a country population of 145 million."

"Tell 'em I'm coming, and hell's coming with me," General Chilton said, and exhaled through clamped teeth. "Jack, if what it's carrying is as potentially inimical to life as you say it is, we need to think about some sort of physical quarantine for the entire continent."

"Quarantine Russia?" Hammerson glanced back at the map. "Some sort of hard border might work if Russia was an island, Marcus. But it borders China, whose population is close to one-and-a-half billion. Quarantining, even if it is possible, might be able to slow it but not stop it."

"That's not what I meant, Jack. The commander in chief is prepared to order a full cauterization if need be. You know what that means. But we must have proof that what is on that lander is as deadly as you say. Do we have that proof, Jack?"

Hammerson knew then how this was going to go. "Sir, I believed Lieutenant Sam Reid when he told us it decimated both lunar bases, he warned us not to let the craft land in any circumstances."

"Do we have *any* concrete proof, colonel?" Chilton's voice was soft.

"No, sir." Hammerson sat down, his hand tight on the phone. "But by the time we get it, it'll be too late."

"We've swiveled all available satellites within complementary orbits and have activated all our internal operatives. We have all eyes in and over Moscow watching. We watch and wait, and say a prayer for a miracle, Jack. It's all we can do." Chilton hung up.

Hammerson returned the phone to its cradle and then turned to watch the Russian lander's telemetry as it entered the Earth's atmosphere.

CHAPTER 64

Baikonur Cosmodrome Spaceport, southern Kazakhstan

Bilov paced nervously as he and the assembled technicians monitored the lander's approach from a remote location close to Red Square. His arms were folded tight across his chest as nervousness caused the bile in his gut to rise and burn the back of his throat.

The president would not be dissuaded from allowing the craft to land, and now he, and a few dozen other assembled politicians and military personnel, were waiting several hundred yards back from Mokhovaya Street right on Red Square in front of the Kremlin. The president still planned to shake the hands of the intrepid astronauts as they came out of the lander's cabin.

The assembled media were also waiting, cameras trained on the cleared street. Or rather almost cleared, as Bilov had at least persuaded the covert Special Forces that they should be ready – there were soldiers, tanks, and also trucks with mounted flamethrowers that could deliver gouts of fire for a hundred feet to incinerate anything *unnatural* that stepped from lander P23–09.

He also had full authority to deploy a regiment of S400 Triumph surface-to-air missiles on the outskirts of the capital. But soon they would be ineffectual.

Even with all that, Bilov's gut told him that the firepower probably wouldn't be enough if whatever exited that cabin was as bad as what his imagination conjured.

He paced a little more before his lead ground crew technician, Janus Androv, turned to him. "This is not a good idea."

"No shit." Bilov kept his head down.

"Remember what Doctor Ivanov told us of the lunar reports before she left? It seemed that their little test subjects' adaptability was exceeding expectations. That they were 'evolving'. Just before everything went dark." Androv exhaled and trained field glasses on the air for a moment before lowering them. "Do you know what Krasnodar's test of intelligence is?"

Bilov shrugged.

"The use of cunning, deception, planning, and anticipation – that is, the ability to adapt to change." Androv watched him. "I have to tell you, I'm not just a *little* scared, major." His eyes were dead. "I'm *very* scared."

Bilov turned away, thinking. Seconds mattered now.

Androv read from the screen. "Ten miles and closing from the west. Any minute now." He frowned. "Wait, something is happening. The override commands for the external door are being engaged. This is madness; they're trying to open the lander in the air." He frowned. "Why?"

Bilov felt his stomach churn. "I can guess why."

Seconds mattered, seconds mattered, seconds mattered, his brain repeated over and over.

He turned back. *Fuck it*, he thought, and lifted the phone.

"Colonel Ursovich, emergency order, 739-Kronos. The incoming lander represents a direct threat to the president and the people of Moscow. By order of President Petrov, target and destroy it. Launch at will."

The executive override order was received and acknowledged.

The craft was slowing as it approached but still traveling at nearly 500 miles per hour. It didn't matter, the S400 SAM had a range of 250 miles, could reach an altitude of fifty miles, and had a target velocity of Mach 14 – 11,000 miles per hour.

With dead eyes, Bilov watched the screen as the blip of the lander headed toward Moscow and dropped lower in the atmosphere. Then another blip appeared on the screen, chasing it, moving at a blistering speed.

Soon the two blips intersected, and then they were both gone, undoubtedly in a fireball that for a few seconds would have been hotter than the sun.

Bilov sank into his chair and exhaled loudly.

Androv wiped his eyes. "Thank you, sir. They never understood the risk."

Bilov nodded, but his own eyes were glassy and unfocused. "Go home, Androv." He raised his voice to the room full of technicians. "Everyone go home, right now. What I did was my decision alone."

The room cleared, and Bilov sat staring at nothing, but not in silence, as phones rang, screens lit up, and radios squawked. He didn't care anymore. He knew he was as good as dead. He just hoped he'd acted in time, because *seconds mattered, seconds mattered, seconds mattered.*

The door exploded inward and he smiled brokenly.

"What kept you?"

CHAPTER 65

Near Side of the Moon, edge of the Copernicus Crater

Nearly 240,000 miles away, a lone figure, charred and black-ened, sat on the edge of a crater watching the Earth.

It had taken her a while to walk around the moon so she could see her home. On her way, she had seen the orange bloom of a low atmospheric explosion over Moscow. Seems they were doing a little spring cleaning of an unwanted guest.

Sophia knew they wouldn't be back, probably, and as she would most likely still be functioning for another thousand years, she would be the sole witness to the blue planet's changing face, and fate.

She turned to stare at America as it came around again. She used her amplified vision to focus in on Massachusetts, then Boston, and then Buchanan Road, where Alex lived. Watching it gave her a strange sensation in her chest, and she gently touched it with slim, silver fingers.

"Love hurts," she said softly.

Human emotions were just a side effect of her programing, she had been told. And one they wanted to eradicate. "Because for love, sometimes you have to sacrifice everything."

Sophia dropped her hand. She sat. And watched. And waited.

CHAPTER 66

Buchanan Road, Boston, Massachusetts – two months later

Alex sat on the back step of his porch with Joshua next to him. It was early evening, and the moon was just rising.

He closed his eyes and listened to the crickets chirping and simply enjoyed the warm night air against his cheeks while inhaling the sweet scent of blooming star jasmine flowers climbing the porch railing.

"I heard that the moon used to be part of the Earth." Joshua looked up at his father. "Before we got hit by this big rock and it was blasted off into space."

Alex looked down at his son. "Yep, you're right. The Theia impact." He smiled. "And only happened about four and a half billion years ago."

"Awesome," his son intoned solemnly, and then snorted. "I can't believe you were actually up there."

Alex nodded. "So far, yet so close."

"I couldn't … I couldn't read you. It was as if something was blocking me." He put his hand on his father's forearm. "I was scared."

Alex placed his hand over his son's. "Don't worry about me. Never worry about me." He leaned closer. "Rumour has it, I'm the man who can't be killed." He winked.

Joshua grinned and looked back at the huge rising moon. It was glowing silver and seemed so close and clear they could see the individual lakes, seas, and craters.

"You were there, but on the other side. It's not the same as the side facing us, is it?"

"No," Alex said. "The dark side has its secrets. And as far as I'm concerned, it can keep them."

"Who has secrets?" Aimee came and sat next to Joshua, throwing her arm around both of them.

"The moon does," Joshua said and looked up at Alex from under her arm to share a cheeky grin.

"Oh, really?" Aimee playfully pushed his head. "That's an odd name for your father."

Alex kept quiet. He knew Aimee was intuitive enough to know his mission was more arduous than he had let on. But he was home, and it was over now. He glanced up at the moon again. Would they ever go back to re-establish the bases?

He doubted it; the risk was too great. For now, the 240,000 miles between Earth and the moon was the best firewall in existence. Let it stay that way.

Alex stood and held his hand out to Aimee. "This Saturday night, best restaurant in Boston, on me."

"Yay." Joshua threw his arms up.

"That'll do." Aimee gave him a half smile. "For a start."

EPILOGUE

The clump of cordyceps spores still burned at its outer edges as it floated down. In the Moscow sky it was a single snowflake among billions that glowed as it descended.

By the time it reached the marshlands on the outskirts of the city it was just a single spore that touched down on the edge of a reed and stuck there. The pond below was frozen, and it was quickly covered over with snow.

It would be months yet before the land would begin to thaw. And then the frogs and insects would emerge and begin to get active. And following them, would come the foxes and the birds.

It only needed to touch one of them.

Once.

AUTHOR'S NOTES

Many readers ask me about the background of my novels – is the science real or imagined? Where do I get the situations, equipment, characters, and their expertize from, and just how much of it has a basis in fact?

As a fiction writer I certainly create things to complement my stories. But mostly, I'll do extensive research on the science behind my tale.

In regard to my novel *The Dark Side*, there are no moon bases established just yet. However, China, Russia, and the United States all have plans to establish a permanent presence there before 2040.

Besides the strategic advantages of a base being established to "look down" from the near side of the moon, I envisage it also being the ultimate fire wall for storing and experimenting on hazardous biological materials. But there are always accidents in laboratories, human error persists, and in my novel, I hypothesized about what those accidents might entail if you gave the spark of intelligence to something that was already an efficient predator and/or parasite.

And there are none more efficient and deadly, and alien like, than the cordyceps fungal parasite.

CORDYCEPS – The Fungal Parasite from Your Nightmares

Mind control is real. Zombies are real. To find examples of one of the most terrifying living things on the planet, you can either read about them in horror novels, or you can travel deep into a humid rainforest jungle like in Brazil, and then look underneath a leaf hanging just ten inches above the ground.

You might see a deformed-looking ant hanging there, clinging tightly to the leaf with its jaws clamped tight. But the ant isn't alive. Oh, it *does* contain life, just not its own. Its body was infiltrated and taken over by the *Ophiocordyceps unilateralis*, the cordyceps zombie-ant fungus. When the spores touch the carapace of the ant they stick, and then single cells of the cordyceps penetrate the exoskeleton armour. Once breached, the cells move around in the ant's bloodstream, budding off new copies of themselves.

At this time, the ant doesn't even know its fate and that it is already condemned. But just like in John Carpenter's *The Thing*, a single spore cell of the fungus is enough to eventually infect the entire insect.

The next stage of growth for the fungus is for the cells to work together – they connect to each other by a webbing of filaments and begin to work as a single organism – think of a living creature inside another living creature. They then invade and insert themselves into the ant's muscle cells or ingest and replace them with their own cells.

So far, the parasite has left the brain untouched. Even after invading the entire body, the fungus basically turns the ant into a zombie slave, its mind trapped in its own shell that now is under the control of the invader.

If you continued to observe the ant, you'd see this internal life begin to bloom from the body – a long stalk grows out through the ant's head, swelling into a bulbous capsule full of spores. And because the ant is commanded to scale a leaf that overhangs one of its main hive's trails, the fungal spores rain down onto its ant kin below. And the horror cycle continues.

This behavior is not unique to the cordyceps as there are other parasites that manipulate their target hosts while leaving their brain untouched. Examples are a species of flatworm that form a net-like layer over the brain of the California killifish, leaving the brain untouched while making the fish swim erratically at the surface to bring it to the attention of birds – the flatworm's next host.

Some researchers believe that the cordyceps fungus acts as another brain and exerts direct control over the ant's muscles, literally controlling them like a puppeteer controls a marionette doll. This is where the name "the puppet master", comes from.

Sadly for the ant, it ends its life a prisoner in its own body. Does the ant know? Does it try and warn its kin that it is in effect a Trojan horse held hostage inside its own body? Without doubt, it would be a horrible way to die.

What Would Happen to You on the Moon with No Suit?

As far as we know, no one has died on the moon due to being without a suitable spacesuit. Or at least, no country owns up to it. However, through simulations and research where similar conditions were generated, we have a pretty good idea what the results would be.

The first thing you would notice is the lack of air. But more than likely you wouldn't immediately lose consciousness; that might take up to fifteen seconds as your body uses up its oxygen reserves in your bloodstream, and as long as you don't hold your breath, you could probably survive for up to two minutes without significant injury.

However, if you do hold your breath, the external vacuum would cause the gas inside your lungs to expand, which would cause hundreds of tiny ruptures in the lungs and release air into the circulatory system. Therefore, the first thing you would need to do if you ever find yourself in the vacuum of space is to exhale every bit of air out of your lungs.

But the other effects are out of your control. After around ten seconds, your skin would start to swell as the water in your body vaporizes in the absence of external pressure. Also, the moisture on your tongue would begin to boil. And we know this due to the case of Mr. Jim LeBlanc, who was exposed to a moon-like atmosphere in a test chamber in 1965. LeBlanc's suit had a leak, and though he remained conscious for about fourteen seconds, the last thing he remembered was the feeling of his tongue bubbling and popping in his mouth.

The other interesting thing is that if you did die in space or on the moon, your body would not decompose like it would on Earth, since there is no water nor oxygen, and therefore no bacteria. You would either be frozen solid, or if subjected to warmth, mummified for eternity, perhaps becoming an artefact for some future alien race to discover.

A NASA Moon Base – When, Not If

> *"If you can imagine it, you can create it."*
> — William Arthur Ward

When I started planning *The Dark Side*, I knew that using the moon base as a situational concept was going to be a stretch for believability. That was until I started doing more research. Seems a base has been planned for the moon for nearly half a century. I'm now convinced it's a matter of *when*, not *if*.

The Lunex Project was conceptualized in 1958 as a U.S. Air Force plan to construct an underground Air Force Base on the moon, and just a year later, the U.S. Army's Ballistic Missile Agency organized a task force called Project Horizon to assess the feasibility of such a project. Bear in mind that it would be still be another decade before humans ever set foot there (July 1969).

Project Horizon planned to use a relay of Saturn-2 rocket launches to pre-build the base while still in Earth's orbit. Then the almost fully constructed base could be towed to the moon for anchoring and final assembly. Monthly rockets would then ship the base crew and supplies.

A funding boost for the lunar outpost was delivered by George W. Bush in his Vision for Space Exploration, which was later replaced with President Barack Obama's space policy. NASA was to construct the inhabited outpost over the five years between 2019 and 2024, and Congress directed that the U.S. portion would "be designated the Neil A. Armstrong Lunar Outpost".

On 4 December 2006, NASA concluded its Global Exploration Strategy and Lunar Architecture Study. What resulted from the study was a basic plan for a lunar outpost near one of the poles of the moon, which would permanently house astronauts in six-month shifts.

Just recently, traces of water ice in a polar crater initiated a reassessment of plans (I can't find out why). However, the discovery of water doesn't make the lunar base less likely, in fact, it makes them more likely.

Bottom line: watch this space!

Torben and the Canine Guardian Program

In the latest Alex Hunter adventures, I have included more scenes with the dog Torben, from the U.S. Military's Guardian

Program. Readers of my other stories will recognize the huge and enhanced Guardians from the Valkeryn series and how they became the dominant intelligent species in a strange world of the far future.

Could canine guardians end up a real thing? Well, dogs have a long history of working with mankind on the battlefield and have played a role in war since ancient times, when Romans sent dogs with leather armor and razor-sharp collars into their enemies' ranks.

Today, war dogs are among the most valuable military assets and can detect scents more than a thousand times better than any human or equipment, which makes them ideal for patrols, finding bombs, and chasing down terrorists. But for all their natural strength, intelligence, and loyalty, there is a desire to make them more than what they are.

In 2015, a team of scientists in China announced they had created the world's first gene-edited dogs, which possess increased heart and lung capacity and also twice the amount of muscle mass than that of a non-engineered dog. These superdogs have great potential for police and military applications, according to Liangxue Lai, a researcher involved with the project at the Guangzhou Institutes of Biomedicine and Health.

In the past, changes to the size, strength, or temperament of animals were achieved through selective breeding. But for rapid and extraordinary results it is now done by manipulating the genome. According to the Chinese scientists, the impressive achievement of superior strength and stamina was attained through the simple deletion of a gene responsible for the production of myostatin, a muscle-inhibiting protein.

To date, the U.S. has relied on dogs it is forced to buy from mostly European breeders, and given the best stock is needed to ensure they are the strongest and smartest and provide the best return on the investment over their lifespan, they can cost around $5000 to purchase and $60,000 to train. The Defense Department wants to breed the dogs domestically to have a secure and stable supply and also cut costs. When they do, will the U.S. ever have a Guardian Program? Maybe – it makes sense to ensure any potential adversary programs are matched or outmatched by our own.

And will they ever be like Tor, or his ancestors as described in the Valkeryn Series? Well, I'll leave the last word to the American writer William Ward, who once said: "If you can imagine it, you can create it."

Milton Keynes UK
Ingram Content Group UK Ltd.
UKHW011302211123
432986UK00001B/209